TAGGERUNG

BRIAN JACQUES

TAGGERUNG

ILLUSTRATED BY PETER STANDLEY

PHILOMEL BOOKS ❧ NEW YORK

First American Edition published in 2001 by
PHILOMEL BOOKS
a division of Penguin Putnam Books for Young Readers,
345 Hudson Street, New York, NY 10014.
Philomel Books, Reg. U.S. Pat. & Tm. Off.
Published in Great Britain in 2001 by
Hutchinson Children's Books, London.
Printed in the United States of America

Library of Congress Cataloging-in-Publication Data
Jacques, Brian.
Taggerung : a tale from Redwall / Brian Jacques ;
illustrated by Peter Standley.— 1st American ed.   p. cm.
Summary: A young otter, kidnapped in his infancy and raised as
a warrior-thief by a band of vermin, leaves the tribe and goes off
to seek adventures of his own.
[1. Otters—Fiction. 2. Animals—Fiction. 3. Fantasy.] I. Standley, Peter, ill.
II. Title.   PZ7.J15317 Tag 2001   [Fic]—dc21   2001021468
ISBN 0-399-23720-8
1 3 5 7 9 10 8 6 4 2
First American Edition

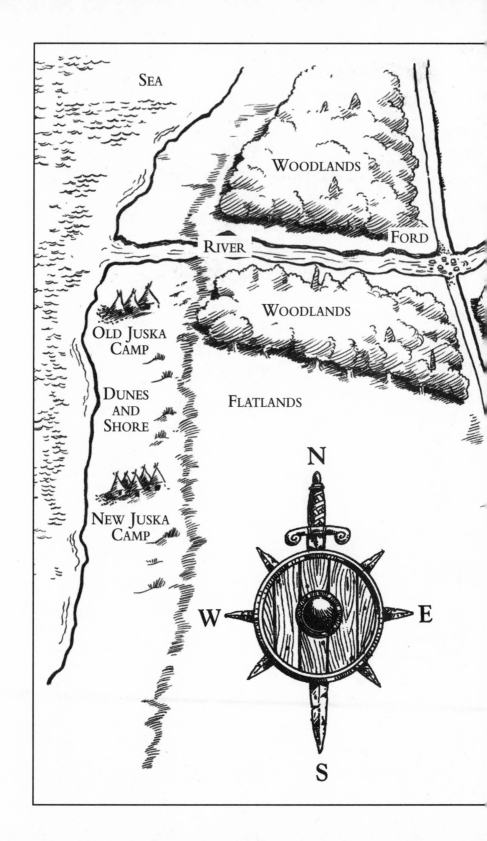

Prologue

My father always says that the life of a scholar is more rewarding than that of a cook. When I asked him why, he told me it is better to have ink on your paws than flour on your nose. But then he grew serious and explained to me that to be a Recorder at Redwall Abbey is a great honor. He said that my writings will form part of our Abbey's history. They will remain there for all creatures to see, forever and ever. Then he laughed and said that no matter how much care goes into the making of a piecrust, it disappears in the space of a single meal. So I am serving my apprenticeship under that good old mouse, Brother Hoben, our senior Recorder. Old Hoben sleeps a lot these days, so I get lots of practice. I am finding more and more that I like to write. My mother thinks my writing shows a great talent. But mothers are like that, aren't they?

I have been working since last winter on the strange tale of the Taggerung. I have spoken to many Redwallers about it in the evenings, and spent my days writing it up. What a story it is! Brother Hoben says that every good tale should have the proper ingredients and they are all here, believe me. Sadness and joy, comedy and tragedy, with a little mystery sprinkled throughout and quite a good dose of rousing action. Sounds a bit like a cooking recipe to me. Be that as it may be, I have finished writing the account. This evening I am due to start reading my narrative to all the Redwallers, in Cavern Hole. Winter is the best time for stories: a good warm fire, some tasty food and drink, and an attentive audience. Who could ask for more? I can see the snow lying deep on the ground outside our gatehouse; icicles are hanging from the trees instead of leaves. Daylight is fading as night steals in early. All that remains for me to do is to wash this ink off my paws, get my scarf . . . oh, and wake Brother Hoben. The old fellow is in his armchair, snoozing by the embers of the fire. Then it's off to Cavern Hole to read the tale to my friends. I'm really looking forward to it.

Would you like to come and listen? I'm sure you'll be welcome. If you don't know the way, then follow me and Brother Hoben, though it will take a while, as he shuffles quite slowly and has to lean on me. By the way, don't forget to wipe your paws before entering the Abbey. Oh, and another thing, please compliment my dad on his Autumn Harvest soup; I know that will please him. Right then, away we go. Watch out for Dibbuns throwing snowballs. Come on, we don't want to be late. Silly me, how can we be late? They can't start without me. I'm the one who will be reading the tale of the Taggerung, you know. But I've already told you that. Sorry. Up you come, Brother Hoben, you can sleep by the fire in Cavern Hole. But don't snore too loud or my mother will wake you up and tell you not to interrupt her talented daughter's wonderful story. That's mothers for you, eh!

Sister Rosabel,
Assistant Recorder of Redwall Abbey.

BOOK ONE

The Babe at the Ford

1

The clan of Sawney Rath could feel their fortunes changing, much for the better. Grissoul had predicted it would be thus, and the vixen was seldom wrong. Only that day the clan foragers had caught a huge load of mackerel that had strayed into the shallows of the incoming tide. Fires blazed in the scrubland beyond the dunes that evening, as the fish, skewered on green withes, blistered and popped over the flames. Sawney was not as big as other ferrets, but he was faster, smarter and far more savage than any stoat, rat, weasel, fox or ferret among his followers. Anybeast could lay claim to the clan leadership, providing they could defeat Sawney in combat, but for a long time none had dared to. Sawney Rath could fight with a ferocity that was unequaled, and he never spared the vanquished challengers. Sawney's clan were nomads, sixty all told, thieves, vagrants, vagabonds and tricksters who would murder and plunder without hesitation. They were Juska.

Many bands of Juska roamed the coasts, woodlands and byways, but they never formed a united force, each choosing to go its own way under a strong Chieftain. This leader always tacked his name on to the Juska title, so that Sawney's clan came to be known as the Juskarath. Though they were little more than dry-land pirates, Juska vermin had quite a strict code of conduct, which was governed by seers, omens and superstition.

Sawney sat beneath the awning of his tent, sipping a vile-tasting medication that his seer Grissoul had concocted to ease the stomach pains that constantly dogged him. He watched the clan, noting their free and easy mood. Sawney smiled as some of the rats struck up a song. Rats were easily pleased; once they had a full stomach and a flagon of nettle beer they would either sing or sleep. Sawney was only half watching the rats, his real attention focused upon the stoat Antigra. She lay nursing her newborn, a son called Zann. Sawney could tell Antigra was feigning slumber from the hate-laden glances she threw his way when she thought he was not looking. Sawney Rath's eyes missed very little of what went on around him. He pulled a face of disgust as he sniffed the mixture of feverfew and treacle mustard in the cup he held, and, spitting into the fire, he muttered the newborn stoatbabe's name.

"Hah, Zann!"

Grissoul the Seer stole up out of the gathering darkness and placed a steaming plate of food by his side. He glanced up at the vixen. She was an odd-looking fox, even for a seer. She wore a barkcloth cloak that she had covered in red and black symbols, and her brow, neck and limbs were almost invisible under bracelets of coral, brass and silver. About her waist she wore a belt from which hung a broad pouch and bones of all kinds. One of her eyes was never still.

Sawney tipped the plate with his footpaw. "Am I supposed to eat this mess?"

She smiled coaxingly. "Yar, 'tis the mackerel without skin or bone, stewed in milkweed and dock. Thy stomach'll favor it!"

The ferret drew from his belt a lethally beautiful knife,

straight-bladed, razor sharp, with a brilliant blue sapphire set into its amber handle. Delicately he picked up a morsel of fish on the knifepoint, and tasted it.

"This is good. I like it!"

Grissoul sat down beside him. "None can cook for thee like I." She watched him eating awhile before speaking again.

"Th'art going to ask me about the Taggerung, I feel it."

Sawney picked a sliver of fish from between his teeth. "Aye. Have there been any more signs of the Taggerung?"

Antigra interrupted by leaping up and thrusting her baby forward at them. "Fools!" she shouted defiantly. "Can't you see, my Zann is the Taggerung!"

The entire camp fell silent. Creatures turned away from their cooking fires to see what would happen. Sawney stood up, one paw holding his stomach, the other pointing the knife at Antigra.

"If you were not a mother nursing a babe you would be dead where you stand. Nobeast calls Sawney Rath a fool!"

Antigra was shaking with rage. The baby stoat had set up a thin wail, but her voice drowned it out.

"I demand you recognize my son as Taggerung!"

Sawney gritted his teeth. Thrusting the dagger back into his belt he turned aside, snarling at Grissoul. "Tell that stoat why her brat cannot be called Taggerung!"

Grissoul stood between them, facing Antigra, and took a starling's skull, threaded on thin twine, from her belt. She swung it in a figure of eight until the air rushing through the eye and beak sockets made a shrieking whistle.

"Hearken, Antigra, even a long-dead bird can mock thee. Shout all thou like, 'twill not make thine offspring grow to be the Taggerung. You it is who are a fool! Can thou not see the omens are all wrong? Even though you call him Zann, which means Mighty One, he will never be

5

the chosenbeast. I see all. Grissoul knows, take thou my word now. Go back to your fire and nurse the babe, and be silent, both of ye!"

Antigra held the newborn stoat up high, shaking the babe until it wailed even more loudly. "Never!" she cried.

Sawney winced as his stomach gave a sharp twinge. He turned upon the stoat mother, roaring dangerously, "Enough! You have heard my Seer: the omens are wrong. Zann can never be called Taggerung. Unless you want to challenge me for the leadership of the clan and change the Juskarath law to suit yourself, I command you to silence your scolding tongue and speak no more of the matter!"

He turned and went into his tent, but Antigra was not prepared to let the matter lie. Everybeast heard her shout after him: "Then you are challenged, Sawney Rath!"

His stomach pains immediately forgotten, the ferret Chieftain emerged from the tent, a half-smile hovering around his slitted eyes. Vermin who had seen that look before turned away. Only Antigra faced him as he asked quietly, "So, who challenges me?"

He saw the creature, even before Antigra replied, "Gruven, the father of Zann!"

Gruven stepped forth from the shadows. In one hefty paw he carried a small round shield, in the other a tall slim spear, its point shining in the firelight. He struck a fighting stance, his voice loud and clear.

"I challenge you, Sawney Rath. Arm yourself and face me!"

Sawney had always liked Gruven. He was a valuable asset to the clan. Big, strong, but not too intelligent. Sawney shook his head and smiled patronizingly.

"Don't do it, Gruven. Don't listen to your mate. Put the spear and shield down; live to see your son grow up."

Antigra whispered something to Gruven that seemed to embolden him. He circled away from her, jabbing the spear in Sawney's direction. "I'll live to see my son become Taggerung. Now fight like a Juska, or die like a coward!"

Sawney shrugged off the insult. "As you wish." He turned, as if to fetch his weapons from the tent, then half swung back, as though he had forgotten to say something to the challenger. "Oh, er, Gruven . . ."

There was a deadly whirr as the knife left Sawney's paw. Gruven coughed slightly, a puzzled look on his face, then fell backward, the blade buried in his throat up to its decorative handle. Sawney finished what he had been saying. "Don't ever hold your shield low like that, it's a fatal mistake. Grissoul, I'll see you in my tent."

Ignoring Antigra's wails, Sawney beckoned the vixen to sit beside him. "What have you seen?"

Grissoul emptied her bag of stones, shells and bones on the ground, nodding sagely. "See thou, my omens have fallen the same since the end of the last rain. Our Taggerung is born at last. There are other Juska clans abroad in the land, and any of these would deem it a great honor to count him as one of them. Such a beast is a talisman of great power. The Taggerung can change the fortunes of a clan. Nobeast is mightier; none can stand before a Taggerung. Long seasons have passed since such a warrior lived. Who would know this better than thee, Sawney, for was not thine own father the chosen one? Ah, those were glorious days. Our clan was the largest and most feared then. Everybeast had to bow their heads to your father. Zann Juskarath Taggerung! Can you not remember the respect he commanded wherever we went—"

Sawney cut the Seer off impatiently. "Cease your prattle about my father. I know how great he was, but he's long dead and gone. Tell me more of this new Taggerung. How do you know he's born, and where do we find him?"

The vixen studied a single speedwell flower, which she had picked earlier that day. It was pale pink, with three fat petals and one thinner than the others. She smiled slyly.

"My visions tell me a mark shaped like this little blossom will be upon him, or maybe her, for who can tell if Taggerung be male or female?"

7

Just then a weasel called Eefera entered and gave Sawney his knife back, cleaned of blood traces. Sawney dismissed Eefera and placed the blade lightly against the Seer's nose.

"You said any clan would deem it an honor to count *him* as one of them. The Taggerung will be a male creature. Stop playing your little games and get on with it!"

Grissoul turned the knife blade aside with one paw. "He will have the speedwell mark on him, where I know not. See thou these two bones, fallen next to each other, with this shell across the ends of both? That means a river, or a stream, and the shell is for a place where those who dwell not in the waters may cross the stream. Do thou see it also?"

Sawney nodded. "That means a ford. The long path from north to south has such a ford, where the stream crosses it in Mossflower country, a good five-day march from here."

Grissoul closed her eyes, swaying back and forth. "Today I saw a hawk strike a dove in the air. Their cries mingled, and they gave out together a bell-like sound."

Sawney gave a start. "You mean the old Abbey of Redwall! That's the only place that gives out bell sounds in all that region!"

The Seer kept her eyes shut. "Methinks that would be it."

Sawney grabbed Grissoul's shoulder so tightly that her eyes popped open. He pulled her close, his voice like a rasp. "Speak not to me of Redwall. I would not go within a mile of it. I have listened to the talk around the campfires since I was nought but a whelp. The place is accursed!"

He released the quivering vixen and gestured dramatically. "I am not stupid. The history of Redwall Abbey has taught me a lesson. I know how many warlords and conquerors, with vast hordes and mighty armies to back them, have been defeated by the woodlanders who dwell behind those walls. Even in the seasons long before our great-grandsires' ancestors were born. You've heard their

8

names, everybeast has. Cluny the Scourge, Slagar the Cruel, Ferahgo the Assassin and many others. All of them defeated and slain. But I'll tell you one name that won't be added to the list. Sawney Rath, Chieftain of the Juskarath!"

Grissoul spoke soothingly to calm Sawney's rising ire. "Nay, fret thou not. The bell sound omen is a warning, telling thee not to go near yon red Abbey. Beware the sound of the bell!"

Sawney spat neatly into the fire. "Hah! I already knew that. I'm as wise as any omen. Just tell me what part Redwall Abbey plays in all this?"

Grissoul gathered up her paraphernalia and cast them a second time. She stared at them, then pointed. "See thou those bones that fell foursquare with that red piece of stone at their center? Watch!" She lifted the red stone slightly, and an ant crawled from beneath it and ran over the bones. The Seer smiled triumphantly. "It means that the Taggerung will be a creature from the Abbey!"

Sawney placed a paw on the ground, and the ant ran onto it. The ferret held the paw close to his eyes, watching the insect circling a claw. "What manner of creature will it be?"

Grissoul pursed her lips. "Who can tell?" She inspected the pawprint Sawney had left in the sandy ground. "Five days from here, at the ford where waters cross the path. Then will thou see what sort of beast the Taggerung will be."

Sawney stood up and patted his stomach. "I feel better. Tell them to break camp; we travel tonight. To have a Taggerung in my clan will be the greatest of honors. My Juskarath will make the journey in four days. I want to be there early, in case other clan Seers have had visions. I'll slay anybeast who comes near that ford. Tell the clan to hasten or I'll leave them behind . . . aye, the same way I'm leaving Gruven here."

Grissoul stared at him, almost fondly. "Th'art a wise Chieftain, and ruthless too!"

Sawney checked her as she went. "One other thing. Once

9

we have the Taggerung we travel back this way fast, to the sea and shores. Nobeast at Redwall must know 'twas my clan that took him. If the tales about them are true, they must be fearsome warriors, with a long paw for vengeance. I need to avoid a conflict with such beasts."

He waved a paw, dismissing his Seer. As he did so, the ant was hurled from its perch and fell into a basin of water. Sawney failed to notice it, but the ant swam!

2

"After spring's soft rain is done,
At waning of the moon,
Four dry solid days of sun,
Will bring forth growth and bloom."

Drogg Spearback, Cellarkeeper of Redwall Abbey, patted the soft headspikes of Egburt and Floburt, his little grandhogs. "Well said, young 'uns. You finally got it right!"

Squinching her snout and tugging at her grandfather's heavy cellar apron, Floburt, the inquisitive one, piped up. "But Granddad, we ain't growthed an' bloomed. I'm still only likkle, an' so is Egburt. Why is that?"

The stout old hedgehog winked knowingly at his grandson. "Cummon, Egburt, you tell 'er why."

Egburt sucked the tassel of the girdle cord that circled the waist of his smock, pondering the answer. "Hmm, er, 'cos us isn't veggibles, we 'edgehogs, not plants."

Drogg chuckled until his stomach wobbled. Rummaging two candied chestnuts from his apron pocket, he gave them one each. "You've got a brain 'neath those spikes, young 'og!"

The hogbabes sat either side of their grandfather, on an upturned wheelbarrow in the orchard, enjoying the late-spring noontide sun. Drogg spread both paws, gesturing around and about.

"See all that? Well, that's growth an' bloom for you! Plants, grass, fruit'n'flowers, springin' up like wildfire after the rains. Come midsummer we'll be up to our spikes in apples, pears, plums, damsons, strawberries, blackberries an' all manner o' berries. Lookit the salad crop, o'er yonder by the redcurrant hedge: radish, cucumber, cress, scallions, lettuce. Ready for gatherin' in, those are. Remember this, my liddle 'uns, you be plantin' stuff in the earth an' it'll grow quick-like. Save for the great trees like those in Mossflower Wood. They grow slower, stronger, just like us creatures, though trees live much longer'n we do."

Both little hedgehogs sat listening as they munched candied chestnuts. Drogg expanded his lecture, telling them of their heritage, Redwall Abbey. He loved the place with a fierce pride, which he communicated to them. "Plants, trees an' creatures, they come'n'go sooner or later. Not this ole Abbey, though! Lookit all this wunnerful red sandstone. Shines like dusty pink roses in late-noon sun. Nobeast who comes wantin' trouble can pass those big rampart walls of the main gate with the liddle gate'ouse beside it. I couldn't even guess 'ow old our great Abbey buildin' is. Bell tower, gables, columns, Great Hall, Cavern 'Ole, kitchens, dormitories, an' my cellars too. They must've been 'ere forever an' a day!"

Floburt dug her tiny paw into his broad apron pocket, searching for more nuts. Her granddad usually carried a goodly supply. "Have you been 'ere forever'n'aday, Granddad?"

Smiling, he shook his great spiked head. "Dearie me no, though I been an Abbeybeast longer'n most, save for ole Cregga."

Egburt joined his sister in rummaging in the apron pocket. "Ole Cregga the Badgermum? 'Ow long's she been 'ere, Granddad?"

Drogg pondered the question, chewing the milky sap

12

from a grass stalk. "Hmm, let me see. Cregga is wot they call the last of the old 'uns. I think she's older'n some o' the trees 'ereabouts. Great warrior she was, but blinded in some ancient battle. Brother Hoben, the Recorder, says that Cregga has outlived two Abbesses, Tansy an' Song, both long gone. He says that she knew Arven the Champion an' my great-grand'og, Gurgan Spearback, many seasons afore I was born. So figger it out yoreself. 'Ow old d'you think Cregga is?"

Egburt's eyes grew wide as he tried to calculate the answer in hedgehog manner, by counting on his head-spikes. "Phwaw! She mus' be eleventeen thousing seasons old!"

Drogg allowed them to find the rest of his candied chestnut supply before he rose slowly. "Aye, at least that much, I'd say. I got to go now an' broach a barrel of October Ale for the counselors' meetin' tonight. You Dibbuns stay out o' trouble, an' don't go gettin' those nice clean smocks muddied up, or yore mum'll dust yore spikes with an oven paddle. Why don't you go an' see if there be any news of Filorn ottermum's babe? But mind, don't make a nuisance of y'selves. See you anon."

Both Dibbuns giggled at the idea of their mother spanking them with an oven paddle. She was far too gentle. Being sent early to bed was the limit of punishment for Redwall babes. When Drogg had departed, they clambered from the wheelbarrow and ran squeaking and jumping into the orchard. A tiny mole was exploring a clump of bilberry stalks, searching among the pink globe-shaped blossoms. Waving a pudgy digging claw in greeting, he called out in the quaint mole accent, "Burr, goo' day to ee. They'm bilbeez ain't a growed yet. Taken ee toime they be's!"

"My mum sez you get tummy ache from eatin' bilberries afore midsummer," Floburt commented sagely.

Gundil, the Dibbun mole, flicked his stubby tail scornfully. "Moi mum sez ee same thing, but oi loikes bilbeez, h'even if'n oi do gets tumbly h'ache." He ambled out of the bilberry clump and shrugged. "Bain't none thurr, tho'. Whurr us'n's be a-goen?"

Egburt pointed toward the Abbey. "We goin' t'see if Filorn ottermum's new baby be a-borned yet. Cummon!"

The three little chums wandered off paw in paw toward the Abbey. Once inside, they stopped off at Great Hall to play a favorite Dibbuns game. Almost lost amid the vastness of stone and timber beams, they hopped about on the floor, in and out of harlequin hues of sunshafts from the stained glass windows far above them.

Gundil gave a deep bass giggle, holding a paw to his face. "Hurrhurrhurr. Luk ee! Oi be's all purkle!"

Floburt twirled about in a pool of amber light. "An' I'm all gold, a solid golden 'ogmaid!"

Egburt chose a shaft of aquamarine blue, floundering upon his back as though he were drowning. "Save me! I'm unner the deep deep water! 'Elp!"

Floburt and Gundil dutifully rescued Egburt and all three fled downstairs into Cavern Hole, where preparations were under way for the counselors' meeting. Friar Bobb, a stout old squirrel, shooed them out with a rush broom.

"Come on, out out. You'll get trodden on, wandering about under everybeast's paws. Go and play elsewhere, you rascals. Quick now. Scoot!"

He made as if to run after them. The little pals thought it was great fun to be chased, and trundled off helter-skelter. Halting on the dormitory landing above the first flight of stairs, Gundil stifled his chuckles and peeked down the spiral stairwell. He tapped a paw against his velvety snout.

"Ee Froyer woan't foind us'n's oop yurr. Hurr, boi 'okey ee woan't!"

Shaking with glee, Egburt pointed to a door. "Let's 'ide in there unner the beds!"

Gundil stood on Egburt's back in his effort to reach the latch, but it still proved too high. Floburt was trying to clamber up on top of them both when somebeast inside heard and opened the door.

The trio of Dibbuns fell tail over ears into the room. Filorn the ottermum stood holding the door, smiling down at them.

"Well, well. To what do we owe the pleasure of this visit?"

Gundil tugged his snout respectfully. "Uz cummed to see if'n ee likkle h'otter was borned, marm."

Rillflag, Filorn's husband, their daughter, a pretty little ottermaid named Mhera, and the great Badgermum Cregga were standing around a woven rush cradle in one corner. Mhera, who was four seasons older than the three Dibbuns, beckoned them over.

"He was born this morning. Come and see. He's beautiful!"

Cregga looked so huge and intimidating that the trio backed away slightly. A deep rumbling laugh came from the blind badger as she sensed their trepidation. Turning her sightless eyes in their direction, she whispered gently, "Oh, do come and look at him. He won't bite you. Neither will I. It's Gundil and the two little Spearbacks, isn't it?"

Floburt trotted dutifully over to the crib, with the other two trailing behind, wondering how the blind badger knew who they were. Standing on tip-paw, they gazed at the tiny new otterbabe. The little fellow stared solemnly back through sleepy dark eyes. Soft infant fur fuzzed out from his chubby cheeks, and a small pink tongue-tip showed as he yawned contentedly.

Mhera stroked his fluffy paw. "Isn't he the prettiest little cub you ever saw?"

Egburt looked up at her inquiringly. "Is that 'is name, Cub?"

Rillflag stroked his son's downy head, smiling. "No, cub

15

is just a word for a babe. His name is Deyna. My great-grandsire was a warrior called Deyna, and he carried a mark from birth just like this little fellow, see."

He turned the babe's paw pad upward. Instead of being all black like the other three, this one only had black edging. In the center was a pink mark, like a four-leaf clover, with one piece thinner than the others. Gundil touched it.

" 'Tis loike ee likkle flower. Can ee babby coom owt an' play with us'n's, zurr?"

Rillflag shook his head in amusement. "Not yet. Next season, maybe."

Filorn took a box from the mantelpiece and let them each choose a piece of preserved fruit from it. "I'm sure you'll make good friends for little Deyna when he's old enough to be up and about. Run along and play now."

Cregga enveloped all three Dibbuns in her massive paws. "Not so fast there, rascals. I could hear you outside. You only came in here to hide from Friar Bobb, didn't you?"

Floburt shook her head vigorously. "Ho no, marm, 'onest we didn't. Us was comin' to see if Deyna was borned. Ole Friar Bobb chased us out o' Cavern 'Ole."

The blind badger tapped a paw against her forehead. "Of course, I'd almost forgotten, the counselors' meeting. Right, you three can help me manage those stairs. Slowly, now; my paws aren't as young as yours!"

"Hurr, doan't ee wurry, marm. Uz'll get ee thurr noicely!"

Hiding a smile, Cregga allowed the three to grasp her robe and guide her to the door. "Thank you. I'm sure you will!"

When they had gone, Mhera picked her new little brother up and walked around the room with him, talking softly to him as she had seen her mother doing.

"Who's going to grow up into a great big riverdog like his dad then, eh?"

Rillflag shook his head. "He ain't a real riverdog until his back's touched runnin' water."

Filorn took the baby from Mhera and held him close. "Don't you think he's a bit young for that?"

The big male otter snorted. "Not at all. My father took me to the river when I was his age, just as I took Mhera when she was born. Deyna will feel the running water on his back too!"

There was a note of pleading in Filorn's voice. "But he's so small. Perhaps you could wet his back in the Abbey pond, at the warm shallow edge?"

Rillflag was adamant. "The Abbey pond has no current; it doesn't run on to the sea. It's got to be running water. The ford, where the stream crosses the path, that's the place."

"I'll go with you, Father. I'll carry little Deyna."

Rillflag patted his daughter's shoulder. "No need for that. You stay here and help your mother. I can carry that little rogue, he weighs nothing. Me and Deyna will bring you back some fresh watershrimp and good long watercress. Maybe some hotroot too, if we spot any."

Filorn resigned herself to the fact that argument was useless. Her husband could be a very stubborn creature.

"Your father's right, Mhera. You'd only slow him down. We'll get a nice naming party organized while he and Deyna are away. Then, when he's made a real riverdog of our baby, we'll name him properly, like any other Redwaller."

Mhera took to the idea eagerly. "Yes! The moment you set off, Dad, we'll get organizing with Friar Bobb, Drogg Cellarhog, the Foremole and Sister Alkanet. I can start gathering mushrooms and scallions for pasties, Mama can get the ingredients ready for her fruit and honey cake, and we'll ask Drogg if he has a cask of strawberry fizz . . ."

Filorn held up both paws against her daughter's onslaught. "Enough, enough! I'm starting to feel worn out just listening to you. We'll make a start after your father's left. Er, when will you be setting off, dear?"

Rillflag took an old traveling cloak and fashioned it into a carrying sling across one shoulder. He selected a stout ash-handled spear, which would double as a traveling stave. "As soon as you've packed some food and drink for two warriors. Enough for three days should do. We don't plan on wasting time at the wayside, do we, Deyna?"

From his mother's arms, the baby otter gave a rough squeak. Rillflag nodded in his direction. "He said no."

All three burst out laughing.

Down in Cavern Hole the meeting of Redwall counselors was about to begin. A supper of spring vegetable soup, new-baked oatbread and wedges of white cheese studded with hazelnuts, with October Ale and apple flan, was being served to the counselors seated around the big table. Foremole Brull, Cregga Badgermum, Brother Hoben, Friar Bobb, Sister Alkanet and Drogg Cellarhog were present. Brother Hoben indicated an empty seat as he recorded the members' names.

"Where's Rillflag this evening? Anybeast seen him?"

Cregga leaned forward to accept a tankard of October Ale. "Otter business. I think he's got to take the little 'un for some ceremony or other. You know the way he is about otter rituals. Anyhow, I'll make his apologies for absence."

Friar Bob tapped the tabletop with his ladle. "On with the meeting, then. Sister Alkanet?"

The Sister was a thin, severe, no-nonsense type of mouse. She bowed formally to the others and began.

"Friends, this Abbey has been without Abbot or Abbess for far too long. I suggested this meeting so that the situation might be finally remedied. Have you any ideas?"

Foremole Brull held up a sizable digging claw. It was unusual for the moles to have a female leader, but Brull was solid as a rock and full of good common sense. She was liked by all.

"Yurr, oi doan't think et aportant. Ee Abbey be runnen noice'n'smooth unner Cregga Badgermum. Nowt amiss wi' urr; she'm gudd!"

A general murmur of agreement confirmed Brull's mole logic. Before Sister Alkanet could object, Cregga spoke for herself.

"You all know I'm not a real Abbess, never wanted to be. But when old Abbess Song went to her reward I took up the job of caretaker, in the absence of anybeast's being elected officially. I'm countless seasons older than the oldest among you, I'm blind, sometimes I ache all over and I sleep most of the day. However, as Brull says, the Abbey runs nice'n'smooth. I merely guide or advise. Redwallers are trusty, responsible creatures; they usually know what needs doing to keep the place up to the mark. I'm quite happy to leave things as they are, though even I won't last forever. If you're content with an ancient, blind badger sitting in as substitute, then I'll continue to do so. With your kind permission, of course."

Amid the applause from the counselors, Sister Alkanet, who was always the mouse to raise difficult issues, raised her paw. "Then what about a Champion? Redwall needs a defender like Martin the Warrior."

Friar Bobb's snort of impatience was heard by all, as he wagged his ladle at the Sister and gave vent to his feelings. "I've got four great plum puddings steaming in the kitchens, and I've also got a sleepy assistant. Young Broggle will probably let the puddings boil dry if I'm not there soon. Sister Alkanet, marm, you brought up this same question at this same meeting this time last season. I'll give you the same answer now as I gave you then. Redwall is strong. Tyrants and vermin warlords have broken their skulls against our walls. The Abbey is too hard a nut to crack, vermin everywhere know that. Only a fool would try to test our might. These days there is no need of perilous warriors and great swords—"

Alkanet was up on her paws, pounding the table and

19

objecting. "But what if there were, Friar? What if the day came when we woke to find the foe at our gates and no brave one to lead or defend us? What then, sir? What then?"

Cregga's big paw hit the tabletop, silencing further argument. "Enough! We are supposed to be responsible elders, not squabbling Dibbuns. Friar Bobb, you may return to your kitchens. I'm very fond of plum puddings; they mustn't boil dry. Now, Sister, in answer to your questions. Champions and Abbey Warriors have always arisen when the need is great. It would be presumptuous of us to appoint one; that is something nobeast save Martin the Warrior can do. Martin was the founder Warrior of Redwall. His sword hangs over the picture of him on the tapestry in Great Hall, and there it will stay until he chooses the next Warrior. When our Abbey is in danger, the spirit of Martin will enter some young Redwaller, and he or she will pick up the sword of Martin to defend us. So let us hear no more talk of electing a Champion. Sit down, friends, and let's do this good food justice. Brother Hoben, pass me the bread and cheese, if you please. Sister Alkanet, would you like to pour me some October Ale?"

As Alkanet leaned across to pour, Cregga whispered, "Come on, friend, smile. It doesn't hurt to look happy!"

The Sister was mystified as to how Cregga knew she was wearing a frown. She tried a smile as she filled the tankard. The blind badger smiled back and tapped her paw. "Thank you, Alkanet. That's much better!"

Soft perfumes of dog rose, vetchling, red clover and nightdewed grass lingered upon the still night air with hardly a breeze to disperse them. Rillflag strode energetically north on the old path, glancing up at the star-pierced vaults of the skies above. Slung upon his back was a bag of provisions; in one paw he held the spearstaff, the other rested beneath his cloak cradle, protecting the sleeping babe therein. He breathed deeply, listening to the distant tolling of Redwall Abbey's twin bells, Matthias and Methuselah, sounding the midnight hour.

Deyna moved slightly in slumber and gave a small growl. Rillflag felt a shudder of delight course through him, and he hummed an old otter tune to his son. Life was good. So good!

3

Sawney Rath chose his spot carefully. Within a half-day's march of the ford, he camped the clan on the broad stream's north side. Morning sunlight filtered through the trees as the band of assorted vermin sat, weary and miserable after their forced march from the coastal scrublands. Clad in his usual plain leather tabard, belted by a strap fashioned from fine brass links into which was thrust his amber-hilted knife with the sapphire pommel stone, Sawney, however, looked vital and eager, ready for anything. The only decoration he had was the Juskarath clan mark, a black stripe of dye running from skull to nosetip with two lines of red dots running parallel on either side. These moved as his mobile face did while he issued his orders.

"Rawback, you stay here with the others. Grissoul, Eefera, Dagrab, Felch, Ribrow and Vallug Bowbeast, you come with me. Remember this, Rawback, for I'll hold you responsible. No fires, not even a wisp of smoke. Any food must be eaten as it is, no cooking. No tents or lean-to shelters, or sleeping either. Stay alert on your paws, everybeast. We'll be coming back this way fast when we do, so be ready to move. Antigra, Wherrul, I want no sign left that Juskarath have been here. You'll be in charge of cleaning up pawprints and tracks. When we return with the Taggerung we travel back west to the shores. I've no need to tell you what'll happen to anybeast who disobeys my commands, or tries to cross me. Understood?"

There followed a jangling of bracelets and earrings as the vermin touched their left ears in silence, the clan sign of understanding. Sawney's quick, vicious eyes roved back and forth over them, and then, without flinching, he drew his dagger and nicked the point against his own left ear in a challenging gesture.

"See how easily I shed my blood. I am Sawney Rath, and I can shed your blood far more easily. Keep that in mind!" He nodded to the six he had picked. "Come on, let's go and get a Taggerung for our clan!"

Rillflag was astounded. He was muttering to himself as he laid little Deyna down on a bed of soft mosses by the streambank.

"Hoho, what a riverdog you're goin' t'be! Not only got that back wet in the runnin' water, but you nearly swam away from your ole dad. I never knew a cub your size that'd swim right off. Mhera wailed enough t'frighten the birds when her back was wetted, but nary a sound out o' you, Deyna!"

He tickled the otterbabe's stomach roughly. Deyna doubled over and bit his father's paw with tiny white milk teeth. Rillflag roared with laughter as he released his paw.

"Hahahahohoho! Proper liddle shark you are. Lucky there weren't any tasty fishes swimmin' in the water, or you'd 'ave ate 'em all, eh, son!"

He sat awhile, fondly watching the cub, trying to remember an otter streamsong as the babe's eyes began to close in the warm midday sun.

"Ho if I was a stream I'd chance to go,
A-racin' to the sea,
Yonder way fresh waters flow,
An' that's the way for me.

Leapin' an' boundin',
Splashin' an' soundin',
Rudder 'round rock an' log,
With pike an' trout,
I'd frisk about,
A good ole riverdog!

Through leafy glades the waters call,
Across the open meadow,
An' when I sight a waterfall,
Why down will go me head oh!"

Deyna's eyes flickered as he fought against the slumbers that threatened to overcome him and he yawned aloud, giving out a squeaking sound. Rillflag turned his attention to the shallows, where movement had caught his eye.

"Hah, I see watershrimp. What do you say, liddle matey? Shall we catch some to take back to Redwall? You stay there an' watch your ole dad. I'll show you the way 'tis done!"

Sawney crouched behind a broad elm trunk on the other side of the stream, Grissoul at his side. He pulled the Seer close, whispering in her ear, "That's no Taggerung, he's a full-grown otter. What do we do now?"

"That one is no part of my vision," the vixen Seer whispered back. "Thou canst do what thou likes with him; he is none of our concern."

Felch the fox, Dagrab the rat and Vallug Bowbeast were hiding on the other side of the stream, behind a high-banked bend. Sawney slid back toward them, staying on the opposite bank until he was out of the big otter's eyeline. Then he waved to Vallug, attracting his attention. Sawney pointed to Rillflag and made a gesture with both paws, as if firing a bow. Vallug nodded. It was a simple task for a skilled bowbeast.

Standing waist deep in the water, the otter straightened

up with a double pawful of watershrimp. Too late he saw the ferret standing on top of the bank with bow drawn and a shaft notched onto the string. Vallug Bowbeast could hit a dragonfly on the wing; the big otter standing still in the stream presented an easy target. He fired and Rillflag lay dead in the water, an arrow in his heart.

Felch and Dagrab dashed along the bank toward Rillflag's body. The fox pulled up sharply, almost tripping over the otterbabe that lay on the mossy bankside. He grabbed at the little creature, scrabbling to pick it up, but Deyna growled and bit his paw, drawing blood. Felch yowled and grabbed for the axe he carried in a shoulder strap.

"Yowch! Yer liddle savage. Bite me, would yer?"

Sawney was crashing through the shallows on the far side of the ford when he saw Felch raise the axe. Quick as lightning Sawney threw his knife, and Felch lay screaming beside the otterbabe, his right paw fixed to the axe handle by Sawney's blade. The ferret Chieftain was across the ford in an instant. Stamping down on Felch's wrist, he pulled the knife free, hissing dangerously in the fox's agonized face, " 'Tis your lucky day, Felch. I let you live. But if you even look at that babe the wrong way again I'll carve you a new mouth, right across your stupid throat!"

Sawney picked up Rillflag's cloak from the bank and wrapped the otterbabe in it, chuckling as it snapped at his paws. "You're the one, all right!"

Vallug nodded at the slain Rillflag. "Warra you want doin' with 'im, Chief?"

Sawney was happy. He smiled at the bowbeast and winked. "Push him out into center stream. He'll float down to the sea and never be seen again. Good work, Vallug. Great shot!"

The ends of the cloak trailing in the water, Sawney waded across the ford to where his Seer was waiting.

"So then, Grissoul, is this what we came seeking? Tell me."

The Seer opened the cloak and inspected Deyna. She held up the infant's right paw, showing Sawney the marked pad. "See!"

The four-petal mark was pink and clear, like a tiny blossom. Sawney looked anxiously at Grissoul. "Well, is it really him?"

For answer the Seer took Sawney's paw and placed it against the otterbabe's footpaws. Then she spoke.

"Zann Juskarath Taggerung!"

Sawney recognized the ancient words, and translated them.

"Mighty warrior of our clan. Taggerung!"

Rawback the stoat climbed down from his lookout perch in an oak. "Break camp, Sawney's comin'. Get ready t'move fast!"

Swift and silent the clan began breaking camp, though there was not much for them to do other than pick up their belongings. Shortly thereafter Sawney and the six vermin came hurrying in. The ferret made it clear he was in no mood to linger or display the prize he had taken.

"Stir yourselves, come on, move! Move!"

He stood watching as they packed gear on their backs and hastened to obey. To add extra menace to his demands he embellished the facts a little.

"If you don't move sharpish there'll be a horde of Redwall warriors on your tails before noon, and I hear they don't take prisoners. 'Tis your own loss if you don't keep up!"

Checking the last ones from the deserted campsite, Sawney walked backward as he followed them, the better to observe the two who were bringing up the rear. Wherrul and Antigra bent to their task of clearing up the tracks, dusting over the ground with clumps of groundsel that they had twined with stalks of strong-smelling wild watermint to dispel the vermin odors. Antigra could sense Sawney's eyes upon her. She kept her gaze down and her back bent, one paw steadying the baby stoat who scrabbled about in the sling upon her back. Like Sawney, the pair walked backward, following the ferret Chieftain as he left the camp and took the trail in the wake of the Juskarath clan.

Half asleep on his back in the cloak hammock, Deyna gave a growl. Antigra heard it, and raised her eyes slightly. Sawney was staring at her, patting his precious bundle.

"Oh yes, I've got the Taggerung. Do you know how to greet him in the old Juska tongue? Zann Juskarath Taggerung, that's what you say. Let me hear you say it, Antigra."

Antigra's eyes blazed hate as she spat out the phrase. "Zann Juskarath Taggerung!"

The smile on Sawney's face was far more fearsome than any hateful glance she could give. Antigra felt herself tremble as he drew the blade from his belt.

"Zann. Great warrior. That is one of our new Taggerung's titles by right. I won't have another creature taking the name. You will call your brat Gruven, after his foolish father. It's either that or I bury you both here. Take my word for it!"

Antigra lowered her eyes, bowing to Sawney Rath's will. "Gruven he shall be."

A moment later the camp lay deserted, the dust motes drifting down on to the sun-warmed ground. There was not a trace of anybeast in the silent glade. It was as if Sawney Rath and his Juskarath clan had never been there.

Ten times the sun had set over Redwall Abbey since Rillflag's ill-fated journey. Old Hoarg, the ancient dormouse Gatekeeper, held his lantern high. A brawny Skipper of Otters and eight of his crew entered. Hoarg pulled up the cowl of his habit as damp spots fell from the dark cloudbanked night sky.

"Hmm, that rain is goin' to get heavy. Wouldn't

surprise me if a storm broke soon. Well, Skip, still no sign of 'em, eh?"

The big otter placed his tattooed paws against the gate and slammed it shut, knocking down the long wooden bar and locking it. He shouldered his javelin wearily and prepared to follow his crewbeasts up to the Abbey. "Not a trace, matey," he called back to Hoarg. "Not a single flippin' whisker. An' this rain ain't goin' to improve our chances tomorrow!"

As the crew seated themselves around a table in the kitchen a flash of lightning illuminated the stairway to Great Hall. Skipper waited until he heard a distant rumble of thunder. "'Twill hit 'ere afore midnight, I reckon."

Friar Bobb hovered anxiously about a fat young squirrel who was pushing a food-laden trolley into the kitchen. "Watch what you're doing, Broggle. You'll spill the watershrimp and hotroot soup. And mind that dip in the floor, you dozy beast!"

Skipper turned his gaze on the hapless Broggle, lowering his eyebrows and showing a row of clenched teeth in mock menace. "Is somebeast spillin' good watershrimp'n'hotroot soup?"

Broggle pushed the trolley to the table, trembling. "N-n-n-no, sir. I ai-ai-ain't spilled a drop, sir!"

Skipper's face broke into a huge grin as he hugged the young kitchen assistant to him. "Well done, bucko. Serve it up an' have some y'self!"

Broggle shook his head vigorously as Skipper released him. "N-n-no, sir, 'tis too 'o-'o-'ot for me. I m-made it jus' the w-way you like it!"

The soup was served, with onion bread to dip in it and special cold mint and dandelion tea to cool the otters' mouths. Friar Bobb placed another bowl on the table, this one containing extra hotroot essence, for those who liked their soup good and fiery, which the ottercrew did. When the soup was finished Broggle served dessert: an immense heavy fruitcake, with blackberry wine to wash it down.

Cregga and Foremole Brull joined them at the table. The Badgermum had only the usual question to ask.

"Still no trace of Rillflag and the little one?"

Skipper shook his big scarred head. "Sorry, marm. Ten days now, an' anybeast'd think they vanished off the face of the earth. Where's Filorn an' the liddle maid Mhera? They usually comes down t' see me."

Foremole drummed on the tabletop with her heavy claws. "They'm oop in ee room, zurr, a-grieven an' a-weepen sumthin' turrible, pore h'otters."

"They heard the main outer gate shutting, you see, Skip," Cregga explained. "Now if Rillflag and the babe were with you they would have come straight up to see Filorn and Mhera. So they know there's been no sign of them. No point in coming down just to hear bad news, is there?"

Skipper put aside his food. Blinking hard, he turned away and sniffed. "My 'eart an' paws goes out to 'em, marm. Nobeast could 'ave searched 'arder than me'n'the crew 'ere. I feel as if I knows every blade of grass 'twixt 'ere an' the ford, every rock'n'boulder. I'd give my rudder to find 'em alive an' well!"

Cregga put out a paw and touched the otter's craggy face. "I know you would, Skipper. You're a goodbeast and a true friend. 'Tis a sad thing to say, but perhaps we may never find them. Maybe someday . . ."

Skipper nodded. "Aye, marm, I know what you mean. Maybe someday somebeast will come across their bones. Even then we won't know the full truth. Be that as it may, me'n'the crew'll be out searchin' on the morrow, storm or fair. Rillflag was a matey o' mine, an' if'n he is dead then I'll find his bones, just to give peace o' mind to pore Filorn an' young Mhera." Skipper's paw sought the javelin he had placed nearby, and his eyes grew hard as flint. "But if'n Rillflag and the babe was murdered, I'll find the scumbeast who did it, on my oath I will. There won't be enough of 'im to leave bones when I'm done with the coward. Nobeast I know could've bested that otter face-to-face. He would've fought twice as fierce, protectin' the liddle cub. I wager you an acorn to an oak Rillflag was murdered by ambush!"

Sister Alkanet had been listening from the stairs of Great Hall. Now she entered the kitchen and came to the table.

"I've got an idea that might work. Why don't you stop searching for Rillflag and the babe? Concentrate on scouring Mossflower for any creature you find there. Bring them back to Redwall. We can question them here; somebeast surely must have seen or heard something!"

Broggle appeared with his trolley to clear the platters away. "Th-th-that's what I'd do, too. G-g-good idea, S-Sister!"

Skipper shrugged. "Well, we've tried everythin' else an' got nowheres. Maybe yore idea'll work, Sister."

Cregga rose from the table, politely stifling a yawn. "As you wish, then. Do you need any help from us, Skipper?"

The otter stroked his rudderlike tail reflectively. "If this storm's blowed itself out by dawn we'll start the search for anybeast roamin' Mossflower then. Aye, marm, we could do with some Abbeybeasts to lend a paw. I never refuse a willin' offer. If'n they want to volunteer I won't refuse 'em!"

"S-sir, I—I'd like to vo-vo-volunteer!"

Friar Bobb shook his head. "Your job is here with me in the kitchens, Broggle, not scouring the woodlands."

The blind Badgermum reached out and ruffled Broggle's ears. "We can't refuse a willing heart, Friar. Let him go."

Skipper chuckled, pressing his big hardwood javelin into the young squirrel's chubby paw. "That's the spirit, matey. You'n'me between us, we'll be a right pair o' terrors!"

Broggle nearly overbalanced trying to lift the big javelin. "Any v-vermin'd better w-watch out for us, s-sir!"

Cregga began to feel her way to the door, smiling broadly. "Aye, Broggle, woe to the villains who run into you, but take good care of Skipper. He's not a Redwall Warrior like you."

Thunder exploded over Great Hall just as a vivid lightning flash illuminated the place in sudden white light. Cregga ran her paw along the walls, each stone familiar as she made her way toward the dormitory stairs. Over the din of the rain battering against the high windows, the badger's keen ears detected another noise. It was the sound of somebeast weeping aloud, over by the far wall, where the great Redwall tapestry hung. Silently the blind Badgermum moved in that direction, holding out her paw until it came into contact with the tear-wet face of a young ottermaid. Drawing her close, Cregga held her comfortingly.

"Mhera, my pretty, I thought you were upstairs with your mother. What are you doing down here all alone?"

Mhera allowed the Badgermum to stem the tears with her apron. "Mama knew there'd be no news of Dad and little Deyna. She cried herself to sleep, and I did too. But the thunder woke me, so I came down here to ask Martin the Warrior if he knew what had happened to my dad and the baby."

Cregga touched the tapestry, feeling the beautiful embroidery that countless paws had worked upon. Martin the Warrior mouse, Hero of Redwall, there had never been one braver than he. Martin was depicted standing in his armor, holding the great sword, whilst terror-stricken vermin fled from him in all directions. The Warrior had a strong but kindly face, and wherever anybeast stood in Great Hall he seemed to be looking at them, eternally watching over his beloved Abbey.

Cregga placed her paw on Mhera's head. "My poor little one. Did he tell you anything?"

Mhera wiped a paw across her eyes. "Not really. I just stood here waiting for an answer, but none came. Then I began to feel happy and sad just looking at him. I decided

31

to cry all of my tears out for the last time. I felt determined not to spend my life weeping, but to comfort and help my mama as best I could. I think Martin was trying to tell me to be strong. Does that sound silly, marm?"

Cregga felt her spirit lift. Mentally she thanked Martin. "No, little one, it sounds good and brave. Well, seeing as you have the desire to help others, you can guide me up to my room."

Mhera managed a tiny smile. "Now *that* sounds silly, marm. Nobeast knows their way about the Abbey better than you. What need do you have of me?"

Cregga took Mhera's paw and patted it. "I don't tell this to every creature, but I'll let you in on a secret. I'm a very very old badger whom everybeast relies upon for advice, about all sorts of things, especially Abbey matters. So I try to help as much as I can, but nobeast ever seems to ask if *I* need anything. Old Cregga can take care of this and old Cregga can sort that out. But who is there to help old Cregga? I tell you, Mhera, the older I get the more I need a friend."

The ottermaid clasped the Badgermum's big paw tightly. "I'll be your friend, marm, forever."

Cregga opened the door to her room and ushered Mhera in. Rain pattered heavy and drumlike on the window. The badger found her massive overstuffed armchair and collapsed into it with a grateful sigh. There was lots of room on the arm for the young otter to perch upon.

Cregga put her footpaws up on a worn buffet. "This room once belonged to a great friend of mine, Abbess Song. She passed on seasons before even your mother was born. Ah me, the times Song and I spent together. She was a happy creature, always singing; that's why her name suited so well. If she were here now, looking at two miserable creatures like us, I know what she'd have to say."

"Go on then, marm, tell me what Abbess Song would say."

"She'd say, if that young otter's your friend, tell her to stop calling you marm and call you by your name, Cregga. Then she'd say that the way to stop feeling sad and sorry is to think up an excuse for a feast. One involving all the Redwallers. Get everybeast feeling happy and you'll feel happy yourself, that's what Song always said."

Mhera thought about this, but only for a second. "What a wonderful idea, Cregga! Let's have a great feast. It'll be summer's first day when the new moon appears, six days from tomorrow. Is that a good excuse for a feast?"

A lightning flash lit up the badger's silver-striped muzzle. "It's a marvelous excuse, young 'un. We always have a feast at change of season, so let's make this one an extra special feast. We'll call it . . . er . . . what shall we call it?"

Mhera clapped her paws. "The Summer of Friendship feast!"

Cregga drummed her footpaws on the buffet. "Splendid! What a lovely idea, the Summer of Friendship feast. Now, besides the food we want lots of games, singing, dancing, poetry and musicians. We'll be in charge of that part, and leave the food and drink to those who know best, the Friar and Drogg Cellarhog. First thing tomorrow the preparations begin. We'll make this a feast to remember, eh, Mhera?"

The ottermaid agreed wholeheartedly. "We certainly will. My mama can help Friar Bobb; she's a great cook, you know. It'll help to take her mind off things."

Cregga could fight her weariness no longer. A huge yawn escaped her lips. "Oh, dear. Wish I was as young as you again!"

Mhera plumped the pillows behind her friend's head. "Sleep now, Cregga. You can get a lot of things done in dreams. Start planning our festivities. I'll see you in the morning."

Listening to the door close as Mhera crept back to her mother's room, Cregga mused to herself in a drowsy murmur, "Get a lot of things done in dreams. What a wise young creature my young friend is. Yes, just the type Redwall needs . . . wise."

Thundersound grew more distant, the lightning less frequent. The volume of rain decreased to a drizzle as the storm moved east from Redwall and the green vastness of Mossflower Wood. Peace fell over the Abbey. Cregga in her armchair, Dibbuns in their dormitories, grown creatures in their beds, slept on through the night hours calm and undisturbed. New-baked bread, flat oatcakes, scones and turnovers lay on the warming shelves in the kitchens, ready for breakfast. Red embers glowed in the oven fires, casting flickering shadows in the silence. Friar Bobb, who never left his beloved kitchens, snored gently upon the truckle bed in the cool larder. Skipper and his crew snored uproariously in Cavern Hole, sprawled on forms, tables and makeshift mattresses. Broggle, the fat little assistant cook, lay on the first stair, still gripping Skipper's big javelin. He growled and showed his teeth in slumber, hunting evil foebeasts through the woodlands, and, of course, subduing and capturing every one of them.

You can get a lot of things done in dreams.

4

Grissoul had a fire going in a small cave on the riverbank, a tiny island of light in the darkness. Outside, the clan huddled in their hastily erected shelters, mostly frayed pieces of canvas draped over branches and spearshafts. They ate what they had managed to forage that day on the journey westward. Squatting in any dry place, the vermin cursed the storm under their breath, hoping for fairer weather with the arrival of dawn.

Warm and dry inside the cave, Sawney Rath ate the remainder of a poached dace, which the Seer had caught to feed the otterbabe. Sawney watched the little creature with a fondness that was almost fatherly.

"Look at him, sleeping like a proper old riverdog. Did you see him tearing at the fish? Not much wrong with his appetite!"

Grissoul turned the babe's paw lightly, exposing the birthmark. "It is interesting that fortune chose an otterbeast to be Taggerung. An intriguing choice."

Sawney drew his knife. Holding it by the point, he placed the handle between the tiny paws. Deyna clasped it in his sleep. The Chieftain's fierce eyes turned to the vixen Seer.

"Aye, it's not usual, but otters grow big and tough, full

35

of muscle and sinew. I'm sorry he wasn't a ferret like me, but an otter will serve the purpose just as well. We have to live by the prophecy and the omens. Thank your fortunes it wasn't a toad we found bearing the mark you foresaw!"

Grissoul agreed. "Aye, thank the fortunes!"

Sawney chuckled quietly, so as not to disturb his charge. "Look at him, holding the knife like a true assassin. This one will be a powerful force when he grows, mark my words."

Rain pattered on a canvas groundsheet that had been fixed to the riverbank side close to the cave. Beneath it Antigra lay nursing the babe she now had to call Gruven. Two other vermin shared the shelter, Wherrul the rat and Felch, the fox whose paw Sawney had crippled with his blade. Wherrul had his nose close to the fox's ear, complaining bitterly.

"It ain't right, cully. We've carried the tents from the scrublands to the ford, an' now we're carryin' them back the way we came. Where's the sense in it, if we ain't allowed to use them? Sittin' out 'ere in the rain under bits an' scraps o' canvas, while Sawney's got a dry cave, a fire an' good cooked vittles. My back's killin' me from bein' bent double all day, wipin' out tracks. It ain't right, I tell yer!"

Felch held up his injured paw, whispering a reply. "Lookit that. Me axe paw ruined for life. Sawney didn't even allow me t'stop an' bandage it. I 'ad to make do with a dollop of bankmud an' a dock leaf. All because I looked the wrong way at that otterbrat. Huh! Taggerung! I never 'eard of no otter becomin' a Taggerung. But I'll bide me time, Wherrul, wait'n'see. One day Sawney'll pay for what 'e did to me, I swear it!"

Hugging Gruven, Antigra closed her eyes, ignoring the whines and complaints of her companions. By listening hard she could hear Sawney and Grissoul's voices echoing from the cave. Sawney was speaking of the otterbabe's future.

36

"As he grows I'll teach him all I know; the use of the blade, the teeth, the claws. I'll teach him never to turn his back on an enemy, to be more tough and savage than anybeast. Vallug can instruct him in archery. Little Taggerung'll be twice as fierce and fast as my father ever was. He's my lucky charm; since the time I found him my stomach hasn't troubled me."

Grissoul stared into the fire, trying to extract messages from the flame-shapes and the pattern of the ashes. "Aye, the fortunes of the Juskarath grow by the way. Thou did well to heed the omens, Sawney Rath. But the babe must be taught speed. Quickness of the paw is everything. Give him a short and fast name to remind him of this."

A thought caused Sawney's eyes to light up. "Tagg! That's what we'll call him. Tagg!"

Grissoul brought forth certain objects from her pouch. "Now is the time to speak the ancient words and confirm him. Cover thine eyes when I put my paws o'er the flames."

The Seer placed a hawk feather, a piece of flint and the gleaming skull of a small pike on the ground beside the otterbabe. Holding her clenched paw above the flames, she opened it suddenly. A blue flare rose from the fire for a brief moment, intense and bright, and Grissoul began to chant.

"Who can outrun the wind
Yet turn on a single leaf,
Stand silent as an amberfly
Or steal the breath from a thief?
The Taggerung!
Who can outswim a pike
Whose eyes are keen as the hawk's,
Who brings death in his wake
Yet leaves no mark where he walks?
Zann Juskarath Taggerung!"

Sawney watched as the Seer painted the clan sign on the sleeping infant's face. A black stripe flanked by red dots, with a small added lightning flash of blue on his left cheek, to denote that he was no ordinary creature. The little one slept through it all. Sawney lay down beside him, sharing the cloak. Grissoul had never seen the ferret Chieftain show tenderness toward any living thing, so she was astonished when Sawney spoke gently to the babe.

"Zann Juskarath Taggerung. My son Tagg!"

Outside, under the sheltering canvas, Antigra bit her lip until she tasted blood.

"Take the life of my mate, take the name from my son. I am strong, I can bear it. One day I will take it all back and add the title Taggerung to my son's name. I hope you are strong then, Sawney Rath; strong enough to face a slow and painful death along with your new son Tagg. It will happen, I swear it on the memory of my mate Gruven!"

Within the hour following dawn over Mossflower Wood, mist tendrils rose from the treetops. Heralding a fine warm day, the sun stood high in a sky as blue as a kingfisher's tail plumes. Skipper took his javelin from Broggle's paws. Ears and whiskers twitching, the big otter signaled by waving the weapon at the searchers nearby.

"Down, mateys. Lie still'n'quiet!"

Broggle dropped to the damp grass, his eyes wide. "Wh-what is it, S-S-Skip?"

The otter threw a paw about Broggle's shoulder. "Ssshhh, an' listen!"

It was the strangest of sounds, like three or four creatures all playing instruments, jangling but tuneful. It sounded even odder when a wobbly voice warbled along with the music in an off-key tenor.

As whatever it was drew nearer, Skipper and Broggle had to stifle giggles at the ridiculous song.

"Collop a lee collop a loo,
Oh what I wouldn't give to
Be eating a filthy great plate o' salad,

38

Instead of composing this beautiful ballad.
A collop a lollop a lee oh loo,
Life's hard without scoff 'tis true,
You can always eat a lettuce, but
A lettuce can't eat you. Oooooohhhhhhh
Collop a lee a loo!

Hey ho for the life of a fool,
I recall my mater's wise rule,
Eat at least ten meals a day,
Or else you'll waste away she'd say,
Poor dear Mater so old and grey,
And fat as two bales of hay, hey ho. Ooooooohhhh
Father said to me, 'M'lad, you know,
She's goin' to explode one day . . . I saaaaaaay.'
So both of us ran away. Hey!"

Crashing and stumbling through the undergrowth came a hare. On his head he wore what had been a three-pointed jester's cap, but only the top point with its bell remained. The sides had been cut away, and in their place the hare's ears formed the other two points, each with a small round bell attached to it. His outfit defied any accurate description; it was a flowing, trailing ragbag of harlequin silk, with bits catching on the bushes and tearing off as he toppled and staggered through the woodlands. The reason for his awkward gait was apparent: he was carrying a gigantic musical instrument. The thing had strings and levers, bells, small bugles, flutes and even a drum attached to it. He finally tripped and fell flat on his back. It did not seem to put him out a bit. He lay there, struggling with the instrument and still composing his ridiculous song.

"Oh the saddest sight on earth,
I'll tell you for what it's worth,
Is the sight of a chap with an empty tum,
Laid low in the grass without a chum,
A jolly pal, who'd stay close by,

An' feed a poor fellow some apple pie,
Or perchance a slice of onion pastie . . ."

He stopped and gazed up at the faces of Skipper's crew surrounding him. "I say, what rhymes with pastie?"

Broggle offered a suggestion without thinking. "Fastie?"

The hare looked thoughtful. "D'you think so? Let's give it a try. *Or perchance a slice of onion pastie, with which to break my morning fastie* . . . hmm. Many thanks, old scout, but it'll need a bit of workin' on, wot!"

Two of the ottercrew lifted the instrument from the hare. Skipper grabbed him and pulled him upright. "Tell me, how long've ye been in these woods? Have ye seen anythin' of a growed otter an' a newborn otterbabe? Or did ye cross the path of any vermin lurkin' 'ereabouts? Speak up!"

The hare blinked and flopped his long ears to either side. "Bit of a tall order, old lad, but here goes, wot! I'm merely a wayfarin' traveler, passin' through, y'might say. As for otters, big or small, haven't spotted any, aside from your goodself. Not a sign of a vermin either, lurkin' or disportin' their scummy hides t'me view. Sorry I can't help you, sah!"

Skipper eyed the odd creature up and down. "I think you'd best tell us yore name, matey, and what yore doin' 'round here."

Before he could stop him, the hare had seized Skipper's paw and was shaking it heartily. "Matey? Do I detect a nautical twang, sah? Well, me name ain't matey. Boorab the Fool at y'service, bound to take up an exalted position as Master of Music, Occasional Entertainer, Composer, Melodic Tutor and Instructor in all things lyrical. Without payment, of course. My services are rendered purely out of the kindness of my heart, y'know. The only remuneration I require is vittles. Food, sah. Grub, tucker, scoff, call it what y'will, as long as they're not stingy with the portions, eh, wot wot! By the bye, do any of you chaps

40

know the way to an establishment known as Redwall Abbey?"

Skipper broke the furious paw-shaking grip of Boorab. "Yore goin' to Redwall Abbey?" He turned to Brother Hoben, who had volunteered for the search. "D'you know anythin' about this, Brother?"

Hoben, being Recorder, had his paw on all Abbey business. He shook his head in bewilderment. "First I've heard of it. Tell me, Mr. Boorab, who appointed you?"

Boorab waggled his ears nonchalantly. "Nobeast really. One hears these things, y'know. Did you treat a goose with a bashed-up wing pinion last summer, perchance?"

Hoben recalled the incident. "We did! He spent quite a bit of time with us until Sister Alkanet got him flying again. Why do you want to know?"

Boorab relieved Drogg Spearback of a candied chestnut he had taken from his apron pocket, and chewed on it reflectively. "That was the very chap. Big white feathery cove, honked a lot. It was him who told me that your jolly old Abbey hasn't got a hare, or a music master in residence there. So I thought I'd nip down an' fill the post, wot. Hope no other bally hare's beaten me to the blinkin' job. Got to keep the old eye out for cads an' rotters an' job pinchers these days, y'know, wot!"

Drogg drew Skipper to one side. "I thinks we'd best take 'im t'the Abbey," he murmured. "Cregga will decide what to do with 'im. What d'ye say, Skip?"

The brawny otter smiled as he shot a glance at the quaint beast. "Hmm. Hares are good mates, 'cept when yore sittin' next to one at dinner. I think we'll 'ave to take Boorab back with us, Drogg. Supposin' 'e fell over again. With that thing lyin' atop of 'im the pore creature might never get up. I couldn't 'ave that on me mind an' sleep easy. Makes y'feel responsible for 'im, don't he?"

Drogg turned back to Boorab and gave him the good news. The hare was delighted, but he changed mood swiftly. Facing the ottercrew, he puffed out his narrow chest and acted as though he were challenging them.

"Right, laddie bucks, any of you think you're stronger than me?"

Otters are fiercely proud of their agility and strength. Two hefty young ones sprang forward, a male and a female, and spoke together as one. "I am!"

Boorab clapped them on their backs. "Splendid. Two towerin' figures of otter muscle, wot! I'll wager you could lift that instrument with me jolly well sittin' atop of it, right?"

It was the otters' turn to swell their chests and flex their muscles. They chorused in agreement. "Right!"

Skipper knew what was coming, and he chuckled as Boorab answered, "Good, then I won't sit on the instrument. You two carry it an' I'll walk. I'm not lazy, y'know!"

Skipper walked alongside Boorab. He was developing a liking for the comical hare. "Boorab the Fool, eh? You ain't such a fool, matey, I can tell. That's the queerest ole instrument I've ever clapped eyes on. What d'ye call it?"

Boorab stumbled slightly, and gathered up his flapping robes. "That, sah, is a haredee gurdee. Made it m'self. Mandolin, drums, fiddle, flutes, bugles an' harp, all in one. With a space in the mandolin bowl to carry one's vittles. Empty now, as ill luck an' a healthy appetite would have it."

Broggle trundled along between Skipper and Boorab, carrying the big otter javelin. Boorab cast an eye over the fat little squirrel. "Ah, my friend the rhymester. What do they call you, young sir?"

"B-Broggle, M-Mr. Boorab s-sir!"

Boorab glanced across at Skipper. "How long has the little chap had that stammer, wot?"

Skipper shrugged. "Long as I've knowed 'im."

Boorab turned back to Broggle. "Say ah!"

"Ah!"

"Now longer. Say aaaaaahhh!"

"Aaaaaaahhhhhh!"

"Excellent. Now sing out like this." The hare composed a small tune on the spot. "My name is Broggle, Mr. Boorab saaaaah!"

Skipper nodded at the young squirrel to do as he was bidden.

Broggle took a deep breath and sang forth. "My name is Broggle, Mr. Boorab saaaaaaaah!"

The hare smiled. "Very good. Did y'notice anything, Broggle?"

"N-no, s-sir?"

Boorab chucked him lightly under the chin. "You never stammered once when y'had to sing."

An expression of awe and delight framed the young squirrel's face. "I d-didn't, s-sir?"

"No, of course y'didn't, laddie buck. Try singin' instead of talkin'. It'll help, you'll see, wot!"

Suddenly Broggle brandished the javelin and sang out in a clear little voice.

"I didn't stammer once when I had to sing,
So now I'm going to sing everything!"

Boorab winked at Skipper. "Told you that chap was a good rhymester. We'll soon get rid of that stammer, wot wot!"

Skipper grinned from ear to ear. "I think ole Cregga Badgermum's goin' to like you, matey."

Broggle skipped ahead, waving the javelin and singing lustily.

"I work in Redwall kitchens, with old Friar Bobb,
'Cos I'm the cook's assistant, that's my job!"

The hare raised his eyebrows. "Assistant cook, wot? A fine chap t'know, I'd say. I think I'll give the little grubslinger his singin' lessons in the kitchen. Marvelous places, kitchens. Full of food, y'know."

Cregga was in the kitchens with Mhera, Filorn and Friar Bobb, beginning to work on a menu for the feast. Filorn

43

realized that the others were trying to cheer her up, and to please them she joined in with the proceedings, her enthusiasm rising every time Mhera smiled at her.

"Oh, Mama, say you'll bake your apple and raspberry flan, with meadowcream and the pattern of mint leaves on top. Oh, please, we haven't had it for ages!"

Filorn fussed with her apron ties. "I'm not sure I can remember how to do it. The apples are very important. But it's the wrong season for apples, is it not, Friar?"

The fat Friar chuckled. "Not at all, marm. What sort o' Friar would I be if'n I didn't keep a good stock of last autumn's russet apples in my larders? Nothin' like a nice russet!"

"Oh yes there is. Two nice russets, wot, hawhawhaw!"

They were startled by the sudden appearance of the quaintly garbed hare. Friar Bobb grabbed his biggest ladle. "Who are you and what're you doin' in our Abbey?"

Broggle marched in and pointed at the hare with Skipper's lance.

"Boorab is my friend,
On that you may depend,
He's come to stay awhile,
Be nice to him and smile!"

Mhera went into a fit of chuckles. "Broggle, what are you singing like that for?"

The bells on the hare's cap and ears jingled as he did a hopskip toward the ottermaid and gave a low sweeping bow. "Why, my pretty one, well may you ask. But observe, when my pal Broggle sings he doesn't stammer. Simple, wot?"

Cregga's booming voice brought the hare to instant attention. "Stand up straight, sah, ears upright, whiskers t'the front, paws in position an' tail well fluffed. Identify y'self!"

The hare threw a smart salute and rattled off his reply. "Boorab the Fool, marm! That's B for Bellscut, O for

44

Oglecrop, O for Obrathon, R for Ragglewaithe, A for Audube, B for Baggscut. Marm!"

Cregga beckoned the hare to her. She put out a paw and ran it over his face and ears, nodding sagely. "Hah! That's a Baggscut face all right. I should know, after commanding more than a thousand hares when I ruled the mountain of Salamandastron. Your grandfather, Pieface Baggscut, served under me as a leveret runner."

Boorab chuckled. "Stap m'whiskers, old Grandpa Pieface, eh wot? Now there was a beast who c'd lick his weight in salad, wot wot! I remember one time, I must've been no bigger'n young Broggle there . . ." His voice faltered as the realization of whom he was addressing hit him. He gulped.

"Oh corks! Oh crumbs! Marm, oh, marm! You must be Lady Cregga Rose Eyes, Ruler of Salamandastron, the wild-eyed Warrior Queen, the Belle of the blinkin' Bloodwrath, the kill—"

"Silence! That's enough of that, young Baggscut. And who told you to stand easy? Come to attention, sah!"

Skipper, who had been listening from the doorway, came forward. The otter Chieftain held a long whispered conversation with Cregga, who held a huge handkerchief to her face. To anybeast watching it looked as if she had been taken by a fit of coughing, but in fact Cregga was bravely striving to stop herself roaring out with laughter. Mhera felt sorry for the odd hare, standing nervously to attention, ear and cap bells tinkling faintly, awaiting the pronouncement of his fate, and whispered, "Don't worry, sir, it'll be all right."

It took Cregga a considerable time to get her mirth under control, but at last she wiped her eyes and cleared her throat portentously.

"I am informed that you are applying for the post of Redwall Abbey's Master of Music, Occasional Entertainer, Composer, Melodic Tutor and Instructor in all things lyrical. I understand that you have come on the

45

recommendation of a goose that was treated here some while back. Is that correct?"

Boorab the Fool brightened up instantly. "You've got it in one, marm! Y'won't regret it, I promise you. Why, I'll have the whole flippin' Abbey singin' an' dancin' from dawn to bally nightfall, just you wait'n'see, wot!"

Cregga shut him up with a wave of her paw. "But you haven't got the job yet. I'm not too sure we are in need of your services. Tell me, what would you want in return?"

Boorab sucked his stomach in, trying to look like a beast who ate virtually nothing. "Want in return, marm? Merely a place to rest the old head an' the odd pawful o' fodder. I'm more of a dedicated artist of m'trade. The thought of food makes me sick sometimes. Why, a butterfly with no appetite eats more'n I jolly well do."

Cregga turned her face to Filorn and Mhera. "Hmm. What do you think? Shall I hire the hare?"

Mhera was surprised her opinion had been asked. "Oh, please do, Cregga marm. Look at the way Mr. Boorab is helping Broggle. Mama, say you want him to have the job."

Filorn could not help smiling at the look of noble dedication that Boorab was radiating in her direction. "I'll go along with my daughter. I think you should let Boorab have the position, Cregga."

The badger sat stroking her chin until the tension grew unbearable for Boorab, and he flung himself at her footpaws. "Merciful marm, say y'will, I bally well beg you. Don't leave a benighted Baggscut blunderin' about in the storm an' snow without a kindly crust to keep fur an' ears together! Oh, me little furry friend Broggle, sing a line on my behalf!"

The young squirrel obliged.

"He wants to work in the kitchens,
With me an' Friar Bobb,
So please Cregga Badgermum,
Give him the blinkin' job!"

Cregga drummed her paws on the tabletop, then nodded. "Here's my decision. I'll put you on one season's probation, Boorab, under the supervision of Filorn, Mhera, Broggle and Friar Bobb. Now, you four, keep your eyes on this hare. His meals must be the same size as any other Redwaller's, no secret snacks or midnight feasts. If he is reported just once for raiding the larders, out of the gate he goes! Also, he will sleep and rise at the same time as everybeast. Unless he is ill, there will be no lying late abed, or nipping off to shady spots for a snooze. We will see how he behaves throughout this coming summer season. Do you agree with our terms, Boorab? That's the offer, take it or leave it."

For answer, Boorab bowed formally, did a somersault of joy and began serenading them on his haredee gurdee, which two of Skipper's crew had just brought in. It jangled and booped wildly as Boorab made up the words as he went along.

"Derry cum day foll deeh,
I pray you listen to me.
I'll compose this ditty upon the spot,
To say you're a jolly decent lot,
Then you can judge for yourself or not,
What an Abbey asset I'll be,
Derry cum day foll deeh!

You lot won't know you're born,
I'll be up before each dawn,
To serve you crumpets'n'tea in bed,
To wake you gently I'll stroke your head,
I'll warble sweetly until you're fed,
And you'll never feel forlorn,
'Cos I'll do this every morn!

Sing derry cum de all day,
What a splendid hare you'll say,
He's handsome, happy an' modest too,

An' what a cook, why I'll tell you,
There's nought this super chap can't do,
Let's never send him away,
Yes, I'll wager that's what you'll say!"

Boorab finished his song with a winning smile, made an elegant leg, bowed, picked up his haredee gurdee and overbalanced. He fell amidst a discordant crash of bugles, drums and twanging strings. Foremole Brull covered her eyes with a huge digging claw, patting Cregga sympathetically with the other.

"Hurr, marm, oi bets ee be deloighted we'm gotten uz ee hurrbeast. Yurr, Skip, lend oi ee paw to 'elp 'im oop."

Boorab struggled from under the mammoth instrument. "Soup? Did somebeast mention soup? I say, you chaps, it must be time for dinner, wot?"

Friar Bobb placed his head mournfully on Filorn's shoulder. "My ole dad used t'say that feedin' a hare was like chuckin' pebbles down a deep well. You never fill it in a thousand long seasons!"

5

Though it was still only early summer, hot noontide sun beat down on the shore. Below the flotsam-wreathed tideline clear turquoise shallows gave way to a bright blue sea. A mild southerly breeze chased the creamy spray atop swelling wavebanks as they rolled in to break noisily amidst rockpools and sandy coves. Juskarath tents had been pitched on the beach, where dunes met the strand. Sitting on a blanket, the otterbabe waited hungrily for the next mouthful of food, which Grissoul was feeding him from a large scallop shell. Sawney hovered around them like an old mother hen, watching anxiously.

"Be careful there's no fish bones in that concoction!"

The Seer used a mussel shell to transfer food to the babe's mouth. "Fret thou not, there is nought in this but goodness, the white flesh of sole and young seaweed, cooked with a pinch of sea salt. I made it myself. See how he likes it?"

Sawney tweaked the otterbabe's stomach. The infant growled at him for disturbing its feed, and the ferret Chieftain chuckled. "Hoho. Did you hear that? My little Tagg has a temper. Eat it all up and grow strong, my son. Did they bring in some fresh young scallops for his supper?"

Grissoul shrugged. "They say the tide is strong yet. When it ebbs they will search for some among the rocks."

Sawney's mood changed. He whirled on a group lounging nearby. "Juskarath clanbeasts frightened of a few waves? Up, up off your idle backs and get foraging. Our Taggerung needs only the youngest, most tender scallops for his evening meal. You, Felch, take Antigra and the rest of your lazy crew. Get out of my sight, and I warn you, don't come back with empty paws!"

They hurried to obey. Sawney turned his back on them, to face four rats who came stumbling hot and tired down a steep dune. "Well, did you cut any sign of creatures tracking us?"

Shaking his head, the lead rat hunkered down in the sand. "Nah, nary a pawmark or a bruised leaf. 'Tis more than twoscore days now. If they was comin' after us we'd 'ave spotted 'em long since, Chief."

Sawney drew his blade and pointed it at the rat. "I asked for your report, not your opinion, Grobait. How far back did you search? Tell me the truth!"

Grobait cringed visibly under Sawney's ruthless eyes. "Close on a day back upstream, Chief. There wasn't a sign of anybeast, I swear it on me oath!"

Sawney toyed with the trackers as they nodded agreement with Grobait and sat waiting on their clan leader's word. He turned, as if dismissing them.

"A day upstream, eh? Well, let's see you try a little further afield this time. Say two days upstream. Get going!" He tossed his knife, catching it by the point, ready to throw. "Now go!"

Allowing himself a humorless smile, Sawney strode off, listening to the labored grunts of the rats as they clambered wearily back through the shifting sand to the dunetops.

Standing shoulder-deep in a rockpool, Antigra shielded her eyes as a wave cascaded over the stones. The other vermin who had been sent with her and Felch to gather scallops coughed and spluttered seawater. Antigra kept her gaze riveted on the ferret Chieftain, who was swaggering about among the tents, issuing orders. The stoat mother gritted her teeth.

"Look at him, Sawney Rath the high and mighty clan chief, giving out commands like the warlord of a battlehorde. Run here, run there, fetch me this and give me that, bring the best of scallops. And what for? The supper of an otterbrat!"

A weasel named Milkeye tossed a scallop into the bag slung about Wherrul's neck and turned his one good eye on Antigra. "Better not let him 'ear yer talkin' like that!"

Antigra hurled a scallop against the rock, smashing the shell. "An ottercub, a mewling puking little riverdog, lying on a blanket in the shade, getting the choicest vittles specially cooked and fed to it. Look at my babe Gruven. I had to leave him lying there alone, out in the sun, while I forage for the next meal of a so-called Taggerung!"

Milkeye rescued the broken scallop and sucked the contents from its smashed shell. " 'Tis agin the clan law to speak like that about a Taggerung."

Antigra curled her lip in contempt. "You'll see who the real Taggerung is when my son grows. He'll be ten times tougher and faster than that spoilt little ruddertail, you wait and see. Since Sawney brought that creature to our clan he's changed. Treading roughshod over us, killing and injuring his own tribe."

Felch held up his useless paw. "Aye, Antigra's right, but who's goin' to challenge Sawney? He's like lightnin' with that blade of his."

Antigra flattened her back against the rocks, avoiding another shower from a breaking wave. "Sawney Rath's father was even harder and swifter, but time caught up with him. I remember him being the Taggerung when I was a young 'un. He lived on his legend. Sawney is older than us, growing out of his prime, more every season. We

51

can wait. The time will arrive when his paw isn't so strong, nor his eye so keen. That's when I'll take my revenge, aye, me and my son against him and his parentless brat!"

Wherrul nudged Antigra. "Hush. 'Ere comes the vixen!"

Grissoul came to the pool's edge, calling to them over the booming surf. "Bring enough scallops for Sawney Rath too, and don't be all day about it. I want thee to forage for wild celery and onion in the dunelands. Bring any fresh herbs ye see growin' there also!"

Wherrul hauled himself from the water, the bag of scallops clacking against his chest. "Young scallops cooked in wild celery'n'onion an' herbs," he muttered under his breath. "I wouldn't mind a bowlful o' that meself."

Milkeye elbowed the rat aside. "Huh! You'll git wot yore given, like the rest of us, a lick of Sawney's temper an' leftover scraps!"

Antigra reached out a paw and helped Felch ashore. "Don't fret. It may take seasons yet, but we can wait. One day the tables will be turned, and then 'twill be us eating off the fat of the land!"

At Redwall Abbey there was no shortage of good food. That same evening Redwallers shared the best of everything as they sat in a lantern-lit orchard to celebrate the Summer of Friendship feast.

Before the food was served, the elders, counselors and parents took their places. Smiling and nodding to one another, they watched as the newly formed Dibbuns' choir filed in and stood in order of height, tallest standing at the rear, a line kneeling in front of them, and the front row, of the smallest, sitting cross-legged. All were holding tiny lanterns, and their clean robes and well-scrubbed faces were bright in the soft reflected light.

Boorab strode majestically to the rostrum, which was the old upturned wheelbarrow decked out in summer blossoms. The hare made a dignified bow to the elders, and then, taking out a bulrush baton, he coughed formally.

"Lady Cregga, respected elders, good creatures all, may I present tonight for your delight an' delectation—"

"Wot's a dite of lectation?" little Floburt piped up, much to everybeast's amusement. Boorab silenced her with a severe twitch of his nose.

"Without further ado the Jolly Dibbuns Choir of Redwall will render for you, under my expert direction, a recently composed masterpiece, written by m'goodself, wot wot . . ."

"Wot wot!" several Dibbuns chorused together. The hare waggled his ears fiercely at them before continuing.

". . . entitled, 'Welcome to the Feast'."

Boorab produced a small reed pitch flute and blew upon it, then attempted to get the key right. "Fahfahfah . . . Soooooooodomeelah . . . Lalalalahhhhh. One two . . . !"

The little ones made a ragged start but soon picked up the air.

"Welcome to the feast, the feast,
Oh welcome one and all.
Good creatures that you are, la la la,
Who dwell within Redwall.
The lark descends unto its nest,
The sun has sunk into the west,
And we are left all evening long,
To bring you light and song.
Sing out sing out each joyous beast,
Oh welcome to the feast, the feast,
We wish you happy seasons long,
And hope you liked our sooooooong!"

Applause broke out as the final note drifted clear upon the summer night air. Boorab took a hasty bow and turned back to his Jolly Dibbuns Choir.

"Well done, chaps an' chapesses. Dismiss to your seats

now. Not you, young Egburt. Come here, sir, this very instant!"

The little hedgehog quailed under his hare conductor's gaze. "Er, heehee, I sorry, sir. I sing d'right words nex' time."

Boorab held the quivering baton under Egburt's snout. "Fiend! Lyric wrecker! What were those words y'were singing? C'mon, spit it out. Recite 'em back t'me, sah!"

Egburt remained silent until his Grandpa Drogg growled, "You do as Mr. Boorab sez, young 'un, or 'tis straight up t'bed for ye. Go on, what were you singin'? Tell the truth!"

Egburt was left with no choice. Raising his spikes, he boomed out in a fine baby baritone:

"Ho welcome to the feast, you beast,
I hopes you trip an' fall,
I've got a fat grandpa, ha ha ha,
Who'll prob'ly eat it all.
The lark defends his feathery chest,
The sun has sunk into his vest,
If he don't bathe before too long,
There'll be an awful pong . . ."

Boorab snapped the baton and covered his eyes. "Enough! Enough I say, you small spiked song destroyer!" The outraged hare turned abruptly to Drogg Spearback. "Well, sir, what the deuce d'you think of your grandson, wot?"

Stroking his grey headquills, Drogg eyed Egburt pensively. "Hmmm. If'n you ask me I think the liddle 'un shows a rare talent for rhymin' words together."

Boorab pondered Drogg's answer a moment, then he laughed. "Hawhawhaw! Well, frizzle m'whiskers, sah, y'could be right there. The rogue does have a certain turn of phrase, wot?"

Drogg patted his ample stomach proudly. "I reckon he

gets it from me. Us Spearbacks was always good poets, fine singers too. Comes nat'ral to us!"

Brother Hoben, the old Recorder, had a wry sense of humor, despite his serious and learned look. Not averse to a bit of mischievous fun, he tapped Boorab.

"Excuse me, sir, but if I were you, being the official Abbey poet and musician, I'd say that Drogg was issuing a challenge!"

Cregga and several others caught on to Hoben's idea. They pounded on the tables, calling out, "A contest! Let's have a contest!"

Drogg shrugged. " 'Tis fair enough wi' me. I don't mind."

Bells tinkled on Boorab the Fool's ears as they stood erect. "I accept the challenge, sah. A contest it is, an' may the best creature win, wot wot!"

Hoarg the dormouse piped up. "A contest then, but what's the subject to be?"

Cregga's keen ears detected the creaking of trolley wheels. "They're bringing the food to serve for our feast. Let's make that the subject. A musical verse praising our cooks' efforts!"

Boorab waggled his ears confidently. "Ask me t'sing about scoff? Pish tush, sah, a piece of cake. You're on a loser, me old pincushion. Like to go first?"

Drogg waved a paw airily. "Nay, sir, if'n yore so good, don't let me stop ye!"

Boorab stood to one side, striking a fine dramatic pose, one leg behind the other, ears laid soulfully back, paws bent at chest height in true hare singing fashion. Casting his eyes over the contents of the carts as the servers trundled them up to the tables, he coughed politely and launched into a speedily delivered verse.

"How can one count the praises of the vittles at
        Redwall?
Oh pure delight, oh wondrous night, I'll sing to one
        and all.

Thaaaaaaat blackberry pudden looks such a good 'un,
All covered in meadowcream.
And the hazelnut cake, well for goodness' sake,
I hope it's no jolly old dream.
That huge apple pie, oh me oh my, the crust is pipin'
hot,
Good creatures be nice, an' save me a slice,
Or I'm sure I'll die, wot wot!"

Foremole Brull nudged a cart with her footpaw. It rolled gently to rest, right under Boorab's nose. The hare tried bravely to carry on singing with a hot mushroom pastie, dripping onion gravy, simmering under his nose.

"What rhymes with pastie, I'll try to sing fastly,
My nose tells me 'tis wrong,
This soon will grow cold, if I may make so bold,
Pray excuse a chap endin' his song!"

Unable to stand it any longer and disregarding cutlery, the gluttonous hare hurled himself barepawed upon the pastie. "Grmmff, I say, sninch grrmm, rotten ole mole cad, grmmff grrawff, put me off my ditty completely, grrmff snch, bounder!"

Drogg the Cellarhog fell off his chair laughing. "Ohohoho! Nobeast could follow that. Mr. Boorab, take a tankard o' my finest October Ale an' wet yore whistle. You win!"

Sister Alkanet helped herself to a plate of summerfruit salad and a mint wafer spread with soft white cheese. Looking prim and severe, she remarked to Brother Hoben, "That hare! What a bad example he's setting to the young ones!"

On the Dibbuns' table many Abbeybabes were imitating Boorab. Little Gundil was practically washing his face in a portion of deeper'n ever turnip'n'tater'n'beetroot pie, the moles' favorite dish. A tiny squirrel and an infant mousemaid were feeding each other pawfuls of summer vegetable soup. It looked as if they were trying to paint one another. Egburt and Floburt were at either end of an applecream flan, munching away, eager to see who would get to the center first. Table manners, spoons, forks and serviettes were completely ignored as each Dibbun went at it paw and snout, enjoying the fun and the food.

Sister Alkanet was about to rise and deal with them, but Brother Hoben pressed her gently back into her seat. "Please, Sister, let them be. Dibbuns don't remain babes forever. To them 'tis all a game. Let them play it and have a good time."

Alkanet picked daintily at her salad and fumed. "It's not good manners. Look at the mess they're making. Look at those smocks, clean on this evening. Who'll get the job of washing them? Certainly not me!"

A fat kindly mole called Wummple poured a beaker of dandelion cordial and passed it to the Sister, chuckling. "Hurrhurrhurr. Doan't ee fret, marm, oi'll be ee washerbeast. You'm let they likkle h'infants be. They'm full of 'arpiness. Oi wishes oi cudd join 'em, burr aye!"

Cregga sat back, sipping at a small cup of elderberry wine, letting the festive feeling wash over her. Everybeast tried to press different delicacies upon the Badgermum, and she acknowledged them all pleasantly.

"Yurr, marm, oi saved ee summ turnip'n'tater'n' beetroot poi. Foremole Brull sez et makes ee grow big'n'strong!"

"Thank you, Gundil. I hope it makes me grow big and strong as you."

"Try some o' my best October Ale, marm. It's a new barrel."

"Put it down there, Drogg, I'll sample it later, thank you."

"Cregga, I saved you a slice of plumcake, it's delicious!"

"I'm sure it is, Friar. I was hoping you'd save some for me."

The big badger accepted everything graciously,

knowing that her friends thought she did not know what was on the tables because of her blindness. Cregga, however, had extra-keen hearing and an amazing sense of smell and touch. Hot scones she could detect by their aroma, even before they were brought to the festive board. Cheese, ale, salads, bread, trifles, cakes and puddings: she could place them all in position uncannily, at their exact location in relation to where she sat.

Somebeast touched her paw, and without thinking she identified who it was. "Enjoying yourself, Skipper?"

The otter shook his head in amazement. "Aye, marm, 'tis a grand ould party. I brought you some o' the watershrimp an' 'otroot soup wot Mhera an' Filorn made. Stripe me rudder, I never tasted better in all me life, marm!"

Cregga mentally chided herself. She had not heard the voices of the ottermum and her daughter at table for a considerable time. She patted an empty space on the tabletop, indicating where Skipper should place the bowl of soup.

"Tell me, Skip, have you seen Mhera and Filorn anywhere?"

"In the kitchens last time I clapped eyes on 'em, marm. Why?"

Cregga rose from her seat carefully. "Sit in my chair and keep it warm for me, Skip. I'll not be gone for too long."

Cregga merged back into the orchard trees, not wanting anybeast to offer a paw to guide her. Silently, her paws touching familiar objects, she made her way back to the Abbey building. Like a great moonshadow she drifted noiselessly through Great Hall and down to the kitchens. Filorn and Mhera did not hear her enter. They were hugging each other, seeking comfort as their bodies shook with grief. No sooner did Cregga hear them weeping than she was at their side, holding them in her huge embrace.

"There, there, now, my good friends, what's brought all this about?"

Mhera turned her tearstained face up to the sightless eyes. "Oh, Cregga, I tried my best, I really did . . . but we miss Dad and little Deyna so much . . ."

Sobs overcame the ottermaid's voice. Filorn continued haltingly where her daughter had left off.

"I knew that Mhera was trying to cheer me up after our loss, so I tried to be brave and not think about it. We busied ourselves and helped to organize the feast, and it worked for a while. But Skipper was so pleased with our freshwater shrimp and hotroot soup that he reminded us of poor Rillflag. It was my husband's special favorite, you see. So we couldn't help . . . oh, dear!" A fresh burst of tears overflowed from Filorn.

Cregga herded them both into a corner. Sitting them down on a bundle of empty sacks, she whispered, "Stay there. I'll be back in a tick." She returned shortly with a flask and three tiny pottery cups, and sat down with the two otters. "This is very old strong damson wine, so sip it carefully."

The Badgermum filled the three cups, then waited until they had taken a couple of sips and dried their eyes.

"Tastes like sweet fire, doesn't it? I usually have a drop on winter mornings, just to get me up and about. There, that's better. I've seen lots of winters, you know, far more than anybeast I know. Every grey hair on my black stripes is a winter. Aye, I've seen friends too, good companions, die and pass over to the silent streams and sunlit glades. Oh, I'm not the hard old blind warrior everybeast thinks I am. I've grieved and shed tears, long and loud, for my departed loved ones. Don't be ashamed to weep; 'tis right to grieve. Tears are only water, and flowers, trees and fruit cannot grow without water. But there must be sunlight also. A wounded heart will heal in time, and when it does, the memory and love of our lost ones is sealed inside to comfort us."

Filorn clasped the badger's paw. "Thank you for your kind words, Cregga."

The Badgermum could not resist pouring them another small tot of the damson wine. "Oh, don't thank me, I'm speaking for all our Redwallers. 'Tis they who want to thank you for arranging and cooking most of this feast. Friar Bobb and young Broggle had almost the entire evening off because of your splendid efforts. As for me, well, I don't want to see you both hiding in these kitchens, and neither would your dad if he was here, Mhera. Isn't that right, Filorn?"

Drinking her wine off in one draft, the otter mother lost her breath for a moment, then stood up, nodding. "Whooh! Yes, that's right. Rillflag always used to say that time heals everything and life must go on."

Skipper was standing on a chair. He spotted the lantern Mhera was carrying and called out in a hoarse whisper, "Belay, mates, 'ere they come. Are ye ready?"

Loud cheers resounded as the trio entered the orchard. Redwallers gathered around to thank Filorn and Mhera.

"Many many thanks for the wonderful spread, ladies!"

"Hurr aye, missus, et wurr greatly impreciated boi all!"

"Never had a blinkin' scoff like it in me jolly old life, wot!"

While a molemaid presented each of the otters with a bouquet of flowers, Drogg tipped the wink to Boorab, who had the Jolly Dibbuns Choir ready with a song. Giving Egburt a swift warning glance, Boorab tapped his baton against the upturned wheelbarrow and started them off on the background harmony.

"Rum be diddle dee dum, be diddle dee dum, dee diddledy dum . . ."

The hare pointed an ear at his soloist. Broggle stepped to the front and sang out beautifully into the lantern-lit orchard.

"Ladies dear oh ho we thank you,
For this evening's wondrous feast,

Every Dibbun every elder,
From the greatest to the least.

We can say with paw on heart,
That your efforts did you proud,
So in tribute to your art,
Let us sing with joy aloud.
Ladies dear oh how we thank you,
And in truth we always will,
Knowing that your gracious beauty,
Is in keeping with your skill!"

Amid the applause, Foremole Brull pounded Broggle's back. "Gurtly dunn, young maister. Ee doan't be a-stammeren when ee singen. 'Tis ee marvel!"

The young squirrel flicked his bushy tail triumphantly. "No, marm, an' I don't stammer when I speak anymore, as you can see. Completely cured, thanks to my good friend Mr. Boorab. I sang the words in my mind as I spoke them at first, but now I don't even have to do that anymore. I just speak as I like an' out it comes, without a stammer or a stumble or a trip. Talk? It's the simplest thing on earth! Would you like to hear me recite the alphabet, forward, backward or sideways as you please? 'Tis quite simple, listen . . ."

Broggle was forestalled by Boorab's thrusting a honeyed hazelnut slice into his mouth. The hare pulled Brull to one side.

"Confounded young bounder found his voice earlier this evenin', an' now I can't shut him up. Lackaday, he's babblin' like a bally brook. There's no stoppin' him. Humph. Wonder if I did the right thing, givin' him my special lessons, wot?"

Brull poured the hare a tankard of strawberry fizz. "Nay, zurr, you'm can't teach ee young Broggler to stammer agin. Us'n's ull 'ave to put up wi' et. Hurr hurr hurr!"

Broggle buttonholed Mhera and Filorn. He had decided

to practice his newfound speech powers on anybeast who would listen.

"Ahah, a very pleasant evening to you both. What a magnificent and sumptuous feast, or as my friend Mr. Boorab would say, super scoff, wot wot? Sumptuous. Now, there's a word I could never say when I stammered, but now it's sumptuous, superior, superlative, splendid! What a splendid word splendid is, just like the food you made for us and this smashing summer evening in our Abbey's awesome orchard. It's all too splendiferous for words, ladies!"

Filorn put a paw around Broggle's shoulder and laughed. "It certainly is, young squirrel, and all the better for hearing you speak properly for the first time. Congratulations!"

"Huh, easy for your mum to say," Friar Bobb muttered to Mhera out of the corner of his mouth. "She doesn't have a bedspace near Broggle in the kitchen larder. I'm going to kip down on the Abbey roof if he starts talking in his sleep. What are you laughing at, missie? It's not funny, y'know!"

Mhera took a drink of strawberry fizz from Boorab's tankard. "Oh, hahaha. Sorry, Friar, I'm not laughing at you. Hahaha. It's just that I feel happy all of a sudden!"

Boorab cast a jaundiced eye into his near-empty tankard. "Er, excuse me, my pretty young gel, but next flippin' time you start feelin' happy would you mind standin' next to some other chap's drink, wot!"

Little Gundil offered his beaker to Mhera. "Yurr, miz, you'm can taken ee drink o' mine."

The ottermaid was about to accept the offer when the hare neatly relieved the molebabe of his beaker.

"My turn to pinch somebeast's drink, old chap, wot!"

He swigged down a good mouthful, swallowed it and clapped a paw to his throat. A look of horror spread across his face. He charged off toward the Abbey pond, roaring, "Yaaaagh! It's 'orrible! I'm poisoned! I'm on fire! Whoooaah!"

Gundil stuck out a bottom lip as he inspected the empty beaker. "Hurr, et wurr only summ 'otroot zoop'n'dannyline wine an' 'ot minty tea wi' roasted cheshutters a-floaten in et. 'Tis moi fayvert drink. Vurry tasty, hurr aye!"

Mhera, Filorn, Friar Bobb, Cregga and Foremole Brull fell about laughing helplessly. Broggle wandered amongst them, waving a paw in the air and declaiming airily, "Taken aback was my unfortunate instructor, stricken by a cunning concoction, whilst about him many mingled in mirthful merriment. Truly the Summer of Happiness and Friendship was off to a memorable start, or should that be splendiferous start? I like that word, it's splendiferous!"

BOOK TWO

Fifteen Seasons On

6

Felch the fox had run, taking the blade of Sawney Rath with him. Trees, shrubs, bushes and grass merged into a green blur in the dawn rain as the fox staggered along on leaden paws. Felch had been running since midnight. He was glad of the rain, hoping that it would obliterate his tracks and throw his pursuer off the scent. Instinctively he knew that Sawney would send only one creature to hunt him down. The Taggerung. Blundering into nettlebeds and crashing through groves of fern, Felch felt a numbing terror constrict his aching chest. Who could escape the Taggerung? Now the weariness was pressing upon him; he could feel himself making stupid errors. Rain or no rain, he was leaving a trail that a one-eyed toad could follow. But the sound of a river in the distance drove him onward through north Mossflower. It was the only place where he could possibly stand a chance. Rainwater dropped from his nosetip onto his parched tongue, and he blinked away the raindrops that broke against his slitted eyelids. A fat woodpigeon, which had been feeding on the ground, whirred up in front of him. The startled fox let out a ragged yelp and tripped over an elm root. Ignoring the blood seeping from an injured footpad, he struggled upright and continued a crazily weaving course. River noise grew loud in his ears as he skirted a yew thicket, his heart rising at the sight in front of him: a high riverbank with alder and willows overhanging it. There were rocks sticking up from the water, which was deep with no shallows. Felch grabbed a leafy bough and scrabbled down. Cold swirling currents took his breath away for a moment as he landed shoulder-deep in front of a rock ledge. Pushing through the overhanging willow foliage, he wedged himself safely under the bank, out of the main current. Rain dappled the river surface, its noise making hearing difficult. The fox was bone weary, hungry, wet and miserable, but at least he was alive. His eyes flickered from side to side as he watched for any unusual movement around him, some inner sense suddenly telling him there was another creature nearby. From above, small fragments of rock and earth splashed into the water, and overhanging willow branches swayed, dipping downward into the current.

Felch held his breath, one paw inching underwater to the knife thrust in his belt. He could not see the banktop because of the jutting ledge he was hiding under, but he knew somebeast was up there, casting about in the rain for signs of him. It had to be the Taggerung! The fox brought Sawney's blade slowly out of the water, and with his good paw held it ready for an upward thrust. Felch had never been so afraid, but he was desperate. Taggerung or not, he was prepared to sell his life dearly, rather than be dragged back to the Juska camp to face Sawney Rath's vengeance.

His eyes flickered upward. On the bank above he could hear movement over the rain noise. A shower of pebbles hit the water, along to his right, then he caught the sound of a dead twig breaking underpaw further away. Felch, his heart pounding, remained motionless beneath the ledge for a long time, his vulpine sense stretched to the limit as he listened and watched. After what seemed like an eternity, he finally knew. The Taggerung had gone, he was sure of it. Shuddering with a mixture of relief, cold and exhilaration, Felch relaxed. He had escaped the Taggerung!

However, he knew that he would have to stay hidden until night. If the Taggerung was hiding somewhere nearby, waiting for his quarry to break cover and run, he would be disappointed. Felch was no fool. Having got this far, he was not going to betray himself with any sudden silly moves. Lowering the dagger until it was level with his face, the fox saw his breath misting the bright blade. He cursed inwardly. Maybe if Sawney's blade had not been in question the Juska Chieftain might not have sent the Taggerung to hunt him down. Perhaps he might have let Felch desert the clan, not thinking the fox of any great importance, merely an old follower with a useless paw.

The fox's eyes hardened as he recalled how mercilessly Sawney had ruined his paw with that same blade. A fierce determination swept over him, and he thrust the knife back into his belt. It belonged to him now! If he was no longer one of the Juskarath, he would take something with him, for all the long seasons of unrewarded service to Sawney Rath. Aye, the ferret would remember Felch the fox, every time he looked at the space in his belt where the blade used to be.

Since late spring Sawney had been harassing Antigra and her companions, as if expecting some sort of mutiny within the clan. He had come down hard on Felch, abusing and humiliating the fox at every possible opportunity. It had come to a head on the previous evening. Felch had been out foraging in the north sector of Mossflower's sprawling woodlands, and was returning to camp with a meager offering, a small trout he had found floating dead in a stream. Sawney stood watching him trying to slink into camp unnoticed. The Juska Chieftain was tossing his knife idly, catching it by the blade, just below its tip. He looked to be in a foul mood.

Sawney's rasping voice had stopped the fox in his tracks. "What's that dirty piece of rubbish you're sneaking back with?"

Felch avoided the ferret's irate stare. "It's a fish, a young trout I caught."

Sawney sniggered nastily, pointing with his knife. "You must've had a hard battle bringing in a monster like that. Hold it up so we can all see it. Go on, hold it up."

Felch raised the small dead fish halfheartedly, his eyes fixed on the knife Sawney was toying with. He could guess what was coming by the tone of Sawney's voice.

"I told you to bring a bird back, a big fat woodpigeon. I know an idiot like you has trouble telling the difference between a bird and a fish. But maybe I'm wrong, perhaps you didn't hear me right, Felch. Is it your ears?"

The fox didn't answer. Sawney, who was more than thirty pawsteps away, raised his blade, ready to throw. "Aye, I think it must be your ears. Let's take a look at one. Stand still, now. This shouldn't hurt . . . much!"

Felch ducked as the blade flashed from Sawney's paw. Even as fast as he moved, the fox could not avoid the blade's nicking his left eartip. Zipping past him, the knife disappeared into the woodland foliage.

Grissoul, who was squatting at a nearby campfire, cackled. "A goodly throw, but thou gave him too much warning. Felch did well to avoid thy blade. Let him live."

Sawney ran across to the cringing fox and kicked him. "If you don't find my blade, you'll die slowly, for 'twas you who lost it by moving when I told you not to. Find the knife, Felch, and I'll let you live. Though I'll still take that ear as a punishment for disobedience. Now get searching, addlebrain!" Another savage kick sent the fox scurrying off into the bushes on all fours.

70

It was not until nearly midnight that he discovered it, a fair distance from the camp. Rain had started to fall when the fox glimpsed a shaft of moonlight glimmering off the wet sapphire pommel stone. Felch tugged on the knife, which had buried its point deep in a sycamore trunk. He pulled it free, falling over backward in the process. Behind him the camp lay still, firelight gleaming hazily through the closed tents. Sawney and his clan lay sleeping. Felch knew his prospects were bleak. Sawney Rath would take his ear if he returned. Without thinking further, he thrust the blade into his belt and ran.

Beneath the bank ledge, with rainwater beating constantly on the river surface, Felch wedged himself tighter in. Weariness and fatigue overcame him, and despite the water's cold embrace he fell asleep.

Throughout the day the rainfall began to slacken from downpour to drizzle. By midafternoon the skies had cleared, giving way to warm sunlight. Steam rose from the banksides, wreathing around trailing willow fronds. Small flies began hovering close to the bank where the current ran more slowly. It was one such gnat, wandering around on the fox's nosetip, that wakened him. The first thing Felch saw was a tail rudder, decorated with two white fishbone tailrings. Fearfully he raised his eyes. Standing on a rock not a whisker-length out from the bank was a barbaric-looking young otter. His only clothing was a short barkcloth kilt, girdled by a broad eelskin belt. He wore two patterned flax wristbands and a single hooped gold earring. The eyes, piercingly dark, stared back at Felch from behind the face tattoos of the Juskarath clan. The otter carried no weapons, save for the knife, which he had removed silently from the sleeping fox's belt. Felch did not notice when the gnat stung his nosetip. He was not even aware that the rain had stopped and the sun was out. The young otter reached out gracefully and took hold of the fox's shoulder with his sinewy paw. Felch tried to shrink further back against the ledge. But the tremendous

71

pawstrength wrenched him savagely forward, almost completely out of the water. He was dragged up onto the rock, his ear right next to the hunter's mouth. The voice he heard was a gentle whisper that chilled his blood more than any rivercold.

"Nobeast escapes from me. I am the Taggerung!"

7

Rainwater drummed against the high stained glass windows of Redwall Abbey. It had poured down since midnight of the previous day. Even the hardiest of workbeasts had left their outdoor tasks for dry ones indoors. Mhera and her faithful friend Gundil emerged from the kitchens to sit upon the cool stone steps to Great Hall. Brushing a paw across her brow, the ottermaid blew a sigh of relief. "Whooh, goodness me, it's hot in there, Gundil!"

The mole undid his apron and wiped the back of his neck. "Yuss, marm. If'n oi'd stayed thurr ee moment longer they'm be 'avin' ee roastified mole furr dinner. Hoo aye!"

Filorn's call reached them from the kitchens. "Mhera, Gundil, come and take this tray, please."

She met them just inside the kitchen entrance. Filorn was no longer a young ottermum. Her face was lined and she stooped slightly, but to her daughter she still looked beautiful. Mhera, who was now much taller than Filorn, touched her mother's workworn paw gently.

"Why don't you finish in there for the day? Go to the gatehouse and take a nap with old Hoarg in one of his big chairs."

Filorn dismissed the suggestion with a dry chuckle. "Food doesn't cook itself, you know. I'm well able for a day's labor. Huh! I can still work the paws from under either of you two young cubs!"

Gundil tugged his nose in courteous mole fashion. "Hurr, you'm surpintly can, marm. Boi 'okey, you'm a gurt cooker, all roight. But whoi doan't ee take a likkle doze?"

Filorn presented them with the tray she was carrying. "If I listened to you two I'd never get out of bed. Now take this luncheon up to Cregga Badgermum, and be careful you don't trip on the stairs. Gundil, you carry the flagon and Mhera can take the tray."

Cregga was dozing in her chair when she heard the approaching pawsteps. "Come right in, friends," she called. "Gundil, you get the door. Put the flagon down in case you drop it!"

They entered, shaking their heads in wonder. Cregga patted the top of the table next to her overstuffed armchair. "Put the tray down here, Mhera. Mmmm, is that mushroom and celery broth I can smell? Filorn has put a sprinkle of hotroot pepper on it, just the way I like it."

She checked Gundil. "Don't balance that beaker on the chair arm. Put it there, where I can reach it easily."

The mole wrinkled his snout. "Burr, 'ow do ee knoaw, Creggum? Anybeast'd think you'm 'ad ten eyes, 'stead o' bein' bloinded."

She patted his digging claw as he replaced the beaker. "Never you mind how I know. Hmph! That door has swung closed again. Open it for me, please, Mhera my dear. This room can get dreadfully stuffy on a rainy summer's day."

Mhera opened the door, but it would not stay open. "Warped old door. It's starting to close again, Cregga."

The badger blew on her broth to cool it. "Have a look in the corner cupboard. I think there's an old doorstop in there, on the bottom shelf."

Mhera did as she was bidden, finding the object immediately. "Oh, look, it's a little carved squirrel, made from stone, I think. No, it's made from heavy dark wood. Where's it from?"

Cregga dipped a barley farl in her broth and took a bite. "It belonged to Abbess Song. Her father, Janglur Swifteye, carved it from a piece of wood he found on the seashore. That was longer ago than I care to remember. Though I do recall that when Song was old she used it as a doorstop too. She gave it to me before she passed on. Why don't you take it, Mhera? When Song was young she was a lot like you in many ways. I was going to leave it to you when my time comes, but you might as well have it now."

Mhera took the carved statuette to the window and turned it this way and that, admiring it. "Thank you, Cregga, it's lovely. Abbess Song's dad must have been a very skilled carver, it looks so alive. What a pity it ended up as just a doorstop. Here, Gundil, take a look."

The mole took hold of the carved squirrel and inspected it closely, sniffing and tapping it with his digging claws. "Burr, wunnerful h'objeck. 'Tain't no doorstopper, tho'. This 'un's a bokkle."

Mhera looked at her molefriend curiously. "A bottle? You mean a sort of flagon?"

Gundil nodded sagely. "Ho urr. Oi see'd one afore. Moi ole granfer 'ad one shapened loike ee moler. Kep' beer in et ee did."

Cregga poured herself cold mint tea. "Tell us then, Gundil, how can a statue be a bottle? How would you get anything into it? Where's the top, where's the neck?"

The mole grinned from ear to ear with delight. "Hurrhurr, marm, see, you'm doan't be a knowen everythin' arfter all. Ee top is ee head an' you'm turn ee neck. Lukkee!" He twisted the statuette's head, and it came away from the neck. Inside had been cunningly carved out to form a bottlelike container.

Gundil passed it to the badger, and Cregga felt it all

75

over with her huge paws. The Badgermum's voice went hoarse with excitement. "Mhera, your paws are daintier than mine. There's something inside. Can you reach in and get it out?"

Mhera's paw fitted easily into the cavity. She brought forth a scroll, held by a ribbon with a red wax seal. "It's an old barkcloth parchment with a ribbon and seal!"

Cregga abandoned her lunch and sat up straight. "Is there a mark upon the seal?"

Mhera inspected the seal. "Yes, Cregga, there's a letter S with lots of wavy lines going through it. I wonder what it means?"

The Badgermum knew. "The Abbess's real name was Songbreeze. Her sign was the S with breezes blowing through it. Can you see properly, Mhera? The light in here means nothing to me. Gundil, run and fetch a lantern, please. Hurry!"

Clearing the tray from the table, they placed both lantern and scroll upon it. Cregga felt the seal with her sensitive paws. It had stuck to both scroll and ribbon.

"What a pity to break this lovely thing. I would have liked to keep it, as a memento of my old friend Abbess Songbreeze."

"Yurr, you'm leaven et to oi, marm, oi'll get et furr ee!" From his belt pouch, Gundil took a tiny flat-bladed knife, which he used for special tasks in the kitchen. It was as sharp as a freshly broken crystal shard. Skillfully he slit the faded ribbon of cream-colored silk and slid the blade under the wax, cleverly lifting it away from the scroll in one undamaged piece.

Mhera held it up admiringly. "Good work, Gundil. It looks like a scarlet medallion hanging from its ribbon. Here you are, Cregga."

Taking it carefully, the Badgermum smiled with pleasure. "I'll treasure this. Thank you, Gundil. I'm sure nobeast but you could have performed such a delicate operation!"

Gundil scratched the floor with his footpaws, wiggling his stubby tail furiously, which moles will often do when embarrassed by a compliment. "Hurr, et wurrn't nuthin', marm, on'y a likkle tarsk!"

Mhera was practically hopping with eagerness. "Can we open the scroll now, Cregga!"

The blind badger pulled a face of comic indifference. "Oh, I'm feeling a bit sleepy. Let's leave it until tomorrow." She waited until she heard her friend's sighs of frustration. "Ho ho ho! Go on then, open it. But be sure you read anything that's written down there loud and clear. I wouldn't miss this for another feast. Well, carry on, Mhera!"

The barkcloth had remained supple, and Mhera unrolled it with meticulous care. There were two pieces. A dried oak leaf fell out from between them, and she picked it up.

"There's two pages of writing. It's very neat; Abbess Song must have been really good with a quill pen. A leaf, too."

Cregga held out her paw. "Give me the leaf." Holding it to her face, she traced the leaf's outline with her nosetip. "Hmm, an oak leaf. I wonder if it's got any special meaning? What does Song have to say? Come on, miz otter, read to me!"

Mhera began to read the beautifully written message.

"Fortunate are the good creatures,
Dwelling within these walls,
Content in peaceful harmony,
As each new season falls.
Guided in wisdom by leaders,
One living, the other long dead,
Martin the Warrior in spirit,
And our chosen Abbey Head.
'Tis Martin who chooses our Champion,
Should peril or dangers befall,

77

But who selects the Abbess,
Or Abbot to rule Redwall?

I was once your Abbess,
A task not like any other,
To follow a path in duty bound,
I took on the title of Mother.
Mother Abbess, Father Abbot,
They look to you alone,
For sympathy, aid, and counsel,
You must give up the life you've known.
To take on the mantle of guidance,
As leaders before you have done,
Upholding our Abbey's traditions,
For you alone are the One."

There was a brief silence, then Cregga repeated the last line. "For you alone are the One!"

Mhera looked perplexed. "Me?"

Gundil climbed up and sat on the arm of Cregga's chair. "Wull, et surrpintly bain't oi. This yurr moler wurrn't cutted owt t'be no h'Abbess, no miz, nor a h'Abbot noither!"

Cregga chuckled, stroking the mole's furry head. "You've got a point there, friend. I couldn't imagine you in the robes of an Abbot."

Gundil folded his digging claws over his plump stomach. "Nor cudd oi, marm, gurt long flowen garmunts, oi'd trip o'er an' bump moi 'ead!"

Mhera held up a paw for quiet. "There's writing on this other page too, that's if you want to hear me read it?"

Gundil spoke out of the side of his mouth to Cregga. "Yurr, she'm a h'Abbess awready, bossen uz pore beasters abowt. We'm best lissen to miz h'otter!"

Mhera gave them a look of mock severity and coughed politely. "Ahem, thank you. Now, there are several things written down here. First of all it says this. Oak Leaf O.L."

Cregga passed her the leaf. "Here's the oak leaf. Take a close look at it, Mhera."

The ottermaid inspected it. "O.L. It's a bit faded, but Abbess Song wrote those two letters here on the leaf."

Gundil cast his eye over the two carefully inked letters. "Ho urr. O.L. stan's furr h'oak leaf. Wurr ee h'Abbess a-tryen to tell us'n's sumthink?"

Cregga gave his back a hearty pat. "That's sound mole logic, my friend. Read on, Mhera!"

The next lines Mhera read affirmed what Gundil had guessed.

"Though I am no longer here,
I beg, pay heed to me,
O.L. stands for Oak Leaf,
A.S. leaves you her key.
                              A.S."

Cregga caught on fast. "A.S. Abbess Song! It's simple really."

Mhera interrupted her. "Not as simple as you think. Listen to the second verse.

"If you would rule this Abbey,
G.H. is the place to be,
At the T.O.M.T.W.
Look to the L.H.C."

Gundil scratched his snout in puzzlement. "Hoo urr, they'm a gurt lot o' letters!"

Mhera smiled confidently. "Let's go down to the gatehouse and find out, shall we!"

Cregga eased herself from the big armchair. "Gatehouse?"

Mhera took her friend's paw. "Of course. G.H., gatehouse. Lend a paw here, Gundil."

Even with their help, the Badgermum had great difficulty managing the stairs. When they reached the bottom step Cregga sat down, shaking her huge striped head.

"You two carry on to the gatehouse. I'll wait here. I'm

not as spry as I once was. Don't get that parchment wet with rain."

Mhera tucked the scroll carefully into her apron pocket. "But Cregga, don't you want to come with us and find out what it all means?"

The blind badger sighed wearily. "I'll only slow you down. You can let me know what you found out when you come back. Go on now, you two."

When they had gone, Boorab, who had been banished from the kitchens, sauntered by. The gluttonous hare was munching on a minted potato and leek turnover, which he hid hastily as he caught sight of Cregga.

"Er, how dee do, marm? Bit of inclement weather, wot wot?"

She held out her paw. "Help me up, please." As the badger was hauled upright, she sniffed the air. "I smell mint. Have you been plundering in the kitchens again?"

The hare's look of injured innocence was wasted on a blind badger. His earbells tinkled as he shook his head stoutly. "Shame on you, marm. I haven't been within a league of your confounded kitchens. I was down in Cavern Hole, composing a poem to your wisdom an' beauty an' so forth. But I'll bally well scrap the whole thing now. Hmph! Accusin' a chap of my honest nature of pinchin' pastries, wot!"

Cregga shrugged. "But I can still smell mint and I know that Friar Bobb is baking minted potato and leek turnovers for dinner tonight."

Boorab sniffed airily. "Well, of course you can jolly well smell mint. I always put a dab or two of mint essence behind each ear after my mornin' bath. Gives a chap a clean fresh smell, doncha know?"

Cregga inclined her head in a small bow. "Then forgive me. I apologize heartily. We'll share a turnover or two at dinner this evening. I like them best when the crust is dark brown and the potatoes have melted into the leeks."

Boorab fell into the trap unthinkingly. "Well, they're not

quite at that stage yet, marm. The potato is still a bit lumpy and the crust is only light brown."

As he bit his lip, the badger patted Boorab's pocket, squashing the turnover against his stomach. "Aye, I'd leave them to cook properly, if I were you," she growled. "As far as I'm concerned, you're still on probation at Redwall."

The hare watched her lurch slowly off. Dipping his paw into the mess inside his pocket, he sucked it resentfully. "Fifteen blinkin' seasons' probation. Bit much for any chap, wot!"

Grass squelched underpaw in the rain as Mhera and Gundil hurried across the front lawns to the little gatehouse by the Abbey's main outer wall entrance. Gundil was about to knock when old Hoarg opened the door.

"What're you two doin' out in this? Yore wetter'n fishes in water. Come in, come in!" He tossed them a big towel to dry their faces. "So then, what brings ye here, Miz Mhera?"

Taking the parchment from her pocket, Mhera spread it on the table and told the ancient dormouse gatekeeper the whole story to date. Placing small rock crystal spectacles on the end of his nose, Hoarg inspected the document, staring at it for what seemed an age. The two friends maintained a respectful silence. Hoarg sat in an armchair and mused awhile. "Well then, you've come to my gatehouse to search for clues?"

Gundil sounded a trifle impatient. "Yurr, uz 'ave, zurr. May'aps you'm 'elp us'n's?"

The old dormouse nodded sagely. "Oh, I'll help ye all right. But first tell me, Mhera, do you think wisdom, patience, an' the ability not to rush at things would be good qualities in an Abbess?"

Mhera was very fond of the old gatekeeper. "Oh, I do, sir. Why d'you ask?"

Pursing his lips, Hoarg stared out of the window at the rain. "Hmm. Learning, too, I wouldn't wonder. Gatehouse is one single word, you know, not two separate ones. So this place would only be referred to as a single G on your scroll. Now I want you to take your time and think. Name me a place at Redwall Abbey that starts with the two letters G and H."

Mhera slammed her paw down on the table as realization hit her. "Great Hall, of course. Come on, Gundil!"

Hoarg's voice checked them as they dashed for the door. "There you go, rushin' off without thinking. I never make a move before I think anythin' out. I've solved the next bit of that puzzle. I know what T.O.M.T.W. means."

Mhera grabbed the scroll and stuffed it in her apron pocket, her paws aquiver with excitement. "Oh, tell us what it is, sir, please please tell us!"

"Only if you promise to go a bit slower in the future and stop to reason things out, instead of hurtlin' 'round like madbeasts."

"You'm roight, zurr. Us'n's be loike woise snailers frumm naow on, oi swurr to ee!"

Hoarg removed his spectacles and put them away slowly. "I could be wrong at such short notice, but I think that T.O.M.T.W. means Tapestry Of Martin The Warrior."

With his cheek still damp from the kiss Mhera had planted on it, Hoarg sat back in his armchair. He heard the door slam and the two sets of footpaws pounding away over the drenched lawn toward the Abbey building. The dormouse chuckled. "Ah, the speed and energy of younger ones. I'm glad I lost it a long time ago."

Closing his eyes, he went into a comfortable doze.

On entering the Abbey, wet and panting, the two friends spied Cregga. She was sitting on the floor of Great Hall, gazing up at the tapestry. Mhera skidded to a halt beside her.

"Cregga, how could you! Listen to that rain out there. You let us run all the way to the gatehouse and back!"

The Badgermum turned her sightless eyes toward them. "It came to me while I was sitting on the stairs, but you two had already charged off. What did Hoarg have to say?"

Gundil flopped on the floor and began drying his face on Cregga's habit sleeve. "Lots o' things abowt gooin' slow an' payin' 'tenshun an' lurrnen t'be woisebeasts, marm."

The badger dried Mhera's face on her other sleeve. "Good old Hoarg. I remember he was slow and methodical even when he was a Dibbun. Well, here we are. G.H. Great Hall, and there it is, T.O.M.T.W., the Tapestry Of Martin The Warrior. But I haven't the foggiest notion of what L.H.C. means, have you?"

Mhera stared up at the likeness of Redwall's greatest hero, armor-clad and armed with a sword. "No, I'm afraid not. There's one other thing that puzzles me also. What are we supposed to be searching for?"

Cregga put out a paw and touched the tapestry. "Wisdom maybe, knowledge perhaps, L.H.C. certainly, but where do we find it?"

"Hurr, marm, mebbe us'n's jus' sit 'ere an' arsk Marthen ee Wurrier. Thurr wurr never ee woiserbeast than 'im."

Mole logic won the day again. They sat staring at the mouse warrior, each with their own thoughts.

L.H.C.

Lower Hall Cavern?

Little Hot Cakes?

Lessons Have Commenced?

Let Him Choose?

The image of Martin began to swim and shimmer in front of Mhera's eyes. It had been a long hard day, working in the kitchens, dashing about with trays, helping Cregga downstairs, rushing to and from the gatehouse. Cregga was already dozing as Mhera leaned her head against the badger's lap and fell into slumber, still pondering the puzzle.

8

Sawney Rath had not slept well. He was awake long before dawn, wincing and rubbing at his stomach. Taking a beaker of boiling water from the cauldron that bubbled over the glowing embers of his fire, the Juskarath Chieftain sat down outside. Stars still studded the aquamarine sky, and the camp lay still and silent. Sipping at the steaming water, which seemed to relieve his aching gut slightly, Sawney mulled over the past fifteen seasons.

In many ways, Tagg was a puzzle to him. Maybe it was because Redwall Abbey had spawned his adopted son. Perhaps things might have been different if he had taken a wife from his own clan and fathered the future Taggerung. However, the omens were not to be denied, so he had done his best with the otterbabe from the ford bank, the one whose father he had ordered to be slain. While Tagg was small, Sawney had been enormously fond of him. The little otter showed all the physical signs of a Taggerung, swift as lightning and frighteningly strong. He was obedient too, not only to Juska laws and customs, but always to Sawney's wishes. Then he began to grow and think for himself. At first, Sawney admired Tagg's independence. However, gradually it began to cause a rift between them as the otter grew up. The seasons had been good and relatively peaceful, with hardly any killing raids or tribal strife. Then Sawney began noticing things he did not like in Tagg's nature. With a natural talent for weaponry, the knife in particular, the young otter could outfight, outrun or outthink any clanbeast, but in the few quarrels and fights he had he was always merciful at the end. Despite Sawney's urging, he would merely defeat his opponent and release him without punishing him further. Sawney often took him to task about this. Why had he not slain his adversary, or at least crippled him? It was not the way of a Juska, particularly a Taggerung, to show leniency to anybeast he had conquered. Tagg would smile oddly at Sawney and shrug, saying that there was no need for such actions once the challenger was beaten. The Juska Chieftain wanted to see his adopted son become a complete Taggerung, with the same truly barbaric nature he had seen in his own father. What if the clan had to go into battle, or on a killing raid? Sawney had never seen Tagg take a life. Would the young otter prove himself to be a true Taggerung when the moment came? Sawney still felt very close to Tagg, but he felt it was high time his adopted son learned the lesson that would gain him respect through fear. Tagg had to prove himself by slaying somebeast. When he brought Felch back, which Sawney did not doubt for a moment he would, the ferret decided that Tagg would be the fox's executioner. He tossed the remaining hot water away, his stomach suddenly feeling a lot better.

Felch could not believe he was still alive. He sat wet and shivering on the banktop where the Taggerung had hauled him. Soon the strange otter had a fire going. He tossed Felch a small traveling sack.

"Sit there," he ordered curtly. "Warm yourself by the fire, and take a drink. I'm not going to tie you up. Go on, drink. You'll not get far the state you're in. I'll go and get us some food." The fox nodded dumbly as Tagg strode off, calling back. "I won't be long. Keep that fire going."

He dived off the banktop. Felch did not hear a splash as the sleek hunter hit the water. The fox waited a moment, then, shouldering the bag, he crept carefully away from the fire and forced his water-stiffened limbs into a run. As he sped through the bushes, his mind was racing also. Had the Taggerung missed him earlier that day, when he passed along the banktop, above the hideout under the ledge? Maybe the Taggerung was not as skillful as everybeast said, perhaps he had found his quarry through a lucky accident. Felch rushed onward, assuring himself that he would not let himself be captured a second time.

Something flew by him at shoulder level, and the thwack of a hefty rudder laid the fox flat on his stomach. He tried to rise, but the breath was knocked from him as the Taggerung landed upon his back. A paw cuffed his ears soundly, then seized them and dragged his head backward. Felch felt Sawney's blade tickle his throat.

"You don't have much sense for a fox, do you?" the powerful otter snarled menacingly into his ear. "Now tell me, would you like to go on living, or do I slay you right here?"

"Mercy!" Felch managed to gasp hoarsely. "Don't kill me!"

Tagg pulled Felch upright, leading him by one ear like a naughty youngster back to the fire, where he sat him down. The fox cowered fearfully, but the Taggerung merely winked at him. "Right, mate, we'll start again. You stay here, I'll go and get us something decent to eat. Understood?"

The fox groaned as he rubbed the side of his face. "Understood!" Like a flickering sunshadow, the otter disappeared.

Unshouldering the sack, Felch tugged its drawstrings open with his teeth. Inside were four pears and a flask of

86

nettle beer. He drank gratefully and began chewing on a pear. Then he threw some pine twigs on the fire and hunched up close to it, aching all over as life seeped back into his bruised body. Miserably he began to ponder his fate.

The fox's thoughts were interrupted when two nice-sized vendace, slung together by their gills on a reedstalk, landed slap next to the fire. With Sawney's blade, the otter cut two green willow twigs and passed them to Felch.

"Well, come on, do something for your keep. Spit those fish and cook 'em. Plenty there for two. I like vendace." He sat on the other side of the fire, watching the fox. "There's something on your mind, I can tell."

Felch set the fish to sizzling over the fire. "Why didn't you capture me this morning, when you passed by on the banktop? You must've known I was there."

The barbaric-looking otter took a pull at the flask. "Hah! That wasn't me, it was Gruven the stoat. You know, Antigra's son. He's the clumsiest tracker I ever saw. I was watching him from the other side of the bank. Nice soft moss there. I'd been tracking you all night and I was tired, so when I found you I took a nap. You weren't going anywhere. I knew Gruven wanted to make a name for himself by being first to nab you, so I left him a nice false trail. I saw him pass by in the rain. I could see you too, shaking like a leaf under the bank ledge opposite me. Aye, I'll wager Gruven's still tracking away somewhere. He's tough and nasty enough, but slow-witted."

The fish was delicious, and they shared the remaining pears and the last of the nettle beer. Felch felt his nerves returning to normal as he conversed with the Taggerung, aware of the fierce eyes behind the painted face, gleaming in the flames.

"You could've slain me. Why didn't you?"

The otter felt pity for his wretched captive, knowing that Sawney would have some terrible punishment in store for him, but he kept his heavily tattooed face

87

immobile and shrugged, replying as if it were an everyday matter. "Sawney Rath told me to return to camp with two things, his fine blade and you, or your head as proof I found you."

Felch gulped visibly. "My head!"

Tagg twirled the knife in the air and caught it deftly. "I didn't want to mess my supply bag up and have to carry extra weight, so I'm returning you to Sawney alive."

The fox's whole body slumped. There was pleading in his eyes. "If you take me back Sawney will kill me himself."

The otter stared at the amber-handled knife. "I don't make the rules, Felch. You are Juskarath, you know our clan laws. You shouldn't have run."

Felch was about to stand up and reply, but he thought better of it and remained seated. "But Sawney was going to kill me anyway if I hadn't found the knife he had thrown at me. I had no choice, don't you see? There was nothing left for me but to run!"

Tagg pointed the blade at his captive. "You should be dead now, by rights. If Gruven had found you he'd have beheaded you on the spot. Be thankful you are alive, fox."

Felch leaned forward eagerly. "You spared my life. I'll always be gra—"

The otter cut him short. "Save your breath, we've got a fast journey at dawn. Get some sleep, you'll need it. Don't forget, though: one false move and I'll make you wish that Gruven had captured you!"

The Taggerung threw more branches on the fire. He watched the fox until he was sure that Felch was deep in sleep, then he lay down himself and drifted into a light slumber, the blade still held relaxed but ready.

It was the dream that had visited his mind many times over the last fifteen seasons. A beautiful otter face, gentle and kind, and a soft voice murmuring things he could not quite make out. A younger face also, bright-eyed, pretty, repeating the same comforting noises. Soft clean linen against his cheek, aromas of the late spring and delicious food baking. A big male otter standing proudly close by, and the presence of a huge motherly beast hovering in the background. Then there were the walls, old, warm, red stone, everywhere about. Sunlight shafting through a window, turning them to the hue of dusty pink roses. It was a feeling of peace, happiness and safety he had never known running wild outdoors with the Juskarath clan. Tears coursed from under the lids of his closed eyes, dripping down onto the paw that held the knife. Suddenly he was awake, swiftly wiping his eyes and peering out into the still summer night. Behind him he could hear the slow swirl of riverwater. He stayed still as a stone, sensing everything about him, even a wood beetle, trundling by on some nocturnal errand. After a while he relaxed and checked on Felch. The fox was lying on his side, snoring lightly. The Taggerung lay down again, letting slumber wash over him, seeking again those visions he longed to see.

But this time it was a mouse standing in the corridors of his mind. A mouse? Instinctively he knew it to be no ordinary mouse. It was a male, a warrior, clad in battle armor, bearing a sword that was as beautiful as it was fearsome. He knew that if ever he stood against this mouse, he would meet his match. A warrior indeed! But for all that, the mouse smiled upon him, like a father meeting a beloved son. The mouse warrior spoke but a single word.

"Deyna!"

Then he was gone, faded into the dusty citadel of dreams.

Blue-grey woodsmoke from campfires drifted between the sun and shade of woodland trees. Covering his eyes with a paw, Sawney Rath noted the position of the sun standing in the sky at high noon. He turned his gaze onto the two creatures entering the clearing and spoke to the stoat Antigra without even deigning to look at her.

"You see, I told you. Here comes Tagg, my son, right on time!"

Antigra left off plucking the feathers from a dead dove, and threw a hate-laden glance at the Taggerung and his prisoner. Sawney continued to gloat and mock her.

"Nobeast living can hunt like my Taggerung. He was born of the storm and fathered by lightning on a moonless night! Hah! The food you are preparing for your sluggard son will have rotted in the cooking pot by the time *he* returns. Where do you suppose your precious Gruven is? Chasing butterflies ten leagues from here, I'll wager. Huh! He couldn't hunt on his own tail!"

The clan vermin crowded around the Taggerung and his prize, staring at their icon in awe and admiration. Shoving Felch ahead of him, the lithe otter strode through the crowd, like a pike through a minnow shoal. Grissoul stood smiling in front of Sawney's tent. She bowed fawningly.

"Thou did well! Zann Juskarath Taggerung!"

Sawney pushed the Seer aside and embraced his adopted son. "You did it! I knew you would, I said you'd return at high noon with both Felch and my blade, and here you are!"

The otter threw a paw about Sawney's shoulder. "That's the duty of a Taggerung, not to disappoint his Chief. Any food around? I'm famished!"

Sawney gave Grissoul a shove. "Go and get that roasted woodpigeon for my Tagg. Shift yourself, vixen, he's hungry!"

Eefera, one of Sawney's most trusted weasels, had Felch down on the ground, binding his paws with thongs. He pulled the fox upright. "One runaway, Chief, bound an' delivered!"

Sawney brought his face close to the fox, smiling dangerously through slitted eyes, his voice dripping menace. "Last night was your last night, Felch. Enjoy the rest of the day!"

The Taggerung whispered in Sawney's ear. "Punish him good, but don't kill him. That fox is still a useful beast. I think he's learned his lesson."

The ferret Chieftain patted the otter's cheek, still smiling. "Eat now, Tagg, and rest in my tent. Leave this to me. Our clan still carries the name of Rath; I make the rules here."

Tagg was halfway through his meal when Gruven came storming back into camp, thornstung and muddied. The stoat dashed past Antigra without even acknowledging her. Everybeast watched as he confronted the otter, sitting on the ground eating. Gruven pointed at Tagg and yelled, "A false trail! You sent me off on a false trail!"

The Taggerung rose slowly, wiping a paw across his mouth. "And you were clever enough to follow it. Well done, Gruven!"

The stoat was shaking from ear to paw with rage. "If you hadn't laid that trail I'd have taken the fox's head an hour after dawn!"

Grissoul was about to step in and remind Gruven of his lowly position in the clan when Sawney pulled her back. "Let them be. I want to see this."

Tagg shook his head. "An hour after dawn? Really? I don't think so. I'd already spotted Felch before that. Remember this, too. I was the one sent out to bring him back, not you, my foolish friend."

Gruven always carried a sword. Now he drew it in the blink of an eye. "I'm no friend of yours and I'm not foolish either. Huh, Zann Taggerung, you don't even have the guts to carry a weapon. So, who's the fool now, eh?"

The otter moved like chain lightning. He dealt Gruven

91

an awful blow, just below the shoulder. It paralyzed his sword paw. Tagg's rudderlike tail thudded into his opponent's stomach, bending him double. The sword, which was still held loosely in the stoat's paw, its point against the ground, bent too, like a bow. A stunning crack from Tagg's paw to his adversary's chin sent the stoat crashing backward. The sword made a twanging noise as it left his grip and sailed off into the trees behind the clearing. Gruven lay flat on his back. The otter drew Sawney's blade from the back of his belt and threw. It buried itself alongside the stoat's face, clipping off several whiskers in the process. The Taggerung turned away.

Sawney put his footpaw in Gruven's face as he tugged the knife free from the ground. He held it out to the otter. "Take it and kill him, Tagg. He just tried to kill you!"

Tagg shook his head. "Gruven's probably killed me a thousand times in dreams, but he'll never get the chance to do it while he's awake. Why should I kill him? He amuses me. Besides, I'm still hungry."

He went back to his food. Sawney raised the knife to slit Gruven's throat, but suddenly burst out laughing. "Hahahahaha! He amuses you, that's a good one, hahahahaha! What a Taggerung our clan has, and he's still hungry? Hahaha!"

He took his footpaw from the stoat's face, leaving him to crawl off defeated but still alive. Sawney sat down beside Tagg. "I've never known a beast like you, my son, but you should learn to obey me, you impudent riverdog. When are you going to do as I say, eh?"

Tagg tore a leg from the roasted bird and gave it to Sawney. "Next time you give me an order, I promise. Tell me, though, have we ever been inside a building, I mean a real big place, built of reddish stone, with other otters in it, like me?"

Sawney stared at him oddly. "Never! No, we've never been in such a place!"

Tagg sat back, his food forgotten. "What about a mouse warrior, a real tough-looking beast, wearing armor and carrying a great sword, said his name was Deyna? Did we ever meet a creature like that?"

Sawney felt a twinge of his old pain griping in his stomach. His previous good mood began to dissolve. "An armored sword-carrying mouse named Deyna? What's the matter with you, son? Are you losing your mind?"

Tagg lay down and yawned. He gazed up at the sky. "No, it was just a dream I've been having."

Sawney hurled the roast woodpigeon leg into the fire. "A dream? I had a dream the other night, I dreamt I jumped off a cliff and flew, aye, flew like a bird! Who can say what rubbish and nonsense comes into a beast's mind when he's weary and sleeping? You're tired, Tagg. Go into my tent and get yourself a proper sleep, one without stupid dreams!"

Antigra sat watching her son eat. She was angry, but scared and relieved that neither Sawney nor the Taggerung had killed Gruven, who seemed to be taking the whole episode with sullen indifference. Antigra served him mint tea, sweetened with honey.

"You did wrong shouting out like that, my son. The same blade that took your father's life nearly slew you too."

Gruven spat gristle into the cooking fire. "What d'you expect me t'do, go an' thank them for sparing me?"

Antigra put a paw about his shoulder. "We must wait and bide our time until the right moment."

"You've been sayin' that for as long as I can remember," Gruven snarled, pushing aside his mother's paw. "I'm sick of waitin'. The right moment is now!"

"Wouldst thou tell me what moment that would be, Gruven?"

Mother and son glanced up, startled to see Grissoul the Seer standing close by. Guilt was all over Antigra's face,

93

but Gruven replied with a surly scowl, "None o' your business, slybrush. What are you sneakin' around for? Did Sawney send you to spy on us?"

Shaking her numerous bracelets of coral, bone and silver, the vixen rolled her unstable eye in what she imagined was a friendly smile. She sat down between them. "Bold words for one who almost lost his life today. Did thou not teach thy son any sense, Antigra?"

The stoat mother smiled ingratiatingly. "All I could, but wisdom only comes with age. Mayhap you'd like to give Gruven some advice. Who knows, he might listen to one as wise as you, Grissoul. I will pay you for it. Wait!" Antigra went to her tent and brought out four dove eggs in a clay bowl, which she gave to the Seer. "I know you are very partial to these. They are fresh. My son is dining on the one that laid them."

The vixen pierced one with her tooth and sucked its contents down. She stowed the other three in her pouch. "Thou knows my weakness, stoat. The eggs are good. Hearken now, both of ye, an' listen to me. I saw ants this morning, fighting among themselves on their own anthill. I have seen other things of late. The omens are not good for the Juskarath. If I were thee, Gruven, I'd do nought to anger Sawney. His stomach is troubling him again; 'tis a dangerous sign. Make thy peace with Sawney Rath, be one of those in his favor. Mark my words, it could save both thy lives."

Gruven sniffed contemptuously, but his mother jabbed him with a stick of firewood. "Listen to the Seer's advice. What should we do, Grissoul?"

The vixen pointed to the remains of the roast dove. "Take thou a sling an' stones, Gruven, go out into the woodlands an' slay a pair of doves. I'll take them to Sawney as thy peace offering, an' praise thee to him as a good hunter an' a loyal clanbeast. He'll listen to me. Heed my advice, both of ye!" Grissoul rose to take her leave.

Gruven snorted. "Why should you care about us? You

only came 'round here to see what you could get. Four dove eggs just for a pile of mumbo jumbo about ants an' the state o' Sawney's gut. Not bad, eh?"

The Seer gathered her painted cloak about her, staring down at the stoat and shaking her head pityingly. "Thou art a bigger fool than I thought thee to be, Gruven. I care for this Juska clan, not just two stoats. I can tell what is in thy heart, but if thou try to take vengeance on Sawney or the Taggerung, 'twill be the death of thee an' thy mother. My task is to stop our Juskarath being torn apart by strife. Sawney's moods, thy bad temper, they affect all. Where would I go if there were no clan to protect me? Get some sense into thy stubborn head an' heed my words!"

When the vixen had departed, Antigra brought a throwing sling and pouch of stones from the tent. "Do as she says, son. It's good advice."

Gruven spat into the fire and listened to the sizzle it made. "I'm not crawlin' back beggin' for Sawney Rath's favor, or that otter who thinks he's a Taggerung. Leave me alone. I'm tired, wanderin' Mossflower all night an' half the day."

Antigra lost her temper. She lashed the empty sling across Gruven's back. He winced but did not stir.

"As lazy as your father, that's what you are! I'll go and kill two doves myself, you bone-idle beast!"

Gruven called after her as she strode angrily off into the woodlands north of the camp. "Then go. I'm not scared of Grissoul, Sawney or anybeast!"

Cool shades of early evening fell upon the tent as Grissoul shook Tagg gently into wakefulness. "Come. Thy father wishes thee to attend him."

The otter sat up and stretched, flexing his lean sinewy frame. Taking a dipper of water from a nearby pail, he drank some and poured the remainder over his head. A good dreamless sleep had refreshed the Taggerung.

"What's that old ferret up to now, Grissoul?"

95

"He is about to deal with the runaway, an' he wants thee to witness the punishment."

Felch had his paws upstretched, bound to the thick bough of a beech tree. All the Juskarath vermin were assembled there on their Chieftain's command. Sawney stood impatiently twirling his favorite blade, the knife with the amber handle. He watched as the crowd parted to allow his Seer and the Taggerung through.

"Ah. So, did you have a good sleep, my son?"

Tagg noted the curious gleam in Sawney's eye. "Good enough, thankee. What are you going to do to Felch?"

Sawney licked the knife blade, tasting its cold steel. "I think I'll skin him alive. He'd make a nice tent flap, eh?"

A stricken silence fell upon the clan. Nobeast had ever imagined such cruelty, but they all knew their Chieftain was capable of it. Felch moaned pitifully. Though Tagg was horrified at the suggestion, he knew enough not to show it. Sawney watched him closely, waiting for a reaction.

A careless smile showed on the otter's face. He nodded toward Felch, remarking, "A stringy old worthless hide like this? I don't think it'd be worth your time and trouble."

Sawney laughed. "Haha, you're a cool one, Tagg!"

The otter shrugged. "No point getting excited over some mangy old runaway fox. Cut him down and let him go, I say. Make him clean up the camp on all fours for a season, starve him a bit to slow him down. That's what I'd do."

Sawney winced and rubbed his stomach with a paw. "But you're not me, are you? I'm the one who gives the orders and makes the decisions in this clan. Right?"

Tagg tried keeping the mood light. He nodded. "Right!"

To his surprise, Sawney grinned and hugged him fondly. "Zann Juskarath Taggerung! My strong right paw. No, I won't skin Felch alive. Remember when we last spoke, just before you took your nap this afternoon?"

Tagg disengaged himself from the ferret's hug. "Aye."

Sawney tossed his blade up and caught it neatly. "You do, good! Because I recall exactly what you said to me. You promised that you'd obey me next time I gave you an order."

Tagg was forced to agree. "That's what I said right enough."

Quick as a flash, Sawney Rath's eyes hardened. "Then I'm ordering you to skin Felch alive!" He took the otter's paw, closing it over the knife handle. "Obey me!"

The crowded clearing became as silent as a tomb. All eyes were upon the Taggerung, awaiting his reaction to the order.

Tagg turned his back on Sawney and strode to the side of the fox strung up to the beech bough. He raised the blade. Felch shut his eyes tight, his head shaking back and forth as his nerves quivered uncontrollably. With a sudden slash Tagg severed the thongs that bound him. Felch slumped to the ground in a shaking heap. Tagg's voice was flat and hard as he turned to face Sawney.

"I'm sorry to disobey your order. The fox is a sorry thief, but I will not take the life of a helpless beast."

Sawney's paw shot to his belt, forgetting that Tagg was holding his blade. Spittle sprayed from the ferret's mouth as he roared, "You'll do as I say! Don't try to give me excuses! Carry out my command! Do it! Do it now!"

Tagg sliced through the bonds that still held the fox's paws together. He spoke only one word. "No!"

Sawney was beside himself with fury. His voice rose to a scream. "Your promise was a lie! Do it, or I'll make you obey me!"

Tagg ignored him. He lifted Felch upright and rubbed life back into his numbed paws, whispering, "You may as well run for it again, wretched creature."

Felch dashed off into the trees. Sawney rapped out an order to the ferret, Vallug Bowbeast. "Kill him!"

Felch was still visible as he dodged between the trunks. Vallug ran forward a few steps. Keeping the fox in sight, he notched an arrow onto his bowstring and drew the weapon back. Tagg leaped in, a single swipe of his blade parting the string. Vallug saw the look in his eyes and backed off.

Sawney's face screwed up in pain as shafts of agony ran like lightning bolts through his stomach. He waved Grissoul away as the Seer ran to help him. Glowering at Tagg, he pointed an accusing paw.

"Traitor! You are not a true Taggerung to the Juskarath. I made a bad mistake when I took you in and called you my son!"

Tagg gave vent to his feelings. "Look around you, Sawney. Rats, stoats, ferrets, weasels and foxes. I'm the only otter in the whole clan. How can a ferret be father to me? I've never called you father, but I respected you as Chieftain until now. Did you think I am the sort of beast to skin a living creature alive? Well, the fox has run and I won't be the one to bring him back. You can't make me obey what your temper dictates. That isn't true Juska law!"

Sawney curled his lip in contempt. "What do you know of Juska law? This clan is mine! I make the law here. Eefera, Vallug, seize that otter. I'll teach him to defy me. Somebeast bring me a whip!"

Tagg had the blade in front of him. "First beast who tries to lay paws on me dies!"

Vermin who had chanced a pace forward froze. They had seen the otter growing up and knew his awesome strength and skill. Nobeast was prepared to tangle with the Taggerung. Tagg backed toward the trees, his blade still menacing.

"I no longer want to be with you or your clan, Sawney. You've become too dangerous for your own good. I've watched you change over the seasons from a clan chief to a bad old beast. I go my own way now. Our paths will never cross again, so I wish you better times and hope you learn to treat others more wisely!"

Tagg moved so swiftly that the trees soon swallowed him up. "Our paths will cross, otter," Sawney called after him, "oh yes they will. I'm going to track you down and slay you myself!" He wrenched a spear from the grasp of Eefera. "Nobeast leaves this camp. I'll bring him back myself, dead or alive. Well, what are you all staring at, eh? He's old, you're thinking, he's not as fast as that otter. Well, you just wait and see. I've got a brain. I'm smart, smarter than he'll ever be. He's not a Taggerung anymore. But I'm still Sawney Rath!"

They watched in silence as he loped off into the dense fastness of north Mossflower woodlands, hard on the trail of his new enemy. Grissoul sat on the ground and tossed her bones and pebbles. She stared at the way they fell, noting the position of each one. Wordlessly, the Seer shook her head and covered her eyes.

9

The rain stopped somewhere between late afternoon and early evening. Friar Bobb fought his way through a small pack of Dibbuns to open the main Abbey door and let them out to play. They tugged impatiently at his robes and apron.

"Us wanna go out'n'play!"

"Open a door. 'Urry up, Firebobb!"

He swung the doors wide and was almost knocked flat by Abbeybabes stampeding out onto the wet sunlit lawn. Shaking his ladle at them in mock anger, the fat old squirrelcook roared aloud, "Anybeast's late back for dinner an' I'll make soup out o' their tails!"

The fresh breeze from the open door, combined with a broad band of sunlight and the ensuing noise, roused Mhera and her friends from their slumbers. Cregga sat up straight, causing Gundil and Mhera to fall over. The ottermaid rubbed at her eyes as she struggled upright.

"What . . . where . . . oh, dear, we must've slept for ages!"

Gundil shook his head ruefully. "Hurr, an' uz never solved ee probberlem."

Cregga scratched her stripes thoughtfully. "I think I did. L.H.C. could mean the Left High Corner of the Warrior's tapestry. I think we'll need a ladder to reach it."

Suddenly the dream she had been having tumbled in on Mhera. "No, no, it's the Lantern Holder Column. Martin told me!"

"Martin told you?" Cregga sounded incredulous.

Mhera fidgeted with her girdle, slightly embarrassed. "I'm not sure it was him and I don't really know if I was properly asleep. I saw his picture, just like the one there on the tapestry, and a lovely gentle voice echoed in my mind. Lantern Holder Column, that was all it said."

There were two fluted half-columns, flat against the wall, one either side of the tapestry. Both had small iron lanterns hanging from them, to illuminate the image of the Warrior at night. It was still daylight, so they were unlit. Mhera looked from one lantern to the other. "Lantern Holder Columns, but which one?"

She took down the lanterns from their hooked iron holders and examined them with Gundil, whilst the blind badger went carefully up and down each column, sniffing and running her paws over the stonework. It was not a successful exercise.

Brother Hoben the Recorder came toward them, pulling a little cart containing oil, candles, wicks and cleaning equipment. He watched their activities curiously. "What are you doing there, may I ask?"

Cregga immediately recognized the mouse Recorder's voice. "Ah, Brother Hoben. Come to refill the lanterns, I suppose."

Hoben took a pitcher of lilac-scented vegetable oil from his cart and went about his task. " 'Tis the Recorder's job, always has been. To shed the light of knowledge and learning by keeping our Abbey's records, and to shed illumination where it is needed. Every sixth day I come 'round, replacing candles, collecting old beeswax and trimming each lantern and lamp wick. As you can see, I make sure each one is topped up with fresh oil. Why do you ask? Is there something amiss?"

Taking him by the paw, the Badgermum led Hoben to

the column on the left of the tapestry. She guided his paw to a gap between the carved stones, where the cement pointing had been hacked out, leaving a slot. "Did you ever remove anything from here, a piece of paper, a slat of wood, perhaps a flat piece of slate?"

"Indeed I did, marm," Hoben answered immediately. "A flat piece of slate, just as you said. Though it was a while back now, let me see, eight, no nine seasons ago, or perhaps it was nearer ten, let me see—"

Mhera interrupted him. "Pardon me, Brother, but it's not important how long ago you removed the slate. Have you still got it?"

The Recorder responded to her question in his most dignified manner. "Do I look like a mouse who throws things away willy-nilly, miz? As Recorder to Redwall Abbey it is my solemn duty to preserve anything at all that has writing on it in any form!"

"Hurr, then beggin' ee parden agin, zurr, wudd ee koindly take us'n's to whurr et be?"

Hoben directed one of his rare dry smiles at the mole. "Why, certainly. Follow me, please."

They followed him, Mhera wriggling and skipping, all agog. "It's got writing on it, Brother Hoben said so!"

Gundil grabbed her paw and leaned heavily on it. "Stop thoi jumpen an' frulliken abowt. 'Member wot oi said abowt h'Abbesses fallin' o'er on they'm 'eads!"

Old Hoarg stood at the gatehouse door, enjoying the sunny evening. He winked at Mhera and the mole. "Back agin, mates? Two visits in a single day; makes an old dormouse feel honored. What is it now?"

Hoben nodded to him and entered the gatehouse. "Some old records I want to dig out from the archives."

Hoarg held a paw to his lips. "Then dig 'em out quietly, Brother. Mhera's mama is takin' a nap in my big ole chair. Looks like she deserves it, too."

A feather from one of the cushions had lodged itself close to Filorn's mouth. It fluttered up and down as she breathed in and out. Gundil chuckled fondly. "Bless yore mum's 'eart, miz, she'm ee 'ardest wurrken creetur in all ee h'Abbey. Better cooker'n Froyer Bobb, too, hurr aye, but doan't ee tell 'im oi sedd so!"

Cregga stood with Gundil and Mhera in the doorway, watching Brother Hoben chunnering his way through dusty volumes.

"Hmm, autumn of the weeping willow . . . no, 'tis further back than that. Summer of the singing skylark, spring of the swooping swallows . . . ah, here it is. Winter of the ceaseless snows." He brought the book out into the open and dusted it off.

They sat on the lower walltop steps as Hoben flicked through the pages. He produced a wafer-thin oblong-shaped slate of a bluey grey hue and passed it to Mhera. "Is that the thing you're looking for?"

Mhera recognized Abbess Song's precise and well-formed script. She read aloud what it said.

"My first is third, like the sound of the sea,
My second's the center of you, not me,
My third is the end of him but not you,
My fourth starts a picture, not a view,
My fifth is in bean though not in been,
My sixth and seventh start seldom seen.
Sunrise and sunset, warmth and cold,
Put them together a sign will unfold."

Gundil lay flat on his back, holding his head in both paws. "Whoo urr, whutt be a pore molechoild t'make uv thatt? Et be's more'n moi likkle brain cudd stand!"

Mhera smiled at her molefriend. "Wait until you hear the rest. Listen to this.

"The strangest thing you've ever heard,
A point that makes a noisy word,
The other three make quieter pleas,
Let me start you off with 'teas'."

Cregga lay alongside Gundil, she too holding her head. "Move over, friend. That's more than my brain can stand too!"

Mhera tapped her tail on the step in frustration. "That's the second time I've been interrupted. There's another two separate lines to go yet. Will you two sit up and listen!"

Gundil sat up quickly, folding his paws and looking attentive. "Yurr, Creggum marm, us'n's better pay 'tenshun, or ee gurt h'Abbess'll make uz wash pots in ee kitchen."

The badger sat up, folding her paws primly. "Oops, sorry, Mother Abbess. Carry on, we're all ears!"

Mhera stifled a grin. "Stop calling me Abbess, you two, and listen. Here's the last two lines.

" 'Twixt water and stone I stand alone,
Sounding burnt but alive I survive!"

Brother Hoben preened his straggly whiskers thoughtfully. "Well, what do you think of that?"

Filorn had wakened and emerged from the gatehouse. She stood on the path below them and called up, "I think it's dinnertime, but you can sit on those damp steps all night if you like!"

Old Hoarg left the gatehouse and accompanied them across the lawn. "Minted potato'n'leek turnover, now there's a dish to set the ole mouth waterin'. Mmmmm!"

Helping their elders, Mhera and Gundil wended their way slowly over the rainwashed grass in the warm evening sunlight.

"What's for afters, Mama?"

"Oh, I wouldn't be surprised if Broggle and Friar Bobb have made a woodland trifle. They said they were going to."

"With flaked almonds and meadowcream, marm?"

"Friar Bobb always says that's the way a woodland trifle should be, Brother."

"Hurr, be thurr any zoop furr starters, mum? Oi loikes zoop!"

"Well, you should know, Gundil. You and my Mhera chopped the celery and carrots this morning."

"So us'n's did, mum. Oi'd furgotten to amember that, hurr hurr!"

"Cregga, you ole stripedog, can't you move any faster? By the sound of that dinner we'll be lucky to get any if Boorab gets to the tables first!"

"You're right, Hoarg. Come on, let's run!"

They entered the Cavern Hole breathless and laughing. Boorab was already seated next to his friend Drogg Cellarhog. The hare raised an eyebrow as he saw them taking their places.

"Late for dinner an' laughin' like frogs at a fry-up, wot? Not the sort o' thing one does in the mess. Very serious business, eatin'. Only time I laughed at table was one suppertime long ago when my big fat auntie's chair collapsed. She bumped her blinkin' head on the table an' passed out. Only laughed then because I got her bally share. Hawhawhaw, er, beg y'pardon!"

Redwallers were a bit surprised that Cregga had not taken the big chair at the main table, which was the customary place for anybeast acting as leader. Instead, she chose to sit among the younger element, creatures like Gundil, Egburt and Floburt, many seasons out of Dibbunhood but not yet considered adults. At the badger's request, Brother Hoben and Mhera, who was actually regarded as a proper young adult, sat down with Cregga. The big chair remained empty. Gossip hummed about freely. Redwallers liked to discuss the day's events over dinner. As the servers arrived with their trolleys, Cregga tapped the tabletop with a spoon. A respectful silence fell over all. Broggle, who was still called young Broggle for all his size, was selected by the Badgermum to say the grace. However, the squirrel had developed such a fine tenor voice that he always chose to sing it.

"When the day's work is done,
Then gather we all,
To dine in good company,
Here at Redwall,
On the fruits of our labors,
We harvest and tend,
Each helping the other,
As neighbor and friend.
May the seasons' fine fortune,
Roll on without cease,
And grant us fair weather,
In plenty and peace."

The blind badger shook her head in admiration. "Thank you, young Broggle. That was beautifully sung!"

Boorab dipped fresh crusty bread into a bowl of soft cheese and chives, commenting airily, "Indeed it jolly well was. Of course, he had an expert music tutor. Mustn't forget that, wot wot?" Then he abandoned further self-praise to concentrate on his life's greatest interest. Food.

Cregga addressed Brother Hoben so that all at table could hear her. "Tell me, Brother, you taught most of these young 'uns at Abbey School. Would you say they're a pretty bright lot?"

Hoben put aside his soup spoon and looked around. "Hmm. They may be bright now, but most of them were fat-headed dozy little Dibbuns when I taught them."

Mhera silenced the young ones' indignant squeaks and growls by throwing out a challenge. "Right then, let's see, shall we? The creature who can solve most lines of a riddle we have here can sit in the big chair at breakfast tomorrow. Also, with Cregga Badgermum's permission, they can have the entire day off, to do as they please."

The announcement caused a sensation among the young creatures.

"What's the riddle? Bet I can solve it!"

"Go on, go on, tell us what it is, Mhera!"

"Burr, oi'm ee gurtest riggle solverer as ever lived!"

"Oh no you're not, I am!"

Brother Hoben raised his voice. "Then stop chattering and listen to Mhera. Carry on, miz!"

" 'My first is third, like the sound of the sea.' That's the first line. Any ideas as to what it means?"

They stared blankly at Mhera until Floburt inquired, "Are there other lines? Perhaps you could read us one. They may connect up to give a meaning."

Drogg Cellarhog called across from another table. "She's right, miz. Read the lot out, 'tis only fair!"

Mhera had started her dinner. She slid the slate across to Hoben. "I'm famished. You carry on, Brother."

Hoben read the first eight-line poem, slowly and clearly. Immediately they began raising their paws, as if they were still at Abbey School, jigging up and down and calling, "Brother! Brother!"

Hoben pointed at Egburt with a small baton loaf. "You first!"

The young hedgehog scratched his spikes. "I still don't know what the first line means, but the answer to the second line is the letter O. 'My second's the center of you, not me.' O is in the center of the word *you*, Brother."

As Recorder, Hoben always carried a scrap of parchment and a charcoal stick. He produced them and began writing. "Very good, Egburt. Any more answers, please?"

A mousemaid named Birrel spoke up. "Third line, Brother. 'My third is the end of him but not you.' That's the letter M. It comes at the end of the word *him*."

Suddenly Mhera had solved the first line, but she was beaten to the answer by young Broggle.

"I've solved the first line! 'My first is third, like the sound of the sea.' Third letter of the alphabet is C. That sounds like the word *sea*, doesn't it?"

107

Mhera shook Broggle's paw. "Very clever, mate. That first line had me really baffled. Well done!"

Brother Hoben looked up from his writing. "Floburt, have you got an answer for us?"

The hogmaid fiddled shyly with her apron strings. "Aye, Brother, that line which goes, 'My sixth and seventh start seldom seen.' That's two letters. S and S. 'Seldom seen' starts with them. Er . . . is that right?"

Boorab's earbells tinkled as he applauded. " 'Course it's right, m'gel. I say, can I take a look at your funny old rhyme, wot?"

Hoben passed him the slate. The hare scanned it studiously.

"Ahah! Here's one you'd have to read to flippin' well come up with a solution, this fifth line. 'My fifth is in bean though not in been.' First bean's the bally bean you eat, second one's the been where you've jolly well been, wot. Anyhow, the answer's the letter A. Bit of a swizz, that one, if y'have to listen to it."

Boorab sat down and began tucking into his minted leek'n'potato turnover, nodding at Cregga. "You were right, marm, does taste better when the taters cook down into the leeks, all nice'n'mushy, eh wot!"

"Yurr, this 'un be ee letter P. Moi fourth starts ee pitcher but not ee view. Hurr aye, 'tis ee P all roight."

Brother Hoben chuckled at Gundil's great grin of triumph. "There you are, it wasn't more than your little brain could stand." He held up his paws to stop any further discussion. "Well done, class! I'll let you see what I've written down so far."

Hoben placed his notes in the center of the table. Like everything he did, they were perfectly numbered and laid out. Thus:

1 My first is third, like the sound of the sea   C

2 My second's the center of you, not me   O

3 My third is the end of him but not you   M
4 My fourth starts a picture, not a view   P
5 My fifth is in bean though not in been   A
6 My sixth and seventh start seldom seen   S S

Floburt could hardly contain herself. "It's a compass! The next two lines make it even clearer. Listen.

"Sunrise and sunset, warmth and cold,
Put them together a sign will unfold.

"The sun sets in the west and rises in the east. South is the warm country, north is the cold lands. I've put it together. The compass points: north, south, east and west!"

The Redwallers cheered as Drogg Cellarhog bowed and shifted the big chair back from the head of the table for his granddaughter.

"Sit ye down, my lovely. I'd say you was the winner, paws down!"

Foremole Brull confirmed Drogg's proclamation. "She'm wurr allus gurtly clever, h'even when she'm wurr ee h'infant!"

Boorab dragged his haredee gurdee forward and announced, "In honor of our fair winner I will now render the Ballad of the Brainy Duck. Thank you!"

Sister Alkanet pushed her plate away. "That's completely ruined my appetite!"

The hare shot her a haughty glance. "I heard that remark, marm!" Notwithstanding, he tugged levers and wound wheels until the instrument groaned into action. Much to everybeast's hilarity it kept making noises like a duck. Boorab launched into his song.

"Some said his head was full of stones,
Some said 'twas full of muck,
But I tell you, that wasn't true,
Oh Dingle was a brainy duck!

He knew history and geography,
Read books from front to back,
But the poor little fellow with his webs so yellow
All he could say was Quack!
Oh geese go honk and sparrows tweet,
I suppose jackdaws shout Jack,
But the cleverest bird you've ever heard,
Was the duck who just went Quack!

One day there came a cunning fox,
Who said 'I'm Doctor Black,'
And all the ducks believed he was,
'Til Dingle called him Quack!
Oh Quack Quack Quack! Quack Quack Quack!
Brave Dingle Quacked and raved,
So the ducks jumped Quackly in the pond,
And from that fox were saved.
If ever you meet dear Dingle,
Good manners he won't lack,
Just shake his wing, you'll hear him sing,
Quack Quack Quack Quack Quack!"

Midst rousing cheers, Boorab took his bow and, as usual, tripped over the haredee gurdee, rolling under the table with it. Filorn peered down. It was difficult to tell what was hare and what was haredee gurdee, the two were so enmeshed.

"Oh, you poor creature. Are you all right, Mr. Boorab sir?"

His head emerged from between a set of accordion bellows. "Er, hawhaw, quite well, thankee, marm, just makin' a minor adjustment, wot. Me quackin' mechanism overheated, doncha know!"

The friends made their escape to the comparative peace of Cregga's room, where they confronted the remainder of the puzzle. Brother Hoben read it aloud.

"The strangest thing you've ever heard,
A point that makes a noisy word,
The other three make quieter pleas,
Let me start you off with 'teas.' "

Cregga settled into her armchair. "This gets odder by the moment. What's teas supposed to mean?"

Hoben took on a teacherlike air. "Quite simple, really. *Teas* is just the letters of *east* messed around a bit, right, Mhera?"

"Yes, Brother, like *north* makes, er, er . . . *thorn!*"

Cregga caught on quickly. "And *west* makes, let me see . . . *stew!*"

Hoben nodded. "It's an old trick, but it will fool you easily if you don't look out for it. So, that leaves *south*, the point that makes the word *shout*. That's a noisy word, I'd say. Oh, then there's these two final lines. Listen carefully.

" 'Twixt water and stone I stand alone,
Sounding burnt but alive I survive!"

Hoben tapped his paw on the slate. "And that is the important part, friends. That is what we are searching for."

Gundil scrambled down from Cregga's chair arm, where he had been perching. "Boi 'okey, coom on, we'm a goen south'ard!"

The Badgermum's huge paws lifted him back onto the armchair. "It's nearly dark out. No use searching in that."

Mhera stared at the badger's sightless eyes. "How do you know it's dark, Cregga? You can't see."

Cregga chuckled and held a paw in the direction of her window. "I can feel the heat of the stars, it's almost an hour since dinner, and I'm feeling more tired than I do in daytime. Is that explanation good enough for you, Miz Mhera?"

Mhera sat by the chair, resting her head on Cregga's

footpaws. "I don't believe the first bit, about feeling the heat of the stars. That's a dreadful fib for an acting Abbess."

Cregga reached down and stroked her friend's head. "Come on, this old beast's weary for sleep. It's been a long day. We'll continue our search straight after breakfast tomorrow."

Mhera jumped up. "Breakfast tomorrow? Oh dear, Gundil, we promised Mama and Friar Bobb we'd give some help kneading the oatmeal scones for the morning. Come on, mate!"

Brother Hoben stretched out on the bed, which Cregga never used, preferring her big armchair, which was easier to get up from. The Recorder settled himself comfortably.

"Oh for the energy of the young. The speed those two dashed out with, eh, Cregga?"

The Badgermum grunted dozily. "Glad I can't run that fast anymore. Makes me feel exhausted just thinking about it. Nighty night, Brother."

Filorn shooed Mhera and Gundil off as they ran into the kitchens.

"Off to bed, the pair of you. The scones are in the oven. Drogg Spearback and two of Skipper's crew lent a paw. I hardly did anything, so I don't feel a bit tired after that nap in the gatehouse. Go on, you two go up. I'll wait until the scones are baked and help the Friar take them from the ovens."

Broggle poked his head around the pantry door. "Scone pullin' is my job, marm. No need for you to wait about down here. Good night, marm!"

Filorn accompanied Mhera and Gundil upstairs. "Young Broggle is such a nice creature, isn't he, Gundil?"

"Oh, ee'm passen furr, marm, but miz Mhera, she'm the noicest creetur in ee h'entire h'Abbey!"

Mhera shook her head. "No, no. The nicest, most sweet-natured, politest beast in all of Redwall is . . . Gundil!"

Twirling his tail and ducking his head, the mole

shuffled about on the top stair. "Burr, miz, you'm gotten oi all uv a tizzy naow!"

Filorn laughed heartily, throwing her paws about them both. "Why don't you two get off to your beds and dream of fresh compliments to pay each other tomorrow. Nicest, most sweet-natured, huh? That little soilwhumper?"

Gundil grinned. "Thankee, marm, an' gudd noight to ee!"

10

Antigra went north into Mossflower Wood, to the place where she knew that doves nested among the oak and beech trees. It was soft and mossy underpaw, dappled with sunlight and shadow, fern beds reflecting that calm translucent greenish light often found in deep woodlands. Nature's beauties were lost upon the stoat, as crouching low in the ferns she loaded a small hard pebble into her sling. Two doves were feeding on the ground, picking among last autumn's rotted acorns. Slowly, carefully, Antigra stood, her eye fixed upon the fatter of the pair as she began to twirl her sling. The pebble pouch she carried stuffed into her belt slipped loose and stones clacked noisily as they spilled out. The doves flew off to their nest, high up in an old oak. Still twirling the sling, Antigra cursed her bad fortune. Just then the fatter of the doves poked its head out of the nest, and she whipped the pebble off at it. The random throw was unlucky for the dove. Antigra immediately knew she had slain the bird, by the way its head flopped as the pebble struck it. Then it was her turn to have the bad luck. Instead of tumbling to the ground, the dove fell back into its nest, and its partner flew off in fright.

The stoat told herself there was nothing for it but to

climb the tree and retrieve her kill. Fixing the pebble pouch firmly into her belt, she looped the sling about her neck and began climbing. It was very difficult at first, but as she went higher and the branches became more close growing her progress was easier. She reached the nest, and found two eggs in it with the dead dove. Her climb had not been in vain. Straddling the bough, Antigra settled her back against the trunk. The eggs were her bonus. The stoat sat sucking them and gazing about her, interested at how the land looked from a high vantage point. She could not see the Juskarath camp, but far over to the north a glimpse of snow-peaked mountaintops showed beyond the woodlands, bathed in early-evening sunlight. Antigra turned her attention to looking for other nests, but she saw none. She began climbing down, halting when her keen eyes spotted movement below on the woodland floor. She watched from her hiding place in the foliage. A shadow slipped from tree to tree, pausing a moment amid some ferns before hastening silently off northward. It was the Taggerung!

Antigra had no knowledge of what had taken place back at the camp. Instantly a plan formed in her cunning mind. She would climb down and track him. Her aim with a sling was good. Nobeast would know it was she who had slain the Taggerung. If she was careful and accurate, her son Gruven would soon become Taggerung of the Juska. She was almost halfway down when another movement below caused her to freeze. Sawney Rath came loping along, halting momentarily to inspect a bruised fern frond. He smiled grimly, pleased to have picked up the trail of his quarry. Antigra seized the moment. Fitting a large pebble to her sling, she changed her plans.

Whirring the loaded sling until it was a blur, she yelled sharply, "Sawney Rath, I'm up here!"

The Juska Chieftain looked upward, shock stamped upon his face as the stone struck him between his eyes, slaying him on the spot. With the dead dove lying forgotten halfway up the tree, Antigra scrambled down out of the boughs and dropped to the ground. Sawney lay still, one paw still gripping the spear he had been carrying, eyes open wide, staring at the sky. She circled him apprehensively, as if expecting her feared enemy to leap up at any moment. Without warning, sounds of some otherbeast traveling toward the scene reached Antigra. But this was no stealthy tracker or hunter she could hear. It was the labored, staggering noise of some wearybeast, unwittingly heading her way.

Antigra slipped quietly behind the oak tree and waited. Felch came stumbling along, gasping for breath. He ground to a halt in front of the Juskarath Chieftain's body. Like the stoat, he too circled it warily. Antigra stepped out from behind the oak.

"He's dead. 'Twas I who slew him," she said flatly.

Felch exhaled loudly with relief. He knelt at the ferret's side and inspected the wound, then looked at Antigra's weapon. "Aye, so ye did. A slingstone took his life. The Taggerung carried only a knife when I last saw him. I was much slower than either of 'em. I hid myself an' let 'em pass by me, first the Taggerung, then Sawney tracking him." He broke the dead Chieftain's grasp upon the spear and stood up. "You said you'd wait an' get Sawney one day. Hah! The 'igh an' mighty Sawney Rath, eh? You won't be slingin' yer orders 'round no more. You don't look so tough now, ferret-faced scum!"

Felch stabbed the body with the spear. He grinned at Antigra. "Long seasons I dreamed of doin' that. I wager you did, too."

The stoat grinned back. "Aye. Tell me, what happened back at the camp? Why was Sawney hunting the otter?"

As the fox explained, a crafty gleam entered Antigra's eyes. "So, we're rid of them both, Sawney and his pet otter."

Felch brandished the spear. "No more worries, eh?

We'll rule the clan together now, just you'n'me. Chieftains together!"

Antigra pounded the fox's back. "Give me that spear. I want to stab him too!"

Giggling like a naughty Dibbun, Felch passed the spear over. He was still giggling as Antigra whirled and ran him through. A look of pained surprise crossed the fox's face as he stood swaying, grasping the spear shaft with both paws. Antigra stared back at him, her eyes hard and bright as flint.

"My son will rule the clan. There's no room anymore for you, Felch. You've seen and heard too much!"

Fresh wood had been heaped on the campfires. Grissoul sat beside the one outside Sawney's tent, gazing into the night. She felt the spearpoint touch her back, and heard the whisper issuing from the darkness behind her.

"Sawney Rath is dead!"

Without attempting to turn, Grissoul answered, "The omens have already told me this, Antigra."

The stoat's breath felt hot on the back of the vixen's neck. "And did your omens tell you who slew him? Think carefully if you wish to continue living."

Grissoul reached behind her and pushed the spear gently aside. "My omens told me that thou would know the answer to that question. They said no more; it is not for me to guess at the answer."

Antigra kept to the shadows where she could not be seen. "You are a wise beast, old one. I've had a vision that my son Gruven is Taggerung now. Do you agree? Answer me!"

Grissoul shook her head. "It cannot be. Nay, Antigra, put down thy spear and listen. I have had no vision of the Taggerung's death. Juska law says that only he who slays a Taggerung can be called Taggerung in his place. Thy son cannot be Taggerung while the chosen one lives. But a new Chieftain can always take the place of a Chieftain

117

who is slain. I will help thee to have thy son named Gruven Zann Juskazann, leader of this clan. Does my new vision sound fitting to thy desires?"

Antigra liked the idea immediately. "Your vision is good. Tell me what to do, Grissoul!"

The Seer closed her eyes. "Wait awhile before entering camp. Then tell thy story to all. I'll agree with it; the Juska will not doubt my word. I will send thy son off with strong warriors to hunt down and slay the Taggerung, and together you and I will rule the clan until the day of his return."

Antigra nodded. "It is a bargain." She slid back into the darkness.

A short time later, Antigra roused the clan vermin. She staggered into camp, shrieking, "Sawney Rath is dead, murdered by the Taggerung!"

The crowd followed her up to the fire outside Sawney's tent, where Grissoul was still sitting. The Seer got immediate silence by throwing a pawful of something into the flames, which caused them to send up a blue flame.

"I saw the death of Sawney Rath in my omens when he left camp today. Some of you saw me cast the stones and bones."

The stoat Rawback spoke up. "Aye, I saw her. She clasped her head in her paws!"

Gruven sneaked up to his mother's side and whispered, "What's happened? Did you see Sawney get killed?"

Antigra pinched his side between her claws sharply. "Do as I say," she muttered. "Stay out of this and keep your mouth shut until I tell you. Big things are at stake here tonight."

Other vermin were backing Rawback up.

"Grissoul looked as though the omens were bad."

"I saw 'er too. She looked like a creature who'd seen death!"

The Seer leapt up, her painted face taking on a blue tinge from the flames, and swirled her cloak back and forth dramatically. "Let Antigra speak! Tell thy clanbeasts what took place, Antigra!"

All eyes turned on the stoat.

"I was up a tree after birds' eggs and I heard noises. First came Felch, then Sawney, following him. He shouted the fox's name, Felch turned and Sawney slew him with a spear cast. I did not know that the traitor Taggerung was hiding nearby. He saw Sawney unarmed and threw the very blade that was once Sawney's. It did not fly true, but the stone at its handletop struck Sawney 'twixt the eyes and laid him out, unconscious I think. The Taggerung could not see me, so I started climbing down from the tree to defend our Chieftain. But alas, before I reached the ground, the otter had pulled the spear from the body of Felch and murdered Sawney with it. He ran off, north toward the mountains. I could do nought but hurry back here to bring you the bad tidings. It was a treacherous and horrible sight, I'll never forget it!" Antigra slumped on the ground, covering her eyes. "Vengeance upon the traitorous Taggerung," she wailed. "The spirit of Sawney Rath cries for vengeance from the gates of Dark Forest!"

Grissoul's sudden scream rent the night. She began a shuffling dance, holding both paws forth. Vermin shrank from her touch. They feared what they could not understand; it was a night of omens. The Seer's paws finally touched Gruven's face. He looked to his mother, and she nodded at him to stay still. Grissoul cast herself down in front of him, her voice rising to an eerie pitch.

"Is this the one to do thy will, O Sawney Rath?" A great sigh escaped her, and she touched her head to Gruven's footpaws.

"Gruven Zann! Juskazann!
Take our name, rule our clan,
Heed the voice of the Chieftain now dead,
Bring back to this Seer the traitor's head!"

A roar of approval came from the tribe, caught up in the hypnotic ritual. Grissoul led Gruven to the fire, where even his slightly puzzled features looked impressive in the changing hue of the flames. The Seer cast pawfuls of different powders into the blaze. Antigra, who had darted into Sawney's tent a moment before, came dashing out to drape the dead ferret's best cloak about her son's shoulders. She pressed his sword into his paw, hissing in his ear, "Try to look less like a befuddled frog and more like a clan chief, can't you? Say something to them, stir them up. Speak!" She mingled in with the crowd and yelled hoarsely, "Gruven Zann Juskazann!"

Others took up the cry until it became a deafening chant. "Gruven Zann Juskazann! Gruven Zann Juskazann!"

Gruven held up his sword and they fell silent as if by magic. He repeated every word that Grissoul, who was standing behind him, whispered in his ear.

"Warriors of the Juskazann, fear not. The coward Taggerung cannot run far or fast enough from my wrath. I vow upon this sword that the otter will pay for his treachery. Aye, I will choose from our best to accompany me, and I'll bring back his head. We leave at dawn. I will make the name of our clan feared throughout the land. Tell me, you brave ones, what are you called?"

The clanbeasts roared, waving their weapons high. "Juskazann! Juskazann! Gruven Zann Juskazann!"

Grissoul knew then that her plan was working. The clanbeasts were in a frenzy. The Seer sprang up in front of Gruven and flung more powders into the fire. Blue, red, green, silver and purple smoke wreathed her as she cast her bones and shells on the ground. Everybeast was awed by the sight of her, an eerie multihued apparition, howling like a demon.

"Sawney Rath calls to me from beyond the Hellgates! The otter is a traitor Taggerung, a Chieftain murderer and a cowardly runaway! He is not fit to be Taggerung! Shame will fall on our clan if he lives! Gruven Zann Juskazann must slay him and take his title. My omens say that the one who slays a traitor Taggerung can then be called Taggerung by right! Go now, Gruven Zann Juskazann, bring honor to your new-named clan, avenge our fallen Chieftain, bring death to the fleeing coward and take on the name of Gruven Zann Taggerung!"

Even through the flames and smoke, Grissoul could see the fanatical burning light of satisfaction in Antigra's eyes.

Far north in Mossflower Wood, Tagg surfaced from a broad stream. Shaking himself dry he sat on the bank, trying to define his present mood. He was banished from the company of the only beasts he could remember living with, a loner, an outcast from the clan. Yet he felt light-hearted, free and happy. Sometimes he had admired Sawney, his strength, leadership and determination, but he had never really liked the ferret, never called him father, never loved him. Tagg was not bothered that Sawney was hunting him. He had grown old, slower, and more prone to making mistakes because of his quick-tempered mood changes. The otter felt a shudder of joy pass through his entire body from ear to rudder. He was glad to be rid of the whole Juskarath. Life was his, to do with as he pleased. Exactly where he was going and what he intended to do had not occurred to him. Then he remembered the mountain.

Several times that day Tagg had glimpsed it as he traveled north through the woodlands, its pure white craggy cone standing out against the clear blue sky. He moved further along the bank to a higher point, and standing on tip-paw he saw it again, mysterious and cool, its snows turned soft grey by the starry night. Suddenly Tagg wanted to be there. He had never been on a mountain. Fired by the prospect, he leaped high in the air and shouted at the object of his desire. "I'm coming to see you, mountain!"

As he jumped, his head struck something in the overhanging foliage of a tree. Tagg reached up among the leaves and discovered it was a pear. The fruit was not quite ready; it was still hard, but sweet and slightly juicy. Tagg laughed aloud, shouting through a half-full mouth as he plucked another one. "Aye, you stay there, mountain, I'm coming!"

"Yeek! 'Tis a mad riverdog! Stay 'way from 'im, Krobzy!"

"Yarr, don't fret yore snout, Prethil, I kin deal wid 'im!"

Tagg stood still, instantly alert, looking about to see where the voices were coming from. Two bankvoles were standing at the water's edge below him. He smiled politely at them. "Hello!"

The male was a small fat fellow, clad in a homespun nightshirt. He brandished a club and stood protectively in front of the female, wiggling his nose aggressively, as bankvoles do when they are ready to fight. He pointed the club at Tagg. "Donchew 'ello me, ruddertail, or I'll boff ye a good 'un. Wot's yore name an' wot's yore business on our midden, eh, eh?"

Tagg leaned his paw against the dagger in his belt. "I wouldn't chance trying to boff me if I were you."

The bankvole started up the hill toward Tagg, with the female trying to pull him back. The otter's words had roused his temper. "Hohoh, wouldn't ye now? Lissen, streamwalloper, I've boffed bigger'n you many a time, don't fret yore snout about that!"

Tagg did not want to hurt the bankvole. He tried reasoning. "Now now, what are you getting so carried away about, friend?"

Shaking the female off, the bankvole hopped excitedly about. "Carried away, me? Hoho, that's a good 'un! Yore stannin' up there, bawlin' an' shoutin' an' wakin' the babies. Stealin' an' pinchin' an' scoffin' away at our pears. Wotjer expeck me t'do, come out an' give ye a big kiss, eh, eh?"

He hurled himself at Tagg, who moved swiftly to one side. As the bankvole went sprawling, Tagg disabled him by placing a footpaw on the back of his head and pinning his clubpaw to the ground with his strong rudderlike tail. Facedown and helpless, the angry creature snuffled his snout against the earth.

The female sat down, weeping into her nightie. "Ahoohoo hoo! I tole ye the riverdog wiz mad. Now 'e'll murdify both of us an' eat us all up. Oh, 'elp us, somebeast. Ahoohoohoo!"

Taking the club away from the male, Tagg picked him up and sat him down next to his blubbering partner. "Hush now, marm, I'm not going to murder or eat either of you. I wouldn't hurt you, I'm a friend. Come on now, dry your eyes."

She pushed his comforting paw aside. "Go 'way an' don't even speak t'me, ye villigan!"

The male seemed to compose his temper rapidly. He winked at Tagg before throwing a sympathetic paw around the female. "Yarr, cummon, muther, turn the waterfall off. 'E ain't goin' to 'urt us, are ye, sunshine? I'm Krobzy an' this is me missus, Prethil. Wot's yore name?"

Tagg held out his paw. "Oh, just call me Tagg. Pleased to meet you."

Prethil scrubbed at her eyes with the nightie hem. "Pleased to meechew like . . . ler . . . hic! Ler hic! Hic! . . . wise. Hic!"

Krobzy hugged his little fat wife. "Lookit, ye've gone an' gived yoreself 'iccups now wid all that cryin'. Grab 'old of yore snout an' bang yer tail aginst the floor, that always stops the 'iccups. Are you 'ungry, Tagg? Is that why yore scoffin' our pears, eh, eh?"

The otter helped them both up onto their paws. "Sorry, I didn't know the pears were yours. Yes, I am hungry. I haven't eaten since midday."

Krobzy dusted Prethil down before attending to himself. "Well, why didn't ye say so, ye great rudderwhacker? Come on back to the 'omestead. We'll feed yore big famine-stricken gob!"

The homestead was actually built under the hill Tagg had been standing on, with a tunnel leading to it from a secret entrance on the bank. It was a big comfortable place with pear tree roots tracing their way across the ceiling and down the walls. There were other bankvoles living within, alongside a big family of watervoles and another family of fieldvoles. They gathered around the otter, touching the amber-hilted knife with its blue pommelstone. Little ones rode Tagg's tail by sitting on it, others felt his paws and strong limbs admiringly.

"Big feller, ain't 'e!"

"Aye, fine pow'ful beastie!"

"Wouldn't like t'meet 'im up a creek on a dark night, eh, eh?"

"Phwarr! That'n would swipe the tail offa ye wid that blade!"

"Oh aye, fine sharp blade that'n is, eh, eh?"

Prethil shooed them away and led Tagg to a table. "Will ye leave the pore beast alone? 'E's 'ungry!"

This statement caused even more speculation from the voles.

"Bet 'e could wade through a fair bit o' grub?"

"Yarr, so c'd you if'n you was 'is size!"

"No use givin' 'im a small bowl an' a liddle tankard, eh, eh?"

Krobzy pushed them aside and sat down with Tagg. A bushy male watervole joined them. Krobzy introduced him. "Tagg, this is Sekkendin. We calls 'im that 'cos 'e's my sekkendin command 'round 'ere."

The table moved as a pile of younger voles pushed in against it, trying to get closer to the newcomer. Sekkendin glared at them. "Goo 'way, g'wan, the lot of ye. Go an' show Tagg 'ow youse kin dance. Rakkadoo, make some gob music for 'em, willyer!"

A kindly-looking fieldvole placed hot nutbread and a

pan of vegetable stew in front of the otter, commenting, "Bowl'd be too liddle for the likes of ye, sir. Eat 'earty now."

Krobzy poured out tankards of a fruity-tasting beer, which the voles called bankbrew. Tagg ate and drank as he witnessed the voles' pawskills at dancing.

Two elders began twanging on jawharps and the one called Rakkadoo rattled out a curious melody. It was very fast and comprised of odd sounds interwoven with words.

"Ho rang tang rattledy battledy,
Twirl y'tails an' kick up y'paws,
Flibberty flabberty rumple dee doo,
Which 'un's mine an' wot one's yores?
Y'jump like a trout an' y'caper about,
An' don't dare stamp on anybeast's tail,
Roll like a vole playin' toad in an 'ole,
An' rackit an' rampit an' fetch the good ale!
Rubbledy dubbledy fleas never troubled me,
Fiddledee faddle an' diddle dee doo,
Slugs never 'it me an' bugs never bit me,
I'm far too fast so I'll leave 'em t'you.
A rap tap tap I jump so 'igh,
There's birds beneath me flyin' by,
Flippin' an' flappin' me paws are a-tappin',
To beat a vole dancin' y'never should try. Hi!"

Apart from seeing a few rats sing the odd verse around the campfire, Tagg had never known anything like the voles' dancing. His own footpaws felt weary from rapping the floor in time with them. Even the smallest of infant voles could dance expertly, and not only that but they could somersault, backflip and perform the most amazing acrobatics without missing a beat of the gob music. They came crowding around the table again, but Prethil appeared brandishing a stone and a branch in her paws.

"Last beast a-snorin' gets rubbed down with a rock'n'a root in the river!"

125

With fearful yowls the little voles fled into another chamber, where they flung themselves on the moss-strewn floor and began making small snoring noises. Krobzy smiled.

"Yarr, that's got rid o' the pests fer the night. Now then, Tagg me ole sunshine, tell us all about yoreself. We got all night an' us voles do like a good yarn!"

The otter took a draft of bankbrew to moisten his throat. "Let me see, now. How did it all start . . . ?"

Dawn broke clear and quiet. Gruven was still slumbering deep when his mother's footpaw stirred him awake. "Gruven Zann, up now. There's big things for you to do!"

The stoat sat up, picking at the corners of his eyes. "It's not properly daylight yet. I'm tired!"

He rolled aside as Antigra slammed the swordpoint into the ground beside him. Bringing her face close, she hissed, "I didn't wait all these seasons for you to be tired. You are a clan Chieftain now. Get up!"

He rose hastily and donned the cloak he had been given the previous evening. It was a dark red dyed barkcloth, a touch short for Gruven, but it added slightly to his bearing as a new Chieftain. Recalling the events of the last few days, he tugged the sword free, allowing anger and hatred to build inside him. Antigra straightened the cloak about her son. She stared into his vengeful eyes, murmuring in a low voice, so that those waiting outside could not hear, "That's more like it. Remember this: as long as the otter lives you cannot really call yourself leader of the Juskazann. Keep that in mind, and hunt as you have never hunted before. When you do catch up with him, slay him by any means, fair or foul. Only then can you return here to claim your full title. Go now!"

Grissoul awaited Gruven outside the tent. The Seer had eight vermin with her, fully armed. She waited until Antigra came out to join her before speaking.

"Gruven Zann Juskazann! I have chosen eight of our

126

best to go with thee. Eefera, Dagrab, Ribrow, Grobait, Milkeye, Rabbad, Rawback and Vallug Bowbeast. Command them well and bring back the head of the traitor Taggerung. Thy mother and I will go with thee as far as the spot where Sawney Rath lies slain. You will pick up the trail from there. You warriors, guard your chief with your lives. If you return here without him you will all die."

From their open tents and around cooking fires, the clan watched as Antigra and Gruven led the hunting party out of the clearing. Through the summer-dappled trees of Mossflower they trotted, heading north for the oak tree where the murders occurred. Grissoul traveled at the rear, with one of Sawney's most trusted lieutenants, the weasel Eefera. He was a big taciturn beast, well versed in the art of death. Grissoul had instructed him precisely. He knew what to do should Gruven shrink from his mission or show fear. Accidents could always happen out among the woodlands.

11

Brother Hoben woke late next morning in Cregga's room. The Badgermum's empty chair was evidence that she was already up and about. The Recorder muttered to himself as he sluiced down his face in the bowl of water on a cornerstand. "Huh! Might have given me a shake. Leaving me to lie abed half the morning. Not like Cregga at all."

He hurried downstairs, only to find the dining tables deserted. There seemed to be nobeast about; the place was silent. Hoben stood gnawing his whisker ends, completely perplexed. Then he heard a sound. The squeak of trolley wheels sent him scurrying to the kitchens from whence it issued.

Young Broggle was loading the trolley with jugs of cold mint tea and blackberry pies, which he was pulling from the ovens with a long paddle.

"What's going on around here?" Hoben demanded indignantly. "Where's everybeast gone?"

Broggle elbowed him gently to one side as he loaded his cart. "Going on, Brother? I'll tell you what's going on. Mhera and Cregga's search has turned into a full-scale picnic. Since we solved that riddle poem last night there's not a creature in the Abbey who doesn't want to be involved with it. At the moment they're all down at the south wall having breakfast in the open. I just came up here for more supplies. Fresh air makes them ravenous, apparently. Did you oversleep, Brother?"

Hoben began lending a paw to finish loading the trolley. "Aye, I slept like a log, it was so quiet and peaceful in Cregga's room. Her bed is absolutely massive. She never uses it, sleeps in her armchair all the time. Quiet and peaceful that room, no Dibbuns playing 'round the door an hour before sunrise. Come on, Broggle, I'll push and you pull. Easy now, watch those jugs."

Around the south wall was a scene of merry chaos. Boorab came to meet them, a beaker of pennywort cordial in one paw and a half-eaten oatmeal scone, dripping honey, in the other. He appeared to be in fine fettle. "What ho, here's two gallant chaps bearing munchable reinforcements to the front, wot. Well done, chums. You can leave that trolley to me now. I'll see to it, wot wot!"

"Get your plundering paws away from that trolley this instant, you flop-eared reprobate!"

The hare evaded Friar Bobb's ladle with a sideskip. "Only tryin' to help, old scout. Offerin' one's services, y'know!"

Filorn caught up with Boorab and took his paw. "Come and help me to get the Dibbuns down from the walltops, sir. I'll shoo them off and you can stand sentry on the wallsteps to make sure they don't get back up again."

Boorab strolled off gallantly, holding the ottermum's paw on his in courtly fashion. "Never refuse a pretty gel, wot. Duty is me second name, marm. I'll guard those wallsteps against the little blighters with my very life. Hi there, you midget savages, down off the bally battlements. Down I say, sir. Yowch!"

A well-aimed apple core bounced off the hare's scut tail. Filorn struggled to keep her face straight as Boorab closed one eye and glared fiercely up at a molebabe. "Assassin!

You leave me no alternative but to declare war on you and all your fiendish crew, sah!"

Hoben found Mhera and Gundil with Cregga, breakfasting sitting on an old rug spread close to the wall. He sat down with them, helping himself to barley toast, quince jam and a beaker of cold mint tea. Cregga waved away an inquisitive wasp.

"A beautiful morning, Brother. Before you start telling me off, I left you asleep on the bed because it seemed a shame to waken you. Your breathing sounded so peaceful I hadn't the heart to disturb you. I hope you'll forgive me."

The Recorder felt abashed that he had misjudged his friend. "What's to forgive, marm? I had the best night's sleep I've known in many a season. Well now, how far have we got with our latest riddle? What was it? Ah, I remember. All the clues ran south, until those last two lines.

" 'Twixt water and stone I stand alone,
Sounding burnt but alive I survive!"

Gundil picked daintily at a candied plum. "You'm gotten ee gurt membery, zurr. Oi surpose et's 'cos ee be's an Accorder. We'm bain't gotten no furtherer with ee riggle."

Mhera poured more mint tea for the Badgermum. "But 'tis not for want of trying, Brother. We've sat here racking our brains since dawn, without a result."

Cregga shook her head sorrowfully. "Look around if you want to see the reason why. We've had a hare filching our food, Dibbuns racing around us like wild things, Sister Alkanet complaining about this, that and the other, and young Broggle fracturing our ears with his ceaseless chatter. Hardly a good place to sit and solve problems, is it?"

Brother Hoben pointed upward. "Then let's adjourn to the walltop. Mhera's mama has cleared it of Dibbuns and

Boorab's guarding the steps. It should be quiet enough for us to do some thinking up there."

Boorab's spear was a window pole. He stood on the second step, barring their way. "Who goes there? State y'business, wot?"

Brother Hoben tapped an impatient paw on the bottom step. "Come out of the way, please. We're going to the walltop."

The hare twitched his whiskers officiously. "No Dibbuns allowed up here. You're not Dibbuns, are you?"

Cregga took hold of the window pole he was clasping and lifted both Boorab and the pole, with one paw, down onto the grass. "Do we look like Dibbuns? Don't try my patience, sah!"

"Just doin' one's duty," he muttered up the steps after them, somewhat crestfallen. "I was only jolly well askin' a civil question, wot. Humph, some creatures!"

Hoben was right. The broad walkway of the ramparts, backed by the battlemented wall, *was* more peaceful. Mhera liked being up high. She could see the land to the south unfolding below her and the path meandering off into the distance.

Cregga took a deep breath of the fresh morning air. "Ah, that's better! Mhera, my pretty, let me borrow your eyes. Which way are you facing and what can you see?"

"I'm looking south, Cregga, and I see the woodlands to my left and the open space below, then the path. Off to my right there's the flatlands and a few hills over toward the horizon."

The badger leaned her back against the battlements. "That's all? Nothing out of place, no unusual objects sticking up you'd not noticed before? Come on, you two, get looking and help her out."

Brother Hoben and Gundil searched the scene carefully. "Not a thing, Cregga. It all looks fairly normal."

"Burr aye, et be's a noice purty soight though, marm!"

The Badgermum issued her next instruction. "Now turn 'round, right 'round, facing into the Abbey grounds. Tell me, what do you see now?"

They pieced together the picture for their blind companion.

"Mossflower Wood's treetops and the north wall, the beehives and the flower gardens, then the lawns."

"Burr aye, then ee gurt h'Abbey buildin' an' ee path frum et runnen to ee gate'ouse an' ee west wall wi' main gate in et."

Cregga stopped Gundil with an upraised paw. "Take it from there, Mhera. Slowly and carefully. Leave nothing out, and remember, we're looking for something that sounds burnt but alive, whatever that's supposed to be."

Mhera started from the east wall. "Well, I can see the south side of the Abbey and the orchard between that and the east wall, and further west more lawns running right down to the west wallsteps, south of the gatehouse . . . Wait. We're looking for something that stands alone 'twixt water and stone, aren't we?"

Cregga suddenly became alert at the ottermaid's tone. "Yes, yes. Have you seen it?"

Mhera concentrated hard, feeling she was on the edge of a solution. "Not exactly, but it occurred to me that I might narrow it down a bit. 'Twixt water and stone. Suppose this wall . . . the one we're standing on . . . is meant to be the stone, between here and the south side of the Abbey is the pond. Maybe that's the water we're looking for!"

A slow smile of satisfaction spread over the badger's broad face. "Now we're getting somewhere. 'Twixt water and stone, between this wall and our Abbey pond. What else is there?"

"Hurr, marm, on'y ee gurt ole tree."

"What sort of tree?"

Brother Hoben shrugged. "Probably an ash tree, I think. Why?"

Mhera spotted Drogg Cellarhog down below and called to him. "See that tree I'm pointing at? What sort is it, please?"

The stout old hedgehog replied without even looking. "That'n's an ash, miz. I gets all my tool shafts from it. Fine timber, 'tis; makes goodly furniture too!"

Mhera patted the rough greyish-hued bark as they stood around the tree in question. "What a bunch of puddenheads we are. Ash! A living tree which sounds by its name as though it had been burned. What next?"

Brother Hoben had a suggestion. "We inspect the trunk and the ground around it, to see if we can find out what Abbess Song meant."

Cregga had an even better idea. "I am taller than any of you and my paws are extra sensitive. I'll inspect the trunk all around as high as I can reach. You three stand back a bit and look at the trunk and the ground. Use your eyesight to examine the ash."

Filorn and Foremole Brull passed by the tree with a crowd of Dibbuns around them. The otter waved to her daughter. "Brull and I are taking the babes for a paddle in the pond. It'll give Friar Bobb and Broggle a chance to get cleared for lunch. Please don't swing on my apron strings like that, you'll pull me over. Let me go, Durby!"

The molebabe trundled over to Mhera and attached himself to her smock. "Oi be goen a-skwimmin' in ee deep ponder!"

Mhera laughed as she detached the tiny creature. She wagged a paw at him and replied in mole dialect. "Ho no you'm bain't, likkle zurr, ee be's goen a-pagglin'. Skwimmin' bain't furr ee, lessen you'm a h'otter!"

Durby sucked on a digging claw as he thought about it, then trundled off chortling. "Hurr, miz, you'm a-tryen to cloimb ee gurt tree, an you'm bain't ee squirrler. Hurr hurr hurr!"

His logic struck the ottermaid immediately. "Cregga, he's right! We need a squirrel. Who better to examine a tree? Come on, let's get ourselves a squirrel!"

Friar Bobb was too old and young Broggle, by his somewhat well-fed girth, was not quite in athletic trim. The good Friar gave thought as to whom he could recommend.

"Hmm. What you want is a first-class treewhiffler, a specialist climber. 'Tis a bit of a problem, friends. Overweight parents, old 'uns like me, and some Dibbuns. They're the only squirrels we have at the moment. Broggle, can you think of anybeast who'd fit the job?"

Curling his tail soulfully, the assistant cook spoke one word as if it were a prayer. "Fwirl!"

Mhera stared at the dreamy-eyed Broggle. "Just tell me two things, please. What do you mean by a treewhiffler, and who in the name of seasons is Fwirl?"

Broggle was tongue-tied. Friar Bobb replied for him. "A treewhiffler is the squirrel name for a champion climber. There's a young squirrelmaid, called Fwirl, living alone in the woodlands. She's quite shy, but Broggle knows her. He often takes a few goodies up to the east battlements as a gift for her. We're hoping that someday she'll join us as a Redwaller."

Gundil was grinning at the adoring look on Broggle's face every time the name Fwirl was mentioned. "Hurr, may'aps you'm'd loike t'fetch miz Ferl to meet us'n's? She'm sounden loike ee roight h'aminal furr ee job."

Young Broggle dug into his apron pocket and produced a neatly wrapped package, tied with a fancy bow of chamomile stalk. His tail curled over his eyes and he scuffed the ground with his footpaw as he explained. "I was, er, just going to see her. I'll, er, ask Fwirl if she wants to help. No need to come with me. I can go myself, thanks. Oh, an' if she is good enough to come, please don't refer to me as young Broggle, just Broggle will be sufficient. Wait here, I'll be back."

Brother Hoben watched the chubby figure ambling off

to the east wall. "Our young Broggle looks as if a barrel of October Ale just fell on his head. He's evidently smitten with Miz Fwirl."

Cregga shook her great striped head in wonderment. "Young Broggle, eh? Who'd have ever thought it?"

Gundil gave a deep bass chuckle. "Hurrhurr, that'n lukken loike 'is stummick be full o' buttyflies an' 'is 'ead be full o' bumblybees!"

Mhera spoke up in defense of the assistant cook. "Now just stop that talk, please. I won't have Broggle made fun of, poor creature. It's obvious he thinks a lot of Fwirl, so let's not do anything to embarrass either of them!"

Friar Bobb bowed his head courteously to the ottermaid. "Thank you, Mhera. That was kindly said. I knew that Broggle was visiting the squirrelmaid, I've known it a while now, but I never told anybeast, lest they made fun of him. I've practically reared Broggle, and he's a hard worker, loyal to our Abbey. If he were my son I couldn't think more of him!"

Cregga held a paw to her mouth. "Ssh! I hear him coming back!"

Broggle marched up with a jaunty swagger. "I spoke to Fwirl, and she's agreed to help us."

Brother Hoben looked about and spread his paws wide. "Thank you, Broggle. But where is she?"

The tubby squirrel folded his paws and smirked. "Up in the ash tree. Where did you expect her to be?"

Cregga gave an involuntary start. She took Broggle's paw. "Just a moment, sir. I never heard a thing. To do as you say she'd have had to dash around to the west wall, scale it, and come up behind us so silently that we didn't hear. Then she'd have had to climb that tree without us even seeing her."

Broggle winked at them and nudged Cregga. "Well, you said you wanted a good treewhiffler! Fwirl, would you like to come down and meet my friends?"

Fwirl was not just pretty, she was startlingly beautiful,

135

with huge almond eyes, dainty paws, snow-white teeth and a curling redgold tail unlike that of any squirrel Mhera had ever seen. She was clad in a short belted tunic of soft green.

Mhera welcomed her with an outstretched paw. "Well, hello, Fwirl. You must be the champion treewhiffler of all Mossflower!"

Fwirl's smile lit up the bright summer day even more. "Haha, you've been listening to Broggle. He's told me all about *you*. I feel as though I know you all. How can I help you? I do climb a bit."

Cregga ran a paw over Fwirl's perfect features. "That's what I like to hear, a squirrel who doesn't beat about the bush. We've examined the ash tree and the ground around it as far as we can, Fwirl. But I think whatever we're after is much higher than the trunk. Could you take a look up in the boughs and foliage for us? 'Twould be a great help."

The squirrelmaid shot away like lightning, her tail swirling in a blurring circle. Halfway up the trunk, which she covered in the blink of an eye, Fwirl turned and addressed Cregga. "What am I looking for, Badgermum?"

Cregga liked the squirrelmaid's friendly manner. "Well, it could be anything at all: a carved message, a slip of parchment, or an object you wouldn't normally find in an ash tree. By the way, I hope you're going to join us for lunch?"

Fwirl vanished into the foliage, calling back, "It would be my pleasure, but let's take a peep up here first!"

The friends sat on the grass in the welcome shade of the old ash. Broggle sighed. "Isn't she just . . . just . . . Isn't she?"

Gundil lay flat on his back peering up into the foliage. "She'm surrpintly is, zurr. You'm a gurt lucky beast!"

Broggle plucked a blade of grass and chewed on the stem. "I hope Fwirl decides to come and live at our Abbey, if that's all right with you, Cregga marm?"

"All right with me? We'd be delighted to have her, eh, Mhera?"

Mhera threw a paw about her squirrel friend's shoulder.

136

"I'm sure Fwirl will come to live at Redwall. Especially as she knows you're here, pal!"

Fwirl was back down among them in a surprisingly short time and made her report. "No carvings or secret messages, I'm afraid. No parchments either. However, I did come across this."

Brother Hoben took the object she produced from her belt. "It's like half a pair of glasses with an old bit of cord hanging from it. What do you make of it, marm?"

Cregga took the object. She sniffed it, ran her paws gently over it and smiled wistfully. "Long long ago, a gallant and perilous hare gave this to me. His name was Perigord Habile Sinistra, the most dangerous saber fighter ever to come from the mountain of Salamandastron. Alas, the dust of long seasons has blown over his brave bones now. This is a monocle. You wear it in one eye, with the cord looped around your neck, so as not to lose it. Let me tell you, Abbess Song was a little vain. She would not wear glasses, even when she was very old. I gave her this monocle, and she kept it hidden in the sleeve of her habit. If ever she had to read anything, she would slip it out and use it secretly. I often wondered what became of it. Where exactly did you find it, Fwirl?"

With the exception of Cregga, they all looked up to where the squirrelmaid's paw was pointing. "On the north side, near the top of the tree. It was lodged in the joint of two boughs. Somebeast had cut two little slots into the bark so it would stay in position. I hope I did the right thing by bringing it down here?"

"I'm sure you did, missie," Friar Bobb reassured her. "But you say there was nothing else up there whatsoever?"

Fwirl shrugged expressively. "Nothing, Brother. Only the monocle."

Friar Bobb excused Broggle from cooking duties so that he could sit next to Fwirl at lunch. Taking advantage of the

137

good summer, Redwallers liked to dine outside. Cregga had the food served on linen cloths in the orchard, away from the search site. Fwirl enjoyed everything that Broggle put in front of her, particularly some little farls of warm bread, which she ate with her cream of mushroom soup and salad. Filorn served her some more, extolling Broggle's reputation as a baker.

"That's Broggle's nutfarls, my dear. He made them this morning. There's hazel, beech and chestnuts in them. They're my favorite too. Nobeast bakes a nutfarl like our Broggle!"

The squirrelmaid bit into another one. "Mmm, they're delicious. I could make a full meal of just your nutfarls. What a wonderful skill you have, Broggle!"

Boorab had fallen asleep whilst guarding the steps. He came hurrying in late and plonked himself down between the two squirrels. Halfway through loading a platter with salad, cheese and nutfarls, he suddenly noticed Fwirl.

"Wellwellwell. Howdy doody, m'dear. I say, what an absolute corker your charmin' pal is, Broggle. A real spifferoo, wot wot. Come on, Broggle, y'old rascal, you lucky grubslinger, how's about introducin' a chap to your stunnin' luncheon guest, wot, wotwot?"

Cregga's massive paws descended on the garrulous hare, and she lifted both him and the plate he was holding clear of the two squirrels. "I thought you were left to guard the south wallsteps, sah. Skipper, escort this malingerer back to his post. Let him take that plateful of vittles with him. Back to your duties now, you horrible hare!"

The brawny Skipper of Otters chivvied Boorab along. "Right y'are, marm. Come on, Mr. Boorab. Remember, yore still on probation 'ereabouts. One two, one two, eyes front, that's it!"

Boorab's protests faded into the distance, amid general laughter. "I say, you rotten old riverdog, get y'paws off me. Still on probation? Pish tush, sah, flippin' length o' time I've been at this confounded Abbey, I should be on pension, not bally probation. The nerve o' that great stripe-muzzled mauler, eh, wot?"

Gundil ruminated as he worked his way through a turnip and gravy pastie. "Whoi wudd ee h'Abbess be a leaven ee mononokle oop in yon tree?"

Brother Hoben selected a maple wafer spread with white cheese. "Yes, and why in that one particular place?"

Mhera spoke the answer before she had realized it. "Monocles are for seeing through. Maybe she placed it there so somebeast could climb up there and look through it."

Cregga smote a paw against her forehead. "Of course! It was placed facing north, Fwirl said."

The squirrelmaid allowed Broggle to fill her beaker with cordial. "From the position of the monocle in between the boughs, I'd say anybeast looking through it would be viewing the Abbey building on its south side, if that's any help."

Gundil wiped a serviette across his mouth. "Us'n's ull foind that owt doireckly arfter lunch, hurr aye!"

The second visit to the ash tree involved taking along one of Drogg Cellarhog's stout ropes. Fwirl took it up into the tree, and looping it around a high bough she let the end down, scampering to the ground behind it.

"Have you got the monocle, Mhera? Come on, I'll help you up."

Cregga gave the ottermaid final instructions. "Place the monocle back in its slot and look through it. The instant you see something, shout down and tell me. Up y'go, friend!"

Assisted by the treewhiffler, Mhera climbed into the spreading ash, hauling herself up on the rope whilst allowing Fwirl to find holds for her footpaws. She chanced a glance down. "We're getting rather high up, aren't we?"

Fwirl placed her shoulder under Mhera's footpaw to steady it. "Don't look down, Mhera. Keep going. Nearly there now."

The friends below on the ground stood patiently waiting. After a while they heard sounds.

"Hurr. Et's Miz Mhurra an' she'm larfin' fit t'burst."

Cregga turned her face upward. "Mhera, have you found anything? What are you laughing at?"

Ottermaid and squirrelmaid were both chortling. Mhera called back down to the bemused Badgermum. "Hahahaha! You, haha, you'll never believe it, Cregga. Ahahaha! I'm staring straight into your bedroom window. Hahahaheeheehee!"

12

Rain drizzled lightly through the early-morning mist rising from the surface of the broad stream. The two voles Krobzy and Sekkendin emerged from the secret tunnel with Tagg. The otter carried a small sack of supplies and a cloak, which they had presented to him. Krobzy blinked up at the indifferent milky sky.

"Yarr, drizzlin' won't last long; my ingrowed paw claw ain't twingein' enough. 'Twill clear up afore noon an' the sun'll smile on us again. Tagg, I wish ye wouldn't go, mate. Stay 'ere wid us. Ye could make an 'appy 'ome midst our voles."

Tagg clasped the bankvole's chubby paw fondly. "I've never had such a happy time as I spent with your tribe, friend, but I must go. There's bound to be Juska beasts following me, Sawney for one, and I don't know how many others. It would not be the act of a friend to bring trouble upon your creatures. Juska are thieves and killers. Stay out of their way. Keep to your homestead and be watchful for the next few days."

Two more voles emerged from the tunnel, carrying what appeared to be a large basket. Sekkendin showed it to Tagg. "This is a coracle. When yer finished wid it, just cast it out into the stream. 'Twill drift back 'ere by itself."

Tagg tried to hide a smile as he inspected the flimsy craft. "A coracle? Are you sure I'll fit into it?"

Krobzy chuckled. "Ye've still gotta lot t'learn, big feller. A coracle's a good liddle craft, light an' easy on the paws. There's just one paddle, see, wid a blade on each end. Yer paddle's a mast, too, when y'slip it atwixt those two blocks." Two small chunks of sycamore had been tied into the woven rushes of the craft's base. Tagg stood the paddle end up between them.

"Good idea, but where's the sail?"

Sekkendin indicated the cloak Tagg had been given. "That ain't just a cloak, matey. 'Tis a sail, too, an' I'll tell ye somethin' else. Our cloaks are special made, wid beeswax an' secret plant oils soaked into the weave. Ye'll find rain an' water don't affeck them. They'll keep ye dry anywheres!"

Krobzy tossed the sack of supplies into the small round coracle. "Yarr, those vittles too, they're travelin' rations. Full o' goodness t'keep yore strength up."

They launched the coracle into the water and Tagg got in. Despite his size it floated well, and he pushed off into the current, dabbing left and right with the double-ended paddle.

"This is wonderful! 'Tis so easy to steer, even going upstream against the current. Thanks, friends. My best wishes to you and all your tribe. I'll never forget your kindness. Please don't stand waving on the bank. Go in, and keep your heads low for a while. Keep a weather eye out for Juska vermin. Goodbye, and may your seasons be long and happy!"

The voles scuttled into their secret tunnel, calling back, "Yarr yarr, Tagg, call back an' see us agin. Yore allus welcome!"

Krobzy stayed at the entrance for a time, watching the

sturdy otter paddle his coracle off into the drizzly mists. "Good fortune to yer, Taggerung. I 'opes you meets friendly beasts like us along yore way!"

Drizzle was still falling in moist curtains when the hunters woke, damp and uncomfortable, in unfamiliar woodland after a night spent out in the open. Gruven huddled into a dry space beneath a fir tree, irate and hungry. He snarled at the weasel Milkeye. "What's the matter with you, deadlamp? Did y'never learn to light a fire properly? You'll be all day puffin' an' blowin' there!"

Milkeye turned from his flint and tinder, so that his good eye could see the stoat. "Wood's all wet with the rain. Can't make a fire with damp wood."

Gruven turned his bad temper elsewhere. Vallug Bowbeast was gnawing some dried fish from the meager rations they had brought along. Gruven tossed a pinecone at him. It missed.

"Hey, Vallug, are you goin' to sit there stuffin' your face 'til it bursts? Where's my breakfast? I'm clan Chieftain."

"Not yet you ain't," Vallug commented with his mouth half full. "Sawney always said that a leader had to prove 'imself first. We ain't seen you do nothin' yet except complain. I'm not yer mother. Get yer own vittles!"

Gruven sat glaring at the big ferret. Vallug was a killer, a dangerous beast to get the wrong side of. He wished he had picked on somebeast weaker. He tried to save face by growling, "When I catch up with that otter, then I'll prove myself all right!"

Eefera strode into view. He had been up before dawn, searching for tracks. Without reporting to Gruven, he threw himself down and grabbed some dried fish. He addressed himself to Rabbad, a small, sly-looking fox. "Waste o' time tryin' to track in this weather. There's a stream over yonder. Otters favor streams."

Rabbad collected water, dripping from the trees, onto a

dock leaf. He poured it into his mouth and swallowed. "Ye reckon we should follow the water course, then? Which way d'ye think the streamdog went?"

Vallug shouldered his bow and quiver of arrows. "Prob'ly north. That's the way he was travelin'."

Gruven decided the time had come to assert his authority. Leaving his shelter, he strode off purposefully, snarling orders. "Right, we're headed north. Break camp, you lot, no time for squattin' 'round eating. Follow me!"

There were definite sounds of gruff laughter from the group. He wheeled around to see Eefera pointing in the opposite direction. There was a hint of contempt in the weasel's voice. "It's this way . . . Chief."

Gruven found himself trailing at the rear. It was too narrow a trail to push past the others and regain the lead.

By midmorning they were well along the riverbank, traveling at a fast lope. Though Gruven was big and well built, he found it difficult to keep pace with the others. They were older than him, but lean and hardy for the most part. He was silently relieved when Vallug stopped them for a short rest on the bankside. Eefera scouted ahead whilst the others sat under the shade of some weeping willows, out of the continuous drizzle. Dagrab nodded northward. "Riverdog'll be makin' for the big mountains."

Gruven felt argumentative. "Where's the sense in that? Why should he want t'go there? It's stupid if you ask me."

The rat Grobait replied without even looking at him. "Mountains is made o' rock. 'Tis 'arder to track a beast over rock. That's the way I'd go if I was 'im."

Gruven spat into the stream. "Huh! Who asked you?"

Further conversation was forgotten as Eefera reappeared. "Come an' look at this. I was right."

They followed him to a spot on the bank further upstream. Eefera pointed out the signs. "I said otters favored streams. See? This is where he came out. There's part of a pawprint, in the mud, under that stone, an' 'ere, this's where the riverdog's tail flattened an' broke two young ferns. Sometime late last night, I'd say."

Gruven was prepared to argue the point. "Sometime last night, huh? How d'you know that?"

Eefera did not answer. He strode off, further up the bank. Gruven smiled at the others, shaking his head. "The great tracker, eh? Couldn't give me an answer, could he?"

Milkeye felt the bottom part of the broken fern stems. "Didn't 'ave to. Feel that. It takes a good few hours fer the rain to wash away the sticky sap that leaks out, an' these ain't sticky. They been stannin' 'ere broke in the rain since it started late last night. Come on, Eefera's on ter sumthin'."

Gruven drew his sword and raced ahead of the others, making certain he was in the lead this time. "Aye, come on, mates. Follow me!"

He dashed off as Eefera's voice called back through the bushes, "Stop 'im! Grab ahold o' the vole!"

Gruven turned this way and that, saw the bushes shake and hurled himself forward, crashing through them. Something dodged by him; he tripped and collided head-on with Eefera. They scrambled together in the bush cover until Eefera kicked him aside and leaped up, blood streaming from his mouth as he yelled, "In the water! The vole's in the water. Gerrim, Vallug!"

Swiftly the Bowbeast loosed two shafts at the shadowy figure before it disappeared underwater, speeding downstream with the current. He fitted a third arrow to his bow, then turned away in disgust, calling back to Eefera, "Shoulda let me know quicker. I only got 'im in the back paw. No use chasin' after 'im; that vole's well away by now!"

Eefera wiped blood from the corner of his mouth and spat into the stream. He turned slowly upon Gruven, controlling his temper with great difficulty. "I nearly caught the vole. You made me miss 'im!"

Quailing under the weasel's icy glare, Gruven

blustered, "Well, it was you who yelled out for me to stop 'im."

Eefera picked up Gruven's fallen sword from beneath a bush. His tongue probing at a loosened tooth, he answered, "Sorry . . . Chief. I didn't know it was you I was shoutin' to. I thought it was one of the others, a beast with a bit o' sense."

Gruven shrugged, trying to dismiss the sarcastic reply. "It was only a scummy little vole. What would y'want with a vole?"

Eefera looked at him as if he were totally stupid. "Information?" He made as if to give Gruven's sword back and thought better of it, tossing the weapon carelessly away over his shoulder.

Gruven took a little time locating the sword, and when he hurried back to the others it was to find them moving off. Joining them, he noticed they were eating pears. The stoat grabbed hold of Milkeye, one of the few he could bully into obeying him.

"Where'd you get those pears?"

Milkeye gestured back to the place they had just left. "Top of an 'ill yonder. There's a pear tree there, Chief."

Gruven spun the weasel around forcefully. "Run back an' get me a few. Go on, get moving!"

Milkeye avoided a slap from the flat of Gruven's swordblade. "All right, Chief, I'm goin'!"

Krobzy crouched in the secret passage entrance with Sekkendin, bandaging the watervole's footpaw with a dressing of sanicle, dock leaf and hair moss. Sekkendin placed his paw gingerly on the ground and smiled.

"Yarr, I'll live! Take more'n some ole Juska arrow to kill me."

Krobzy picked up a reed blowpipe and a tufted dart, its point smeared with laburnum and agaric fungus juices. "Aye, mate, but the vermin that gets this in its behind won't be able t'say the same thing. You lay 'ere an' rest. No Juska varmint's goin' t'do that to a vole an' live t'brag about it!"

Milkeye grabbed two pears from the tree and dashed off, not wanting to be left adrift in strange country.

"Ouch!" He felt the sting on the back of his neck and slapped at it. "Scummy liddle gnat, take that!"

He continued his hurried progress to catch up with the others. Krobzy followed until he found his dart lying in the grass. Picking it up gingerly by the tuft, he dropped it into a tiny box and thrust it into his belt pouch.

"Yarr, dat's one liddle gnat you won't ferget, varmint!"

Midnoon sunlight sparkled off the waters, fleecy white clouds decorated the bright skies. Krobzy had predicted the weather accurately. Tagg shipped his paddle. Reaching up, he grabbed an overhanging alder branch and pulled his coracle into the still shallows of a small cove. Beaching the little craft amid some concealing bushes, he waded ashore and stretched his limbs. It was a pleasant spot, with blackberries growing in profusion. Tagg made a leisurely meal of some flat cakes with dried fruit baked into them and a flagon of pear cordial from his vole supply sack, and a few pawfuls of the ripest berries he could find. In a patch of sunlight amid the alders, he spread his cloak and lay down upon it, humming an old tune that had always been with him, though he could not remember from where. The otter fell into a doze, trying to recall the words, his eyelids slowly closing.

Dim kindly faces hovering about him, soft clean linen touching his cheeks, the scent of spring flowers. He was in the magic place, the room of old red stone where peace and happiness lived. Two female otter voices were singing to him from far far away, a young one and an older one, singing sweetly, gently. Calm and serenity, safety and peaceful joy.

147

"Where glides the butterfly,
O'er some still pond,
There is my little love,
Dear one so fond.
Hush now you humming bee,
Soft shadows creep,
Silent in summer's eve,
Sleep baby sleep."

The happiness Tagg felt was intense, yet, as in all dreams, elusive. Even though he was in the realms of slumber, he realized this and sought to retain the feeling. He strove to make it clearer, to see more, to understand the dream, so that he could recall it at will and experience its joyous warmth. But the dream faded, like smoke on the wind.

How long he lay curled on the cloak in that silent glade, Tagg did not know. Then the mouse warrior was standing in his mind, pointing at him with the wondrous sword and calling, calling . . . "Deyna! Deyna!" It stirred him to wakefulness for a brief second. Eyes half open, he began to sit upright. Then he felt a heavy blow across his skull, and fell backward into agonizing darkness.

Eefera studied the bank edge, close to the water, and called back to the stoat Rawback, who was following behind with the others. "Still no signs near the shallows. What about you, any luck?"

Further back and higher up on the bank, Rawback, who had taken the lead, shouted his reply. "Nobeast been along 'ere 'cept us. Nary a trace!"

Eefera waited until they caught up. He was staring at the water. "He's on this stream, though, I know he is. I think he must 'ave some sort of light boat, a fast 'un."

Gruven sat cooling his paws in the shallows, cynical as ever. "Where would he get a boat? He's an otter, isn't he? Otters are supposed to be great swimmers."

Eefera did not dignify Gruven's ignorance with a reply. Rabbad the fox sat down to wet his footpaws in the stream. Gruven looked at him triumphantly. "Well, I'm right, aren't I?"

Rabbad enlightened him. "Even otters can't swim at full speed all the time, especially agin the currents. We're makin' good time, travelin' fast. If'n 'e was swimmin', we'd 'ave caught up with 'im afore now. So the otter must be usin' a fast boat like Eefera sez."

Gruven turned their attention away from his stupidity by sniggering as Milkeye, who had fallen far behind, came staggering crazily along the bank to join them.

"Oh, look who's arrived! What're ye pantin' an' slobberin' for, deadlamp? Is the goin' too tough for yer? Don't go lyin' down. We're movin' off soon. Where's the pears I sent yer for?"

Milkeye collapsed on the bank, unable to move an inch further. "Water, mates . . . water!"

Gruven looked up at the weasel, huddled on the banktop. "Idle hound. There's plenty o' water right here. Come an' get it yoreself. What d'ye think we are, skivvies?"

Eefera made his way up the bank. Crouching beside Milkeye, he raised the weasel's head. "Wot's wrong with ye? Have y'taken a sickness?"

Milkeye's face was beginning to bloat, and his one good eye was half shut and red-rimmed. He clasped Eefera's paw feebly. "Pain, all over . . . I'm burnin' up . . . Water!"

Eefera cast about until he found a large dock leaf. "All right, mate, I'll get ye some water."

He was halfway down the bank when Milkeye made a horrible gurgling noise. His paws thrashed about momentarily, and then he went still. Grobait prodded him with a footpaw.

"Milkeye's dead! By the blood'n'fang, wot d'ye think of that?"

They weighted the body down with a few stones lashed

149

to its middle and threw it into the stream. Eefera and Vallug then conferred as to the group's next move. Gruven joined the rest, foraging for berries and birds' nests, smarting with resentment because the two self-appointed leaders were ignoring him. He returned with a pawful of dandelion roots and two apples and boldly sat himself down next to the Bowbeast.

"Well, what's our next move?"

Vallug pointed with one of his arrows at the far bank. "We need to scout both sides o' the water. The otter could be leavin' tracks on the other edge."

Gruven chuckled nervously. "I'm not swimmin' across there. 'Tis deep an' fast."

Vallug shot him a glance that dripped contempt. "You won't 'ave to, yore stayin' this side with me . . . Chief. For all the use you'll be," he added under his breath.

Eefera waded into the stream to test the current. He was almost swept off his footpaws, and Vallug had to reach out his bow to help him back to the bank. "Young mudbrain's right," the weasel muttered to Vallug, out of Gruven's hearing. "It is too deep'n'fast, an' there's trailin' weeds that wrap around the paws, too. I think I stepped on ole Milkeye's carcass trapped in 'em. We'll ford it further along."

They spent the remainder of the afternoon trekking along the bank, searching for a spot where a crossing could be made. Unwittingly the hunters went right past the place on the opposite side where Tagg had pulled in and hidden the coracle. Toward evening, they halted beyond a bend where the stream eddied, prior to increasing its speed when it hit the straight. Eefera favored the spot.

"Water swirls a bit 'ere, but it ain't so bad. See, there's reeds stickin' up near t'other side, no current there. This'll do to cross. Ribrow, Grobait an' Rabbad, you come with me. The rest of ye stay this side with Vallug."

Holding paws, the four vermin entered the stream, with

Eefera in the lead. At the center they had to hold their heads back, chins up. Rabbad spat out a mouthful of water. "I didn't think it'd be this deep. We might 'ave t'swim fer it!"

Eefera, who was slightly taller, silenced the fox. "It gets shallower from 'ere to the bank. Keep goin'. You let go of anybeast's paws an' we're all in trouble!"

There were no shallows on the other side. The bank was a rock ledge that dropped straight down, so the stream remained the same depth as at its center. However, there was little or no current near the far side. Eefera entered the reeded area, which slowed progress. "Nearly there now . . . Yowch, I'm bit!"

Disregarding his own instructions, Eefera loosed Grobait's paw and floundered as fast as he could to the bank. Grabbing the rock ledge, he hauled himself out with panicked energy.

His actions caused chaos among the other three. They let go of each other; it was everybeast for himself. The water began threshing with big ugly mottled brown fish as a shoal of burbot attacked from their base in the reedbeds. Lying flat on the bank, Eefera extended his spearpole to Grobait. Shrieking aloud, the rat grabbed the spear, hauling himself along on it. "Yaaaargh! One of 'em's got me!"

As he clambered up the bank, Eefera took a rock and pounded on the broad frightening head of a big burbot, which had its teeth sunk into Grobait's backside. The stoat Ribrow, who had been last on the chain of linked paws, pushed away from the reeds and swam awkwardly, but fast, back to the other bank, pursued by two burbot, their rounded backfins cutting the water behind him. Vallug Bowbeast dispatched one expertly with a well-aimed arrow. Rawback and Dagrab ran into the shallows, beating off the other with sticks as Ribrow stumbled ashore, his eyes wide with fear.

Rabbad was the unlucky one. He screamed in agony as

151

several of the huge fish attacked him. Turning, he tried to emulate Ribrow by swimming back to the far bank, only to meet the one who had been driven away by Rawback and Dagrab's sticks. Gruven stood horrified as he watched the fox being pulled down by the burbot shoal. Monstrous heads, with two short spikes protruding from their nostrils and a long one trailing from the chin, reared open-mouthed out of the water to rip at the helpless fox. He screeched shrilly as the water reddened around him. More burbot, and two large pike, came skimming to the fray, attracted by the blood swirling in the stream. Rabbad went under, the water stifling his last cries.

The bedraggled vermin stood stunned, staring at the eddying, bloodied waters where he had disappeared. Vallug was the first to move. Wading in, he reached out with his bow, trapping the arrow that was sticking out of the burbot he had shot. He pulled it in to shore, inspecting the long heavy body with its sharp dorsal fin and fan-shaped tail, and called across to Eefera, "Bad fortune on Rabbad, dinner for us. I see you got a fish too!"

"Aye, but it nearly ate Grobait's be'ind," the weasel answered, pointing to his companion. "We'll stop 'ere t'night an' start trackin' again at dawn."

Gruven gazed hungrily at the burbot grilling over a fire, spitted on a green willow branch, watching Vallug prod it with an arrow to see if it was ready. "Wot sort of fish d'ye call that ugly monster?"

Ribrow had seen them before. "Burbot."

Gruven nodded, drawing closer to the fire. "Burbot, eh? It should make good eatin'."

Vallug continued prodding the fish as it sputtered over the fire. "Well, I'm the only one who'll find that out, 'cos I killed it. Go an' catch yer own fish if'n you want one. This 'un's mine!"

Gruven's voice went shrill with indignation. "Lookit Eefera. He's sharin' his with Grobait."

Vallug chuckled dryly. "So 'e should. They caught it t'gether, an' Grobait's bottom was the bait. Huh huh! Grobait . . . bait! That's a good 'un!"

Rawback, Dagrab and Ribrow knew better than to ask Vallug Bowbeast for a share of his fish. They remained silent, gnawing roots and apples. But Gruven felt a sense of injustice, and he said so.

"Lissen, Vallug, I'm supposed to be yore Chief. I should get a share of that fish!"

The big ferret had just taken a piece and was chewing on it. He spat out a bone and turned to face Gruven. "Then try an' take it . . . Chief!"

Gruven knew the others were watching him. He decided the moment had come to show them who was leader, and his paw strayed to the sword thrust through his belt. Vallug leaped forward and floored him with a hefty punch to the nose, then stood over him. "I'll tell yer who they'll call Chief, the beast who brings back that otter's 'ead! An' I tell yer, snotnose, it won't be you. We all saw the Taggerung give you a wallopin' back at camp. You ain't no Chief, Gruven; yore mama's tougher'n you. Ole Grissoul will make up a load of mumbo jumbo fer the one who slays the otter, the one who's tough enough t'do it, an' that'll be the clan leader. So you keep outta my way, unless ye want to die. I got no time fer bigmouthed fools, see! You was nothin' but a snivelin' cub when Sawney brought that otter into our camp. I was the one who slew 'is father, an' I'll be the one to slay the son too!"

On the opposite bank, Eefera could hear Vallug's every word on the still night air. Licking fish scales from his paws, he murmured to himself, "Oh, will ye now? We'll see about that, Bowbeast."

Gruven lay where Vallug had felled him, wiping blood from his nose and planning how he was going to kill the Bowbeast. Vallug sat with his back to him, wolfing fish. The ferret spat a bone into the fire and spoke, as if he was reading the other's thoughts.

"You ain't got the guts t'kill me, Gruven. Put one paw near that sword an' I'll stuff it down yer neck!"

Gruven made no reply, just lay there alone with his thoughts of murder. As did Vallug, who liked the idea of being a Chieftain. Eefera sat on the other side of the stream, watching them both. His plans involved a double killing. He had learned a lot and his teacher had been one of the best. Sawney Rath.

13

Cregga sat exhausted in her big armchair. Her bedroom was teeming with Redwallers, plus the tiny mole Dibbun called Durby. He had installed himself on the Badgermum's lap and was amusing himself by repeating everything she said. Every other beast was searching, for it stood to reason that if the monocle in the ash tree focused on the room, then there should be something of interest within. Boorab opened the corner cupboard, as numerous others had done that day. The hare poked his head inside, to find Floburt rummaging about busily.

"Jolly hungry work, missie, wot? Found anything, have you?"

The hogmaid brushed dust from her apron and sneezed. "Kerchoo! Only a lot of dust an' cobwebs. It'd be nice to know what we're searching for."

Boorab whispered secretively to her. "Some ancient map to a secret hoard of crystallized scoff. Prob'ly all sorts of super chuck preserved in lashings of honey!"

Sister Alkanet pushed past them both. "Tch tch. Just the sort of a senseless idea that only a hare could think up. Let me take a look in there!"

"This is the sixth time you've searched my room today," Cregga pleaded wearily, with Durby acting as echo. "Will you please go away and leave me in peace? There's nothing here!"

"Hurr, thissa sixy time you'm be's a surchin' moi room. Go eeway an' leaven oi en pieces. Thurr bain't nuthen yurr!"

Boorab tripped over Drogg, Alkanet got locked in the cupboard, and an argument broke out between two mice who were stuck beneath the bed. Mhera decided that enough was enough. "Stop!" she called sternly. "Stop what you are doing, be quiet and stand still. Now!"

She was pleasantly surprised when they did, even the Counsel elders. Mhera changed to a reasonable tone. "Friends, please, have some respect for your Badgermum's feelings. This room has been searched thoroughly several times without success. Leave Cregga in peace now, I beg you. Go about your tasks or leisure time elsewhere. The only creatures who really need to stay are the original searchers."

Cregga smiled as she listened to them filing out in sheepish silence. She waited until the door closed. "Thank you, Mhera, that was beautifully done. You were quite firm and you used a considerable amount of tact."

"Hurr, thankee, Murrer, ee were bootiful undunned. Mmmmf!"

Mhera placed a paw gently over Durby's mouth. "What will we do about this little terror?"

Broggle put on a gruff voice. "Chop off his tail and stick it in his mouth to keep him quiet. I'll take him to Friar Bobb's kitchen and we'll make molesoup of him!"

Durby scuttled down from the badger's lap. Hurling himself on her bed, he began to make snoring noises. Then he opened one eye. "Whurroo, you'm wuddent chop ee tail off'n ee sleepin' choild! Nay, zurr, you'm a gurt koind beast, an' oi be a-sleepen."

Cregga chuckled. "Thank goodness for that!"

Mhera began tidying things back into place. Fwirl lent a paw, and together they got the room back to normal. Fwirl sat down beside Broggle on a paw hassock, looking glum. "Phew, Redwallers don't mess about when they search a room! Your friends certainly scoured this place from top to bottom. For a while there it was enjoyable, because I've never been inside a building before. But I feel unhappy now that we didn't find anything."

Mhera stared at the pretty squirrelmaid in astonishment. "You've never been inside a building before? How is that, Fwirl?"

They listened sympathetically as she told her story.

"I don't remember much of my early seasons. I must have been only a babe, for I can hardly recall my parents' faces. I can remember cries in the night; I think we were attacked by foxes. I was thrust into a hollow log, and I could hear fighting, then screams, followed by foxes laughing. I must have stayed inside that log almost all night and half a day. When I crawled out my mother was lying quite still, with a deep wound on her head and blood everywhere. My father was gone, the foxes too. I sat with my mother for a long time, but she didn't move. I was hungry and couldn't stop weeping. Next morning I wandered off into the woodlands to search for food. Being only an infant, I got lost. That was as far back as I can recall. There's not much more to tell. I've lived in the woodlands, fending for myself ever since, always keeping on the move. Then one day I came upon your Abbey. At first I was afraid, not knowing who lived here. I used to climb the high trees so I could see inside. I watched you all; you seemed so happy and peaceful. I stayed close to the walls, and that was when I met my friend Broggle. He brought food which he had prepared for me, told me all about his Redwall friends. It must be like a dream living here."

Mhera was smiling, though her eyes were bright with unshed tears at the squirrelmaid's tale. She spoke to Fwirl, knowing the others would welcome her decision. "Then dream on, friend. Redwall Abbey is your home from now on!"

Fwirl clapped a paw to her mouth. "But I . . . you mean I can . . . live here forever?"

Broggle took the liberty of giving her paw a squeeze. "Haha. Nobeast lives forever, but you can stay here until you grow older than Cregga Badgermum!"

"You impudent young rip!" Cregga growled jovially. "Fwirl, my dear, let me be the first to welcome you to your new home. You are now a Redwaller!"

Durby poked his head from beneath a pillow. "An' oi be ee secund to wellcum ee, missus. Ee be gurtly wellcumed to moi h'Abbey, ho aye!"

The Badgermum nodded toward the bed. "And as your first official chore you can take that little rip down to Cavern Hole. His mother will be looking for him. Go with Fwirl and show her the way, Mhera."

They had to play Durby's game. Holding a paw apiece, Fwirl and Mhera bounced the molebabe's footpaws on each stair as they descended, the ottermaid reciting an old Abbey rhyme.

"Where's the naughty Dibbun, tell me where?
Is that him upon the stair?
Hear the little pawsteps, one two three,
And the Dibbun shouting, 'Can't catch me!'
What's for dinner, dumplin' an' pie,
Nice an' hot for you an' I,
If you don't come down those stairs,
Guess who'll eat it, two fat hares!"

Durby's mum wagged a paw at her babe. "Whurr you'm been, rascull? Oi'm out'n moi moind lukken furr ee."

The molebabe crinkled his button nose at her cheekily. "Yurr, doan't ee take on so, moi ole mum. Whurr be's moi vikkles?"

The two friends had to stifle their laughter as the molemum seized her son and hauled him off to the tub. "You'm bain't gettin' vikkles until oi barth ee, Durby Furrel!"

"Woaw!" Durby wailed aloud, trying to reason with his mother. "Keep oi out'n ee warter or oi'll be a-shrunkened. Woaw!"

Durby's mum appealed to Fwirl and Mhera. "Missus, will ee tellen this choild ee warter woan't shrink 'im?"

They helped the molemum to bathe Durby as they assured him, "No, no, water doesn't shrink you. Look at me and Mhera, we both get lots of baths, and we haven't shrunk, have we?"

Durby allowed them to bathe and dry him, then he waved all three imperiously aside and marched to the door lintel. "Oi'll just be a-measurin' oi t'see if'n oi shrinked!"

His mother measured him against the marks she had made to check his growth. She patted his head fondly. "Thurr thurr, choild, ee bain't shrunken, ee growed summ, lookit!"

The molebabe eyed her suspiciously. "Oi 'opes you'm bain't tellen ee fibs!"

Broggle was deep in conference with Brother Hoben, Gundil and Cregga when Mhera and Fwirl returned to the bedroom. Cregga held out her paws, and Gundil and Broggle heaved her out of her chair.

"Come on, let's go down to dinner. I've had enough of puzzles and riddles for one day. Are you hungry, Fwirl?"

"I'm always hungry, the food's so good at Redwall!"

"Ooh, my old bones!" Cregga complained as they negotiated the stairs. "Ah well, what a pity Abbess Song's clue led us nowhere. Dearie me, they did give my room a good search, though. It's feeling tidier than ever now, thanks to you two."

Mhera allowed the Badgermum to lean upon her as they entered the dining room. "We'll take another look tomorrow. Mmmm, smell that!"

Fwirl did. "Delicious! Wonder what it is?"

159

Cregga sniffed the air briefly. "What? You mean the damson and plum pudding Mhera's mum is steaming off, or the hazelnut, mushroom and turnip casserole Friar Bobb's taking from the oven, or the dandelion and burdock cordial Drogg Cellarhog is pouring from its barrel?"

Broggle seated Fwirl at the table, chuckling. "That Badgermum's sense of smell is better than the eyesight of a dozen Redwallers. Oh, look out, here comes trouble!"

Boorab bounded up and struck an eloquent pose between the tables. "And now, my good creatures one an' all, a delectable appetizer of the muse before we strap on the old nosebags, wot wot. A poem, composed by m'goodself. Pray attention for the official poet.

"I beg you listen to my verse, Ode to a damson plum
  pud,
"Tis not much better than it's worse, in fact it's jolly
  good!
Oh queen of puddens as ever was born, a gentle
  ottermum called Filorn,
Has made to grace our scoff this night, by steamin' pot
  an' oven light,
A pudden to tempt the hungriest tum,
Full of flour an' honey an' nuts an' all sorts of
  gorgeous scrumptious an' absolutely spiffin'
  ingredients from the kitchens where she's worked
  like a blinkin' madbeast all day long . . . an' of course
  from damson an' plum!
Pass me a plate, an' I'll say it's great!
Bung me a dish, an' I'll say what you wish!
Slip me a large platter, oh what does it matter!
Slide me a basin, with lots of space in!
Sling me a bowl, as deep as a hole!
Chuck me a pail, an' I won't wail!
As long as it's full of what does a chap good,
Heroic hare-sized portions, of damson an' plum pud!"

Boorab made a long and leggy bow, flourishing both ears and tail. In the silence that followed, he stalked majestically to his seat, but tripped and fell before he reached it. Midst laughter and applause he poked his head out from under the table and tried to silence them with a dignified glare.

"Perfect poetry's wasted on you lot, bounders! Tchah, laughin' at a chap's misfortunes. Small things amuse small minds, my dear old mater used t'say. Some of you never grew up from bein' blinkin' Dibbuns if y'ask me, wot!"

"That's it, that's the answer!"

Everybeast turned to see what Mhera was shouting about. She smiled self-consciously. "Er, sorry, but something just dawned on me. It was hovering in my mind when Durby measured himself against the door lintel. It came to me fully when I heard what Mr. Boorab just said. Growing up, that's the key. The ash tree has grown up since Abbess Song placed her monocle there. We were looking through the lens in the wrong place!"

Cregga started out of her seat. "Of course! Why didn't we think of that earlier?"

Boorab was still sulking. "Huh, why indeed? 'Cos you were too busy titterin' at a poor chap who'd just fallen an' fractured his flippin' tail, that's why!"

Filorn began serving him a massive portion of damson and plum pud. "Poor Mr. Boorab, I never laughed at your fall. Thank you for the lovely poem you composed about my pudding. I think you deserve a double . . . no, a treble helping for your pains."

The hare's mood lightened considerably. "Gracious marm, you are truly a gem among otters, not like these other bucolic bumpkins. Er, excludin' Miz Mhera, wot!"

Fwirl had been thinking of the next move. "As soon as it's daylight tomorrow we'll explore the wall below the window. Whatever it is that could be seen through the monocle back then should be lower down. Leave it to me. Let's see if I'm as good a wallwhiffler as I am a

161

treewhiffler. I'll need a long thin cord and a heavy knife." The squirrelmaid winked at her bemused companions. "Don't ask me what I need them for. You'll see tomorrow!"

Regaining consciousness was a slow and painful experience. Every time Tagg moved his head he was aware of the lump on the back of it, painful as a knife thrust. However, he could not reach a paw to touch it because he was bound securely. Somebeast was moving nearby. Tagg kept his eyes shut, listening as he tried to locate the position of the creature. The floor he was lying on shook frequently. Tagg groaned and rolled onto his side, facing away from where he reckoned the other beast was. He heard it move, felt its breath on the side of his face, then sensed it going back to its former position. Slowly, Tagg opened an eye, the one closest to the floor. It was night. He glimpsed the darkened foliage and realized that he was up in one of the alder trees, on a platform between two main branches, laid with boughs lashed securely together. It was open to the sky, having neither walls nor roof, only the foliage to shelter it.

"Stinkin' scum-splattered vermin, kill 'em all!" The creature was talking not to him, but to itself. "Rotten slime, festerin' spawn, don't deserve t'live. Kill 'em!"

Tagg lay quite still, listening to the hoarse voice raving on.

"Dirty foul vermin, nothin' on their minds but evil an' death. Death, eh? I'll show 'em death, I know a bit about that. Death!"

The creature began crawling toward him. Tagg lay quite still, the hairs on his nape prickling as it got nearer.

"Death, the best thing that can happen to vermin. Death, the slower the better. Make 'em suffer like I did. Yes, yes, oh yes!"

Tagg decided to make his move swiftly. As soon as he felt the other one's breath close to his back he lashed out hard with both footpaws. The creature gasped sharply as Tagg's bound footpaws kicked the breath out of it. Rolling over, Tagg pursued it across the narrow platform, still kicking out furiously, hoping to stun his captor. Whatever species the beast was, it was a tough creature, clawing and mauling him roughly. What was really odd was that it was talking and chuckling to itself as they tussled upon the platform.

"Hahaha! Death's the thing for you, bully, good'n'slow, hahaha!"

Tagg saw its bared teeth flashing close to his eyes. Rearing his head back like a striking snake, he butted it hard, the impact of colliding heads almost stunning him. Then they both rolled off the platform, the strange beast's claws locked into Tagg's belt. He got a fleeting glimpse of leafy foliage rushing by as they plummeted earthward. Tagg twisted, his lightning reflexes putting him on top of his attacker. They struck the ground with a hard thud. Both lay completely stunned.

A long interval passed before Tagg stirred. The creature beneath him was still unconscious, though it was groaning and muttering through its stupor. He realized that his foe would soon regain its senses; he would have to work quickly to free himself. Tagg rolled off the beast, shaking himself until its claws came loose from his belt. The otter's mind was racing, with one thing uppermost. His knife, where was it? An idea occurred to him. Using his footpaws he rolled the beast over, facedown. There was the blade, thrust into the back of his adversary's belt. Tagg's teeth closed around the handle, and with a mighty effort he tugged the knife free. The beast groaned and rolled over onto its back. It was coming slowly awake; there was no time to lose. Holding the knife point forward in his mouth, Tagg worked his head up and down, sawing away at the bonds on his paws, which were tied tightly in front of him. It did not take long. Sawney Rath's blade could slice a leaf floating in the air. Keeping an eye on the

163

fast-reviving beast, Tagg sliced through the thongs about his footpaws.

Still holding the knife in his teeth, Tagg massaged the life back into his limbs. The otter's head was banging and he was sore all over from the fight. But he was alive. Sheltered from the moonlight, it was totally dark in the tree shadow. Tagg still did not know what type of creature he was up against. It was not quite his height, but much bulkier. Suddenly it sat bolt upright, laughing madly.

"Hahaha! So you stayed t'get yourself killed, eh?"

Tagg did a forceful twirl. His rudderlike tail thwacked hard, right across his opponent's forehead, sending it down again. Like a flash he was upon it, straddling the creature's chest, his blade across its throat. "Be still! Still, I say! Don't move, or you'll be the one who gets killed. Be still, I warn you!"

Two glittering eyes grinned wildly up at him. "Hahahaha! Kill me then, vermin. Go on, get it over with!"

Reversing the knife, Tagg thwacked his opponent between the eyes, stunning it again. Piecing together the thongs that had bound him, he tied an end around one of the beast's paws. He dragged it upright and slammed it face forward against the nearest alder. Running the thong around the trunk, he tied it to the beast's other paw and let it slump down into a sitting position, paws spread, embracing the tree it was bound to. Tagg staggered down to the water's edge and lay flat in the shallows, letting the cold streamwater wash the aches from his body. Then, feeling refreshed, he went to where he had hidden his coracle and found the pack of supplies given him by the voles. Having eaten a few small cakes of oats and dried fruit, he drank some pear cordial and felt much better.

Tagg curled up in the coracle and dozed away the remaining night hours with his blade held ready. At dawn's first light he strolled cautiously back up to the clearing. His prisoner was still there, bound to the tree, sitting with its forehead resting against the trunk, muttering away.

"Vermin won't escape me, oh no, I'll track him an' bring him back an' watch him die, nice an' slow. Beggin', pleadin' an' moanin', just like all scum-mouthed vermin do."

As Tagg got closer, he realized it was a squirrel, a big old strong female, clad in a tunic of what looked to be skins of weasels, rats and foxes. Tagg sat down in a spot where the squirrel could see him and spoke to her quietly. "Why did you try to kill me? I'm not a vermin."

She stared at him scathingly awhile, then answered, "Painted face, gold earring, eelskin belt, fancy patterned wristbands, an' you tell me you're no vermin. You even carry an assassin's blade. Don't tell me you ain't a vermin. Go an' take a look at yourself in a shady pool down by the stream. Go on, then come back here an' tell me what you see . . . vermin!"

"Karrr, she be right, she be right, vermin you be!"

Drawing his blade, Tagg whirled around to face the eavesdropper. A large male bittern, practically invisible because of his brown, black and fawn plumage, came up from the riverbank reeds. Stalking gracefully along on thick green legs, he halted between Tagg and the squirrel, splaying his strong talons and poking a long needle-pointed beak in the otter's direction.

"Kaburrrrr! You fool, not Botarus. I see verminbeasts, hunting the banks they be. On this stream, both sides. Kurrrrrr!"

Tagg nodded, knowing now that hunters had been sent after him. "How many of them? Where are they now?"

The black iris of the bittern's umber eye widened. "Think you I be fool? I tell and you be calling them to you."

The squirrel gave an insane chuckle. "Hahaha! Let him call 'em. You free me, Botarus, an' I'll kill 'em all, every murderin' vermin mother's son of 'em!"

Tagg stowed the knife in his belt. "The last thing I want to do is call them. I'm not a vermin, they're the vermin. They've been sent to hunt me down and slay me!"

Botarus put his head on one side, the bright eye questioning. "You they hunt, these vermin? For why?"

Tagg did not want to go into the long story, so he made up an answer that was not far from the truth.

"I am an otter, see. I am not ferret, fox, rat, weasel or stoat. I was captured by them, and they tried to make me a vermin too. I escaped, and now they hate me and want to kill me."

The bittern pondered Tagg's answer before replying, "Krrrrrrum! Then why want you to kill my friend?"

Tagg pointed to the squirrel. "Her? I had no intention of killing her, she wanted to kill me! I was only protecting myself. That's why I had to tie her up!"

Botarus looked at the squirrel and nodded toward Tagg. "Krrrror! Riverdog he be, truth I think he speaks!"

Tagg tapped his rudder impatiently on the grass. Drawing his blade, he slashed through the thong, freeing the squirrel. "There, is that good enough for you two?"

The squirrel bounded upright, pointing an accusing paw at him. "Then why d'you look an' dress like a vermin, eh?"

Botarus held his position between both creatures. "Krrrrrrr! Told you that already the riverdog has. Where be you going on yonder volecraft?"

Tagg pointed north. "To the mountain."

Botarus preened his chest feathers carefully. "Karrrrr. Go ye not by water in the volecraft. Ahead of you they be, the vermin. Seeing not your craft, passed by here yesterday they did. Here leave your craft. Overland go, sweep 'round west by north. To the path I will take you myself."

Tagg bowed his head politely. "Thank you, Botarus. Wait, please, I'll get my food."

Tagg went back to the coracle and collected his stores,

Botarus and the squirrel following him. The squirrel watched him shoulder his supply sack. "Give me the food. I want it!"

Tagg did not like the tone of his former foe's voice. However, he emptied some food out onto the ground, adding a flask of drink. "Here is half of what I have. I need food for myself. You can take the coracle too, and if any vole asks you how you came by it, tell them it was a gift from me, Tagg."

The squirrel inspected the boat as Tagg gathered up his cloak. He turned to see her brandishing the paddle.

"Your blade, it's a good one, I'll have that too!"

Botarus shot out his long leg and knocked the paddle out of the squirrel's paws. He glared fiercely at her. "Enough you have, Madd. Stop you here now. With me Tagg goes, back I'll be by eventide. Riverdog Tagg, come you!"

The otter gave a wary berth to the squirrel, who picked up the paddle and shook it at him.

"Hahaha! Come back this way sometime an' visit me. So that I can kill you, vermin. Hahahahahaaaa!"

Tagg and Botarus made their way through the alders and into sparser woodlands. Tagg sighed with relief.

"Thank you, Botarus. I'm glad to be shut of that beast. I heard you call her Madd. Is that her name?"

The big bittern shrugged. "Mad she be, so Madd I call her. She knows not any other name."

Tagg strode swiftly to keep pace with Botarus. "Madd is a good name for her. She's a nasty dangerous beast."

"Krrrror, so would you be, were you her," Botarus commented dryly. "Killed her family, vermin did, for dead they left her. Three days lay she there. Found her I did, wound in her head, deep, so deep. Any otherbeast 'twould have killed outright. Together now we've been, long long seasons. Not easy to get along with is Madd."

Tagg smiled at the bittern. "Then why do you stay with her?"

Botarus smiled back, the gleam in his eyes sudden and savage. "I like not the vermin either. As mad as her I am sometimes."

Approaching midday they reached the limits of the woodlands. Tagg could see the mountain clearly slightly off to his right, still far off. Botarus pointed his beak out across the flatlands and outlined the route.

"Go you that way, 'twill keep ye clear o' the stream and your enemies. Krrrr, watch you, Tagg, there be drylands an' wetlands before foothills you reach. Live there many reptiles do, active in summer they be. Tread you careful an' fare you well!"

Botarus went into an ungainly run, but once he took to the air there was nothing awkward about his graceful flight. He soared and wheeled to gain height, then flew off with a long cry. "Krrrrrrooooooooommmmmmm!"

14

It was baking hot out on the flat scrublands. Dry heather, furze and teasel dotted the landscape, grasshoppers everywhere kept up a dry chirruping, butterflies in swarms visited every scrap of flowering vegetation. Bees hummed busily as they bumbled around the blossoming heathers. Tagg strode out energetically, tasting the light lemonish tang of some dandelion buds he was sucking, his eyes on the cool white of the snowcapped mountain, shimmering in the distance. The place belied the name flatlands. Hollows, hummocks and rises, combined with dry watercourse beds, made it extremely lumpy going. At midnoon he found sheltering shadow in the lee of an oddly shaped hillock. Conserving his meager rations, Tagg ate sorrel, wild onions and some cornsalad leaves. He drank sparingly from his remaining flask of pear cordial and dozed off with the background noises of the heathlands lulling him into slumber.

It was not shouts or screams that wakened him, but a series of smothered grunts, mingled with hissing noises. He listened until he located the sounds, which came from the other side of the hillock where he was resting. Tagg drew his blade and went to investigate.

He had seen smooth snakes before, but this one was a

particularly large specimen, light grey in color, with a narrow head and a dark stripe across both eyes. The snake had a harvest mouse in its coils and was trying to crush it to death by constricting its slim smooth-scaled body. However, the mouse was a game little fellow, and he kept struggling loose and inflicting some sharp bites upon the predator's flanks. Never once did he shout or cry out for help. Tagg admired his courage and jumped smartly in to help. Stamping down, he pinned the snake's head to the sandy ground and grabbed its tail firmly, straightening it out. Once the reptile had nowhere to anchor itself for purchase it was virtually helpless. Tagg winked at the harvest mouse.

"Best get out o' the way, friend. This villain's not going to be very pleased when I let him go!"

The harvest mouse straightened his little yellow tunic and bared his teeth. He performed a dance of rage. "Then pass me that dagger o' yourn, mate, an' I'll chop that stringy mouse mangler into bite-sized bits, the scaly-nosed scumtail, the fish-eyed field forager, the legless land lizard! Just gimme the blade, an' I'll show that 'un how t'make a new tunic out of snakeskin!"

Tagg was taken aback at the mouse's ferocity. He flicked him aside with his rudder. "I said stay clear. I'll deal with this."

The mouse was practically doing somersaults in his anger. "Well, gerron with it an' quit jawin', will ye? You came along just when I had that snake well an' truly whipped. Don't stand there like a weasel on a washin' line. Kill it!"

Tagg twirled his knife so he was holding the blade, and dealt the smooth snake two sharp blows on its head. It went limp.

"There, that's put him to sleep for a while, though he'll have a rare old headache when he wakes. Come on, let's get going."

The mouse stamped his footpaw and ground his teeth.

170

"Y'mean you ain't going to slay the blaggard? Are ye soft in the head or wot? Fine big lump of an otter like you an' you can't even kill a rotten reptile! Wot's wrong with ye, eh?"

Tagg swung the mouse up onto his shoulders and strode off. "Bloodthirsty little scoundrel, aren't you? No reason to kill the snake; you got away all right. By the way, my name's Tagg."

A tiny paw appeared for him to shake. "Please t'meetcher. I'm Nimbalo the Slayer. Next time y'see me finishin' off a snake, just leave us alone, will ye?"

Tagg tried his best to stop laughing. "How did y'come to be out here alone, Nimbalo?"

"Got taken by an eagle," the harvest mouse replied airily. "Caught me asleep, y'know. Anyhow, he was flyin' me off t'the mountain, so I broke his claws an' dropped off down here. I fell into some soft sand, an' that's where that overgrown worm found me. Huh! Lucky for it I was a bit dazed!"

Tagg now had his laughter under control, and merely nodded. "It certainly was, Nimbalo, but where did you come from? I mean, your tribe, your family, where do they live?"

Nimbalo gave the otter's ear a tug. "Bit nosy, ain't you? Where do I come from? Oh, 'ere an' there, y'know. I've been 'round the rocks a few times, matey. As for families an' tribes, huh, who needs them? They ain't nothin' but a load o' bother. Nimbalo the Slayer travels alone!"

Tagg raised his eyebrows as the mouse shifted position. "Except when you're traveling with me, eh?"

Nimbalo leaned over Tagg's head and stared down into his eyes. "Don't contradict me, riverdog. It don't pay to cross Nimbalo. Any'ow, what're you doin' 'round this neck o' the land? Let's 'ear you doin' a bit of talkin' fer a change."

The otter told Nimbalo the story he had made up for Botarus and the squirrel, about being captured by vermin

171

and trying to escape being one of their tribe. The harvest mouse chuckled.

"Yore right there, Tagg. Steer clear o' tribes an' families, they'll only bring ye grief. So, why are ye goin' to the mountain?"

Tagg stared longingly at the snowy peak ahead. "It's hard to say, really. It looks so cool and clean, sort of free and away from it all. I think the mountain might be a good place to live, though I've never been there. Have you?"

Nimbalo spread his paws expansively. "Mountains, I've been 'round 'em, down 'em, up 'em an' about 'em. I've crossed more mountains than you've ate dinners, me ole mate!"

Tagg halted. He took the harvest mouse down from his shoulders and faced him. "You've certainly led a long and adventurous life, my friend. Tell me, how many seasons old are you?"

Nimbalo started to count upon his whiskers, then dismissed it. "A lot older'n you, pal, by a good stretch. Ho yerss, us 'arvest mice could fool anybeast. We're usually about ten times older than ye'd think!"

The otter put his next question flatly. "Why do you tell so many lies, Nimbalo? Don't you ever tell the truth?"

Nimbalo punched Tagg's paw lightly and grinned. "Truth? What's the truth, eh? Just a pack o' lies made up by otherbeasts so you'll believe 'em. Of course I always tell lies. What's wrong wid that, Tagg? They don't 'urt you, do they?"

Tagg stood bemused, stuck for an answer. His companion swaggered jauntily onward, in his odd hopskip manner.

"Come on, me ole riverdog. Life's too short t'worry about things like that. I'll go to the mountain with ye. Hah, suppose I'll 'ave to. Big honest streamwalloper like you, ye need a smart 'un like me to look after ye. Well, are you comin'?"

172

Over the remainder of the day, Tagg grew quite fond of Nimbalo, who was an excellent traveling partner and never at a loss for words. At one point he had Tagg cut him the thick stem from a gentian flower. Nimbalo gnawed holes in it, hollowed it out and made a whistle. As they trekked along a dry streambed he kept Tagg amused by tootling tunes on it and singing comic ditties in between.

"I'm the fiercest mouse livin' in all the wide land,
Me fur is so fine an' me muscles are grand,
If I ever meet with some ole vermin band,
I give all the rogues a good towsin'!

For although I'm real savage, me temper I'll bide,
But beware of me dander, ye'd best step aside,
Or you'll find out why so many blaggards've died,
Givin' lip to Nimbalo the Slayer!

When I meet a bad crew all the warriors do hide,
'Cos me fame goes afore me both far an' both wide,
But to mothers an' young 'uns I bow with great pride,
That's the way o' Nimbalo the Slayer!

So take care when you see this mouse passin' by,
I can knock ye out flat with the wink of me eye,
You just ask any mousemaid, she'll blush an' she'll
    sigh,
He's a hero, Nimbalo the Slayer!"

Nimbalo turned and winked at Tagg. "Oh, I fergot to mention, I'm modest too!"

Summer evening shades began falling as the hot day drew to a close. The two friends made camp in a hollow on top of a rise. Tagg was pleasantly surprised by Nimbalo's foraging and cooking skills. Gathering dried turf, the otter lit a fire and awaited Nimbalo's return, as the harvest mouse had insisted on finding food by himself. Purpling layers of cloud backed the mountain, tapering off to gold and red toward the west, sweet aromas came from the turf fire. Tagg settled himself comfortably on the sandy slope of the dip, savoring the beauties of twilight. Nimbalo broke the spell on his return. He tossed a bunch of roots and vegetation onto Tagg's chest, leaping over the top of the rise and shouting, "Halloo the camp! Stir yore stumps, big feller, let's get supper goin'. I'm starved!"

Tagg inspected the tangle of vegetation. "What's all this, mate?"

Nimbalo rummaged cheerfully through the mass. "I can see yore used to woodland vittles. These are flatlands food. See, whitlow, tastes just like cabbage, pennycress, touch bitter, but nice. There's comfrey roots, pepperwort an' bindweed flowers. You'll like them, they're sweet."

Tagg sniffed the flowers appreciatively. "Hmm, lovely smell. Hope they taste as good. Ah, dandelion leaves and roots, wild strawberries and some blackberries. I've got some fruit and wild oatcakes the voles gave me and most of a flask of pear cordial."

Using both paws, Nimbalo hauled the blade from Tagg's belt. "Sounds good, mate. I'll start choppin' the salad with this sword of yours. Keep that fire low, though. Turf don't give off much smoke, it just glows. Those vermin you said was trackin' you, any idea where they might be?"

Tagg gestured to the mountain's east side. "Probably over that way. They were following a stream, so I went off in the opposite direction. I can't see them troubling us yet awhile. Maybe when we're on the mountain we might run into them. Do you carry a weapon, Nimbalo?"

Baring his teeth in a ferocious grin, the mouse replied, "These is all the weapons I need, mate, teeth an' paws. If I needs more you can cut me a big stick."

Their meal was frugal, but enjoyable. Nimbalo played a few tunes on his whistle and they sat by the fire, watching the night draw in. When Nimbalo stopped playing, the otter went to the top of the rise. He ducked as a group of swifts winged low over him, then he listened carefully. Nimbalo sprawled in the hollow, watching him.

"Wot's the matter, big feller? Somethin' up?"

Tagg slid down beside him. "Birds flying low, I thought I heard a far-off rumble, and the air feels heavy. There may be a storm on the way."

Dusting sand from his tunic, the harvest mouse stood up. "I've been in more storms than an ole gull at sea. We'd better make a move an' find shelter. I tell ye, Tagg, you don't wanna get caught in a storm on these flatlands."

Lightning flared briefly beyond the mountain. Tagg gathered his cloak and pack together, hearing the distant thunder rumble. "Sounds like it'll be a bad one, mate. Come on!"

Complete darkness fell as the moon became shrouded by heavy cloud. They hurried along the dry bed of a stream, feeling the first heavy raindrops strike their heads. Tagg pulled his waterproof cloak over them both. Nimbalo pointed. "Lucky ole us, matey. There's a little cave in the side of the bank, I can just make it out."

Rain was sheeting straight down, lightning splitting the night skies in spectacular jagged rips and thunder booming overhead. Nimbalo skipped smartly up the bankside and held out a paw to his friend. "C'mon, ye great lump, inside afore ye get soaked!"

Tagg huddled in alongside Nimbalo. There seemed to be plenty of room. They lay in the entrance, the cloak draped over their heads, watching the awesome spectacle of the huge summer storm. Tagg shuddered and wriggled with pleasure.

"It's great to watch a big storm, especially when you're nice and dry and not caught out in it!"

The harvest mouse elbowed him roughly. "Be still, willyer? Near rolled over an' crushed me then!"

Tagg pulled himself back from the cave entrance. "Sorry, pal. I'll get back in here a bit. Hmm, this is quite a

175

sizable cave. Maybe we could light another fire, what d'you think?"

Nimbalo turned around. He sniffed the interior air and froze. "Stay still, Tagg, stay still, fer pity's sake!"

Tagg answered him from the darkness. "Why?"

Rustling coils and venomous hissings told him the reason even before Nimbalo whispered it into the menace-laden blackness.

"Snakes!"

Following both sides of the stream course up into the foothills, the hunting party came together again. Vallug found a broad shallow expanse where he was able to lead his followers across by a series of stepping-stones that showed above the surface. They joined up with Eefera on the opposite side. Gruven saw Grobait resting, clutching a paw to his bottom, and sniggered. "I wouldn't let any fish take a chunk out o' my behind."

Eefera pushed roughly by him. "Easy fer you to say. You didn't even have t'get yore paws wet. Any luck with tracks on yore side, Vallug?"

"None. What about you?"

"None, same as you. What d'ye think? Will we be wastin' our time climbin' the mountain to look for 'im?"

Gruven interrupted them to air his opinion. "If no tracks lead up here, I reckon we're on a fool's errand. What's the point of climbin' a mountain? I said it was a stupid idea from the first!"

Even Grobait could not keep the patronizing tone out of his voice as he took it on himself to answer Gruven. "He was travelin' upstream, not down. This is the only place he could go. So wot's the use comin' this far an' not lookin' on the mountain fer the otter? Mebbe we didn't find any tracks, but he could've left the stream an' found an easier way up. We'd be the ones lookin' stupid, to come this far an' not even bother takin' a look up there!"

Gruven indicated Grobait's injury with a nod. "Well, you won't get far with that wound. Wot d'you plan on doin'?"

Grobait spat into the stream. "I'll keep up, don't fret yerself!"

Vallug had been sniffing the air. He turned moodily on them. "You'd better keep up, both of yer. See that rock ledge up yonder? I'm gettin' under it. The rest of ye'd best do the same if'n you don't want to get caught in the storm!"

Disregarding everybeast, Vallug started climbing. Gruven was about to make a smart retort when the first drops of rain splattered on his head. He joined the others following Vallug.

"Lend us a paw 'ere!" Grobait called as he struggled upright.

Gruven could not resist snickering an answer. "Why? You've already got four like the rest of us."

They huddled under the ledge as the rain began sheeting down. A thunderclap caused Ribrow to jump, and he touched the ledge above him nervously. "This mightn't be a safe place t'stay. S'pose the thunder an' lightnin' struck this mountain an' collapsed it down on us? We'd all be crushed to death by these rocks!"

Gruven snorted at the idea. "If yer frightened you don't have t'stay 'ere. Go an' sit out there with Grobait."

The injured rat had hardly moved. He lay by the swelling stream almost battered flat by the heavy downpour. Eefera stared callously at the prone figure. "That wound must've gone bad on 'im. He's been limpin' all day. Looks like 'is back leg's stiffened up an' gone useless."

A lightning flash illuminated Grobait's pitiful figure. "Don't lay out there," Dagrab shouted to him. "Come up 'ere!" None of them made a move to help the wounded rat. Vallug sneered.

177

"Grobait ain't goin' anywhere, unless the stream swells up an' sweeps 'im away in the night. Save yer breath, Dagrab."

Gruven peered through the curtain of rain spilling from the ledge. "Yore the Bowbeast, Vallug. Put Grobait out of 'is misery."

Turning to Gruven, the big ferret smiled wickedly. "That 'un ain't worth wastin' an arrow on. But if it was you out there, well, I'd use an arrow, mebbe even two or three. I wouldn't consider 'em wasted on you . . . Chief!"

15

Very slowly Tagg drew his blade, whispering to Nimbalo, amid the hissing and slithering, "Pass me my cloak, mate. Do it very carefully; don't make any quick or sudden moves. When I shout, you must jump right out of this cave. Don't hang about for me. I'll be right behind you."

The otter put a paw behind his back, feeling Nimbalo pass him a corner of the cloak from his position at the cave mouth. Outside, the rain continued its onslaught. Below the cave there was a swirling, gurgling sound. The storm was filling up the dry bed of the stream. Tagg felt something dry and scaly slide over his footpaw. The weight and breadth of the reptile could mean only one thing. Adders!

The vicious hissing increased. He figured there were at least six snakes in the darkened cave. Now that they had scented other creatures and felt movement stir the air, they would be ready to strike with their poisonous fangs. Tagg acted with every fiber of his great strength and uncanny reflexes honed to their limit. Flinging the blanketlike cloak where he judged the adders to be gathered, he slashed low all about him and yelled, "Jump! Quick!"

The harvest mouse was actually in midair when,

propelled by a massive back somersault, Tagg cannoned into him. With a resounding splash they both hit the water. The otter grabbed Nimbalo with one paw and shoved him high, clear of the flood. Tagg slashed out with the blade held in his other paw, right down the ugly head of a big adder, with almost half its body length extended as it struck. Hissing madly, it pulled back into the cave, its skull sliced to the bone.

Tagg shoved off, swimming strongly, following the current, with Nimbalo still held high, yelling shrilly, "Don't drop me! I can't swim!"

The otter was a powerful swimmer, even with one paw holding the harvest mouse clear of the swollen streamrace. He continued for quite a while, then his head broke the surface close to Nimbalo. "Are you all right, little mate?"

The mouse kicked and squirmed. "All right? I'm near drowned by this rain! Get me ashore!"

As soon as he spotted a rock, sticking sideways out of a fern patch a few lengths from the bank, Tagg abandoned the stream and set Nimbalo down. Slithering and sliding, they made their way up the bankside and stumbled to the welcome cover beneath the large stone chunk. Rolling thunder sounded more distant now; lightning flashed far off. Tagg wiped mud from his paws onto a fern and lay back.

"Storm's moving away now. The rain should slack off before dawn. Well, mate, we've lost our supplies and the cloak, but we're lucky. We could've lost our lives to those serpents back there."

Using his tail as a probe, Nimbalo dug mud from his left ear. "Gave me a good ride, didn't ye, big feller? I was foolin', y'know; I'm a champion swimmer really. Faster'n a fish, that's me!"

Tagg went along with the joke, knowing his friend was lying. "Well, you scoundrel, I never knew you could swim, and me carrying you all that way, swimming with three paws an' a rudder. Rascal!"

Nimbalo tweaked Tagg's ear affectionately. "Never mind, pal. Next time I'll swim an' hold *you* up over the water, I promise!"

Tagg chuckled. "I'll keep you to that promise, you rogue."

Sleep was out of the question. They sat watching the rain. It had slackened somewhat, but was still quite heavy, with a light breeze beginning to drive it sideways. Tagg sat Nimbalo on the lee side, taking most of the wetness on his right side. Nimbalo peered out onto the rainswept plain. "Can you see a light out there?"

Tagg saw the dimly flickering glow. "Aye, and it's coming this way."

They sat still and silent, the otter gripping his blade, as the light got closer. Nimbalo screwed his eyes up against the rain. "It's some ole beast carryin' a lantern!"

Tagg slid the blade back into his belt and moved over a bit, to make room for the newcomer. It was an ancient shrew, bent almost double, covered in a blanket cloak and hobbling along with the aid of a blackthorn stick. Groaning faintly, he put the lantern down and sat between them. Throwing back his cloak hood, the shrew dug a spotted kerchief from it and wiped his whiskers.

"Filfy night 'tis, plain filfy. Yew nearly fell into me den as youse climbed the bank back there. Hoho, that woulda been wot y'call droppin' in fer a visit, wouldn't it, me ole cullies?"

He tapped the side of his lantern, and about six fireflies flared their tiny lights in response. The ancient shrew cackled. "Heeheehee! I'd got 'ere sooner, but I 'ad to feed me pals. A liddle 'oney'n'water, that's all they needs. Sparky bugs, they are. Now, wot are youse two doin' out 'ere on a night like this?"

Tagg allowed Nimbalo to act as spokesbeast. "We was about to ask you the same, me ole greysnout."

The shrew tapped Nimbalo's paw with his stick. "Yore an 'ardfaced liddle 'arvest mousey. Wot's yore name, eh?"

181

"Nimbalo the Slayer. Everybeast 'round 'ere knows me!"
The shrew sucked his toothless gums, looking Nimbalo
up and down. "Well, I don't, but I'll tell ye why I'm 'ere,
Lamino, I come t'see if'n youbeasts was needin' shelter in
me den. 'Tain't much, but it's all mine, an' 'tis dry too. So,
wot d'ye say, Limbow? Does you an' yore big silent
brudder want a night's lodgin', eh?"

Tagg touched his paw to his nose politely. "Thankee,
that'd be very nice. My name's Tagg, sir."

The old one arose creakily and picked up his lantern.
"Well, my name's, er, er, Ruskem. Hah, 'tis so long since
anybeast spoke it I'd almost forgotten. Come on, then,
Tugg, foller me. Come on, Minaglo, you can carry the
lantern."

As they made their way back to the bank, Nimbalo
whispered, "Wish he'd get me name right!"

Tagg wiped rainwater from his eyes. "Don't get too
upset, mate; Ruskem has trouble remembering his own
name, poor old beast. He must live all alone."

Ruskem's den entrance was near the banktop above the
waterline. He ushered them in with his stick. "In 'ere,
Togg an' Ninnybo, this is me ole den."

It was tiny inside. Tagg had to bend his head to avoid
the ceiling. However, it was homely and comfortable, with
a turf fire glowing in a stone hearth, an armchair, a bed,
and thick rugs of woven moss and reeds carpeting the
floor. Ruskem produced a ladle and two polished elm
bowls, which he proceeded to fill from a big cauldron
hanging over the fire.

"Shrewburgoo, that's wot 'tis, an' don't ask me wot's in
it. That pot ain't been empty since I don't know when. I
just adds to it aught I c'n find, berries, fruit, roots an' all
manner o' things. One fer you, Numbowl, an' the big bowl
fer Tigg. There's a kettle o' mint'n'comfrey tea on the
'earth, so 'elp yoreselves."

The shrewburgoo tasted wholesome and filling, though
some parts of it tasted sweet and other bits were definitely

savory. Ruskem poured them tea, and saw Nimbalo's eyelids start to droop.

"Yore in need o' slumbertime, Binflow. I'll sleep in me chair, you take the bed. Fogg, yore too big fer either. You kin sleep on the rugs, they're nice an' soft."

Nimbalo swigged his tea off, flopped on the bed and fell asleep without further ado. Ruskem sat in his chair and sighed. "Don't tell me yore story, Wagg. It'll tire me ole brain out."

Tagg was gazing around the walls, which were filled with pieces of slate. Each one had a skillfully executed portrait of a shrew's face on it, some male, others female. The otter smiled. "Oh, I won't tell you my story, Ruskem, it bores me listening to it. These are good pictures. Who did them?"

The shrew pointed to a lot of flint shards on the mantelpiece. " 'Twas me. I like makin' pitchers, got a good eye fer it. Those are my kin, ma, pa, grandma an' grandpa. That 'un's my ole missus, seasons rest 'er pore 'eart, the rest are me sons an' daughters. Gone, all gone now. Those that ain't died 'ave packed up an' left. There's on'y me now. But 'tis my 'ome an' I likes it enough ter live wot seasons I got left right 'ere. You get some rest now, Flagg. Big feller like you needs plenty o' shuteye. Nighty night!"

Sometime during the night, Tagg woke up. Ruskem was snoring gently in his chair, but Nimbalo was talking in his sleep, sobbing too. In the dim glow of the turf fire, Tagg watched his friend tossing about on the bed, and listened to the harvest mouse's disjointed ramblings.

"But Papa, I've done all the work. I'm hungry. Ow! Ow! Please don't beat me, Papa, I've done all the work. Where's Mama? I want my mama! What . . . Oh, Mama, please come back . . ."

Nimbalo sobbed heartbreakingly. Tagg rose quietly and stroked his friend's head as gently as he could, murmuring, "Hush, matey, sleep easy now. Hush, hush."

Nimbalo's eyes opened wide, and he sat up with his

paws clenched. Tagg could tell he was still sleeping. Nimbalo's voice grew hard. "Put that belt down, Papa! I said put it down, you ain't goin' to beat me with it no more. No more, I say!"

Tagg pushed him back down and passed a paw over his eyes. "Sleep, now. Tagg's here, mate. Sleeeeeep."

Nimbalo uttered a single word. "Tagg." His eyes closed and he slept peacefully for the remainder of the night. Tagg dozed off sitting by the fire. So Nimbalo was a runaway who had received a hard upbringing from a cruel father. Now Tagg knew why his friend presented a tough exterior to all. He wanted to show he could not be bullied or beaten anymore.

Tagg woke late next morning. Nimbalo was still asleep, but Ruskem was up and about. He added mixed oats and barley and some strawberries to the shrewburgoo. Stirring in a chunk of honeycomb, he nodded to Tagg.

"G'mornin', Trogg. Wot d'ye think? Shall I toss in some wild celery an' onions to this lot?"

The otter wrinkled his nose and shook his head. "No, I think the strawberries an' honey should be enough, sir. What's the weather like outside, I wonder?"

The ancient shrew poured tea from the kettle for his guest. "Fresh as a daisy an' prettier'n a rosebud. Rain's all gone, stream's runnin' muddy but full. What more could a beast want?"

Tagg went to the bed and shook the snoring harvest mouse. "A traveling partner who's awake, that's what I want."

Nimbalo sat up, rubbing his eyes and lying in his teeth. "I'm awake, I'm awake! Been awake fer blinkin' ages, watchin' youse two makin' breakfast. Fooled yer, eh?"

Ruskem passed him a steaming bowl. "Then try foolin' yore stomach wid some o' this, Bongbul!"

When they had breakfasted, the old shrew sat back in

his chair. Reaching down among the cushions, he pulled out two pieces of slate, with fair likenesses of Tagg and Nimbalo etched on them. He displayed them proudly.

"Hah! I was up long afore youse pair. Well, wot d'ye think?"

Tagg studied them. "They're very good, sir, very good!"

Ruskem was pleased with the otter's verdict. "Heeheehee! Thankee, Blogg. I'll put 'em up on me wall after yore gone. Youse kin be part o' me family, eh!"

"I don't wanna be part o' no fa—"

Tagg clapped his paw over Nimbalo's mouth and picked him up. "Let's go outside and stretch in the fresh air, matey!"

Ruskem put the portraits aside. "Wot's wrong wid young Bimbo?"

"Tummy trouble. He bolted down that hot breakfast."

Tagg swept Nimbalo out onto the sunlit bank. "No need to be insulting to the old fellow. He was honoring us by putting our pictures on the walls with his kin."

The harvest mouse looked shamefaced. "I better go back in an' say I'm sorry to Ruskem."

Tagg patted his friend's paw. "No need to. I don't think he heard you. Just remember to be nice to him. He wasn't obliged to help us, but he did."

Blinking against the sunlight, the ancient shrew hobbled out. "Heehee! See, I told ye. 'Tis a mornin' to be alive on. Nothin' looks prettier'n these 'ere flatlands after a summer storm!"

Nimbalo politely helped the old fellow to sit at the stream edge. "Yore right, sir. It certainly is!"

Ruskem waved his stick back at the den. "Ye'll find some liddle fruit loaves that I baked an' two flasks o' dannelion an' burdock cordial in there. I take it yore bound fer the mountain? I was up there once. A strange an' wunnerful place 'tis, but mind 'ow you go, especially you, young Bungalo."

185

Nimbalo seemed a bit distracted as he answered. "Aye, sir, we'll take care . . . Tagg, can you 'ear a bumpin' sound?"

The otter listened carefully, turning downstream. "Sounds as if it's coming from down that way. What d'you think?"

Ruskem turned in the opposite direction. "I think 'tis a-comin' from upstream, but yore ears are younger an' better than mine, Trigg."

They chose to search downstream, around a bend. A gaunt pine tree trunk was floating there, its thick end bumping the bank, trapped in the shallows as the stream rushed swiftly by.

Tagg tested it with his footpaw, leaning down hard.

"Good fortune for us, mate, a ready made boat. This'll save our footpaws for a day or so. We can make it to the foothills on this."

Ruskem pointed up the mountain's north face. "Stream starts up there, in the north foot'ills. When there's been a storm it swells, an' one part branches off to loop down here before circlin' 'round t'the mountain again. Dries up after a score o' days. Yore right, though, Cragg; if ye can free that trunk while the flood's this high it'll take ye close t'the west face in no time."

Tagg trimmed spare branches from the pine and held the trunk steady, whilst Nimbalo boarded with their provisions. Wading waist deep, the otter pushed the makeshift craft out into the current and leaped aboard. Ruskem waved his stick as they were swept speedily away.

"Fare ye well, Frogg an' Numble. May yore stummicks be full an' yore path smooth!"

They shouted back as the log raced downstream.

"Goodbye, Ruskem. Take good care o' yourself!"

"Aye, an' thankee for yore 'ospitality, mate!"

The ancient shrew watched until they were out of sight, waving his stick and murmuring to himself, "Wish I was a-goin' with ye. Heehee, there's two young rips bound off adventurin'. Ah no, I'm 'appy where I am. Did enough rovin' in me younger days. Oh well, time fer me nap."

Ruskem went into his den without bothering to look beyond the upstream bend, where he thought the noise had come from. Had he taken a glimpse there he would have seen the bloated carcass of Grobait, washed up and stuck to the bankside as the sun dried the mud, baking it hard as rock.

16

Broggle had been on breakfast duties in the kitchen. Filorn watched him hastily stacking dishes and wiping tables. The kindly ottermum relieved him of his tasks.

"I'll finish off here. You're anxious to be with your friends in Cregga Badgermum's room, aren't you? Go on, off with you!"

Wiping his paws on his apron, Broggle backed off, bowing politely. "Thankee, marm, very kind of you, marm, you're a real mal, parm, er, I mean a real pal, marm!" He turned and dashed away upstairs.

Boorab, who was last at table, rose and began collecting dishes. "Allow me to assist you in these menial chores, O fair one."

Filorn smiled at him and curtsied deeply. "My thanks t'you, kind sir. Pray, what's the reason for this sudden rush of helpfulness?"

The hare winked broadly as he loaded a tray with bowls. "Just my sense o' duty, marm, an' of course there's always lots o' nice leftovers from brekkers, wot!"

Filorn picked up a tray of beakers and followed him out to the kitchens. "Oh, I'm sure we can find you somethin' to tickle your palate, sir. I'll put the kettle on and we'll have a nice cup of rosehip tea together."

Bells tinkled on Boorab's ears and cap as he shook his head in admiration of Filorn's understanding nature. "You, marm, are an opal among otters, if you'll allow a chap t'speak poetically. A diamond midst the dreary dross of daily duties, wot!"

Fwirl placed her paw on the windowsill, judging it as accurately as she could. "There, that's about dead center, I'd say."

Mhera approved her decision. "Right, put the nail right on that spot, please, Broggle."

With a stone-headed hammer, Broggle drove a small clout nail into the woodwork, to about half its length. Fwirl explained her plan as she worked. "This is how you make a plumb line. I tie one end of the thin cord to this knife hilt, and now I let it out over the windowsill."

Gundil scrambled up onto the sill. "Ee knoife be's goen' daown an' daown on ee corder, miz."

Fwirl played the cord out slowly. "Tell me when 'tis almost near the ground, Gundil."

The mole watched the knife's steady descent. "Jus' ee likkle bit more, miz . . . Stop! That be furr enuff!"

Fwirl tied the cord around the nail as Cregga called from her chair, "What's going on? Keep me informed, please."

Brother Hoben did the explaining. "Fwirl has made a plumb line. It runs straight and true, right from the center of your window to the ground below."

Cregga levered herself up out of the chair. "Of course! The clue that Song could see through the monocle before the ash tree grew will be somewhere on that line, probably between the cracks or on the wall itself!"

Gundil thought he had found a flaw in the plan. "Oi' bain't a-climberin' oop ee gurt 'igh walls. You'm be needen summ turrible long ladders furr ee job!"

Cregga lifted Gundil down from the windowsill. "Who needs ladders when we've got our Fwirl?"

"But that'n be ee flatted wall, et bain't ee tree," Gundil protested. "Miz Furl be a-fallin' off on she'm skullbones. Hurr!"

Fwirl reassured the doubting mole. "Don't fret, Gundil. I can walk up a wall as easily as you can walk about on the ground, you wait and see."

Gundil scurried to the bed. Burying his head beneath a pillow, he cried out in a muffled voice, "Ho no, luvly mizzy, oi cuddent burr to watch ee. Moi 'ead wudd be assidurably dizzied a-wurryin' abowt ee. Burr, lackeeday!"

Redwallers gathered on the grass below, necks craned upward, while those in the bedchamber leaned over the windowsill to stare downward. All eyes were on the squirrelmaid, searching the wall, spreadeagling herself parallel with the plumb line as she moved back and forth. Broggle was practically bursting with pride and admiration.

"Now that's what I call a champion climber. Skillful, magnificent!"

Fwirl stopped moving, concentrating on one particular block of wallstone. She studied it for a moment, her bushy tail twirling with excitement, then she shot upward like an arrow, straight back through the window and onto Cregga's lap.

"I've found it! Writing carved into the stone, but I can't read or write words down. What should I do?"

Mhera and Brother Hoben came up with a simple scheme right away, and shortly thereafter Fwirl scampered back down and found the sandstone block with the carving on it. She spread a clean white table napkin, its four corners smeared with honey, over the writing. Then, taking a stub of beeswax candle, the squirrelmaid colored in the white linen all over and made a perfect rubbing of the characters beneath the cloth. A cheer went up from the onlookers as she pulled it from the wall and waved it like a banner, crying shrilly, "I did it! I've got it!"

Cregga's room became jammed to the door again. Everybeast listened in breathless silence as Brother Hoben read out the message carved into the wall of the Abbey long seasons ago.

" 'Twas I slew the Scourge in days of old,
Then I was one, but now we are two.
We who are dumb, yet sound so bold,
Day and night to order you.
We are those who announce a feast,
Or victories of the brave-hearted.
We are those whose solemn farewell,
Mark sadly a loved one departed.
On our oak see knowledge unfold,
We never speak 'til we're told?
We never speak 'til we're told?"

In the brief silence that followed, Fwirl shook her head. "What a puzzle. Great seasons, what's it supposed to mean?"

Her comment was greeted by roars of laughter. Broggle bristled. "Don't laugh at her, it's not fair!"

Mhera pounded the small tabletop until she restored silence. "Broggle's right, you shouldn't laugh at Fwirl. She's only just come to our Abbey. How is she supposed to know about Redwall?"

Everybeast began explaining at once, until Cregga roared, "Silence, please! Floburt, would you like to explain it all to Fwirl? I don't want to hear a murmur from anybeast except Floburt, thank you!"

The hogmaid recited what every Redwaller had learned at Abbey school.

"The poem means our two Abbey bells. They're called Matthias and Methuselah. A long time ago Redwall had only one great bell, called the Joseph Bell, after its maker. Our Abbey was captured by an evil rat, Cluny the

191

Scourge, but a mouse named Matthias fought him. Matthias took the great sword of Martin the Warrior and cut the ropes holding the Joseph Bell. It fell on Cluny and killed him, but the bell was split by its fall. Later, the metal was melted down and recast into two smaller bells, Matthias and Methuselah, the pair we have in our bell tower today. If you know this the answer becomes clear. Bells cannot speak, yet they make sounds, ringing out at midnight, midday and eventide. They ring for feasts, triumphs and also for a death. The line that's repeated at the poem's end is a clever play on words. We never speak 'til we're told. Think about it. A bell will make no sound until you toll it, so they never speak 'til they're *tolled!*"

Old Hoarg the Gatekeeper sat down on the bed. "Hah! I didn't see that 'un 'til you explained it, Floburt. Very clever indeed. But wot about the line speakin' of knowledge unfoldin' on our oak? Where do we find our oak?"

Mhera whispered something to her mother. Filorn nodded understandingly, then she made an announcement. "You'll learn the answer right after the entertainment contest!"

Everybeast appeared bemused at this.

"What entertainment contest?"

"Hurr, furst oi yurr'd abowt et."

" 'Tis a new one on me too."

"I didn't know about any entertainment contest, did you?"

Mhera restored order. "It's to be held by the gatehouse very shortly. Give your names to Gatekeeper Hoarg if you wish to enter. Any kind of entertainment will be considered. My mum will present the winner with a large woodland fruit trifle, topped with meadowcream. Line up outside the gatehouse if you'd like to put your name down!"

Seconds later, Broggle gazed around the deserted bedchamber. "Well, Mhera, that certainly cleared the

192

place. They went out of here like ants chasing honey. Still, who wouldn't for one of your mum's woodland trifles with meadowcream? Whose idea was that?"

Mhera giggled like a Dibbun. "It was mine. The entertainment contest, too. We don't need that lot following us around all day. Come on, let's go and take a look in the bell tower. That appears to be the place where this riddle is centered."

Cregga shook her great striped head as she rose from her chair. "You're a crafty otter, Mhera. That was cleverly done. Now, I'm too old for climbing bell tower stairs, there's too many of 'em for my liking. But you could drop me off by the gatehouse. I want to hear about this entertainment contest. Who knows, I might put my name down. I'd dearly love one of your mum's trifles all to myself."

The search party assisted the Badgermum down the stairs, joking.

"What'll you do, Cregga? Sing the song of the ancient badger?"

"Ee cudd resoite summ gurt dramatuck vursus, marm!"

"Haha, or play tunes on Boorab's haredee gurdee!"

Cregga sat on the bottom stair to catch her breath. "Insolent wretches! I'll have you know I was very skilled at entertaining in my younger seasons. Maybe I'll perform a quick acrobatic dance, that should do the trick!"

Mhera and Fwirl were laughing so hard that they could not help Cregga upright again.

Inside the bell tower it was dim and cool, but the spiral stairs seemed to go on forever. Halfway up, Brother Hoben had to sit down and rest awhile. "Phew! Lackaday, now I know why Cregga didn't want to come!"

Fwirl's voice came from high above them. "Put a move on down there, I'm already up here!"

Gundil wiped a paw across his brow, trudging doggedly on. "Hurr, easy furr ee t'say, moi booty, but this

193

choild bain't nuthin' but ee pore molebeast, not fitted furr cloimbin' oop sturrs wot goes 'round an' 'round!"

Together they stood up near the small conical roof, astride a massive wooden beam with stout ropes bound around it. Below them was a dizzying drop, with two tolling ropes hanging the length of it. Mhera pointed out the two bells suspended from the beam below their footpaws.

"The one on your left is the Matthias bell, this one on the right is the Methuselah bell. See their names embossed around the edges? A pretty awesome sight, isn't it?"

Gundil's nosetip had gone dry. He turned his eyes aside, moaning, "Bwhurr, oi bain't no burd, an' oi bain't feelen too gudd noither!"

Mhera and Fwirl assisted him off the beam and sat him lower down on the steps. The mole turned his face to the wall. "Oi woan't be 'arpy 'til oi'm saferly on ee gudd furm grownd."

Broggle inspected the beam on all fours. "This is definitely made from a great oak. Look at this huge scar cut across it. Wonder how that happened?"

Brother Hoben, being the Recorder, instinctively knew. "That's where Matthias severed the bell rope with Martin's sword. Such a forceful blow he struck that he scored the beam deeply."

Broggle picked at it with his small kitchen knife. "Must have hit the hem of his habit, too. Look, there's a piece of cloth wedged in the cut."

Mhera saw what was going on as she returned to the beam with Fwirl. "Don't damage it in any way, Broggle. Try as carefully as you can to get the cloth out all in one piece!"

Broggle shaved the wood delicately away, either side of the cloth. "That's easy. See, it just lifts out!"

"He's a real artist with that little blade," Mhera whispered to Fwirl, loud enough for Broggle to hear. "There's nobeast in Redwall more skilled with a kitchen knife than our Broggle."

Blushing with modest pride, the assistant cook gave the cloth to Mhera. It was only a small square of light green material, simple and homespun, nothing elaborate or special. Mhera sniffed it before laying it flat on the beam.

"Hmm. Still got a faint scent of lilac on it. I wonder who it belonged to? Ah, there's letters inked onto it. Let's see . . . HITTAGALL? What's that supposed to mean? The letters aren't even written straight across horizontally, like ordinary writing. They're written vertically. HITTAGALL all in capitals from top to bottom. Brother Hoben, what d'you make of it?"

Folding the material carefully, Hoben slid it into his belt pouch. "Nothing right now, but let me think on it. What do you say we go down and discuss this over lunch? I think Gundil's illness is catching. I'm beginning to feel a bit woozy up here."

Friar Bobb was sitting with the rest of the audience in front of the west wallsteps, by the gatehouse. When the friends appeared he waved for them to sit down by him, whispering, "Sorry about lunch, I'll fix something later. Come and enjoy yourselves. We've had some marvelous entertainment here."

Egburt and Floburt were tootling flutes and performing a jig, while Grandpa Drogg beat a small drum as he sang for them.

"We never have to comb our spikes,
Because they won't lie flat,
An' that is why you'll never see,
A hedgehog wear a hat.

I've seen some hares wear helmets,
And bees in bonnets too,
While molemaids favor mob caps,
All stitched with bluebells blue.

But hedgehogs don't wear headgear,
An' that's my sad refrain,

195

Poor hedgehogs get as wet as frogs,
When left out in the rain!"

They skipped off to great applause, still tootling their flutes.

The next item was a real novelty. Sister Alkanet and three little ones, Durby the molebabe, a tiny mousemaid named Feegle and the smallest hedgehog who could just about toddle, called Wegg, climbed up on to the wallstep, which served as a stage. In her severe and precise tones, the Sister recited a cautionary poem. Much to the hilarity of the audience, the three infants acted out the lines with serious faces and much paw wagging.

" 'Tis often said by otherbeasts,
And trust my word 'tis so,
There are certain manners,
Which Abbeybabes should know!

All Dibbuns must behave themselves,
From break of dawn 'til night,
Tug their ears, touch their spikes,
In general, be polite.

Bid all their elders time of day,
Don't interrupt . . . My word!
Our rule is Dibbuns may be seen,
But very seldom heard.
One must wash one's paws and face,
Before one ventures out,
And up one's sleeve a kerchief keep,
With which to wipe one's snout.

Never sup soup noisily,
Say please and thanks when able,
Remember to excuse oneself,
Before one leaves the table.

If Dibbuns heed these golden rules,
They grow up good and true,

Early to bed, straight to sleep,
And don't hide when bathtime's due . . . Thank you!"

The little ones bowed, to tumultuous applause, though Foremole Brull was heard to remark to Cregga, "Doan't hoide when barthtime be due? Hurr hurr, lookit likkle Durby thurr, larst toime me an' 'is mum barthed that 'un ee water turned to solid mudd, burr aye!"

Before any other contestant had a chance to present themselves, Boorab leaped up, flourishing his long robes dramatically. "I do this not for any triflin' reward, wot wot, get it, trifle? Ahem, pray attention, goodbeasts all, for as Abbey Poet I have composed a small recitation that I shall recitate. These few lines would bring tears to the blinkin' eye of an underwater fish! Mothers, cover your babes' tender ears! For 'ere goes, ear goes? Hawhaw, that was a good 'un, wot wot?"

"Oh, get on with it, you great long-eared windbag!"

Boorab glared at old Hoarg, who had shouted out the remark. "Fie on you, sah. Even windbags have feelin's!" Then, drooping his ears and waving a limp paw, Boorab soulfully began.

" 'Twas winter one summer an' spring was in bloom,
The turnips were twittering gaily
As I cleaned out my humble room,
Three times I do it, twice daily!
When a mole flew in by my window,
He bid me good night and day too.
His eyes were yellow, his nose was green and his tail
	was pinkyblue.
That mole gave me a very odd stare,
Which I put in me pocket for later,
He then asked me if I was a hare,
Or a rascally impersonator?
I replied to him, in accent grim,
'Good sir, I'm a him not a her,
I'm a him that's a hare not a her that's a him,

And the least is as large as the greater!'
'If you're a hare that's a him,' he quoth,
As he left my room with a leap,
'When I return this leap, you'll be,
Not a hare or a him, but a-sleep!' "

Boorab bowed elegantly, tripped over his robes and leaped up in the same instant, calling out to Filorn, "Who could compete with that pulsatin' performance, marm, wot? Deliver the toothsome old trifle to me room at once, so I won't have to share it with these talentless bounders. Don't applaud too loud, chaps. Only doin' me job, y'know. Modest as ever, that's me!"

The trifle was immense, a real beauty. It was displayed in the gatehouse doorway. Helped by Mhera and Fwirl, Cregga mounted the steps, at Filorn's request, to deliver her judgement. She held forth her paws for silence.

"What a wonderful entertainment. You've made my task very difficult. I was going to award the trifle to Boorab, but you all heard him say that he required no trifling reward. So I've decided to give the prize to all the Dibbuns who took part. It's such a huge trifle that I'm sure it's far too much for any onebeast!"

Laughter and cheers greeted the Badgermum's popular decision. The Abbeybabes dragged the trifle inside the gatehouse and slammed the door.

Mhera turned to Brother Hoben. "Well, Brother, have you had time to think about the piece of cloth and the lettering on it?"

Hoben took out the article in question and stared at it. "I've racked my brains until my head's aching, but I'm afraid it's a complete mystery to me. Sorry, Mhera."

Friar Bobb picked the cloth up. "Is this your latest find? What is it?"

Fwirl put her chin in both paws glumly. "We haven't the faintest idea, sir. D'you think Cregga will know?"

They took it to the Badgermum, who sniffed it and felt

198

it. "Faint scent of lilac, that's about all I can say. What is the lettering on it? Read it to me, please, Broggle."

"HITTAGALL. All in capital letters, marm, written in a downward line. Is that any help?"

Cregga passed the cloth back to Brother Hoben. "I'm afraid it doesn't mean a thing to me."

Looking thoroughly downcast, the good Brother sighed. "Then that's it, we're defeated. 'Twas all for nothing."

Mhera slapped her rudder down hard against the step. "Well, I'm not defeated, I'll solve that riddle somehow. I'm not going to give up hope or let it beat me!"

The friends strolled paw in paw back to the Abbey, their air of gloom not even dissipated by Boorab, who was pounding the gatehouse door, pleading with the Dibbuns inside.

"Have a bally heart, little chaps, open up for a poor starvin' hare, wot! I'd have given you a jolly good share if I'd won the trifle, honest I would, cross me ears an' hope to turn blue. Come on, open up an' be reasonable, little bods. At least let me lick the bowl. If I die of the horrible hungers it'll be your fault, y'know. Festerin' bounders! Trifle thieves, meadowcream marauders! I hope you all get the screamin' tummyache. Cads!" He loped off and caught up with Mhera and her friends. "I say, you lot look pretty sad, wot. Did you want to win the trifle too?"

Mhera smiled weakly. It was one thing having plenty of fighting spirit and stern resolution, but she was as baffled as the rest. Brother Hoben was right; all their questing had amounted to nothing. The entire thing was still a mystery.

17

It was the evening of their second day upon the mountain, and still the hunters had not sighted any sign of their quarry. Vallug Bowbeast sat shivering over a small fire made from odd twigs and dead heather. He stared out at the tracks of his own party, crisscrossing the snowfields that ran up toward the peak. His stomach made a squirling noise. It needed food, but there was none whatsoever to be had. Eefera was the first to show over the high ridge. He trudged down to the glimmering fire, long bluish shadows of eventide creeping down after him. White steamy breath issued from his mouth as he sat down beside Vallug.

" 'Tis difficult to catch yer breath up 'ere. Huh, I see you packed in searchin'. 'Ow long've ye been squattin' 'ere warmin' yer paws?"

Vallug stared into the paltry wisps of flame. "Long enough t'do some thinkin'."

The weasel glanced sideways at the big ferret. "Thinkin', eh? Tell me about it."

The Bowbeast nodded up at the peak. "Ain't no vittles up 'ere, we never brought robes or cloaks. We could freeze or starve t'death, an' nobeast of the Juska clan would ever know wot became of us."

Eefera thrust his paws closer to the fire. "Aye, there's some truth in that. We've been on this stinkin' mountain almost two days now, an' not a track, nary a single pawmark that the otter's been even near the place. Vallug, do ye think that 'e could've put one over on us? I mean laid a false trail along that riverbank, jus' to make it look as if 'e was comin' 'ere?"

Vallug said what his companion was thinking. "An' give us the slip so's 'e could go elsewhere?"

Eefera shrugged. "But where's 'e gone?"

Vallug lowered his voice as if eavesdroppers were about. "That's wot I been thinkin' about. You remember ole Grissoul mutterin' about omens an' prophecies? She was the one who saw the Taggerung at the river ford where it ran across the long path. Sawney told me somethin' about a big place with bells. 'Twas a long time back, but I can recall it. Sawney didn't want t'go near that place, said it was dangerous an' filled with warriors."

Eefera nodded impatiently. "Aye, I remember all right. Redwall, 'e called it. Grissoul spoke about the red place like 'twas magic. Wot d'you think, Vallug?"

The Bowbeast curled his lip scornfully. "There ain't no such thing as magic. I never seen nobeast that one o' my arrows couldn't stop. I think that otter I slew, the liddle one's father, I think that 'e came from the Redwall place. I'll tell yer wot else I'm thinkin'. I'll wager that sometime in 'is seasons with the Juskarath, that Taggerung 'eard of Redwall too. If'n that otter's laid a false trail fer us t'follow, then 'e's bound for Redwall, the place where 'e was born!"

Eefera had been listening so intently that his paw strayed into the flame. He drew it back sharply and rubbed snow on it.

"Right, Vallug. Yore right! So, wot's the plan?"

Vallug picked up his bow and shouldered it. "We go after 'im. I don't mean those other fools an' Gruven. Leave 'em 'ere on the mountain. Like I said, they'll freeze or starve t'death up 'ere an' nobeast will ever know, 'cept us."

Eefera smiled wickedly. "An' we won't tell, will we. They was all killed, Gruven too. By pikes, serpents, drownded, all of em. Sad, ain't it, mate?"

It was Vallug's turn to smile. He nudged Eefera. "Aye, 'twas an 'ard job, tryin' to save 'em. We was lucky to get back alive, me'n'you, but we slayed the otter between us, eh!"

Vallug spat on his paw and offered it to Eefera. "No sense in 'angin' 'round 'ere, mate. Let's git goin' afore those other block'eads come back. I couldn't stand another night of Gruven's company, braggin' one moment, whinin' the next . . ."

Eefera spat on his paw and gripped Vallug's to seal their pact. "Yah, the cold an' 'unger'll take care of 'em. Come on, back t'the sunny woodlands an' a chance o' some decent vittles!"

Vallug stood to one side deferentially. "Good idea, mate. After you."

Eefera did a mock bow, but stayed where he was. "Nay, friend, you go first."

They stared hard at one another, eye to eye, then both broke out into false hearty laughter and strode off together. Neither of the two vermin wanted to expose his back to the other.

The stream did as many turns as a switchback, rambling and meandering hither and yon. Tagg and Nimbalo were not in any hurry, each enjoying the other's company. Eventide of the second day found them camped on a grassy spur where the waterway forked, one branch disappearing into the flatlands and the other rounding a fairly swift-flowing bend that took the water back into the base of the mountain.

Tagg tested the flow with his footpaw. "Shall we go this way tomorrow? It looks as if the current flows into some underground caves. Would you like to try it, mate?"

The harvest mouse threw more turf on the fire. " 'Twill be a bit of a bumpy ole ride on our log. Aye, let's try it. In the mornin', though; we'll rest tonight. Y'know, these fruit loaves wot Ruskem gave us, they're pretty good. I like 'em!"

The otter cut a chunk from one with his blade. "Ruskem's dandelion an' burdock cordial's very tasty too. Try some."

Nimbalo took hold of his friend's paw as he passed the flask. "Where'd ye get that mark on yore paw from? It's like the shape of a speedwell flower. Is it a tattoo?"

The otter glanced at the mark, then ran a paw over his heavily marked face. "No, I think 'tis some sort of birthmark. These on my face are tattoos, put there long before I can remember. They're clan marks, to show I belong to a certain tribe."

He allowed Nimbalo to touch the tattoos. The mouse snorted. "Bit silly, ain't it? If'n ye ever want to leave the tribe, then yore stuck wid yore face all marked with a big black stripe an' red dots an' the blue lightnin' flash on yer left cheek."

Tagg's paw strayed to feel the flash. "Juska law says that the only time you leave the tribe is when you're dead. I'm marked for life now, but at least I can get rid of these!"

Tagg pulled off his woven wristbands, unsnipped the big gold earring from his ear, and flung them into the stream. Nimbalo smiled sympathetically at his big friend. "You ain't 'ad much fun runnin' 'round with that tribe, 'ave yer? Well, never mind, Tagg me ole tater, you got a new life now, an' you got Nimbalo the Slayer as a pal, so come on, cheer up!"

Tagg lay back, gazing up at the stars. "I'm tired, pal. Play something for me, a peaceful tune."

Nimbalo tootled his reed flute and played awhile, then, putting it aside, he quietly sang a traditional harvest mouse ditty.

"When the corn is so heavy it bends on the stalk,
See the berries are purple with bloom,
And the wild oats do rustle as if they could talk,
There I watch for the gold harvest moon.

Then if you will help me friend,
Stay here oh do not roam,
And we'll sit by the fire,
In my harvest mouse home.

There'll be lots of good food when the work is all done,
And a barrel of old barley beer,
Mellow cheese and fresh bread, for everyone,
While the babes sleep in peace without fear.

We'll gather the fruit,
And the sweet honeycomb,
And some wood for the fire,
Of my harvest mouse home."

Nimbalo put aside his flute and lay down with a long sigh. "Aaaah. I forget the rest. Pretty, ain't it, Tagg? Nothin' like the real thing, though. My life ain't been no bed o' roses, oh no. Let me tell yer about wot I went through, mate . . ." He glanced over and saw his otterfriend was already fast asleep. "Oh well, maybe some other time."

The fire burned low as four little shadowy figures watched the camp. Three of them wore new belts about their tiny waists, Tagg's two wristbands and his golden earring, which had landed on the wristbands as they floated off downstream. The one who was minus a new belt whispered to his three companions, "Yik yik, 'arvest mousey gotta nice belt. Jus' fitta me!"

The biggest of the four clipped him soundly over the ear. "Shushyerrupp! Yew wakey da biggin an' we get all eated up!" He patted his new gold earring belt thoughtfully before delivering the noisy one a clip across his other ear. "Go gerrem ole Bodjev, tellim bring alla Cavemob. Go go!"

He sloshed resentfully off along the streamshallows, calling back in a loud whisper, "Doncha pinch d'mousey belt while I 'way!"

The larger one sent him on his way with a kick in the tail. "Go on, go on, shout louder, nip'ead. Wake alla mounting up!"

One of the two wearing a wristband belt held a paw to his mouth. "Shushyer, Alfik, dey wakey up an' us don't gerra no likkle snakeyfishes, fryken 'em alla way!"

Within a short while, Bodjev, the tiny fat Chieftain of his pigmy shrew tribe, returned with a large bunch of his warriors, each bearing a pine club, tipped with flint shards, over his shoulder. He threw himself down alongside Alfik, his son, hissing with shock as he caught sight of Tagg.

"Wow wow! Whereja find dat monister? Lookarra size of 'im!"

Alfik wrinkled his long nose in a show of careless bravery. "Ho, I jus' finded d'beast, sleepyin' 'ere. Warra us do now, Daddy?"

Bodjev glared at his son and clipped him a good one on the ear. "You norra Squidjee nomore. Worr I tellya? Chief's name Bodjev, only Daddy when you was likkle. Bodjev now, 'member dat!"

One of the Cavemob tribe called out a warning as Tagg groaned and rolled over in his sleep. "Y'be shushed or d'big fella come awakey!"

Bodjev could not identify the voice, so he satisfied himself by dispensing clipped ears to any shrew within reach. "Who you tella to shushed? Talk t'me like dat! All shushed now, wait for da snakeyfishes to come. Den after dat we catcher d'mousey anna bigga monister!"

Tagg glimpsed the mouse warrior with the beautiful sword, wandering through the corridors of his mind. He pursued him, but, unable to run, he floated helplessly through a warm pink mist, calling out the mouse's name. "Deyna! Deyna!"

The warrior mouse halted and turned, shaking his head and smiling. Touching a paw to his armored breastplate, he spoke one word. "Martin!" Then he disappeared, leaving the sleeping otter mystified. If he was Martin, then who was Deyna?

Further dreams were shattered. Both Tagg and Nimbalo leaped up amid a sea of slithering silver. They slipped and fell flat as the slim shining shapes slid over them. Wild squeaks rent the dawnlight. Pigmy shrews were everywhere, striking wildly at the silvery threadlike mass with small clubs and shouting to one another.

"Dink a dink! Gerra snakeyfishes!"

"Yik yik, chukkem inna water!"

"Dink a dinky dink dink! Plenny snakeyfishes, brudders!"

Tagg grabbed Nimbalo. Kicking his way through the wriggling mass, he made it to the top of a rocky mound and stared in wonder at the scene around him. Nimbalo knew what the glimmering threads were. He had seen them once before on the flatlands.

"Elvers, mate! Those are little tiny eels. They travel on the dewy grass, shoals an' shoals of 'em. They can go fer many a league. But where'd all the baby shrews come from?"

Tagg watched the shrews as they raced about killing the elvers, dispatching each one with a quick blow to the head from their flint-tipped clubs. Dead elvers were tossed into the water and washed away downstream into the mountain caves. As they struck out with their clubs, the shrews squeaked triumphantly.

"Dink! Gorra nudder one!"

"Dink a dink! I gorra two snakeyfishes!"

Expertly they flicked the dead elvers into the water with their clubtips. Tagg shook his head. "They aren't babies.

Some of them have grey whiskers. Those are fully grown shrews. I've never seen anything like it!"

Nimbalo was taller than the tallest shrew by more than a head. He stood on tip-paw and puffed out his chest scornfully. "Huh, I knew that, mate. Crowd o' liddle nuisances if y'ask me, wakin' us up jus' so they can stock up their larders with elvers!"

The shrews did not let up their mass kill until a good while later, by which time most of the elvers had passed. They slid away like mobile tinsel, the morning sun reflecting off their packed masses as they glided into the distance. Their countless numbers were scarcely affected by the slaughter.

Alfik and Bodjev approached the mound, clubs at the ready. The Chieftain's son wiggled his nose ferociously at Tagg. "We be's Cavemobs, my daddy a Chief. Who be's you?"

Tagg was about to reply when Bodjev clipped Alfik's ear. "Wot I tellya, nit'ead? My name be's Bodjev!" He shook his head almost apologetically at Tagg. "Norra brains, norra manners. Yik yik, younger shrews dese seasons alla same. No respecks!"

Nimbalo bristled at the father's treatment of his son. "No need t'be whackin' 'is lug like that, mate!"

This gave Tagg an idea. Very gently he kicked Nimbalo's bottom and rolled his eyes expressively at the pigmy shrew Chieftain. "I know exactly what you mean, sir. They're always speaking when they're not spoken to. Put a latch on your lip, young Nimbalo!"

Bodjev held his fat stomach as he chuckled. "Yikyikyikyik! Go make playplay, yew two's. I be's Bodjev. Wot be's your name?"

Tagg held out his paw courteously. "Pleased to meet you, Bodjev, sir. My name's Tagg."

Bodjev grinned as he looked the otter up and down. "Tagg? Yikyik, be's a likkle name for a big fella. So, Tagg, you an' your son be likin' snakeyfish pie?"

Tagg kept a polite smile on his face as he shook the shrew's paw. "Never tasted it, sir, but I'm sure 'tis delicious!"

Bodjev put his head on one side as he tried to pronounce delicious. "Lishus! Lishus! Yikyik, good, eh? You come a me, bring de likkle son, we alla 'ave snakeyfish pie. Plenny good!"

Tagg waded through the shallows, with Nimbalo on his shoulders. The harvest mouse was boiling with ill-concealed temper at the treatment he had been shown. "Yore son? That flap-'eaded wiggle-snouted pudden-bellied beast thinks I'm yore son? An' another thing. Wot did you think y'were doin', kickin' me tail like that? Who gave you the right—"

Tagg's paw stifled any further remarks. "Safety first, mate. I was only protecting us by making friends with the Chief. Look, I know they're only tiny shrews, but there must be thousands of them, all carrying stone-tipped clubs. We might get a lot of them in a fight, but they'd bring us down in the end, just by their weight of numbers!"

Nimbalo yanked Tagg's paw from his mouth, unappeased. "So ye let 'im whack his son an' yer kicked me tail, just t'make friends. That's very nice, izzenit? We could've battled our way through, betcha an acorn to an oak we could. I remember one time when I fought me way outta a nestful of crows. Hah, slew a good few of them I did, an' I got away safe!"

The otter turned his face to Nimbalo, a no-nonsense look in his eyes. "Where's the point in fighting and slaying if you can make a friend out of anybeast instead of a foe? From now on, while we're the guests of these creatures, we might have to do a few things we don't like. But that's the way it is, mate, and I'll hear no more argument about it. Now straighten your face and smile. You look like a beetle with a bruised brow!"

The harvest mouse kept a grin pasted on his face as he

replied, "An' you look like a blackbird with a boiled behind!"

Tagg smiled sweetly, answering from between clenched teeth, "And you look like duck with a webful of custard!"

"Well, you look like a stoat with a stink up 'is nose!"

"In that case you look like a bumblebee with a boil!"

"Hoho, well, you look like a . . . a . . . a hedgehog with a head h'ache!"

"A head h'ache?"

The two friends burst out laughing.

They skirted a small pool, with a little stream from up in the mountains spilling into it, the cascade hiding the entrance to the pigmy shrews' cave. Dodging through the miniature waterfall, Tagg and Nimbalo emerged into what appeared to be a cathedral-like cavern. It was lit by scores of firefly lanterns and torches and populated by literally thousands of pigmy shrews. The stream continued into the cavern, where it ran into a central lake. Halfway down the stream a net had been stretched under and above the water. Shrews dipped sievelike paddles in and pulled out the dead elvers. These were taken away on a small cart to the kitchen, which was merely lots of cooking fires under wide rock ledges. The cooks there were busy doing all manner of things with the young eels: stewing, baking, roasting and frying. All activity ceased at the sight of Tagg. Every pigmy shrew stood gaping wordlessly at the giant who had entered their domain. Bodjev waddled over to the cooking fires and began boxing ears left, right and center.

"Worra you stan' there for? Thissa my frien' Tagg anna likkle son. You be cookin' lotsa snakeyfish pies for us, quicknow!"

A fat little pigmy shrew pulled a batch of pies out of the crude rock oven with a large wooden paddle. No sooner had she placed them on a cooling shelf than she swung the paddle and caught Bodjev a sharp whack on his behind, shouting fiercely, "Doo a this, doo a that! Kachah! Thissa my kitchen, Daddy Bodjev. You keep 'way, likkle fat lump!"

Bodjev did a tip-pawed dance, rubbing his smarting rear. A combined snigger arose from the cooking staff. The Chieftain backed off, replying savagely, but not too loudly, "One day I bake you inna pie, Chichwife!" He turned to Tagg and Nimbalo with a rueful smile. "Yikyik, my Chichwife, always makin' joke. She love me muchmuch!"

An alcove in the cavern was sumptuously furnished, by pigmy shrew standards, for Bodjev's family and high-ranking friends. He took Tagg and Nimbalo there to dine, away from the main population of Cavemob shrews. The otter could see them from where he sat on a thick mat of springy fernmoss. Their table manners were little better than atrocious. Amid the echoing din of insult and argument, they stole food from their neighbors and engaged in pie fights of amazing savagery.

Bodjev clapped his paws officiously. Four very pretty shrewmaids appeared with lunch, and he nodded at them. "Move youselfs, daughter. Serve, serve!"

His four daughters were quite taken with Nimbalo. Ignoring their father, they served the harvest mouse, fussing about him.

"Thissa rosehip an' almond flower tea, special cold. Yikyikyik!"

"Pies good? Our Chichmum a fine fine cooker, eh? Yikyik!"

Bodjev banged his fork against his empty bowl. "Stoppa gigglin', missies. Poor Daddy be's starvin'!"

Nimbalo was glad when the four shrewmaids left him alone to serve Bodjev and Tagg. He straightened his ruffled headfur and applied himself to the food. The rosehip and almond flower tea was refreshingly cold, obviously made with snow from the mountaintop.

If anybeast had told Tagg that he would enjoy

snakeyfish pies before he had tasted the dubiously named dish, he would have declared them mistaken. But the pies were absolutely delicious, round and flat with a soft white pastry crust and a filling that did not resemble anything that looked, smelled or tasted like an elver. It had a texture of oatmeal and a flavor of salt, parsley and sage. Much to the awe of his host, Tagg ate six. Bodjev's wife Chich beamed pleasurably when she was told, and came straight over to the alcove.

"Daddy Bodjev, these goodbeasts you bring here. Big fella's mighty eater. Yik yik, goldie one very hamsing. Chich like him!"

Nimbalo did not know where to put his face. Evidently his light golden brown fur appeared quite attractive to pigmy shrew females. He applied himself to some leftover piecrust. "Thankee, marm. Yore very, er, hamsing y'self!"

Chich threw her apron up over her face and giggled. "Yikyikyikyik! Lissen, big fella, when you go 'way from here, take fatty likkle Bodjev alonga wid you an' leave hamsing goldie here wid Chich. I cook lotsa snakeyfish pies for that 'un!"

Tagg smiled mischievously. "I'll certainly think about it, marm. What d'you say, handsome goldie?"

Nimbalo scowled as Tagg chucked him under the chin playfully. "Don't even think about it, ye treacherous riverdog!"

The incident was forgotten as a pigmy shrew began battering a huge bronze gong, which reverberated through every corner of the massive cavern. All the Cavemob shrews set up a pitiful wail, then fell silent. Tagg looked to Bodjev. "What's that all about, friend?"

"Izza ole Cavemob law," the Chieftain explained in a subdued voice. "Us gotta make goodsure snakeyfish come back nex' time."

Nimbalo poured himself more iced tea. "Hmm. 'Ow d'yer manage t'do that, mate?"

Bodjev pointed upward at the high cavern ceiling. It

was smooth limestone rock, with one long stalactite hanging down. All the pigmy shrews had drawn back to the cave walls, leaving the area beneath the stalactite, not far from the deep lake's edge, completely clear. In the total silence a drop of water fell from the tip, falling through the air for several seconds.

Plock!

The sound echoed about as Bodjev went on to enlighten the visitors. "Waterdrop will fall on chosen Cavemob shrew."

The gong was struck again, and an old shrew in long robes cried out, "Make snakeyfish line. Dance, now!"

All the shrews formed an immense line, long enough to trail around the cavern interior three times. Bodjev rose and nodded to his family. "Us go now, join line. Fortune keep us 'eads dry!"

"Yo Karr, fortune keep us 'eads dry!" Chich, Alfik and his four daughters repeated solemnly.

Nimbalo took hold of the shrewmum's paw. "What'n the name o' fur'n'feathers is goin' on 'ere, Chich?"

She dabbed her apron at her eyes and sniffed. "Everytime snakeyfishes come, Cavemob must choose one to meet Yo Karr, or snakeyfishes come no more. Drop of water fall on shrew head as we dance. That shrew meets Yo Karr."

Bodjev's family went and joined the line, splitting up and each finding a separate place among the others. The shrews began chanting. "Yo Karr, Yo Karr, Yo Karr!" The line moved off, slowly shuffling, swaying from side to side. As they passed under the stalactite, each shrew shut its eyes tight, paws sliding along through the wet area.

Tagg shrugged. "Probably some silly old ritual that goes back as far as anybeast can remember. Look, the ones who've passed under it are going off to stand by the walls again."

Nimbalo watched with growing interest. "Aye, 'cos the

drop didn't fall on 'em. I wonder wot Yo Karr is? Must be some kind of award, eh?"

Tagg saw the relief on the faces of those who had passed under the stalactite and come away dry. He noticed the looks of fear on those whose turn was yet to come. "Huh. It doesn't appear to be an award anybeast wants to gain."

Plock!

A mighty cry arose from the pigmy shrews as the line broke. "Yo Kaaaaarrrrr!"

One of Bodjev's pretty daughters stood rooted to the spot, the fat drop of water running down her brow to mingle with her tears. An uneasy feeling had been building up in Tagg's chest. He stood up.

"Come on, mate. Let's go out there and see what's going to happen!"

Huddled together, the shrewmaid's family hugged one another and wept. Tagg pulled Bodjev away from them. "Listen, friend, I don't like this. Now tell me once and for all, what's going on? Why are you all blubbering like this, eh?"

Tears ran openly down the fat little Chieftain's face. He pointed to the deep lake near the cavern's center. "It is law. You look, you see."

Picking pawfuls of dead elvers from a bowl, the old robed shrew who had beaten the gong hurled them into the lake. From the bluegreen translucent depths something came rushing up and broke the surface. Tagg felt himself go stiff with fright. A gigantic eel glided about, its needlelike teeth snapping the elvers into its ugly mouth. It swirled back under, lying just beneath the surface, its thick olive-hued back and dirty amber underside clearly visible as it waited on more food.

The fur on Nimbalo's neck was bristling with horror and anger as he yelled at the pigmy shrew Chieftain. "Yore not goin' t'let'em feed yer daughter to that thing, are ye?"

213

Bodjev hung his head and turned away. "It is law of Cavemob shrews, so snakeyfish will return. Dinat must go to meet Yo Karr."

The harvest mouse dashed to the shrewmaid's side and put a protective paw about her shoulders, roaring defiantly, "Not while Nimbalo the Slayer's 'round she ain't. I'll drop the first one who puts a paw on 'er!"

The pigmy shrews rushed him. Tagg bounded into the fray to help his friend. Shrews piled in on the pair until they were completely swamped and subdued. Tagg lay trying to breathe under the masses of small furry bodies, unable to move as much as a single paw. Nimbalo was in the same position. The old robed shrew pointed to the shrewmaid Dinat, then to the lake where the monster eel waited, its long backfin stirring the water. Dinat looked as if she was in a trance as the shrew called out, "Yo Karr waits. Go to Yo Karr. You be chosen!"

Dinat walked slowly forward onto the rock ledge that formed the brief shallows at the side of the deep lake. The eel turned and swam slowly forward, stalking the terror-stricken shrewmaid.

Tagg could feel himself blacking out as the crowded shrewbodies pressed down on him. The mouse warrior was suddenly in front of his mind's eye.

"Deyna!" The warrior spoke the one word, then bared his teeth savagely, opening his mouth wide and snapping his teeth together.

"Yeek! Yahee! Aaaarr!"

Pigmy shrews were sent hurtling off the pile, some of them with blood showing on backs and paws. Furious energy coursed through the big otter's muscles and sinews. Between bites he sucked in mighty gulps of life-giving air. His limbs and rudder together lashed out like steel pistons. Nimbalo felt the shrews being kicked from him and began lashing out, yelling, "Go at 'em, mate! Give 'em the ole one-two!"

Tagg was standing upright, like a colossus, shaking off

214

the Cavemob. He roared at the sight of the shrewmaid, locked in the eel's swirling coils as she was dragged screaming from the ledge. Then he broke free and tore toward the lake, hurtling straight into the air and diving down. He cut the water like a knife, locking all four paws around the huge eel's head and setting his teeth into the back of its heavy neck. Nimbalo booted aside a few venturesome shrews and ran to the stream. Tearing the elver net loose, he grabbed the nearest shrew, who happened to be Alfik, and shouted in his face, "Don't jus' stan' there! Lend a paw 'ere or I'll slay ye!" Between them they began dragging the net toward the lake. Bodjev joined them, seizing the heavy net and dragging with them.

Now the eel had its coils around Tagg. It had released Dinat and was concentrating upon its attacker. Arching its head back, it tried biting at the otter, but Tagg clung on like a grim nemesis, clenching his viselike jaws as he bit deeper into the monstrous neck, seeking bone. Down, down they sank, locked together. Tagg felt the air being squeezed from his lungs as the eel tried to kill him by crushing tighter and tighter. The lake was seemingly bottomless and icy cold. Otter and eel sank farther into a world of aquamarine ribboned with scarlet. Bubbles burst in a stream from Tagg's mouth, and he began to feel certain that he would die in the watery depths with an eel embracing him. Then something brushed against his face. It was the tip of the net.

Freeing his teeth from the eel, he locked them around one of the stone weights woven into the net's hem. Squirming around, the eel bit his shoulder and clung on. Despite the pain, Tagg bent his elbow around and got the monster in a headlock. They began rising swiftly toward the surface, the otter with his neck and jaw muscles rigid as he gripped the net with all the strength he could muster. Looking downward from the corner of his left eye, he could see the eel's gold-and-black-rimmed eye staring

215

back at him, his elbow lock preventing its teeth from reaching his outstretched throat.

Then everything was roaring sound, and Tagg's head broke the surface. He saw Nimbalo and a host of yelling shrews, standing on the shallow ledge, heaving on the net.

"Pull! Pull, ye string-snouted swabs, gerrim up 'ere on the ledge!"

Tagg sensed himself and the thrashing eel being hauled sideways, felt his rudder scrape the ledge and then he was in the shallows. Nimbalo hurled himself upon the eel, kicking, biting and punching. "Ye great slimy son of a greasy rope, let's see 'ow many pies we can make outta you!"

Wrenching its teeth from the otter, the eel went for Nimbalo. Tagg felt the constricting coils slacken slightly. Like lightning he whipped out his blade and stabbed deep into the creature's neck where his teeth had been sunk earlier. Suddenly the monster resembled, in truth, the piece of greasy rope Nimbalo had called it. All power left its body, and the bulky coils fell uselessly away from Tagg. It lay hissing softly, its once bright eyes clouding over.

Bodjev waded in and patted it. "Yikyikyik! Make an' 'undred pies outta Yo Karr; mebbe two!"

Chichwife splashed in and cuffed his ear smartly. "Phwah! I not gonna cook datbeast inter pies. Back inna lake wirrim. Back inna lake, brudders!"

As best they could, Nimbalo, Bodjev and Alfik dragged Tagg from the water onto the cavern floor. He lay there exhausted and watched the shrews roll the eel off the ledge. It sunk limply into the depths until it was lost to sight. The shrewmaid Dinat and her three sisters set about dressing Tagg's shoulder, and then she clasped the otter's paw gratefully.

"Thankee much much, big fella, you save this Dinat's life!"

Nimbalo took the knife from Tagg and cleaned it. "Sorry I took so long gettin' the net to ye, matey. I 'ad t'pull Dinat out wid it first, an' by then you'd gone so far down we could 'ardly see yer. I thought you was a goner that time, on me oath I did."

Tagg grinned. "Well, I'm back now, handsome golden one."

Taking his blade back, he beckoned to Bodjev. "Yo Karr's dead now. Listen, friend, you're the Chieftain here. You should never have let that happen to your own daughter."

Bodjev looked sheepish. He shrugged awkwardly. "Law. It was ole Cavemob law, always be'd thataway."

Tagg jabbed his fat stomach with the knife handle. "Don't let it ever happen again. Sacrificing creatures' lives! What an awful idea. You're the Chief, make some new laws. The elvers'll still come back, you'll see."

Bodjev stuck out his stomach and shouted to the pigmy shrews, "Lissen, alla Cavemobs. I Chief make lotsa new law. Nomore Yo Karr, nomore die, snakeyfish still come back, you see."

Alfik stepped up beside his father amid the cheering. "Nomore Cavemobs die! Good ole Daddy!"

Bodjev cuffed his ear. "Worra I tell you, nit'ead?"

Tagg caught Bodjev's paw as he raised it again. "And no more ear-smacking, or name-calling. Why not be kinder to one another? It'll make life a lot nicer."

Alfik saw his father's footpaw starting to rise. "An' nomore tailkick!" he shouted.

Bodjev stared at Tagg in disbelief. "Nomore tailkick?"

The otter shook his head. "No more tail kicks, ear smacks or name calls. The Cavemob will be polite and live happily together. This is the law now. All who wish it this way, raise your paws and shout aye."

The response was thunderous. Paws waved wildly and roars of "Aye" resounded throughout the cavern. Tagg noticed that Bodjev was looking rather crestfallen, so he waited for the noise to die away and made another announcement.

"This is the new law of Bodjev, mighty Chief of the Cavemob, whose name will be forever remembered among your tribe."

Cheering themselves hoarse, the pigmy shrews waved their clubs and danced around the big otter as he carried Bodjev shoulder high around the cavern.

"Your biggun be wisefriend," Alfik whispered to Nimbalo. "Lookit Daddy, he smile an' smile lots!"

The harvest mouse feigned a yawn and sat himself down. "So 'e should be, mate. I taught 'im everythin' 'e knows!"

18

For the first time since the start of an ill-fated trip, Gruven felt himself really in command. He sat by the replenished fire, which Vallug had made, watching Dagrab, Ribrow and Rawback. Dawn was well up and the three vermin were lying so close to the fire that he could smell singeing fur. Gruven snapped twigs, flicking them at the sleepers until they stirred and sat up rubbing their eyes. Rawback looked around. "So, Vallug an' Eefera never came back durin' the night, Chief?"

Gruven poked at the fire with his sword. "Huh! Did you expect 'em to? Those two are long gone, an' good riddance too, I say. Who needs 'em?"

He listened as the three vermin speculated.

"Mebbe they picked up the otter's tracks an' went after 'im theirselves, eh?"

"Suppose they got lost an' they're layin' out there in the snow, frozen stiff?"

"Don't talk daft. One of 'em lit this fire, an' it was still burnin' when we found it last night. I think somethin' 'appened to 'em!"

"Like wot?"

"I dunno, maybe they was attacked."

"Attacked by who? Vallug an' Eefera are both good fighters, they could take care of themselves."

"Suppose it was somebeast who was better'n 'em. You don't know wot sort o' creatures are livin' on this mountain."

Gruven jumped upright and scattered the fire with his sword. The trio leapt back, brushing sparks from themselves as he snarled, "Yore like a bunch of ole gossipers, sittin' there arguin'. I'll tell ye wot I think, then we'll go an' do somethin' about it instead of sittin' freezin' our tails off!"

By the respectful silence that followed, Gruven knew he was boss.

"If Vallug an' Eefera was killed by otherbeasts up 'ere, we ain't stoppin' 'round t'find out. I always said climbin' this mountain was a waste o' time. That otter was never up 'ere. So this is wot we're gonna do. We'll get off the mountain an' track Vallug an' Eefera, an' I bet they'll lead us to the otter. Then all three of 'em are goin' to die, the otter 'cos that's who we came to kill, Vallug an' Eefera 'cos they're traitors, desertin' their own clanbeasts, leavin' us to perish from cold an' starvation. Come on, let's move!"

The two stoats, Rawback and Ribrow, walked behind Gruven and Dagrab, conversing in whispers.

"D'you think Gruven knows where 'e's leadin' us?"

"No, mate, but anywhere's better'n 'ere."

"Right y'are. Keep yore eyes peeled for vittles. I'm famished."

The rat Dagrab slithered alongside Gruven, warm sunlight on the hard-packed snow making the downhill descent quite difficult. She kept her eyes down, watching the ground underpaw.

"Look, Chief, prints in the snow!"

Gruven inspected the faint impressions left in the previous night's snowfall. "Hah, I was right! Vallug an' Eefera passed this way. Good work, Dagrab. We're on their trail right enough. Scout on ahead a bit, see wot y'can find!"

"Huh, 'e was right?" Ribrow scoffed, covering his mouth with a paw. "Wot 'e means is 'e was lucky Dagrab wuz keepin' 'er eyes about 'er."

Once they were clear of the snow, the going became much easier. By midafternoon Gruven's party were on the lower slopes among huge boulders, scrub vegetation and shale. Gruven and the two stoats rested by a trickling stream, gnawing on some milk vetch leaves. Gruven was feeling cheerful.

"See, warm weather, clean water an' a bit o' food. Good, eh?" Ribrow and Rawback continued eating in silence as Gruven continued, "Dagrab lost the tracks a bit back there, but she'll pick 'em up again. Don't worry, I won't steer us wrong."

Ribrow spat out a hard bit of stalk, nodding downhill. "Oh, we ain't worried, Chief, but Dagrab doesn't look too 'appy. 'Ere she comes now, see."

Scrabbling breathlessly uphill, Dagrab returned to make her report. "Looks like all kinds o' stuff growin' down there on some ledges, Chief. Proper vittles, mushrooms, wild onions, some turnips an' stuff like that. Only thing is there's a load of liddle beasts, look like shrews. Good job they never saw me. There's a lot of 'em an' they look well armed, clubs, knives, spears . . ."

Gruven tossed away a pawful of vetch leaves. "Liddle beasts like shrews, eh, with plenty o' vittles too? Let's go an' take a look."

From their vantage point on a rocky boulder-strewn spur, the four vermin lay looking down. Far below were broad terraces above the foothills covered in deposits of rich alluvial soil. The pigmy shrews were farming, planting seedlings and gathering in their vegetable crops. Between where they were working and the high spur where the vermin lay was a steep wasteland of thistle, fern, scree, boulders and shale.

Gruven's smile was one of pure wickedness. "This'll

prob'ly make a bit o' mess, but we're not interested in next season's crops, just enough fer a few good meals."

Putting his shoulder to a rounded boulder, he pushed it over the edge, calling to the others, "Come on, send some rocks down that slope!"

The boulders hit the steep incline, bouncing and setting other boulders and shalebanks on the move wherever they struck, smashing fern beds, crushing thistles and sending huge masses of scree into a thundering avalanche. Pigmy shrews scattered hither and thither, squealing in panic as the mountain thundered down on them, crushing anybeast not swift enough to avoid the destruction.

Gruven laughed until tears rolled down his cheeks. The plan was working. "Hahahaha! It's like droppin' pebbles an' sand on ants, hahahaha! Lookit 'em, they don't know which way t'run fer the best, hahaha!"

The three other vermin caught his mood and began tipping more boulders over the edge onto the creatures below.

"Whoohoo! Looka that 'un runnin'. Hoho, 'e's tripped an' fell!"

"Watch me get those two 'idin' be'ind that rowan tree!"

"Heehee, that liddle one just vanished under a load o' shale!"

They watched until the massive landslide subsided. Gruven leaned on his sword and smirked at his companions. "That'll teach 'em, fillin' their bellies while there's 'ungry Juska warriors starvin' up 'ere. There's a good few baskets full o' fresh picked food down there that never got buried. Told yer I wouldn't steer ye wrong, didn't I? Let's slide down there an' see wot the pickin's are like."

Nimbalo jumped at the sudden rumbling and clattering that echoed through the cavern.

"Great seasons, wot's that, mate? Thunder'n'lightnin' again?"

Alfik scrambled up the streambank to the curtaining waterfall that shielded the entrance. "Stay. Not thunder'n'lightnin', that rockfall, not safe. Stay!"

Nimbalo made to follow him, but was stopped by Tagg's strong paw. "Best stop here, mate. These creatures know their own mountain best. That rockfall sounds bad!"

They waited until the rumblings ceased. There was a brief silence, then the Cavemob shrews began chattering wildly and moving toward the cave entrance. Bodjev headed them off, calling for calm.

"Shushupp, shushupp, alla beast! Nogo, stay 'ere. Alfik cleverwise son, know best. Wait, wait 'til Alfik comeback!"

The wait was rather a long one. Anxious shrews who had family and friends outside chattered away interminably to one another. Nimbalo covered his ears, screwing his face up.

"The blinkin' noise that lot are makin' is worse than the rockfall."

Tagg nodded sympathetically. "Aye, but they've probably got kin out there and they're worried. I wish Alfik would come back. Hope he's all right."

Virtually as the otter finished speaking, Alfik came splashing hurriedly through the watery cascade and made straight for Tagg. "Death be's out there, lotsa death, much hurted Cavemobs. Four beasts too, biggabeasts, mebbe yore size, big knifes, spear, lookalike bad. Muchbad!"

The big otter drew his blade, his tattooed face grim. "Bodjev, you and your shrews stay here for a while. Wait a bit before you follow me. I know who those beasts must be, and I don't want any of the Cavemob hurt because of me!"

Nimbalo picked up a flint-studded club and followed his friend to the entrance. Tagg shook his head. "Not this time, mate. This is something I've got to do alone!"

The harvest mouse brushed by him. "No mate o' mine fights standin' alone, I don't care wot ye say. I'm goin' with ye, Tagg. If there's four of 'em you'll need somebeast to watch yore back, no arguments!"

Tagg flashed him a quick smile. "You're a real pal, Nimbalo the Slayer!"

Amid the devastation they had caused to the neatly farmed terraces, the four vermin laughed amid fallen boulders and dead pigmy shrews, callously feeding themselves. Gruven stuffed fresh button mushrooms into his mouth, grabbing at Dagrab as she passed with a basket.

"Strawberries! Why didn't ye tell me there was strawberries 'ere? Gimme some o' those, ye greedy rat!" He spat out the mushrooms and began stuffing strawberries.

Ribrow had a basket part filled with scallions. He munched on a bunch and belched loudly. "Nothin' like fresh-picked veggibles. 'Ere, mate, d'yer want some?" He held out the basket to a groaning pigmy shrew, buried to the chest in rubble, with blood crusting upon his brow. "Doesn't know wot's good fer 'im," Ribrow scoffed. " 'E don't want none. Rawback, chuck some of that celery over 'ere, will ye?"

Rawback was nibbling on some tender young carrots. He threw the celery, but it missed Ribrow's outstretched paw, landing on the back of a dead shrew. Ribrow shot him a look of disgust.

"I ain't gonna eat that now. Yore a lousy thrower!"

Gruven pulled a face and stood up, patting his stomach. "Too many strawberries gives me the gripes. Anythin' else that looks tasty 'round 'ere?"

He turned to scan the far end of what had been the Cavemob shrews' terrace field and saw Tagg, still some fair distance away. For an instant, shock rooted the stoat to the spot. But then he sprang into action. Without a word he ran off down the mountainside in the opposite direction. When Dagrab saw him hurtling off through the

224

rubble and into a grove of rowans, she forgot the strawberry in her paw. "Where's the Chief off to?"

Rawback looked up and saw Tagg thundering toward them. "Yaaaargh! The Taggerung!"

They leaped up and fled like sparrows from a hawk, in the direction Gruven had taken. Ribrow was slightly slower than Dagrab or Rawback, and his paw struck a sharp rock. Leaping and yelping, he hobbled as fast as he could, until a sinewy paw caught the back of his neck in a ferocious grip. Tagg spun the stoat around and stunned him with a resounding blow from his rudder.

Nimbalo had now reached the avalanched area and was yelling, "Tagg, mate, there's wounded an' injured all over the place 'ere. Lend a paw, will you? You've got to 'elp me with 'em!"

For a moment Tagg was torn by indecision. He looked in the direction Gruven, Dagrab and Rawback had taken, his eyes blazing hatred, his whole body quivering as he strove to control himself. Then, hauling the unconscious Ribrow over his shoulder, he growled, "You'll do for now. I'll track those other three down. They can't run fast or far enough with a Taggerung on their trail!"

Driven by fear, Gruven ran like a hunted animal. Some distance behind he could hear what he thought to be the furious otter coming after him. Actually it was Dagrab and Rawback trying to catch up with him, but Gruven did not intend to stop and face the enemy. He pushed on, certain that the other three had run in different directions, or had been hunted down and slain. He struggled open-mouthed to suck in air, his paws pounding over rock, grass and earth alike. Behind him he heard the crackle of snapping foliage. Panic swept over him and he dodged to the left, into an area of boulders, stunted trees and a fast-flowing stream, which bordered the flatlands. He tried to bridge the stream with a running leap and failed, coming down with a splash into the shallows below the opposite bank.

His right footpaw was almost skinned to the bone as it shot between a rock and a root under the water. A screech of pain welled from his throat and he overbalanced to fall backward into the stream.

With their tongues lolling and chests heaving like bellows, Dagrab and Rawback tried to halt at the edge of the narrow stream, but their momentum carried them sliding awkwardly on the damp grass into the shallows below. Scrambling upright, they spat out water, staring openmouthed at Gruven in the shallows near the other side. Their leader was lying on his back, trying to scrub mud and water from his eyes and wailing piteously, "Don't kill me, please! It was the others who caused the landslide, I tried to stop them! Let me live an' I'll 'elp ye to hunt 'em down, I'll do anythin', only spare me, please!" He broke down, blubbering and pleading.

Rawback waded across and stood over Gruven, a look of loathing and contempt plain on his villainous face.

"Gerrup, ye whimperin' idiot, an' pack in yer whingin'! 'Tis only us!"

Gruven dried his eyes swiftly. "Where's the otter? Is he comin' after us?"

Dagrab waded across to study the muddy bankside. "We never 'eard 'im followin' us. So there's no need fer all the shoutin' an' cryin'."

Suddenly Gruven was back to his old self. "I wasn't cryin'. I was callin' out 'cos I'm in pain. If'n yer took the trouble t'look, you'd see my footpaw's trapped!"

Rawback grinned wickedly. "Why so 'tis. 'Ere, let me 'elp yer, Chief."

The stoat could have freed the paw instantly, but he pretended it was a difficult task. Leaning down on Gruven's scraped limb, he ignored his leader's cries, wrenching and scraping the hurt footpaw maliciously, but keeping his voice pleasant.

"There there now, on'y babes cry an' moan. So, you was the one who tried ter stop us causin' the landslide, eh?

Ain't you the big brave Juskazann. Young Gruven the terror, eh? All we could 'ear on the journey was 'ow you was goin' to slay the otter. All those 'orrible things you wuz goin' t'do when ye laid paws on 'im. Hoho, soon as ye clapped eyes on the Taggerung you took off, like a butterfly from a jackdaw. Wot 'appened, O Mighty One? Why didn't ye stand an' fight like yore mama told yer to?"

Gruven pushed Rawback aside and wrenched his footpaw free. "Why didn't you, or you, Dagrab? Yore supposed to be veteran trackers an' killers. I'd 'ave taken that otter on if'n you two cowards would've stayed t'back me up. Aye, we could've done with Vallug an' Eefera there too. They ran long afore the otter showed up. Though if'n they ain't trackin' 'im, wot are they up to?"

Dagrab pointed at the bankside. "Well, we'll soon know when we catch up wid 'em. There's Eefera's pawprints. Weasels ain't 'ard to reckernize. Aye, an' Vallug's still with 'im. See the scratches off'n 'is bowtip an' the deep prints 'e made leverin' 'imself over the banktop? They're 'eaded west by the look o' things."

Gruven slapped cooling mud on his scraped limb, binding a dock leaf to it with weed strands, then stood up and tested his balance.

"Right, we're goin' after those two slybeasts. 'Tis all clear t'me now. They knew all along that the otter'd never show 'is face near a Juska camp again, an' no clanbeast'd ever come this far from our territory to check any story they might tell. So all they do is turn up back at camp an' tell Grissoul that we're all dead, the otter too, an' next thing y'know they're clan chiefs. That's it!"

Rawback climbed to the banktop, shaking his head. "Ye've got it right, 'cept fer one thing. Only one of 'em'll make it back to camp. Ain't no room fer two chiefs. I'll wager 'tis Vallug who returns alone. 'E wuz always the deadliest slayer."

Dagrab climbed up beside Rawback. "Huh, that's wot you say, but Eefera ain't no fool. I've tracked alongside that weasel many a time, an' they don't come any slyer. Vallug's big an' powerful, but my bet is that the one who makes it back'll be ole Eefera. 'E's the craftier of the two."

Gruven scrambled to the banktop, motioning them to move off. "I don't care which one 'tis, I'll slice 'is 'ead off with this sword as soon as we make it back to camp. All you two's gotta remember is that I killed the otter. Stick to that story an' I'll promote ye both to Chief Trackers. You can 'ave yore own followers, give yer own orders, an' live off the cream o' the land. Now let's get goin' while there's still plenty o' daylight!"

19

Every fourth summer, Skipper and his ottercrew went off to a Hullabaloo. They would follow streams and rivers down to the shores of the great sea, where they would meet up with other otter crews and many of the sea otters from the far north. Hullabaloo was a festival that could last until autumn, as long as the otters were having fun. Meeting old friends and relatives, sporting in the waves, singing, dancing and lighting bonfires each night on the beach for the inevitable feasts was good rough fun, of the sort that ottercrews enjoy immensely.

Skipper and his crew marched out of Redwall's gates that morning, waving, cheering, and promising to bring back lots of shells for the Dibbuns. Mhera stood out on the path with her friends, calling goodbyes and fluttering kerchiefs until the otters merged into the sun-shimmering distance of the flatlands.

Fwirl accompanied the ottermaid back inside the Abbey. "Why didn't you go with them, Mhera? 'Twould be a lovely holiday for you and your mama."

Mhera shrugged. "We've not been part of any crew for many seasons now. Skipper said we were welcome to join them, but there's too much to be done here, Fwirl. Friar Bobb couldn't do without Mama; she loves the kitchens as much as he does. As for me, well, I've got my riddle to solve and Cregga to watch over. Besides, I like Redwall in summer. There's always something going on."

Fwirl linked paws with her friend. "I do too. Haha, we're both becoming a regular old pair of Abbeybeasts. Come on, I promised Broggle that I'd help your mama and Friar Bobb to get lunch ready. It won't be too difficult, with twoscore otters out of the way. Race you to the kitchens!"

Even though the lunch that day was a splendid one, Mhera sat toying with her plate of celery and chestnut bake, rearranging the salad surrounding it into random patterns. A leaden lump in her chest would not allow her to enjoy the food. Failure weighed heavily upon the ottermaid. Raucous laughter from the far table, where Drogg Cellarhog and old Hoarg were challenging one another to imaginary feats of eating, did nothing to lift her spirits.

Drogg was gesturing airily with a wooden spoon. "I could chase down a chestful o' chestnuts with cherry juice wine!"

Hoarg smiled patronizingly over his glasses at this effort. "I could purloin a portion o' pears an' pop 'em down with a pot o' pennycress cordial!"

And so the banter went back and forth.

"Ho, ye could, could ye? Well, you'd best step aside when I attack an Abbeyful of apples an' ask for an ample allocation of ale afterward!"

"Step aside? I step aside for nobeast, whether it be a hallowed hedgehog, an officious otter, a seasoned squirrel, a mutterin' mole or a befuddled badger!"

Boorab, who was referee, rapped old Hoarg's paw with an oatfarl. "Foul, sah! Infringement of the rules. You changed your initial letter no less than five times an' never jolly well mentioned food once. You lose two points, old chap, an' that slice o' fruitcake. No kerfufflin', penalty must be accepted!"

Amid gales of laughter, the hare stole a slice of fruitcake

from Hoarg's plate and bolted it. The younger element began calling, "You have a go, Mr. Boorab, go on, show 'em how 'tis done!"

Boorab gulped the fruitcake down and obliged. "Ahem! I could simply scoff sixty-six sticks of celery separately, swallow seventeen swigs o' sweet cider an' sensationally scrunch a selection of salad whilst simperin' smilin' and singin' soulfully to serenade Sister Alkanet's stern stares!" Amid hoots of merriment he bowed to the Sister. "So sorry your name didn't begin with an S, marm!"

She rose abruptly and carried her plate and beaker off to another table, where she sat glaring frostily at the funsters. "Ridiculous! Grown Redwallers behaving like naughty Dibbuns!"

Boorab bounded over and plonked himself down alongside Mhera, attempting to cheer her up.

"I say, wot? Pretty young thing like y'self sittin' there with a face on you like a frog who's lost his fiddle. Y'best hurry up an' jolly well smile, or you'll stick like that, ask Sister Alkanet. She knows all about that stuff. Her face stuck like that when she was an infant, doncher know, missed her mouth an' poured a bowl of custard down her ear, never smiled since, wot!"

Cregga's huge paw lifted the hare right out of his seat. "Away with you and leave my friend Mhera alone."

As he rose in the air, Boorab took Mhera's plate of lunch with him. "Er, right you are, mighty marm. I say, you don't mind me taking this with me, wot. Save it bein' wasted. Can't abide waste, y'know."

Mhera relieved him of the plate and returned it to the table. "You can have it if you apologize to Sister Alkanet about the rude and unkind remarks you made about her!"

The Badgermum stroked Mhera's cheek softly. "He's right, you know. Sitting there scowling won't solve much."

Mhera pushed the plate of food away. "I'm sorry, Cregga, it's just that I haven't the time to fool about. I'm just so angry with myself that I can't solve the mystery of the green cloth with the writing on. I need to get away on my own, so I can think clearly. It's noisy in here."

Lifting her head, the badger checked the chattering, the clatter of plates and the scraping of chairs with her keen senses.

"Hmm, it is rather boisterous, but then summer lunchtimes are usually like this. You've never noticed because a certain ottermaid named Mhera is normally part of it all. Would you like to go up to my room for a bit?"

"I'd love to. Thanks, Cregga!"

The Badgermum put her head on one side as if pondering something. "Wait. Maybe it'd be better if you went up and took a rest in the infirmary sickbay. It's nice and quiet in there, you know."

Mhera could not help pulling a wry face at this suggestion. "I don't feel ill. Why should I go to the sickbay?"

Cregga shrugged. "No urgent reason really, but I was just thinking. Abbess Song loved to take a nap up there when it was empty. She liked the room, said it was both cool and clean."

Mhera rose from the table. "Clean and cool. Good. I'll give it a try."

Boorab came to the table when Mhera had left. He reached for the leftover luncheon, but Cregga's paw closed over his. "Well, sah, did you apologize graciously to Sister Alkanet?"

"Yith, marb, I dibb!"

Cregga frowned. "What are you talking like that for?"

"I 'pologithed add webt to kitth hurr paw."

Cregga translated. "You apologized and went to kiss her paw, is that what you're trying to say? What happened?"

"The Thithter thmacked bee inna node wib a pudden thpoon!"

Cregga nodded approvingly. "Sister Alkanet smacked

you in the nose with a pudding spoon. Well, good for her! Does it hurt?"

"Yith. It thmarth!"

"Oh, I see. And do you look unhappy?"

"Udhabby? Ob courth I lukk udhabby!"

Cregga allowed him to take the plate. "Well, there you are, Boorab, but don't forget to smile, or you'll stick like that, remember!"

Boorab wandered off, muttering darkly, "Thmile? Huh, she bight thigg I'b laffig add gibb be anudder thock wib 'er pudden thpoon!"

It was indeed quiet, peaceful and clean in the little sickbay. Mhera lay down on a truckle bed and gazed around. The room had a wonderful old aroma of verbena. A warm circle of sunlight, coming through the small circular window, shone on the far wall like a pink sun in a sandstone sky, the sandy streaks in the stone appearing to her mind as faint cloud layers. She recalled a couple of spring days she had spent in the sickbay, one season when she was very young. Sister Alkanet had treated her for a sprained footpaw. The Sister had not been stern with her, but kindly and considerate. Maybe she was different when not on duty. There was a scroll, opened out and fixed to the back of the door, with a poem written on it in beautiful copperplate script. The edges were wreathed in artistically painted fruits and flowers. Mhera read the poem to herself as she lay there, feeling calm and rested.

White campion rooted from its bed,
Will cure the pains of aching head,
For one who can't sleep easily,
Then use valerian . . . sparingly.
If ague and fever hang about,
Wild angelica hounds them out.
For wounds of sword and spear or arrow,
The plant to heal them all is yarrow,

Placed o'er the scars where cuts have been,
Dock and sanicle keep all clean.
Use waterparsnip and whitlow grass,
On warts and swellings, they'll soon pass.
And when the snuffles and sniffs are seen,
Just drive them out with wintergreen,
And oft the wise ones do report,
Keep them at bay with pepperwort,
Whilst maidens full of health and cheer,
Dab sweet woodruff behind each ear!

Mhera smiled, recalling the time when she and Floburt were fascinated with the aroma of sweet woodruff. They had persuaded Friar Bobb to make them a flask of the wonderful vanilla-perfumed scent. However, both maids used it so liberally on ears, throat and paws that it became overpowering. Redwallers complained at dinner and Cregga Badgermum ordered them both to eat outside in the orchard. Of course, she had been a lot younger then, and Floburt nought but a Dibbun. Slumber overcame the ottermaid as she lay there reminiscing. With her dreams bygone events came back to sadden her: the sight of her mother weeping over an empty cradle, the chubby, fuzzy babe with a flowermark on his paw. Her brother. Had he lived, Deyna would be a big strong otter of almost sixteen seasons now. Her father, lifting her up and kissing her before he left with the babe, so proud of his little son and his pretty daughter. She missed her father so much.

Mhera awoke weeping. There was somebeast tapping upon the sickbay door. Hastily wiping her eyes on the coverlet, she called out, "Please come in!"

Fwirl and Broggle peeped around the door.

"Cregga told us we'd find you here." Fwirl ran straight to Mhera and put a paw about her. "Oh, dear, you've been crying. Are you all right?"

The ottermaid sniffed, dabbing at her eyes with the

worn green coverlet from the bed. "It was just a dream. Silly of me really, I'll be all right in a moment. A creature of my seasons, weeping like a Dib—"

Suddenly, Mhera buried her nose completely in the coverlet, her whole body stiffening.

Broggle tugged the coverlet gently. "What is it, Mhera? What's the matter?"

She thrust the coverlet at her friends. "Smell! It's lilacs!"

As they put their noses to it, Mhera felt the cloth's texture. "It's very old, and homespun. It's green, too, faded green, just like the scrap of cloth from the bell tower beam!"

There followed a shuffling sound, coupled with paws tapping against the wall. Cregga entered the sickbay.

Fwirl could not contain herself. Words rushed from her mouth. "Oh, Cregga, oh, mum, look what Mhera's found. Sorry, you can't look, can you? Feel this, smell it, what does it remind you of?"

Sitting down on the bed, Cregga did as she was bid. "Hmm, now don't tell me. It's a coverlet, the sort Sister Alkanet uses to keep the sheets from getting dusty. Am I right?"

Mhera's voice rose almost to a squeak. "It smells of lilacs and it's old green homespun!"

Cregga lay back against the pillows and sighed. "Think I ate too much lunch. Oh, is there writing on it anywhere?"

Mhera found it immediately, below the hem she was holding. A single word, which she read out slowly. "PITTAGALL. All in capital letters again, running downward." She pursed her lips, seething with frustration. "First we had HITTAGALL, now we've got PITTAGALL. Well, that's a great help, I don't think!"

Cregga nestled her head comfortably into the pillows. "What were you expecting to find?"

The ottermaid gestured helplessly. "Something . . . I don't know. Maybe an object that'll tell us who the next Abbess or Abbot of Redwall is to be. Something solid and positive I could recognize plainly, not all this HITTAGALL and PITTAGALL nonsense!"

Cregga heaved herself from the bed. "Well, I'm not going to get a very good nap here. I think I'll go to my room and rest in my chair." She waved them away as she felt her way out of the sickbay. "No need to help me, I can make it on my own quite easily. I'll leave you young 'uns here to solve your puzzles. Don't get too angry with yourself, Mhera my dear. You'll come to a solution if you give it a little thought and time. Patience, my friend, patience."

When Cregga had gone, Mhera and Fwirl found some shears and a needle and thread in Sister Alkanet's cupboard. They set about snipping the worded piece from the coverlet and sewing a new hem right along the edge. Broggle watched them, a smile hovering on his pudgy face.

"You'll excuse me saying, misses, but you aren't very good seamstresses, are you? Here, you'd better let me do that."

Mhera could not help laughing at the crooked line of stitching she and Fwirl had worked on. She gave the coverlet to Broggle. "Thanks, pal. I was always pretty dreadful with needle and thread."

Fwirl frowned. "I thought we were doing quite well, but I've had no experience of needlework, so how would I know? I'd love to learn how to do it properly, though."

The assistant cook took out his little kitchen knife and began unpicking the haphazard stitching. "Would you really, Fwirl? Then watch me and I'll show you. It's quite simple once you get the hang of it."

Mhera took the lettered cloth to the round window and studied it while Broggle, who was an extremely quick and neat worker, instructed Fwirl in needlework. The ottermaid soon gave up staring at the scrap of cloth and stood gazing out of the window, to where Durby and his Dibbun chums had finished eating their woodland trifle with meadowcream topping. Trundling from the gatehouse, carrying the empty basin between them, they were making for the pond. Mhera could see their happy little faces, all with beards and mustaches of meadowcream, and she wondered what they were up to. They waddled into the shallows and began washing the mess from themselves, knowing that they might be saving themselves from a thorough bathing by any elder who found them covered in cream and trifle. But, being Dibbuns, they quickly found better uses for Abbey pondwater than washing, and a full-scale watersplashing battle soon broke out. Mhera chuckled to herself as she watched the fun. However, her good humor suddenly turned to alarm. Whilst the rest were splashing one another, they had completely ignored the tiniest Dibbun of all, Wegg the hedgehog babe. He had launched the big beechwood trifle bowl onto the pond and clambered into it.

Paws cupped around her mouth, Mhera yelled down at them, "Durby, Feegle! Pull that bowl ashore and get little Wegg out!" But they were splashing and shouting so loudly that they were oblivious of Mhera's calls from the high window.

Broggle looked up from his work. "Is that the Dibbuns? What are they up to?"

Mhera dashed from the room, calling back to the needleworkers, "You carry on with your task. I'll see to this!"

She was across the landing, down the stairs and through the Great Hall like a flash. Whizzing through the open Abbey doorway, she almost collided with her mother, who was coming in from the orchard with an apron full of fresh pears. Filorn bent to pick up the fallen ones, shaking her head.

"Dearie me, the number of times I've told that daughter o' mine not to rush. She's as bad as any Dibbun, even now she's grown up!"

Bounding over the lawn toward the south wall, Mhera

could see the trifle bowl well out on the lake as the splashing Dibbuns sent up waves. They had still not noticed the hogbabe's absence. But Wegg saw Mhera. Standing up in the bowl, he waved his tiny paws.

"Meeler, Meeler, ukka me!"

He toddled to the edge of the bowl and capsized it.

As she ran, Mhera saw the silvery flash rise close to the surface, then the long high purplish dorsal fin of a big male grayling, closing in on the squeaking hogbabe. Durby and the others saw it too. They stopped splashing and began yelling.

"Cumm owt o' thurr, likkle Wegg!"

"Yeeeek, big fish comin' to eat 'im all up!"

"Out of the waaaaaaay!"

Mhera went sailing over their heads in a long powerful dive. It was all over in the wink of an eye. She struck the hunting grayling in its midsection, stunning it. Swirling her rudder, the ottermaid did a spinning turn and grabbed Wegg, then made a beeline for the shallows, with the hogbabe perched on her head, giggling as if it were all a great game.

Filorn had dropped her pears and set off after Mhera, realizing that something was amiss. She was followed by Hoarg, Broggle, Drogg and Sister Alkanet. They arrived at the pool in time to see Mhera come to land with Wegg. Before they could ask what had happened, Durby, Feegle and the other Dibbuns were relating the adventure en masse.

"Ee gurt fisher, bigger as ee h'Abbey, eated Wegg all oop!"

"Meeyra dived up in the air, right right up to th'sky!"

"Boi 'okey, roight daown ee gurt fisher's mouth 'urr go'd!"

"Yehyeh an' she pulled likkle Wegg out an' swimmed away wiv 'im!"

Filorn felt Mhera's sodden robe. "You're soaked, miss. Is everybeast all right?"

Mhera passed the hogbabe to her mother. "They're fine. This one went sailing in your trifle bowl. He fell in and a grayling went after him, but I got him back safe."

Sister Alkanet pointed a paw severely in front of her. "You Dibbuns, form a line, right there. Just look at the dreadful state you lot are in!"

Hanging their heads and shuffling paws, the Abbeybabes fell in line. Drogg Cellarhog eyed them sternly. "Wot've you been tole about goin' in the pool by yoreselves, eh?"

Before they could answer, Sister Alkanet opened Feegle's mouth and peered at her tongue. "Ugh! Pondwater, sand and I don't know what you've been swallowing. Right, follow me to the infirmary. 'Tis a dose of agrimony physick all 'round and a good bath in clean water and soapwort for all of you. Better bring Wegg along too, Miz Filorn!"

The ottermum felt sorry for the Dibbuns, but she knew as well as they did that lessons must be learned. She kept a straight face as she asked accusingly, "And pray tell me, where's my best trifle bowl?"

Durby tried one of his most winning molesmiles. "Et be's daown unner ee ponder, missus. Ee gurt fishes makin' troifle in et, tho' not as noice as yourn, moi dearie!"

Filorn wagged an admonitory paw at the Dibbuns. "Well, I can't make any more woodland trifles with meadowcream if I don't have my favorite bowl, no more ever. Now d'you see what your disobedience and naughtiness have cost you?" The Dibbuns were led off wailing heartbrokenly.

When they had gone, Mhera waded back into the pond. She waved to her mother. "Seeing as I'm wet already, I'll go and get it back."

Boorab touched his injured nose gingerly. "I'b glad deb liddle 'uns're geddin' physicked ad nodd bee. Blurgh! Id tasthes like boiled frogth!"

Old Hoarg agreed heartily with the hare. "I mind one

time she physicked me for a bad tummy. Phwarr! I swore I'd die afore I took the Sister's physick again."

Mhera emerged from the pool carrying the bowl. "That old grayling looks as if he's in need of some medicine. I had to butt him real hard. Couldn't take a chance on letting him get to little Wegg."

Filorn patted her daughter's soggy back gratefully. "You did the right thing. Thank you, my dear. I'd have missed this bowl very much. Your father made it for me. I think you're as good a swimmer as he ever was, Mhera. Up you go now. Dry off and get out o' those wet robes. There's fresh ones in my linen chest."

Drogg Cellarhog watched Mhera squelch off back to the Abbey. "You got a wunnerful daughter there, marm. Anybeast'd be proud to 'ave 'er as kin!"

20

It was evening when Mhera came back down from her room. She had taken a short nap, cleaned herself up and dressed in a soft magnolia robe with a brown cord girdle. She found Broggle and Fwirl sitting together in the orchard.

"Hello, you two. Well, Fwirl, how was your sewing lesson?"

Broggle pulled a face and held his paws up. "Don't even ask, Mhera! We'd just finished with that coverlet when in marches the good Sister with a crowd of muddy wet Dibbuns. She made us help her to physick and bathe them."

Mhera winked and smiled at Fwirl. "That's Sister Alkanet for you!"

"But that wasn't all," the squirrelmaid went on to explain. "She admired our needlework so much that she found us a lot of old sheets that needed repairing. So now I know all about sewing, thanks to you cutting a piece from the coverlet. That started it all!"

The three friends were still laughing when Floburt and Egburt came running along.

"Hi there. Have you put your names down for the wall race?"

Mhera clapped a paw to her brow. "Great seasons, I'd forgotten. Is it this evening? Come on, pals. We'd better get to the gatehouse!"

Fwirl was all agog. "What's a wall race? Can I take part?"

Broggle chuckled at his pretty friend's eagerness. "Of course you can, Fwirl; you should be good at it. Everybeast who enters has to nominate how they'll run, wall or grass. The grass runners run alongside the wall on the ground, but the wall runners go along the parapet of the ramparts. The race starts from the threshold over the gatehouse, and you run right 'round the four walls back to the starting spot. Anybeast can enter, but it's usually the good runners who win. The elders just watch."

They gave their names to Hoarg. Egburt, Floburt, Mhera and Fwirl nominated to go by the wall. Gundil and quite a few other moles, who were not fond of heights, nominated to go on the grass course. Fwirl asked the mole what the prize was, and Gundil touched his snout knowingly.

"Ee'll soon foind owt if'n ee wins, bootiful miz, hurr hurr!"

Foremole Brull marshaled the runners on the grass, kindly allowing the Dibbun entrants a starting line far ahead of the rest. She kept pointing and explaining to the little ones, "You'm goes thataway. Amember naow . . . thataway ee be runnen!"

Up on the parapet old Hoarg was lining the walltop runners in position. Alongside Egburt, Fwirl watched the antics of Foremole Brull and the Dibbuns curiously.

"What's the Foremole telling them, Floburt?"

The hedgehog chuckled as she explained, "She's telling them which way to go. When the race starts, some of the little 'uns are so dozy that they run all over the place, in the opposite direction, back to the Abbey, wherever. Last time some of them ended up dashing into the pool or straight into the gatehouse. You can never tell with Dibbuns, they get so excited."

Fwirl watched the Dibbuns dancing up and down, their faces alight, chattering to one another in baby talk. "Hahaha, bless their little hearts!"

Boorab's nose had recovered sufficiently for him to start the race. He stood on the gatehouse steps, holding a yellow flag, which had once been a grain sack.

"All contestants pay attention please for the annual wall'n'grass race, wot! Y'must observe the jolly old rules. No shovin' or pushin'. Straight 'round the wall boundaries an' back here, no shortcuts or secret routes. Right ho, chaps'n'chapesses, good luck to everybeast an' let's have a good clean race. Ready . . . on y'marks, get set . . . go!"

The runners took off helter-skelter, both on the grass and along the ramparts. Mhera was out in front, with Floburt and a mouse named Birrel, all running neck and neck. Cregga stayed on the threshold with the other elders. She grabbed Friar Bobb's paw, her sightless eyes blinking rapidly. "What's happening? Who's in the lead? Tell me, tell me!"

The Friar began shouting an excited commentary for her benefit. "Mhera, Floburt and Birrel are leading, though only just now, Egburt is nearly up there with them. Oh, look out! Great seasons, here comes our Broggle, and Filorn too. I never knew those two could run like that. Oh, great flyin' fur an' footpaws, what in the name of thunder is that?"

Cregga smiled knowingly. "Our pretty Fwirl, I'll bet!"

Old Hoarg was waving his stick and roaring, "She's whipped right past 'em all, leapin' along the battlement tops. I never seen aught like it. Fwirl's goin' like a streak o' red lightnin'. Go on, young 'un, you show 'em the way 'round!"

Everybeast yelled their admiration for the newest Redwaller. Friar Bobb turned his attention to the grass runners. "The ground racers have just turned the sou'west

243

corner, it's Gundil in the lead, goin' bravely, with three molemaids on his tail. They've just gone behind the bushes on the south wall. Hohoho, Durby and Feegle have skirted the bushes and are running over to the orchard as if they mean business!"

Drogg Cellarhog groaned. "My pore strawberry patch!"

Fwirl was tugging old Hoarg's sleeve. "Excuse me, sir, I think I'm first back."

The ancient gatehouse keeper stared in amazement at her. "But . . . but . . . the others are on'y midway along the north walltop!"

As the last of the wall runners came in there was much paw-shaking and back-slapping. All attention was now riveted on the grass runners down below. Gundil was only leading by a whisker, with two hedgehogs and the three molemaids pounding almost alongside him. Mhera, Broggle and Fwirl cheered their molefriend on uproariously.

"Keep going, Gundil, keep going!"

"Don't look back, keep going, you can do it, Gundil!"

Panting and blowing like a bellows, the worn-out mole staggered past the wallgate to win the grass race, amid wild cheers.

Both winners were carried back into the Abbey shoulder high. Fwirl looked down at Broggle as they went in. "What happens now?"

Broggle had no time to answer before lusty singing broke out.

"Hail both the winners,
Who raced 'round our wall,
On a summer solstice eve,
The longest day of all.
Valiant and fleet of paw,
Tributes they'll receive,
Lord and Lady victors,
On this midsummer's eve!"

A ceremony had been prepared in honor of Fwirl and Gundil, who were both draped in woven reed cloaks, their heads garlanded with wreaths of primrose and kingcup. Drogg Cellarhog, who had donned a clean apron for the ritual, rolled in a barrel, its staves dyed pink, and upended it in the center of Great Hall. Both winners were presented with artistically carved and polished tankards made from the bole of an elm tree. Drogg did not bother knocking a spigot into the cask bung, but raised a big coopering mallet and addressed himself to the winning pair.

"Ten summers ago I laid down this barrel of strawberry fizz to mature, and now you will be the first to taste it. Only those who have your permission may dip their bowls, flagons or tankards into the barrel. For you have won the titles for one night only of Lord an' Lady Strawberry. And well deserved, says I!"

He swung the mallet and stove in the cask head with a tremendous crash, causing everybeast nearby to be drenched in delicious pink strawberry fizz.

"Broggle, come and have some!" Fwirl cried over the cheering.

"Hurr, miz, that bain't ee way to do et," Gundil whispered in her ear. "Us'n's got to drink furst!"

They dipped their new tankards in and quaffed off a good mouthful each. Fwirl squeaked in surprise. It was the first time she had ever tasted the wonderful cordial. "Yeek! I'm full of fizzy bubbles! It's marvelous!"

Gundil instructed her on how to invite others to share it. He held forth his tankard to Cregga and recited:

"Whoi, 'tis so delishus an' so gudd that oi think,
Oi'll h'invite ee Badgermum to join oi in a drink!"

Cregga dipped her bowl into the barrel and bowed to Gundil.

"Why, thank you, Lord Strawberry, I'll drink right
    willingly,
To good health and long seasons, and to your victory!"

Fwirl caught on to the rhyme instantly and called again to Broggle.

"Why, 'tis so delicious and so good that I think,
I'll invite my friend Broggle to join me in a drink!"

Willing paws pushed the bashful young squirrelcook forward. He dipped his beaker in the barrel and bowed to the pretty squirrelmaid.

"Why, thank you, Lady Strawberry, I'll drink right
    willingly,
To good health and long seasons, and to your victory!"

Everybeast stood on tip-paw, raising the drinking vessels and shouting out to the winning pair to grant them permission to sup the fizz. Trays of special nut shortbreads were brought out and served. Fwirl and Gundil, between gulps of the drink, dispensed permissions as speedily as they could. Music and dancing broke out amid the scene of happy revelry.

Fwirl placed her garland on Filorn's head, and threw a paw about Mhera, her eyes shining. "I never realized what a good runner your mama is, for her seasons, that is. You ran a great race, marm!"

Filorn raised her beaker. "But not as swift as you, pretty one!"

Broggle joined them, clapping a paw to his mouth. "Whoo! This fizz is lively stuff. Best old Drogg's ever made, I'd say. Well, Fwirl, if you've decided to stay at Redwall, we'll never win the wall race again, none of us!"

Fwirl draped her cloak about his shoulders. "Well, I'll be the starter next time, I won't volunteer as a runner." She held up a paw and did a very good imitation of Boorab. "Wot wot, I say, you chaps, get in line there, no shovin' or jolly old shortcuts, you rotters, wot wot!"

Mhera joined in the laughter, but stopped when she

caught sight of Trey, the youngest mouse in the Abbey, weeping over by the main door. Pushing her way through the revelers, she reached his side. "Dearie me, a big fellow like you crying? What's the matter, Trey?"

"Us went onna race again, me'n'Durby'n'Feegle," the mousebabe explained between sobs. "We run like big 'uns onna wall. Then Durby'n'Feegle run like Miz Furl onna bakklemints, but they felled off over d'wall!"

Torches flared in the midsummer night and cries rang out over the darkened Abbey grounds as Redwallers dashed to the walls. Throwing little Trey up on his shoulders, Boorab sped along the walltops with Broggle, Filorn, Mhera and Fwirl in attendance, pumping Trey for information as he went.

"Where were they when they fell, old fellah? Here, over there, by the threshold, north wall, where?"

Mhera followed the direction of the mousebabe's pointing paw. "He's pointing to the center of the east wall."

They arrived panting at the location. Fwirl leaped up onto the battlements. "Was it here, Trey?"

The Dibbun nodded dumbly. Broggle looked pale in the torchlight. "If they'd fallen this way they would've landed here on the parapet. Did they fall over into the woodlands, little 'un?"

Again Trey merely nodded. Mhera's voice was laden with concern. "Tell us, Trey, when did this happen? Just now?"

This time the mousebabe shook his head. Mhera questioned further. "How long ago was it? Why didn't you run and tell us straightaway?"

Trey played with the bells on Boorab's ears as he confessed wanly, "It 'appen long ago when all went inna h'Abbey. Durby say notta tell anybeast we playin' onna wall. They felled off an' I come'd inna Hall. Trey frykkinned to tell, get sended uppa bed!"

Boorab shouted down to old Hoarg. "Get the main gate open, old chap. Search party needed outside!"

Fwirl did not need an open gate. She vanished over the wall with eye-blurring speed. Mhera issued instructions as she raced for the east wallsteps. "We'll use the east wicker gate, it'll be quicker. Mama, take Trey inside. Broggle, Mr. Boorab, follow me, we'll need your torches for light!"

The lock on the east wicker gate was stiff, but a solid kick from the hare's long back paws shot it open. The little gate creaked as they dashed out into the woodlands.

Fwirl was already out alongside the trees growing closest to the wall, her pretty face grim as the light fell on it. She spoke the words they were dreading to hear. "There's no sign of them!"

Blazing torches and lantern lights flickered all around the outside perimeter of Redwall Abbey's outer walls. Search parties chased up and down, looking for the lost Dibbuns, hoping that they would naturally have followed the wall around to the main gate. Mhera was rounding a huge sycamore when a big paw fell on her shoulder. She sighed with relief at the sound of Cregga's voice.

"Mhera, is that you? Any sign of them yet?"

"I'm afraid not, Cregga. It's as if the little rogues vanished into thin air."

Worriedly the Badgermum sniffed the night air. "I don't like this, there's too many out here. Those without torches or lanterns could get lost. Mossflower Wood is a very deceptive place, particularly at night. Everybeast is out here, even the elders, and that's not good. One spark from a torch, or a fallen lantern, could cause a forest fire!"

It was a terrible thought, but true. Mhera clenched her paws. "Right, get them to search inside the walls. Durby and Feegle may have wandered back in through the open gate. I'll take Broggle, Fwirl and Boorab, and we'll continue to look out here. Leave the east wicker gate ajar, so we can report in if they're found. Keep Sister Alkanet close, tell her to have medicines ready, and splints too. They might have broken limbs from the fall and could be lying out here unconscious somewhere. Will you do that, my friend?"

Cregga patted the ottermaid's cheek. "Good thinking, Mhera. I'll have Drogg leave some fresh torches unlit, by the wicker gate. Anything else you need?"

Mhera signaled Boorab over to her side. "Only lots of luck and some early dawn light if we don't find those two Dibbuns soon!"

21

Tagg stood covered in dust and soil, his chest heaving and his paws weary from digging. Nimbalo squinted at the setting sun as the last injured pigmy shrews were carried back into the mountain cave, then gazed sadly around at the deep layers of shale, scree and rocky debris.

"Well, mate, we saved all those we could. No tellin' 'ow many pore wretches lie buried under this lot. C'mon, there ain't no more we can do 'ere, Tagg. Let's go an' get cleaned up."

The big otter hung his head in despair. "None of this would've happened if I hadn't come here!"

The harvest mouse cast an eye to their prisoner. "Yer wrong, mate, you mean none o' this would've 'appened if'n that scum an' 'is vermin 'adn't come 'ere. You can't blame yoreself. Wrong 'uns is wrong 'uns wherever they goes. Huh, they would've only brought sufferin' on some other pore beasts."

Tagg nodded wearily. "Maybe there's some truth in that. Come on, you, get moving!" He took out his blade and severed the rope that anchored Ribrow's footpaws to a long, heavy piece of shale.

The stoat stumbled upright, rigid with fear. "Yore goin' to kill me, I know you are!"

250

Tagg kicked him on his way to the water-covered cavern entrance. "Not just yet, scumface. There's some questions I need answers to."

Ribrow had nothing to lose. "An' wot if I don't answer yer questions, eh?" he snarled back at his captor.

Nimbalo smiled amiably at him. "Then we'll turn yer over t'the kin of those you murdered."

The remark took all the boldness out of Ribrow. He collapsed in a sobbing heap, pleading pitifully, "No, please, don't let those beasts gerrat me!"

Tagg grabbed him savagely, pulling him up so fiercely that his footpaws left the ground. He held the stoat at eye level, narrowing his eyes to a deep stare of icy hatred.

"If you don't tell me what I want to know, you'll wish I had turned you over to the Cavemob tribe by the time I'm done with you. So you'd best loosen up that tongue of yours!"

When they reached the cave, Nimbalo took a refreshing shower beneath the cascade of cold mountain water that curtained the entrance. Taking Tagg's blade, he guarded the prisoner whilst the otter did likewise, energetically washing away the day's dirt and grit. It was as they dragged Ribrow to the cascading screen that they made a fortunate discovery. He was afraid of water. The stoat dug his heels in and yowled, "No! No! I ain't goin' inter that! Lemme go!"

Tagg smiled at Nimbalo. "Leave this to me, matey!" Seizing the stoat by his tail and the scruff of his neck, the powerful otter frogmarched him under the waterfall and held him there. Ribrow thrashed about, unable to escape that relentless grip.

"Owowow! I'm drownin'! Yaaaaargh! Don't drown me!"

Tagg pulled him out, allowed him to get his breath, then shoved him under again, shaking him like a rag. "Talk or I swear I'll drown you! Talk, you black-hearted vermin!"

"Yesyesyes I'll talk! Get me out! Waaahahhahaaaargh!"

Tagg pulled him out and hurled him to the ground. Alfik emerged from the cavern to issue a warning. "Not to bring that'n inna Cavemob dwellin', tribe wanna rip 'im inta bits. My daddy holdem back 'til you finish wirrim!"

Nimbalo winked at the pigmy shrew. "Thanks, mate. We'll stay out 'ere t'night an' keep the stinkin' villain with us."

Ribrow did talk. He told Tagg everything that had occurred since he left the Juska, leaving nothing out. Nimbalo heard it all, but not knowing much about Tagg's past he was rather puzzled until Tagg began explaining.

The harvest mouse sat listening, nibbling at the supper that Chichwife had passed out to them. "So, this Sawney Rath, who was pretendin' to be yore father, 'e's dead. Now yore old tribe's got a new chief, Gruven Zann, an' that's the beast who's out t'bring yore 'ead back an' prove hisself boss of the Juska clan, 'ave I got it right?"

Tagg added sticks to the small fire he had built. "That's it, roughly. My next job is to track Gruven and the other two down. I can take care of that. But the other pair, Eefera and Vallug Bowbeast, they're a different sort altogether. Sawney's two best killers they were, real trained trackers and murderers. Trouble is, I don't have any idea where they could've gone. That worries me, because they're ten times as bad as this idiot we've caught. They're very crafty, too; you wouldn't sleep easy with them within a league of you, knowing what type they are."

Nimbalo was still slightly mystified. "But ain't you supposed t'be called the Taggerung? You tole me that meant yore the greatest warrior of 'em all. I bet you must've slayed more beasts than the whole clan put t'gether, eh, mate?"

Tagg drew his friend aside, out of Ribrow's hearing, and spoke low. "Apart from that big eel I've never slain anybeast. I never had to, you see; I was tougher, quicker and more skilled than any Juska. I always brought them

252

back alive. It was only Sawney wanting me to kill Felch the fox, by skinning him alive, that caused me to split from the clan. Beasts feared my name and reputation, but really I was only Sawney Rath's trained errand runner. When I realized that I could never kill just for fun, the way the Juska do, I suddenly wanted to be free of them and live my own life. But it seems they aren't going to let me do that."

Nimbalo suddenly felt sorry for his friend. He winked at Tagg. "Oh, ain't they now? Hah, we'll soon change their minds about that, me ole Tagg. You've got Nimbalo the Slayer with you now, pal. Those Juskas'll be glad to leave ye alone by the time I'm done wid 'em. Then ye can lead any kind o' life y'like; it'll be even better than the time afore you was a Taggerung!"

Tagg smiled at the irrepressible little harvest mouse. "Thanks, but I can't recall how I lived before I was Taggerung." But even as he spoke, a sudden idea was building in the otter's mind. He turned back to Ribrow, who was sitting nearby, wet and sullen. The stoat huddled defensively against a rock, sensing that his captor was going to start interrogating him again.

"I told yer everythin' I know. There ain't no more, see!" Ribrow's throat bobbed nervously as Tagg took out his blade and began tapping it against the boulder. "Wot d'yer want now? I told yer I know nothin'."

The otter honed his blade on the boulder, looking at the razor-sharp edge, speaking softly. "Tell me, how long have you been with the Juska clan?"

"Dunno exactly, thirty seasons, more mebbe, I'm not sure."

Tagg nodded agreeably, his eyes still fixed on the blade. "Then you must remember how I came to be with the clan. Take your time, stoat, think carefully. I wouldn't want you to make any mistakes, that would make me angry, very angry!"

The otter's voice was like his steel blade, there was cold danger in it. Ribrow felt himself trembling, and held out

253

his paws pleadingly. "Wait, wait, let me think. 'Twas all a long time ago!"

Tagg licked the blade, his tattooed face ferocious in the firelight. "Go on, Ribrow, I'm waiting . . ."

Ribrow decided to tell what he knew. "There was talk that Grissoul's omens said a Taggerung was comin' to the Juskarath clan. Antigra claimed 'twas 'er babe, but the omens were wrong for 'im. There was an argument an' Sawney slew Antigra's mate, wid that blade you've got in yer paw now. Grissoul 'ad visions 'twas to be a babe, wid a marked paw."

"How did you know this?" Tagg interrupted.

The stoat shrugged. "Everybeast was gossipin' about it on the quiet. You know wot Juska are like, always keepin' their ears open in case there's summat in it for them. Next thing, Sawney ordered us to break camp an' follow 'im. I tell yer, I never knew Sawney Rath t'be so nervous an' excited. Nobeast'd seen Sawney like that afore. We marched fer days; 'e drove us 'ard. The new camp was in Mossflower Wood, south'n'west as I recall, by a river. Then 'e picked a bunch of us, I was one, me matey Dagrab was anudder. I can't remember who else, 'ceptin' Eefera an' Vallug Bowbeast, 'is pet killers, they was always with Sawney. We went to a place where a path ran through the water, a ford. The orders was to keep our 'eads down an' be silent. An otter came there, big feller like yerself, carryin' a babe. Sawney gave the word an' Vallug slew the big otter, put a shaft in 'is heart. Sawney grabbed the little 'un, that was you."

Tagg's voice trembled audibly. "Go on, what happened then?"

Ribrow closed his eyes, concentrating hard. "We 'ad to run fer it, fast, Sawney out in front carryin' you, an' the rest of us guardin' 'is back."

Tagg could hardly believe what he was hearing. "I never knew Sawney Rath to turn and run from anything in his life. What was he afraid of?"

254

Ribrow's reply was immediate. "The Red Warriors, that was it! Aye, I remember now. Sawney said to us there'd be Red Warriors, or somethin' like that, comin' after us. We ran like blazes, 'cos 'e said that they didn't take prisoners an' 'e'd leave be'ind anybeast who couldn't keep up. We went dashin' off west, t'the dunelands by the sea. Sawney made clanbeasts cover the trail with stalks of wild mint, an' they 'ad to brush the ground be'ind us. One thing, though: Sawney wouldn't let nobeast near you 'cept Grissoul. I saw 'im ruin a fox's paw fer life with that blade, just fer goin' near you. Wot was 'is name now? Lemme see. Felch, that was the fox. Aye, Felch!"

Tagg was intrigued by the tale. Pieces began to fit together. "Tell me more about these Red Warriors who were coming after you. Did you ever see them? Why did Sawney fear them?"

Ribrow shook his head. "Nah, we never seen 'em. Huh, would've took a bird t'keep up with us, we were runnin' that fast. Wait! I remember ole Grissoul sayin' somethin' about a bell. Er . . . the sound of the bell. Aye, that was it. Beware the sound of the bell, the very words she spoke. Lissen, that's all I kin remember. We was never allowed t'come near you when you was growin' up. Sawney saw that you got the best of everythin', vittles an' trainin' too. Only times I ever saw ye, I 'ad to bow me 'ead an' say Zann Juskarath Taggerung. All the clan did too. I've told ye all I know. 'Twas Gruven who started the landslide, not me. You won't slay me, will yer, Taggerung? Say ye'll spare me!"

Tagg grabbed some rope and bound Ribrow tightly for the night. "I'll spare you if you don't make another sound tonight. Now shut up and get some sleep. We'll decide what to do with you tomorrow."

Tagg slept knife in paw by the fire, his dreams teeming with red warriors and clanging bells. Sometimes he saw the mouse warrior, and he too was red. Tagg called after him, "Deyna, Deyna!"

The mouse warrior raised his sword and called back, "Martin!" Everything became jumbled then, the face of Sawney Rath, poor dead pigmy shrews buried beneath the avalanche of debris, then Vallug Bowbeast, grimacing evilly as he notched an arrow to his bow. The Bowbeast loosed the shaft, Tagg's mind flew back to the soft red room, and he saw the otter's face clearly. Except for the tattoos, he felt as if he were looking at himself. It was his father! Tagg felt the arrow strike his heart and water splash his face as he fell back into the ford.

"Wake up, mate. Lookit wot's 'appened to yore prisoner!" Nimbalo was crouching over him in the early dawn, splashing ice-cold mint and rosehip tea from a bowl onto Tagg's face. "Come on, matey, look, they brought us brekkist!"

Bodjev and Alfik were waiting, with a lot of Cavemob shrews, all carrying weapons. Tagg went over to where Ribrow lay dead, stiff as a board. Tagg looked up, his expression hardening. Alfik grinned. "A mornin' to ye, big fella, yikyik! No worry 'bout tharra one, 'e norra comin' wirrus. Ho no. Dink dink, like snakeyfish. Now 'e nomore kill Cavemobs!"

Seeing Tagg's face, Nimbalo stood between the otter and the shrew. "Ye can't blame 'em, matey. Ole Ribrow didn't show much mercy to the pore Cavemob beasts that 'e killed. They want t'come with us an' slay the others. We've got our own liddle army!"

Tagg did not want the Cavemob along with him, and decided to convince Bodjev dramatically. Drawing his blade, he laid it across both paws and held it forth to the Chieftain.

"O great Chieftain of the Cavemob, I thank you for your help. But we must travel alone, far and wide, to find the vermin and slay them. You cannot march off and leave your beloved mountain unguarded. Who is strong enough to rule with you gone? I will seek out your enemies and punish them for you. Because . . ." Tagg performed a mighty somersault, right over the astounded shrews, and landed brandishing the blade and roaring, "Because I am the Taggerung, faster than the wind and more deadly than a serpent's tooth. I am Taggerung, I slew Yo Karr!"

Sweeping Nimbalo up onto his shoulder, the big otter bounded off with massive speed and energy. The harvest mouse clung tight to his friend's neck, dawn breeze rushing past as they dashed through the rowans and rocks, shale spurting right and left. Nimbalo gripped Tagg's neck tighter and tighter, shouting in his ear, "Slow down, ye great madbeast. Don't trip, or ye'll kill us both!"

Pounding over rocks, leaping streams and dashing over turf and sedge they went. The sun was well up when Tagg slackened his pace to a fast lope. "They never followed us, did they, mate?"

Nimbalo brought his head around to stare into the otter's eyes. "Follow us, those fat short-pawed liddle maggots? Are you jokin', matey? An eagle would've 'ad trouble tryin' to foller us!"

Tagg laughed at his friend's windswept face. "Good, so d'you mind not trying to strangle me, please!"

"Right, then put me down. My pore paws've gone t'sleep tryin' to 'ang on up 'ere for so long!"

The otter put his friend down and slowed his pace. They walked along together, enjoying the warm summer morning. Nimbalo stopped. "Lissen, can you 'ear that?"

Instantly alert, Tagg drew his blade. "Hear what?"

Nimbalo patted his stomach and pulled a mournful face. "That! We left a good brekkist and travelin' packs o' food back there when you took to leapin' 'round. I'm starvin'!" Then Tagg's stomach rumbled so loudly that they both laughed.

"Aye, I'm a bit peckish too, mate. Let's keep going and see what we can find. By the way, I think we're completely lost."

Nimbalo took their bearings. "Well, there's the mountain be'ind us. I think I saw a stream up yonder when I was on yore shoulders. So let's make for the stream an' follow it. Might find some eats over that way."

It was a narrow stream, getting dryer as the summer progressed, high-banked and muddied in the shallows, with reeds and marshy-looking plants sprouting through the water. Clouds of midges flew everywhere. Tagg kept brushing a paw across his face and swatting at them.

"Whew! It's not much fun down in this streambed. What d'you say we go back up on the bank? At least we won't get eaten alive."

Nimbalo was a stubborn little beast. He stuck to his original idea. "No, no, let's carry on down 'ere awhile. If it gets no better beyond that bend, then we'll go up on the bank."

As they rounded the bend they were faced with a curious sight. It looked like a huge ball of dried mud, almost as tall as Tagg. The curious part was that it could talk in a well-educated squeak.

"Help! Assistance! Anybeast, please take pity on me. Hello, is there another creature out there? Answer me, I beg you!"

The mud had set, dry and solid in the sun. Tagg approached and knocked on it, his paw making a hollow sound. He put his mouth close. "Hello? Anybeast at home? What d'you want us to do? I'm an otter and I have a harvest mouse with me. I'm Tagg, and he's Nimbalo."

The reply was polite, but with an edge of urgent impatience. "I'll tell you what I require, I want you to dispense with the formalities and get me out of here before I suffocate. Now, can you do that, sir? Answer yes or no, please!"

Tagg got busy hacking away dried mud with his blade. "Yes!"

Nimbalo found a big club, carved from sycamore root, and dragged it across to Tagg. "See wot y'can do with this, mate!"

Tagg swung the club, dealing the mudball several good blows. Dust and dried mud clods showered him. "I'm not hurting you, am I?" he called out. "Are you all right in there?"

The reply was shaky, but still rather urgent. "As well as can be expected, my dear fellow. Kindly continue."

Tagg battered away forcefully until the mud prisoner called to him, "Stop! Desist, I pray. I'd be most upset if you slew me with my own club, sir, most upset!"

When the dust cleared, they were facing a hedgehog, hanging awkwardly out of a half ball of dried mud. Blinking dust from his eyes, he sneezed.

"Kachoooh! Beg pardon. Ah, I see you have a knife. Would you be so good as to cut this rope? But mind my snout, I pray you."

Tagg saw that a rope ran through the center of the hedgehog's face from spikes to chin. He severed it with a swift slice of the blade. The hedgehog began straining and gasping as the mud started to crack from around his spiky bulk.

"Aaaaah, my thanks to you, sir. Uuuuuunh! Stand clear now!" He popped out free, leaving the rope and a considerable number of spikes embedded in his former prison. Splashing into the shallow stream, he lay on his back, wriggling and sighing. "Aaaaah, that's better. Ooooooh, that feels rather good!" Sitting up, he proffered a muddy paw. "Robald Forthright at your service, sirs. May I express my heartfelt thanks for your prompt actions here today!"

Nimbalo shook his paw. "Please t'meetcher I'm shore, mate, but 'ow didyer get into that blinkin' mess?"

Robald shook Tagg's paw, allowing the otter to help him upright. "Not by my own making, I assure you. Come to my humble abode and I will relate the incident to you in its entire dreadfulness."

22

Robald's home was a turf hut up on the bank. It had been plundered and wrecked. The big stout hedgehog dug a broken-down old armchair from the wreckage, righted it, and dusted it off.

"They never found my emergency rations, fortunately for us." Removing a few slats of wood, he revealed a cupboard full of food. "Plumcake, damson cordial, nutcheese, fruit biscuits, spikebeer, candied apples and Great-Aunt Lollery's raisin teabread. They missed this little lot. Oh, don't stand on ceremony, help yourselves, friends. Don't worry about the mess, I'll clear up later."

As Tagg used his blade to slice the plumcake and teabread, the hedgehog told his story.

"Last night I was quietly dozing the sunset away when I was attacked. Can you believe it, set upon in one's own domicile. Three vermin, ruffianly louts they were, came at me whilst I was half asleep. I didn't even get a chance to reach for my club. One villain had a sword, kept jabbing at me, so what else could a body do? I rolled myself up into a ball, as we hogs are apt to do when in danger. But did that stop them? It certainly did not, the fiends! They tied me with my own rope, bound me painfully tight, so I became stuck in the curled-up position. Then without so much as a by-your-leave they rolled me up and down the bank for what seemed like an eternity. Lucky for me I got a hollow reed into my mouth, so I could breathe a little. Well, what more can one say? They played at their wicked game until I became the mudball you encountered today. Then they had the colossal nerve to ransack my dwelling and eat a pot of mushroom soup and a carrot and turnip flan. Just as well that Great-Aunt Lollery had visited a day earlier. She can't stand vermin!"

Tagg felt he had to interrupt. "Who's Great-Aunt Lollery?"

The hedgehog raised his eyebrows as he poured damson cordial. "Silly me, I forgot to mention, she's not my great-aunt really. She was my old nurse in my younger and better seasons. Lives in the woodlands now, won't move out here at any price. She's my cook, you know, and a hog more skilled in the culinary arts I've yet to meet. Dear old Great-Aunt Lollery, what a treasure she is. Goodness me, you don't think *I* made all this food, do you? Hah! Couldn't cook to save my life. She was only saying on her latest visit, as she always does, Master Robald, she says, you'd burn a salad if you didn't have Lollery to look after you! She's right, too. Why, I remember last winter . . ."

Tagg interrupted again. "Did you by chance hear the vermin's names, sir?"

Robald Forthright consumed a fruit biscuit topped with cheese at one bite, nodding vigorously. "Oh, yes, indeed I did. One was called Chief, stoat I think; there was another stoat too, Rawback, and a rat, ratess she was, name of Dagrab. Great seasons, where do they get these odd names, eh?"

Suddenly Robald put aside his food. "Good grief, I've just thought on, if they follow the streamcourse they're bound to come out in the woodlands, right by Great-Aunt Lollery's cottage. Oh dearie me, doesn't bear thinking about, does it?"

261

Tagg stood up, quickly putting together enough food to eat as they traveled. "You'd best show us the way to your nurse's cottage, Robald."

The hedgehog picked up his carved sycamore club. "Do you think I shall need this? It's fearfully heavy and I've never had cause to use it before. I'm not sure I could, really."

Nimbalo stood tapping his tail impatiently. "Sling it away, mate. No use totin' a club if'n ye can't use it."

Robald put the weapon aside gingerly. "Quite! Follow me, please."

He set out across the flatlands. Tagg scratched his head, bemused. "I thought you said your nurse lived in the woodlands close to the streambank. What are we going this way for? Wouldn't it be best to follow the course of the stream?"

Robald wiggled his eyebrows knowingly. "Most creatures would think that, my friend; a common misconception, I fear. Over the seasons I've found this route the shorter by a considerable time. The stream course meanders and winds far too much. Trust me, my way is altogether more convenient."

Tagg could see the woodland fringe through the layers of midday heat haze. "Looks like he's right," he murmured to Nimbalo. "This is a quicker way."

"Aye, prob'ly is, mate," the harvest mouse whispered out the corner of his mouth, "but I jus' wish ole Robald'd give 'is face a rest. Huh, 'e could talk the leg off'n a table!"

The hedgehog smiled patronizingly at Nimbalo. "I could not help but overhear your remark, friend Nimbalo. Quite incorrect, of course; it would take physical force to remove a table leg. However, as to my verbosity, I fear you are right. When deprived of company one tends to practice the art of conversation far more than one normally would. Had you seen my abode prior to its present state, you would have promptly noticed the absence of birds, bees, wasps, midges and sundry other creatures frequenting the area. They invariably leave after listening to my interminable prattling. Forthright by name and Forthright by nature, as Great-Aunt Lollery often says. I speak my mind, you see, always and often, even since infancy."

Tagg and Nimbalo strode out with a will, speeding up their pace and leaving the talkative Robald behind. The otter had to stifle his laughter as Nimbalo impersonated the hedgehog. "Spoke 'is mind since infancy? Hahaha, can you imagine that 'un when 'e was an 'ogbabe, sittin' up in the cradle an' spoutin' away like that? H'I say, Great-Auntie Lollery, frazzle me up a measured portion of the ole oatmeal porridge inna pan, but make certing the fire is at the correct temperature, will ye? Ho yes!"

Robald had now fallen far behind. "I say," he called, "would you kindly do me the courtesy of accommodating your pace to mine? I feel distinctly breathless!"

"Then stow the gab, y'ole windbag," Nimbalo shouted back. "Button up yore mouth an' let yore paws do the work. We ain't stoppin' for ye!"

Robald broke into a scurrying waddle and caught them up. "Point taken. I am suitably chastened, and from hereonin my lips shall remain sealed. Thank you for your comments, friend Nimbalo."

Hot and dusty, they arrived at the fringe of the sheltering trees, entering gratefully into the cool shade of woodlands dappled by the noontide sun. Robald was about to sit on the moss beneath a broad spreading oak when Tagg hauled him back onto his paws.

"If you're worried about Aunt Lollery, there's no time to rest. Which way do we go now?"

Robald gestured with weary resignation. "You are right, of course, friend Tagg. Over that way. The stream grows quite broad there, where it joins the river. In a moment or two of walking you'll hear the watersounds. Extremely soothing to one's nerves after crossing the exposed flatlands."

He was right. Within the space of a short walk they

reached the point where river met stream. Laburnum, willow and spindle trees trailed their drooping branches gracefully into the placid dark waters of a calm inlet. Robald quickened his pace and hurried out onto a spur dotted with cranberry, water mint and flowering rush. A huge raft was moored there, which seemed to upset Robald. He jumped up and down, stamping his paws.

"No! No! Nononono! Why oh why did I pick the same time to visit as those confounded Dillypins?"

Tagg raced to join the hedgehog. "Robald, what is it? Has something happened to your nurse?"

The hedgehog pointed an accusing paw at the raft. "Don't you see, it's those uncouth ignoramuses. Those . . . those . . . great spiked louts. The Dillypins, I mean!"

His rantings were cut short as a small rough-looking hogbabe emerged from the shrubbery behind them and whacked Robald's footpaw with a little club. He hopped about in agony as the hogbabe threw back his head and went into gales of gruff laughter.

"Ahohohoho! Gotcha dat time, h'Uncle Robald. Hohohohoho!" The babe brandished his club and went after Nimbalo's paws. Tagg picked him up in one paw and took his club away.

"Where's your mum and dad? Quick, before I eat you!"

The hogbabe showed no fear, merely pointing along the stream. "Down dere, h'eatin' up Lollery's pancakes. I show ya. Lemme down!"

Robald limped along in the rear as Tagg and Nimbalo hurried through the trees after the speeding hogbabe. Rounding a sharp curve in the streambank, he pointed to a cottage. It was all a woodland cottage should be, built from logs and roofed with sod and moss on larch trellis. A neat little garden of flowers and vegetables with a white rock border skirted the front. Rough laughter, singing and the strains of odd instruments came from behind the cottage. Robald hobbled up, a look of despair and pain on his chubby features.

"Forgive me, but I'd much rather you had found the three vermin here than that ill-disciplined lot. Oh well, you'd better come and meet the other side of Great-Aunt Lollery's family. No relation to the Forthrights, I'm glad to say!"

Chaos reigned in the back garden. Fat rough hedgehogs, their spikes adorned with flowers and trailing weeds, were guzzling down food, drinking and having belching contests, singing, fighting, dancing and completely ignoring the visitors. A homely greyspiked hedgehog, old and thin, dressed in a spotless white smock and a flowery apron, was frying pancakes on top of an outdoor oven. The three newcomers drew close, wordlessly watching her. She tipped a thick paste of ground corn and nutmeal onto the hot stone oventop, where it spread and fried quickly before she flipped it skillfully over with a broad thin slate. As the bottom fried she ladled honey and chopped berries on top, then folded the whole thing in two and served it to a waiting hedgehog. Looking up from her task, she smiled at Robald.

"I think you smelt my pancakes, Master Robald. Would you and your friends like some? Of course you would. Now, what brings you here? I only visited you two days ago. Oh, there I go, chatting on without introducing myself. I'm Great-Aunt Lollery."

The otter bowed politely. "My name's Tagg and this is Nimbalo. Pleased to meet you, Aunt Lollery. We came here because we thought you might be in danger from three vermin we are tracking."

The hedgehog she had been serving was a particularly big, tough specimen. He chuckled scornfully. "Three vermints? Hohoho! Y'mean those three who tried callin' on us as Lollery was cookin' brekkist? Well, ye've missed 'em, mate. Afore they'd even crossed the stream we sent the bullies on their way with a few good lumps t'think about, eh, Lollery!"

Lollery waved a paw at the three newcomers and continued the tale. "It was so funny. There I am, cooking breakfast, when one of the babes comes to me and says that there's three beasts across the stream, who must've smelled my good cooking. So I went out and there they were, two stoats and a rat, all tattooed up, just like you, Mr. Tagg. Hmph! They weren't very polite, I can tell you. One of them wades into the water waving a sword, saying he was going to chop me into fishbait if I didn't give them vittles. Of course he was shouting so loud that Jurkin here heard him. So the whole Dillypin family came out, loaded up their slings and gave those vermin a pounding they richly deserved!"

Jurkin unwound a hefty sling from his waist, fitted a big round riverpebble into it and whirled the thing overhead. "Aye, us Dillypins knows 'ow t'swing a rock. Gimme a target."

Tagg pointed. "Poplar branch sticking out there, see?"

Jurkin whipped off the stone. It zipped through the air and snapped off the poplar branch with a resounding *Crack!* Grinning, he held out the sling to Tagg. "Wanna try it, riverdog?"

The otter smiled and shook his head. "Not really, mate. See that woodrush flower in front of the poplar?"

Jurkin squinted. "Y'mean that 'un growin' low down agin the trunk?"

Tagg's blade flashed through the air. It landed quivering in the poplar trunk, pinning the star-shaped woodrush flower through its center. Tagg winked broadly at Jurkin. "Want to try it, spikedog?"

Robald pulled Tagg away, beckoning him urgently to sit and eat. It was obvious that Robald was no friend of Jurkin.

"Aunt Lollery has made us some of her delicious pancakes. We'd be well advised to consume them before some Dillypin does."

Great-Aunt Lollery served the delicious pancakes,

pouring everyone a beaker of greensap milk. Serving Tagg first, she whispered, "You eat 'earty now, sir, an' pay no heed to that Jurkin."

Nimbalo tucked into his food, remarking to Robald, "Wot's ole Jurkin glarin' at Tagg like that for? Lookit the face on 'im. You'd think 'e was sittin' on a wasp."

"Jurkin's a decent enough type, as far as Dillypins go," Robald explained. "But he's always got to be top hog wherever he goes. You shouldn't have showed him that knife trick, Tagg. He can't do it, so now he's working himself up to challenge you to some silly game that he knows he's best at. If I were you I'd keep my eye on him."

Robald's prediction turned out to be correct. Jurkin and his crew became extra noisy, tussling with each other and bumping into Tagg's table without apologizing. Then they started flicking small pebbles at one another. Jurkin waited until a young hog was between him and Tagg, and then flicked a pebble lazily at the youngster, who was swift enough to dodge it easily. The pebble struck Tagg on his cheek, which seemed to cause great hilarity among the Dillypins, Jurkin laughing loudest.

Tagg picked up the pebble, calling cheerfully to Jurkin, "Not much of a shot, mate. You'd better learn to throw properly!"

The otter tossed the pebble back over his shoulder and batted it hard with his tail. It zinged off, whacking the tip of Jurkin's nose painfully. Clapping a paw to his injured snout, Jurkin waited until the other Dillypins had stopped laughing. He hid the anger in his eyes by smiling at Tagg.

"Good job yore on'y a riverdog, or I'd spiketussle ye!"

Placing a paw against his forehead with the claws spread wide, Tagg smiled back at the big hedgehog. "Oh, don't let that stop ye, spikedog. Will this do for spikes?"

Spiketussling is the hedgehog form of wrestling, in which two hogs lock headspikes and try to throw each other. Tagg was offering his outspread pawclaws as spikes. Jurkin grimaced fiercely.

267

"Claws'll do fer spikes, if'n yore fool enough to try it, mate. I've been spiketusslin' champion o' the Dillypins since I was a babe. Come on, mate, an' I'll teach ye a lesson y'won't forget!"

He charged Tagg immediately, head down, spikes extended. The otter leaped over the table and met the onslaught, locking his claws into Jurkin's powerful headspikes. Dillypins scattered to get out of the way and benches and tables were overturned as the two roared aloud, pushing one another back and forth around the garden. Shrubs cracked, grass flew and leaves showered from low tree branches. Hedgehogs yelled.

"Give it the neckwhip, Jurkin, you've got 'im!"

Jurkin twisted his neck suddenly, but Tagg went with it, turning a somersault and landing upright. He saw the surprise on Jurkin's face as he carried on the maneuver by throwing another somersault in the same direction. Unable to halt his momentum, the hedgehog flew into the air, landing with a heavy thud on the ground. Belying his hefty bulk, he leaped up, and Tagg did it again, somersaulting so that his opponent was immediately floored once more. He repeated the move every time Jurkin rose. Six times the hedgehog hit the floor, then he tried to rise and fell back, panting hoarsely. Tagg leaned over Jurkin, holding him down, grinning into his face.

"Good game, eh? Want to try some more, spikedog?"

Jurkin held his paws up submissively. "Ye've cracked every spike on me back, y'great riverwhomper!"

Releasing Jurkin's spikes, Tagg helped him up. He grasped the hedgehog's paw and shook it firmly, announcing aloud, "I've never tangled with a beast so powerful in all my life. Good job you never got up again, mate, or you'd have licked me!"

Jurkin held Tagg's paw up, calling to all his crew, "This is my matey Tagg. Anybeast wants to fight with 'im 'as got t'fight with me too. Loll, bring more pancakes, will ye!"

Robald shook his head as he watched the pair scoffing

pancakes and swigging greensap milk like brothers. "I'm afraid it's all a bit beyond me, Nimbalo. Just look at them. Only a moment ago I thought they were trying to kill each other."

The harvest mouse shook his head admiringly. "Aye, my mate Tagg's like nobeast ye've ever met!"

Tagg told Jurkin his story. The hedgehog demolished a pancake as he listened, then he grunted approvingly. "So, yore trackin' these three vermin, Tagg? They're 'eaded downstream an' into Mossflower Wood, y'know. That's the way they went when we sent 'em packin'!"

Tagg rose from the table, licking honey from his paws. "Downstream into Mossflower, eh? Then I'm bound to go after them, friend. Goodbye, 'twas nice meeting you!"

Jurkin rose from the table with him. "Then ye'll be sailin' with the Dillypins, you an' the mousey. We're goin' that way too, so save the wear on yore paws, matey. Now I ain't takin' no fer an answer: you sail with us as far as we can track 'em afore they goes off inter the woodlands!"

Before they left, Nimbalo took issue with Robald and Great-Aunt Lollery, whom he had grown fond of. "Now lissen, Robald me ole pincushion, never you mind livin' out on the flatlands alone an' 'avin' this good 'ogwife runnin' after ye ten times a season with vittles. Yore Aunt Lollery ain't gettin' any younger, an' you should be livin' 'ere with 'er. If'n I 'ad a Great-Aunt Lollery, I wouldn't leave 'er defenseless on 'er own, I'd keep 'er comp'ny an' take better care of 'er!"

Robald stood looking shamefaced. "Now you come to point it out, friend Nimbalo, I have been a touch selfish. You're right, of course. I'll stay here with my kind nurse, if she'll have a fat lonely hermit, that is."

Lollery fidgeted with her spotless apron and sniffed. "Oh, go on with you, Master Robald. I promised your mama I'd look after you. Goodness knows 'tis a trek out onto those flatlands, carryin' great baskets o' vittles to ye. You're welcome to stay with me forever. Sometimes a

269

body gets so lonely in this liddle cottage that even the Dillypins are a welcome sight!"

That evening the sprawling raft took off into midstream, loaded with Dillypin hedgehogs of all shapes, ages and sizes. Tagg sat on the tiller rail with Nimbalo and Jurkin, holding several ropes apiece. These were attached to hogbabes, to stop them from falling in the water as they wrestled and played all over the broad deck. At the raft's center was a construction, part hut, part tent, complete with chimney, oven and galley fire, though there would be no cooking done that night, due to the fact that Great-Aunt Lollery had provisioned them out with all manner of excellent food: cheeses, breads, puddings, cakes, drinks, and extra supplies of her renowned pancakes, which were marvelous, hot or cold. Robald and his nurse waved them off from the bank as the peculiar vessel caught the midstream current and sailed off.

"Goodbye, friend Tagg, pleasant sailing, friend Nimbalo, thank you for all your help. I'd still be stuck in a ball of mud if you hadn't chanced along. Take care of yourselves!"

"Goodbye, Mr. Nimbalo, Mr. Tagg; goodbye, Dillypins!" The hedgehogs lined the deck, singing their farewell.

"Off down the streams away we go,
Where we'll land up I don't know,
With good ole grub an' lots o' drink,
We'll sail along until we sink.
Sink! Sink! Sink!
We're Dillypins an' we don't care,
As long as sky an' wind is fair,
An' when we spot the foe we say,
Yore just a good stonethrow away.
Way! Way! Way!
Weigh anchor mates we're outward bound,
But we'll be back next time around,

270

O'er swirlin' stream an' rushin' foam,
To eat you out o' house an' home.
Home! Home! Home!"

Lulled by the watersounds and late-evening sunrays flickering scarlet through drooping treetops, Tagg lay down on a woven deckmat. The little hogs had been hauled in by their mothers for supper and bed, and apart from the first nocturnal birdsong echoing from the dense woodlands things were fairly quiet. Jurkin held the tiller steady. He watched Nimbalo's head starting to nod and Tagg's eyelids growing heavy.

"Best get yore 'eads down, mates; it's been a long day for ye. Go on, sleep. I'll keep this ole scow on course an' watch for signs of the vermin."

Tagg allowed his eyes to close as he answered, "Thankee, mate. I'll wake around midnight and take a turn on the tiller, then you can catch a nap too!"

Nimbalo curled up close to Tagg's footpaws, yawning cavernously. "Ah, this is the life! Wake me next season, but do it gently, an' I'd like some 'ot pancakes an' dannylion tea when y'do. Yowch! Keep that footpaw still, ye great ruffian, or I'll sling yer in the water!"

Jurkin chuckled at the idea. "Savage liddle beast, ain't 'e?"

Nimbalo opened one eye and growled, "One more word out o' you, needlebritches, an' you'll find out why they calls me Nimbalo the Slayer!"

Once more Tagg's dreams were a kaleidoscope of red warriors, vermin faces and inexplicable events. He was running through deep woodlands, trying to catch up with the elusive figure of the mouse warrior, calling out after him, "Deyna, stop, wait for me!"

Amid the trees, the mouse turned, waving his wondrous sword. He called back things Tagg could not understand. There was a look of urgency on the armored mouse's face. Tagg felt a sudden kinship with him, a desire to go with him, to help with whatever needed to be done. Then Vallug appeared, a murderous snarl on his face as he fired an arrow from his bow. It was too late to dodge the shaft, but Tagg thrust out a paw to protect himself. He roared with pain as the arrow pierced his paw.

"Be still, ye great daft lump. Look wot you've gone an' done to yoreself. 'Old 'im still, Jurkin!"

Tagg woke to find the hedgehog pinning him flat, whilst Nimbalo tugged at his paw.

"Pass me that blade, mate, that'll get it out!"

Tagg looked up at Jurkin. "Wh-what happened?"

Shaking his head, the big rough hedgehog relieved the otter of his knife and gave it to Nimbalo.

"Wot 'appened? You tell me, matey. I think you was 'avin' a nightmare. Kickin' an' roarin' away like a madbeast. Pore ole Nimbalo 'ere was near knocked overboard, then you turns over facedown an' slams yore paw right onto a big deck splinter."

Tagg flinched as the harvest mouse released his paw and held a long pine splinter in front of his eyes.

"Lookit that. Size of a blinkin' cob o' firewood!"

Jurkin fetched a herbal paste, cleaned Tagg's paw and put a light softbark dressing on it, talking as he worked.

"Aye, that must've been some kind o' dream, Tagg. Can you remember wot it was about?"

Tagg winced as the paste entered his deep splinter wound. "I can only recall fragments, red warriors, a room with walls of red stone, a mouse warrior carrying a great sword. I think his name is Deyna, I'm not sure."

Jurkin tied off the dressing. "Sounded to me like you was dreamin' of Redwall Abbey."

Tagg felt his neckfur prickle at the sound of the name. "Redwall Abbey? What's that, and why should I be dreaming of it?"

Jurkin's spikes rippled evenly as he shrugged. "Sorry, mate, I can't tell ye that. But from wot you was shoutin' I knew it was summat to do with Redwall Abbey an' Martin the Warrior mouse. I know the place, I was there once."

The otter's eyes went wide with astonishment. "I thought all of this was only some imaginary place in my dreams. But you were there! Tell me about it, Jurkin. Please!"

Jurkin stroked his cheekspikes. "Ain't much to tell. My ole mum'n'dad took me there for a summer when I was just a liddle 'og. We went t'visit some fat ole cellarhog, a first cousin of a second brother twice removed, or summat like that. I remember, though, 'twas the 'appiest season o' my life. What a wunnerful place, Redwall Abbey. There was mice an' squirrels, moles, an' otters an' 'edge'ogs, just like me'n'you, mate, all livin' together there in peace. The vittles, oh, they was better'n anythin' you ever put in yore mouth. Er, that warrior mouse you mentioned, 'is name's not Deyna, it's Martin the Warrior. I saw 'is picture, woven on a big tapestry there, an' the sword too, 'angin' on the wall. Martin was one of the creatures who 'elped t'build Redwall Abbey, long long ago. They say 'e's been dead fer many seasons, but the spirit of Martin still 'elps an' protects that Abbey, aye, an' everybeast in it. Redwall's a very special place, Tagg."

The otter was bewildered by his friend's revelations. "But . . . but who is Deyna?"

The hedgehog's brow furrowed. "I dunno. I'm tellin' ye wot I recall of Redwall, but that was a long time ago, mate. I can't remember everythin', y'know!"

Tagg clenched his bound paw and stared hard at it. "Sorry, Jurkin. Neither can I. That's why I was asking you."

Nimbalo sat looking from one to the other and shaking his head. Tagg caught the look of comic amusement on his friend's face.

"What's the matter with you, grinning away, with a face on you like a mole sitting on a feather?"

The harvest mouse rested his chin on one paw. "Wot a pair, eh? Yore tellin' Jurkin about some ole dream you 'ad, an' Jurkin's tellin' you about the place in yore dream. A

273

place that 'e's been to!"

Jurkin stared hard at Nimbalo. "So?"

Puffing out his little chest, Nimbalo roared, "So why don't ye tell Tagg where the place, this Redwall Abbey, is, eh? Then 'e can go an' see fer hisself!"

It struck Tagg like a hammer blow. "Right! Tell us where Redwall is, mate!"

The Dillypin Chief gnawed thoughtfully on a facespike. "Er, if I can remember . . ."

BOOK THREE

Deyna

23

Dawn had passed, morning was through and Mossflower Woods shimmered gently in noontide sun. Durby and Feegle, however, were not aware of it as they lay bound inside a smelly sack down a dark disused mole tunnel. Poskra the water rat kicked the wriggling sack and snarled.

"Wun more peep out o' yiz an' inter the dinnerpot y'ill go!" He ran his tongue around the one tooth left in his gums. Life was hard, but good fortune had finally fallen on him. He cackled to himself. Fallen on him literally, right from the battlements of the Abbey's east wall.

Poskra was a loner. He had been thrown out of several tribes, lucky to be alive after the petty thefts and malicious acts he had perpetrated. Long seasons of travel and hardship had sharpened his natural cunning, but without leading to any great success, until he stumbled on Redwall Abbey. Knowing the good Redwallers would not even allow one like him past their gates, he had hung about watching, staying well hidden. He knew that sooner or later an opportunity would present itself, and it did. The previous evening he had been dozing in the woodland close to the east wall when he was roused by the shouts and giggling of small creatures, some of Redwall's precious Dibbuns. There atop the battlements, two tiny figures were staggering precariously along, squeaking and laughing. Instantly Poskra knew one or both of them would overbalance and fall, and he hoped fervently that they would fall outward, not inward. The little mousemaid leaped from one battlement to the next, where she stood teetering back and forth. Then the molebabe leaped and cannoned into her. Poskra could hardly stifle his delight as they plunged outward and down. Hurrying to them, he looped cords around their stunned forms and stuffed them both into the empty gunny sack he collected food in, when there was any. A squeak and a cry from inside the wall told him that there was a third Dibbun, who had most likely gone to rouse the Redwallers. He had to hurry. Hoisting the sack on his back, Poskra backed away into the woodlands, obliterating his tracks as he shuffled off. His best night's work in many a long season. Now he would stay hidden, maybe a full day, so that all the Abbeydwellers would be worried as to the whereabouts of the babes. Then he would approach the Abbey and trade for their lives. Damson wine was the love of Poskra's life: warming, rich, fruity and dark. Meat and tough stringy vegetables did not matter to him anymore; his toothless mouth could cope with neither. Mostly he lived off soups, which he made by boiling down any growing thing he came across, and off birds' eggs filched from low-lying nests. But damson wine, that was the stuff to keep warmth in a body on cold nights in the woodlands. He could live on it and would not have objected to drowning in it. Damson wine!

First he would take along some items of clothing, to convince the Redwallers of his position. Four or five flasks of the wine would do to start, then he would demand two casks, one for the safe return of each Dibbun. Poskra cackled again, this time a little louder. No, he would make it two casks ransom for each babe. Why not? He was in command. The things he could threaten to do to the infants would horrify the goodbeasts of Redwall so much that they'd be glad to pay up.

Popping his head out of the tunnel, Poskra made sure the coast was clear, then dragged the sack up after him. Emptying his prisoners out onto the grass, the water rat produced a long, vicious-looking needle, red with rust. He waved it like a wand before the terrified Dibbuns' eyes.

"Wun, jus' wun werd, an' yiz'll never see yer mummies n'more. Yew, mousey, gimme yiz apron. Moley, gimme yiz likkle belt. Look lively now, or I'll stick yiz both wid this bodkin!"

Wordlessly the Dibbuns did as they were bidden.

Eefera watched them from behind the rotting trunk of a fallen beech tree. Vallug lay on his back, fletching an arrow with a woodpigeon feather.

"Wot's the ole slimeskin up to now?"

Eefera dropped down beside the Bowbeast. "Takin' the apron offa the mouse an' the belt from the mole."

Vallug sighted one eye along the arrow shaft, testing its level. "Wot does the fool want t'do that for?"

Always the clever one, Eefera knew the answer. "I think the rat's kidnapped 'em an' he's after ransom from the Abbey. We could use those two infants."

Vallug thought a moment before he caught on to the idea. "Aye, we could use 'em as hostages an' trade 'em for the otter!"

There was no disguising the sarcasm in Eefera's voice. "By the carcass of Sawney, did ye think of that all by yerself?"

The arrow point suddenly nicked Eefera as it pressed against his neck. Vallug smiled coldly. "Aye, I did. I've 'ad a few good ideas lately. Do I really need a partner like you, that's one of 'em!"

The arrow point pressed harder, but Eefera did not

seem impressed. "Cut yore own nose off to spite yer face, wouldn't ye, Vallug? The game ain't over yet; you'll need me. Now, don't y'think you'd best do summat about those babes afore the rat gets away with 'em, instead of lyin' 'ere arguin', eh?"

Poskra was trying to stuff the Dibbuns back into the sack, but he was encountering difficulty doing it. Feegle squeaked in pain as he grabbed her by the neck. Though still bound, Durby launched himself on the water rat and bit his ear.

"Yurr, ratten, you'm leavin' moi Feegul be!"

Poskra let go of Feegle. Clapping a paw to his bleeding ear, he raised the needle, kicking Durby over onto his back. "I make yiz scream loud fer dat, mole!"

Poskra stood for a moment with the rusty needle raised, then dropped it. His eyes turned upward, and he fell upon Durby, with a newly fletched arrow protruding from the back of his skull.

"Hurr," the molebabe called breathlessly from beneath Poskra's body. " 'Elp oi, Feegul. Ee ratten be a-crushen oi gurtly!"

The mousebabe gave a shrill scream of fright. Eefera's evil tattooed face loomed over her as he pulled the carcass of Poskra off Durby and tossed it aside.

"Nasty ole water rat that 'un, wasn't 'e, mousey?"

Durby smiled politely at the murderous Vallug. "Gudd day to ee, zurr. You'm be a-taken us'n's back to Redwall?"

Vallug shouldered his bow and gave Durby a long stare. "Oh aye, we're takin' yer back to Redwall right enough!"

He bundled them both into the sack.

Mhera was beating her way through a fern bed with a willow withe, calling out the lost babes' names. "Feegle, Durby, answer if you can hear me. It's me, Mhera!"

Fwirl came hurtling out of a sycamore, twigs and leaves

falling all about as she landed near Mhera, pointing, "Over that way! I've found them. They're in danger!"

Mhera grasped her friend's paw. "Go back to the Abbey and get help!"

Fwirl clenched her paws resolutely. "There isn't any time for that. I've got a plan. Come on!"

The first stone struck Eefera in the eye. He dropped the sack and clapped both paws to the eye, staring at the very pretty squirrelmaid who was readying another stone to hurl.

"Yer little scum. Get 'er, Vallug!"

The second stone stung Vallug's ear, clacking off the side of his bow. Fwirl chose another stone from her pouch. This time it hit Eefera's left footpaw hard. He danced about, screwing his face up and haranguing the Bowbeast.

"Get the squirrel, don't jus' stand there. Kill 'er!"

Fwirl dodged nimbly, and the shaft quivered in a rowan trunk. She caught Vallug a beauty on the shoulder with a biggish stone. Adding insult to injury, she popped her tongue out impudently. "Nyaah nyaah! Daft old paintyface!"

Eefera began hobbling toward her, but a pebble caught him smartly in the throat. Her next stone clacked hard off the paw that Vallug was using to draw back his bowstring. The arrow fell awkwardly from the bow, and Vallug wrung his paw in the air. Eefera rubbed at his throat, and another stone caught his jaw. He stiffened with rage at his tormentor's merry laughter.

"Hahahaha! I nearly got that one down your big mouth. Hahaha!"

Eefera grabbed the sack and knotted its neck, unsuccessfully trying to dodge the well-aimed stones. He slung it upon a broken branch protruding from an ash tree. Vallug had picked up his bow, though every time he tried to take aim Fwirl took his mind off the task by hitting him

281

with stones. Eefera rushed her, both paws up to protect his face, and a pebble bounced off his forehead. *Thokk!* His paw came away bloody when he touched the spot.

"Why, yer liddle . . . I'll skin yer for that!"

He waved a paw behind his back. Vallug saw it and began circling to get behind their attacker. Eefera advanced, dodging from tree to tree. Fwirl backed skillfully off.

Mhera emerged from behind the ash trunk and unhooked the sack from the broken branch stub. A sound from behind caused her to turn swiftly. Broggle was pointing at the sack.

"Still no sign of them. What's in the sack? I heard a lot of noise over this way, so I came to see. Where's Fwirl?"

Using teeth and claws, Mhera ripped the sack apart. "Broggle, don't ask questions, take Durby, I'll take Feegle. Run for the Abbey, this way, not that way. If you see Redwallers in the woods, tell them to get inside quickly. Now go, as fast as you can. I'll be right behind you!"

Eefera and Vallug kept their eyes riveted on a low bush where Fwirl had gone to earth. Vallug sent an arrow ripping into it, and there was a faint scream. The Bowbeast smiled, notching another shaft to his bowstring, and both vermin advanced slowly. The delivery of the second arrow was followed by a low gasp. Vallug Bowbeast straightened up confidently.

"First one wounded 'er, but that second arrow finished 'er off!"

They arrived at the bush to find both arrows buried in the soil at its roots. Furiously they began destroying the shrub to find their elusive foe. A rain of pebbles dropped on their heads from the upper branches of a nearby elm, followed by a dramatic cry.

"Oooohhhhh! You got me! That first one wounded me, but the second arrow finished me off. Oooooohhhh! Hahahahaha!"

Fwirl shot off through the treetops, too high and fast for

any arrow to follow. Eefera looked stonefaced at his companion.

"I'll wager when we get back to that sack those young 'uns will be well gone."

It was Vallug's turn to sound sarcastic. "Did yer think o' that all by yerself?"

It was late afternoon. All gates had been secured and every Redwaller was safe inside the Abbey. Mhera had lookouts and wallguards posted all around the ramparts. The elders were holding an impromptu meeting in Cavern Hole, and she hurried down to join them. Seldom had she seen Cregga so wrathful. The Badgermum brought her paw down on the table with a blow that almost split it. She bared her teeth, growling ferociously, "Vermin in Mossflower, trying to steal our Dibbuns? Gurrrr, if I had the sight of just one eye they'd wish their mothers never gave birth to them. You saw them, Mhera. What were they like?"

As best she could, the ottermaid described Vallug and Eefera, mentioning the barbarous facial tattoos of the Juska clan.

Boorab waited until she had finished. "Hmm, sound like a right pair o' scallawags if y'ask me. Young Fwirl said there was another, an old rat, but one of those two bounders slew him with an arrow, wot. Scoutin' party, that's what us chaps need, spot of reccying in the jolly old woodlands, wot. See how many more of the tattooed blighters are out there an' so on. Right, I'll volunteer to command said party—"

Mhera took it on herself to interrupt the hare. "I think Fwirl can do all the scouting and spying that's required. She's a very courageous creature, and deserves our wholehearted thanks for her brave efforts. Thank you for your kind offer, Mr. Boorab, but it would be better if you stayed put here. There's few enough of fighting age since Skipper and his crew went off to the Hullabaloo. This Abbey and its creatures' safety is our main concern; we don't want any outside skirmishes. The defense of Redwall is most important."

Boorab's reply was, to say the least, a trifle frosty. "Oh, beg pardon an' chop off my tongue for mentionin' it. Tut! So that's how a gallant chap gets treated for offerin' help, wot!"

Mhera immediately set about appeasing him. "But you misunderstood me, sir. I already had plans for you. We need an officer, one who knows what he's doing, to command the wallguards and see to the outer walls' security. I was hoping that you'd accept the post."

Boorab sprang to attention, knocking his chair over, and saluted with a wooden ladle, almost raising a bump on his head. "Say no more, O fair one, say no more. I'm the very chap you're lookin' for, wot, wot wot! Leave it to me! I'll straighten out that idle sloppy lot on our walltops, or m'name ain't Bellscut Oglecrop Obrathon Ragglewaithe Audube Baggscut. Commencin' duties as of now. Permission t'leave the mess, Cregga marm!"

Cregga made a small salute. "Permission granted. Carry on, sah!"

Boorab performed a smart left turn, tripped over the leg of his fallen chair, went flat and leaped upright in the same movement. He marched off, muttering under his breath in fine military form.

"Right, look out, you bunch of limp lilies, here comes an officer on parade, wot! I'll have your guts for garters, spikes for supper an' snack on your spines, when I've straightened 'em up a bit! Hoho, me bold laddie bucks, eyes front, chests out, shoulders square, backs straight, paws at an angle t'the seam o' the garments, wot wot, wotwotwotwotwot!"

Cregga and the elders waited until Boorab was well out of earshot before the Badgermum nodded to Mhera.

"Well done, friend, that was very diplomatic of you. So, then, what's your next move to be?"

Mhera felt rather flustered. "I'm sorry, Cregga, I didn't mean to interrupt an elders' meeting. I only came to see if I could be of any help."

Cregga turned her sightless eyes toward Brother Hoben. "Well, I for one think Mhera's been an enormous help. Already she's got rid of that babbling hare and taken care of the Abbey defenses at the same time. What d'you think, Brother?"

Hoben watched the other elders' faces carefully as he replied, "I couldn't agree with you more, marm. Quick-thinking heads and sensible decisions are what's needed among us old fogies, a drop of young blood to liven things up. I suggest we allow our Mhera to take charge of things. I've a feeling she won't let us down. Let's put it to the vote!"

There was an immediate chorus of ayes, but Cregga's sharp ears missed nothing. "Sister Alkanet, why do you choose to stay silent?"

The stern Sister made her way slowly to the door. "I won't say yes or no to Mhera's taking charge. However, I must be honest. I think she's far too young. It's too much responsibility, and I think you'll live to regret your decision." And Alkanet swept off up the stairs to her infirmary.

Foremole Brull twiddled her digging claws and fixed her eyes on the table in front of her. "She'm a gurtly h'odd mouse, that 'un, but she'm atitled to urr umpinnyin'. Hurr, 'tain't moine, tho'. Oi loikes miz Mhura!"

Filorn smiled across at the kind Foremole. "Thanks for your confidence in my daughter. Well, Mhera, you'd best answer Cregga. What's our next move?"

The elders' hopeful faces dispelled any nervousness Mhera felt. "At the moment there's not a great deal we can do. If needs be, Fwirl can easily scout the woodlands close to our Abbey. As for the rest, we've got to keep an eye on the Dibbuns, see none of them try straying outside. You all know by now that even a locked gate or high walls won't stop some of those little rogues. The only thing we can do is to sit tight and hope the tattooed vermin will move off sooner or later. Our walls are patrolled, and we can sleep safely knowing Mr. Boorab is commanding the guard."

This last remark was greeted by chuckles from the elders. Friar Bobb heaved himself upright, straightening his apron. "Villains or no villains, I've got cabbage an' fennel bake to make, aye, and raspberry cream turnovers. Redwallers don't quit having supper because there's vermin in the woodlands, oh no!" The meeting broke up amid creatures going off to their chores.

Mhera was helping Cregga from her chair when the Badgermum began rummaging in her belt pouch.

"Oh, I almost forgot in all the excitement. I found one of your pieces of lilac-smelling cloth. I assume it's the same color as the others. It was lying among the fresh torches we put by the east wallgate when we were searching last night." She passed the ottermaid a scrap of the green homespun.

Mhera inspected the cloth. It was exactly the same as the others: rough faded green homespun, with a faint odor of lilacs. Inscribed on it in the same vertical capitals was the word WITTAGALL.

Cregga twitched her muzzle impatiently. "Well, is it one of those pieces of cloth? Does it have any message on it? Tell me, Mhera."

"What? Oh, er, sorry, Cregga. It says WITTAGALL, whatever that's supposed to mean. I wonder who left it there?"

Cregga leaned on Mhera's shoulder as they mounted the stairs. "How should I know? I'm an old blind badger, not a magician or a mystery solver. It's not important how it got there, it's the word and what it means. WITTAGALL. What d'you think it is?"

Mhera stopped, allowing Cregga to rest her paws.

"You're asking me? I'm only a simple ottermaid, not a wise old Badgermum who's lived more seasons than anybeast I know and can tell just by a sound who it is and what they're doing."

Cregga tweaked the ottermaid's cheek. "You, my pretty maid, are an old head on young shoulders!"

24

Across from the path in front of Redwall's main gate, which faced west, was a partially dried up ditch separating the path from the sprawling flatlands. Twilight's last vestiges were gleaming as Eefera stood in the ditch, looking up at the solid red sandstone heights of the Abbey's outer wall.

"Supposin' the Taggerung ain't in there, what then?"

Vallug rubbed beeswax along his bowstring to keep it supple. "Huh, 'e's in there all right, I kin feel it in me bones."

Eefera took out his long curved knife and began digging at some wild ramsons that were poking through the ditch side. "Hmm. Ain't much chance of us findin' out if the Taggerung's in there or not. It's all 'igh walls, locked doors an' guards walkin' 'round betwixt the battlements. We got no chance o' gettin' in there to seek 'im out." He began crunching the garlicky-smelling plant. Vallug turned away in disgust from the weasel's breath.

"Yurk! D'you 'ave to eat that stuff? I'll tell ye a good way fer us to get in. You climb up that wall an' breathe all over 'em, that'll knock the guards out so you kin open the door fer me."

Eefera wiped soil from another clump of ramsons and

bit into it. "Very funny. Yore jokes'll be the death of you one day, I 'ope. But the way I sees it, we don't 'ave to try an' get inter that place, if'n we can make the Taggerung come out to us."

Vallug gagged as he turned and caught another whiff of ramsons. "Go on then, stinkmouth, tell me 'ow we do that. Why should the Taggerung come out if'n 'e knows we want t'kill 'im, eh?"

Eefera picked his teeth with a filthy pawnail. "Simple. Yore the great Bowbeast, aren't yer? All's you gotta do is kill one o' those guards up yonder, just as a sort o' message. Pretty soon they'll want t'know wot we want, so we, I mean you, kill another one. I'll tell 'em we'll slay every Redwaller we see until they gives us the Taggerung. I think that's a pretty good idea, don't you?"

Vallug eyed the figures patrolling the walltop. "Oh, it's a marvelous idea, unless I kills one an' they all comes chargin' out an' chops us ter fish scraps!"

Eefera spat out a soily bit of vegetation. "Yore plan is better, then? Go on, tell it t'me."

Vallug knew he had lost the argument, so he blustered. "D'ye remember wot Sawney said? 'E didn't want ter tangle with the warriors in there. Sawney Rath was a wise Chief."

Eefera laughed scornfully. "Aye, was! But now Sawney's a dead Chief, an' it wasn't no Redwall warriors did it, 'twas 'is own pet otter. So are yer goin' along with my idea, or are ye scared?"

Vallug pushed his face nose to nose with Eefera, despite the smell. "I ain't scared of yew an' I ain't scared of those up there, an' if yer don't believe me then watch this!"

Fitting a shaft to his bowstring, Vallug drew it back, judging the breeze and the height. He fired and hit one of the guards standing left of the threshold above the main gate. Vallug watched the Redwaller crumple below the battlements and sneered. "Now tell me I'm scared. Vallug

Bowbeast ain't afraid of anybeast 'is arrows can slay. That goes fer them an' you too. Hoi! Come back 'ere. Where are yer goin'?"

Eefera turned a pitying smile upon the ferret. "I'm gettin' out of the way, back inter the woods. They'll prob'ly 'ave archers, spearbeasts an' slingers to fire back at us. But don't lissen t'me. You stay there an' chat to yerself all night. I'm off!"

Vallug crouched and followed Eefera at a run, north along the muddy streambed, to where they could make the trees in safety.

Broggle saw the arrow strike, and dashed toward the fallen Redwaller, roaring out in anguish, "It's old Hoarg! They've killed Hoarg the Gatekeeper!"

Boorab was on the spot immediately, calling out orders. "Stay at your posts, keep those heads down, I'll see to this!"

Tears streamed down Broggle's face as he arrived on the scene. "What would anybeast want to slay old Hoarg for? He never hurt a living thing in all his life!"

Boorab swiftly pushed Broggle's head below the parapet. "You'll be next if y'don't keep your bally head down, laddie buck. Stow the tears, he ain't hit that bad, wot!"

The ancient dormouse had been wearing an old copper bucket as a helmet, with the handle under his chin. Vallug's arrow was stuck tight in the side of the bucket, having pierced it. Fwirl came bounding up and peered under the bucket, which was set firmly on the stunned Gatekeeper's head.

"Don't try to remove the arrow or take the bucket off Hoarg's head. The shaft's gone through his ear."

Tucking the ladle tight against his side, Boorab issued more orders. "Listen up in the ranks there, chaps, sound the alarm bells, two stretcher bearers up here on the double, carry this poor fellow up to Sister Alkanet's infirmary. Steady on now, those carrying slings, load 'em up an' wait on my command. When I give the word, heads up, pepper the ditch below the threshold with one good volley, then heads down smartly, an' keep 'em down! Ready . . . slings!"

A sharp rain of pebbles battered the ditch where Vallug and Eefera had been. Two moles hoisted Hoarg between them and carried him down the wallsteps. His eyes opened as he was hustled down, and he groaned woefully.

"Owwww, my pore ear! Wot hit me? Where are ye takin' me?"

"Hurr, you'm be'd shot in ee bucket, zurr. Us'n's be's takin' ee to yon affirmery. Doan't ee wurry, Sister h'Alkurnet'll fizzick ee gudd, you'm feel gurtly well agin then, hurr hurr!"

Hoarg's voice echoed around the bucket as it tipped forward over his eyes. "If I'd knowed I was goin' to be dragged off an' physicked by that ole mouse, I'd have let the vermin kill me!"

In the absence of kitchen staff, who were part of Boorab's wallguard, Mhera and Gundil helped Filorn and Friar Bobb to make the supper. Between them they made cabbage and fennel bake into pasties, which they parceled up with table linen, placing the raspberry cream turnovers on trays and filling a clean pail with dandelion cordial. Filorn helped Mhera to load up a trolley to take out to the wallguards.

As she worked, the ottermaid kept reciting to herself, "Hittagall Pittagall Wittagall! Hittagall Pittagall Wittagall!"

Filorn looked oddly at her daughter. "What in the name of rudders are you talking about?"

Mhera placed a final tray of turnovers on the trolley. "I

wish I knew, Mama. It's the three words from the three strips of cloth. Hittagall, Pittagall and Wittagall. I just keep on repeating them to myself in the hope that they'll suddenly make sense. Trouble is, they don't."

Filorn lowered her voice confidentially. "Then stop saying them or you'll have everybeast saying that you're acting like a Dibbun. Cregga and Hoben have given you a lot of responsibility, and the elders will look to you for guidance. Until this vermin trouble is over, you'd do well to abandon any puzzles and riddles. Don't you realize, Mhera, you are practically in charge of Redwall Abbey for the moment!"

Before Mhera could reply, the irrepressible Boorab came marching in, his nose atwitch at the smell of food.

"What's that? In charge of Redwall Abbey, young feller m'gel? Aha, well you may be, but yours truly is in charge an' command of the defenses, wot. Jolly old outer wall and all who flippin' well patrol it. Responsibility's m'middle name, doncha know!"

Mhera rapped the hare's paw, which was straying dangerously close to the array of raspberry cream turnovers. "Then why aren't you out there carrying out your duties? The kitchen is no place for a commanding officer."

Boorab swaggered over to Filorn, who had always been sympathetic to him, and gave her his best stiff-upper-lip smile. "Very observant of your beautiful daughter, marm. Everything's hunky-dory out on the ramparts, no vermin showin' their lousebound features about, all quiet an' orderly y'might say. Thought I'd take the opportunity of poppin' in to check up on rations for the troops. One owes it t'the lower-rank chaps, y'know, officer has to feed the faces under his command. Me bounden duty, y'see!"

Filorn curtsied to the hare and presented him with a turnover. "I understand, sir. Perhaps you'd like to sample one of these, to make sure 'tis of the right quality for your wallguards?"

Mhera watched in amazement as the turnover vanished into the gluttonous hare's mouth. Licking his paws, Boorab closed both eyes and smacked his lips appreciatively. "First class, ladies, absoballylutely top hole, wot. A and B the C of D, I'd say. Let me help you take the jolly trolley to my starvin' companions freezin' away the bitter night hours on the rugged ramparts, wot!" He trundled the cart off, with Mhera and Filorn hurrying behind.

"You shouldn't encourage him, Mama," Mhera whispered disapprovingly. "Starving companions freezing away the bitter night? It's hardly a long while since they were last fed, and it's a warm summer night without even a breeze!"

Filorn watched the odd lanky figure hurrying across the lawn, taking great care not to spill any food from the trolley. "Don't be too hard on Boorab. His heart's in the right place and he's always been very gallant and polite to me."

Mhera linked paws with her mother as they followed the trolley. "You're too softhearted by far. Oh, and what does Boorab mean by A and B the C of D? Sounds like some kind of code."

"I asked him once. He said it's some old military saying," Filorn explained. "The first letters of the phrase *above and beyond the call of duty*. A and B the C of D. Apparently his grandsire learned it, when he served with a group of hares called the Long Patrol."

When they reached the wallsteps, Foremole Brull detailed six of her moles to carry the trolley up to the battlements. Mhera had always admired the friendly mole leader, and she stroked Brull's velvety paw affectionately.

"Thank you, marm. I was wondering how we'd get a loaded trolley up there."

Brull had a smile so jolly, it seemed to light up the night. "Doan't ee wurry, miz. They'm h'only likkle, but them'm axeedingly moighty. Ho, boi the way, do ee be's cleckin' likkle piecings o' ee greeny cloth?"

Mhera felt her curiosity aroused. "Yes, I am collecting little pieces of cloth. Have you got one?"

Brull produced the object from inside her sleeve. "Oi foinded this 'un stucked to ee bakklement summ whoile agoo."

It was a green homespun strip, still smelling faintly of lilac. Mhera read the writing on it. UITTAGALL.

"Be's et h'any gudd to ee, miz?"

Mhera blinked absentmindedly. "What? Oh, er, yes. Thank you very much, Brull."

Brull helped Filorn to serve the food as they trundled the trolley around the ramparts. Filorn looked down to the gatehouse wallsteps, where her daughter was sitting studying something. "I thought Mhera was going to help us serve? What's she doing sitting down there in the dark?"

Foremole Brull busied herself with the cabbage and fennel pasties. "Ho, leave urr be, missus, she'm lukkin' at one o' ee ole greeny cloths oi foinded oop yurr."

From out of nowhere, Fwirl landed at Mhera's side. She peered over the ottermaid's shoulder. "Found another of your cloth puzzles, eh?"

Mhera shook the fabric under Fwirl's nose. "Foremole Brull found it not long ago, stuck to a battlement. It says UITTAGALL. Now I've got four cloths and I don't know what even one of them means. But there's an even greater puzzle, Fwirl. This cloth couldn't have stayed stuck to a battlement all those seasons since Abbess Song was alive. It would have rotted or blown away ages ago. The riddle may be an ancient and mysterious one, but I've been thinking hard about it and I've come up with something. Listen to this. The first two pieces we found could have lain there since the time of Abbess Song. One was inside the bell tower, high and dry on the beam, the other was part of an infirmary coverlet. However, look at these last two scraps of cloth. One was found by Cregga, out in the open by the east wallgate, the other was found by Brull up on the walltop, again out in the open. Neither of the outside cloths could have survived the sun, winds, snow, ice and rains of many seasons. So what does that tell us, my friend?"

Fwirl caught on immediately. Her tail whirled excitedly. "Somebeast in the Abbey is putting them there. Right?"

Mhera gripped Fwirl's paws and squeezed them. "Exactly! We're going to keep our eyes open from now on, Fwirl. Because whoever it is holds the key to this whole mystery!"

Filorn came down the wallsteps to find Mhera and Fwirl whirling each other around, chanting singsong style, "Hittagall pittagall wittagall uittagall! Hittagall pittagall wittagall uittagall!"

"Mhera, what have I told you, miss?" Filorn whispered urgently. "Redwallers are watching you. Think of your responsibilities!"

The ottermaid halted momentarily and smiled impudently. "Boorab's a commander, and if he can go around saying A and B the C of D, wot wot, then I'm allowed a bit of fun too. Besides, I'm younger than him. Come on, Fwirl, I'm enjoying this!"

Squirrelmaid and ottermaid started whirling around again. "Hittagall pittagall wittagall uittagall!"

Filorn relented. She helped Brull push the empty trolley back to the Abbey, smiling and shaking her head. "Just look at those two young 'uns. Mad as march hares!"

Brull nodded admiringly as she watched the performance. "Hurr hurr, bless ee gudd 'earts, missus, they'm h'only young once. Oi cudd darnce loike that once; wish't oi cudd naow. Hurr hurr hurr, oi'm gurtly fattied. Moi darncin' days be's long dunn!"

25

The Dillypin raft was well into deep woodland, floating leisurely along the broad river. It was one of those halcyon summer afternoons Tagg would always remember. After a superb lunch of pancakes and bilberry cordial, he lounged on the stern rail with Jurkin, keeping the raft on course and watching the current. Smooth flowing and deep the water ran, clear to its bed. Long trailing weed tresses, submerged flat rocks and fleet darting minnow shoals passed beneath the rudder. Dragonflies and other insects patrolled the shallows, sheltered by overhanging trees from swallows and willow warblers. Jurkin studied the land, as did Tagg, both with the eyes of experienced trackers. The hedgehog nodded sagely.

"Aye, see the broken sedge yonder? Yore vermin passed this way. Bound fer Redwall, if'n I ain't mistaken, matey."

Tagg had been following the telltale signs. He looked up. "Redwall? You mean they're going to the same place I'm heading?"

Jurkin kept his eyes on the bank and shallows. He shrugged. "Mebbe so. We'll find out tomorrer when we comes t'the big rocks. We'll stop then, an' if'n y'see their trail goin' off inland, then you'll know fer sure. Great

pins'n'prickles, lissen to that liddle mousemate o' yourn.
'E's a worse fibber'n me!"

Nimbalo was entertaining the Dillypin hogs, who sat
around listening wide-eyed as he related a monologue of
his adventures. Waving a celery stick, he parried and
thrust at invisible foes as he leaped about, reciting
dramatically.

"I'm Nimbalo the Slayer, haha hoho,
A strange ole name ye may say,
So I'll tell ye how I won me title,
Long ago, on a fine summer day.
I was the son of a mighty King,
Me an' two hundred others,
Half of them was sisters of course,
But the other two halves was brothers.
We was out on a picnic one evenin',
In a forest all dark'n'thick,
Some picked ants out the pudden,
While I just picked on a nick.
Suddenly we was under attack,
By ten thousand vermin, 'twas bad,
Some began shoutin' for 'elp an' aid,
An' others for Mum an' Dad!
There was willful weasels, rotten rats,
Fat foxes, fierce ferrets an' stoats,
With swords an' knives, to take our lives,
An' one had a spear in 'is coat!
When this I did spy, 'Hoho,' sez I,
'It looks like you scum wanna fight?'
So I slew a score wid my left paw,
An' another twelve with me right.
'That mouse is a slayer,' their leader cried,
'But by me spear he'll die!'
So I knocked that rat flat,
With a swipe of me hat,

An' the crust off a dead apple pie.
Then takin' a sword, his whiskers I chopped,
All the while he was shoutin' out 'Save me!'
But in the din 'twas hard to hear,
I thought he was shoutin' out 'Shave me!'
Those villains dashed off in a panic,
'Cos they saw I was in a bad mood,
'Go boil yore bottoms,' I shouted,
(an' other things far more rude).
That's why me name's Nimbalo,
An' I'm a Slayer bold,
I'll fight the good fight,
From morn until night,
But not if me supper gets cold!"

"Did you chase da naughty villuns an' catch 'em, Mista
Nimbal?" a hogbabe piped up when the applause had
died down.

The harvest mouse chomped on his celery sword. "No,
they caught me an' killed me, but I'll get 'em next time!"

Tagg shook his head in mock despair at his friend.
"You're a dreadful fibber, Nimbalo."

Patting his well-filled stomach, the harvest mouse
winked. "After that good lunch, matey, I'm a sleepy
dreadful fibber. I think 'tis about time fer me noontide
nap." He stretched out on a deckmat and was soon
snoring.

It was not long after that Tagg noticed the hogbabes and
young ones chattering excitedly.

"We're coming up t'the water meadows," Jurkin
explained. "They likes to paddle in the shallows an' pick
berries. Some good 'uns grow 'round there. But if'n yore
in an 'urry, Tagg, we'll sail on by 'em."

Tagg would not hear of the idea. "No no, let the little
'uns have their fun. We can always make up the time later.
I like water meadows too, you know."

Jurkin chuckled. "So do I, mate. Thankee."

The hogbabes were all agog, dancing and waving their paws. "Warty medders! There's a warty medders!"

The barge hove in to the vast woodland-fringed area. It was a pretty sight. No more than waist deep, the entire expanse was carpeted in water lilies, plant life and bulrushes. All manner of insect life, including many beautiful butterflies, hovered on the still noontide air. Whooping and yelling, the Dillypins scooted off, some to paddle, others to gather berries and fruit. Tagg left Nimbalo sleeping and joined a bunch of mothers and babes with baskets. They found pears, apples, hazelnuts, blackberries, raspberries and wild damsons, all around the far-flung margin.

They returned aboard in the late noon, happy with their harvest, speculating on the flans, pies, puddings and preserves that would be made with them. The otter put down the two babes he had been carrying shoulder high and waved to Jurkin, who had stayed aboard the raft.

"I enjoyed that. 'Twas well worth it, mate. Where's Nimbalo?"

The Dillypin leader nodded for'ard. "Sittin' up yon with a face like stone. 'E woke just after you went, been sittin' like that all afternoon."

Nimbalo did not even look up when Tagg sat beside him. Never had the otter seen his harvest mouse friend so glum and depressed. By the marks on his face he had obviously shed tears. Tagg leaned close and lowered his voice.

"What's up, matey? Are you all right?"

Nimbalo continued gazing into the water. "Aye, I suppose so. It's just this place, I can't stand it."

Tagg was astonished. The water meadow was a place of great beauty. "Why, what's so awful about it? Tell me."

Nimbalo indicated the far margin with a nod. "Jus' beyond there was where I was reared by my papa. I never knew my mother. Maybe she died when I was young, that's wot I like to think. But 'twas prob'ly Papa

299

drove 'er to run off. 'E was a hard cruel beast. I hid in these 'ere reeds many a time, when Papa was goin' to take a belt to me, for not doin' the chores the way 'e wanted 'em done. There was jus' me an' Papa t'keep the farm goin'. I was never allowed any friends. Little food an' lots o' beltin', that was my life. Said 'e did it to bring me up proper. Papa used to trade with beasts usin' the river, like these Dillypins. I never met 'em, Papa made me stay 'ome an' scrub out the farm'ouse. Always took 'is belt off t'me when 'e got back. Said I was lazy an' shiftless. Enny'ow, one night when I'd growed a bit, Papa took the belt off once too often, I fought with 'im an' ran off. Never been back since. That's why I ain't fond o' this place: 'twas my ole stampin' grounds. Will ye do me a favor, Tagg?"

The big otter was almost close to tears himself. "Of course I will. Anything for you, mate, anything!"

Nimbalo stood up, dusting himself down. "Will ye come with me, over t'the farm? I want Papa to see that I never turned out worthless an' lazy."

Tagg forced a jolly laugh for his friend's benefit. "Hohoho, worthless and lazy, you? Come on, matey, we'll show the miserable old sourface how his son looks now. Lead on, Slayer!" He winked at Jurkin as they disembarked from the raft. "Hold the boat for us, will you, matey? We've got a small errand ashore. We'll be back by suppertime."

The Dillypin Chief tightened off a mooring rope. "Righto, Tagg, supper'll be ready an' waitin'. There'll be all kinds o' good vittles cooked up from the stuff we got today."

Beyond the far side of the water meadow, Tagg and Nimbalo made their way through a grove of trees. They emerged on the edge of a small flatland, which was sectioned and cultivated. Directly across the field was a thatched cottage. The harvest mouse halted and gave the scene a brief glance.

"Hmm, things ain't changed much. Same ole patch o' dirt. Strange, though. Somethin's not quite right."

Tagg looked down at his friend's furrowed brow. "Like what?"

Nimbalo gnawed at his lip. "There's no sign o' Papa. 'E usually works 'til dusk. If 'e was in the farm'ouse there'd be smoke risin' from the chimbly, an' there ain't a single wisp. Somethin's wrong, I can feel it!" He took off at a run across the field, his paws sending young lettuce and radishes flying, Tagg hard on his tail.

"Nimbalo, stop! Wait for me! Slow down, mate!"

But the harvest mouse had kicked open the unlatched door and dashed inside. Tagg put on a burst of speed and chased in after him, halting immediately as he crossed the doorstep.

There in a pool of afternoon sunlight from the single window sat Nimbalo, amid the wreckage of what had once been his home. Chairs were smashed, curtains and coverlets ripped and food trampled everywhere. Nimbalo's father lay dead, stretched out with a gaping wound in his chest.

Tagg knelt and studied a bloodstained pawprint in the dust. He breathed one word. "Gruven!"

Nimbalo had been sitting head in paws by his father's body. At the sound of Tagg's voice he looked up at the wall above the fireplace, where two nails were driven. "They killed 'im with 'is own axe. Lookit that wound, only one weapon could've done that. Papa kept an ole battle-axe over the fireplace there. Ohhhh, Tagg! I know 'e was only a mean-spirited misery of a mouse, but why'd they slay 'im like that an' wreck the place they way they did? Ohhhh, Papa, Papa, wot was it made you like ye were?"

Tagg placed a paw gently on Nimbalo's shoulder. "Is there anything I can do, friend?"

The harvest mouse sniffed and scrubbed a paw across both eyes. "No, mate, 'cept leave me alone 'ere awhile. You go an' wait across the field. Go on, I won't keep ye long."

Tagg closed the door behind him as he left.

Sitting in the tree shade at the field's edge the otter stared at the farmhouse, feeling immensely sad for his little friend. Nimbalo had been nervous on the way over from the water meadows. It had caused him to laugh and joke about what a horrible old grouse his papa had been, and how he was going to show him that his son had not turned out the same. Poor Nimbalo. This was the last thing he had expected. What a homecoming for him.

Tagg wondered what his own father had been like, his mother too. He knew from Ribrow that his father was dead, but maybe, just maybe, he had a mother somewhere. Did she ever wonder what had become of her baby son? The otter sat for a long time puzzling various unknown bits of his former life, and then he saw a wisp of white smoke rising from the farmhouse chimney.

Nimbalo emerged, carrying a heavily buckled belt and a nail from the chimney wall. Closing the door, he took a rock and nailed the belt to the doorjamb. Passing the belt through the door handle, he tugged, buckling it tight, locking the door shut securely. He sniffed, scrubbed at his eyes one last time and straightened his shoulders. Tagg rose and greeted his friend as he paced back across the field.

"You look a bit better now, mate. Ready to go?"

The harvest mouse nodded briskly. "I cleaned the place up, made a fire out o' some broken furniture an' dressed Papa in a clean smock. I sat 'im in 'is favorite chair an' then locked the place up with that . . . er, I locked the place up good'n'tight. D'ye think Papa would've liked that, Tagg?"

The otter took his friend's paw as they walked away. "I'm sure he would have, Nimbalo. You did right."

Nimbalo pulled Tagg to a halt. "Don't you ever

tell anybeast about this, especially those Dillypin 'ogs. Promise me ye won't breathe a word!"

Tagg winked knowingly. "Mateys don't tell otherbeasts their secrets."

They skirted the water meadow, making for the raft. Nimbalo waved to the hedgehogs on deck, muttering to Tagg in an undertone, "When we do catch up with yore vermin, one of 'em'll be carryin' a battleaxe. Leave that 'un to me, 'e'll be the beast who slew my father. I'll pay that feller back in full!" Nimbalo's eyes were as hard as ice-coated granite. Tagg nodded.

As long as he lived, Tagg would never be able to figure his friend out. That night aboard the raft, Nimbalo was the very life and soul of things, laughing, singing and bantering with the hedgehogs. Supper was a spectacular affair. Jurkin had baked a massive outsized dish, which he called allfruit duff. It was a huge soft-crusted crumble, with every fruit or berry they had gathered smeared with honey and baked inside it. The whole thing was covered with a thick white sauce that tasted of vanilla and almonds. It was very tasty; heavy, but satisfying.

Jurkin sat with Tagg, laughing at Nimbalo's antics. "That liddle mouse o' yourn, lookit 'im now singin' an' scoffin' with my 'ogs, yet only this noon 'e looked like a thunnercloud. Where did you two go when ye left the raft?"

The otter shrugged carelessly. "Picking up vermin tracks. Seemed they circled the water meadow, but they're still headed downriver. Nimbalo's just happy that we're still hot on their trail."

Jurkin spooned himself another bowl of his allfruit duff. "That's the way all travelers widout a vessel go. We're still on their tails, right enough. But we'll prob'ly part company with them in the mornin' when we reach the big rocks, where the trail splits. Hoho, lookit Nimbalo doin' the pawspike dance. I thought only 'ogs knew 'ow t'do that 'un."

Tagg winked at the Dillypin Chief. "You'd be surprised at what my little mate knows!"

Nimbalo was in his element, standing in line with the hedgehogs, doing all the actions and singing aloud. It was a very old chanting dance, performed only by the Dillypin tribe. However, the harvest mouse was a quick learner.

"Rum chakka chum chakka chum chakka choo!
I'm a Dillypin who are you?
Choo chakka choo chakka choo chakka chah!
River'ogs is wot we are.

Tap y'paws tap y'spikes tap y'snout an'turn,
Bow to y'partner like a swayin' fern,
'Round an' 'round now, tap that paw,
Who's that knockin' on my door?

Rap chakka chap chakka chap chakka chin!
Ho 'tis you, well come on in.
Chin chakka bin chakka bin chakka choo!
I can dance as good as you.

Clap y'paws, shake y'spikes, touch snouts with me,
Sail down the river right to the sea,
Wot'll we find there wild an' free,
Golden sands an' silv'ry sea.

Whoom chakka boom chakka boom chakka—whoa!
Hold on tight an' away we—goooooooo!"

They all dashed forward, clasping paws, and collapsed laughing on the deck. Leaping up, Nimbalo led the scramble for flagons of cold pale cider, which had cooled in the river current, tied in a sack trailing astern of the raft.

"Let me liddle niece Tingle give a song!" Jurkin called.

Tagg joined the rest in encouraging the young hogmaid. "Aye, come on, Tingle, give us a song!"

Tingle obliged shyly. She had an unusual soft husky little voice.

"Old places I traveled long seasons ago,
Kind faces of friends I have seen,
What's 'round the riverbend, dear I don't know,
'Tis a land where my heart's never been.

Will I sit in the shade of tall willows above,
If I gaze in the stream may I see,
There standing beside, the one that I love,
Or all sad and alone must I be?

The tears I have shed here are mingled and gone,
Through waters which flow without end,
And I must drift, ever seeking that one,
Waiting there 'round some far riverbend."

Tingle threw her apron up over her face and scurried off amid hearty applause and shouts of "More! More!"

Jurkin mopped his eyes with a spotty kerchief and sniffed aloud. "That's me favorite song. Ain't she a luvly singer!"

"She certainly is," Tagg agreed, "and that song was beautiful!"

Jurkin stowed his kerchief away quickly. "Aye, an' guess who wrote it? That plum-faced oaf Robald. Wonders never cease, eh? Where'd a fool who's never 'ad a fight in 'is life get the brains to write summat like that? Hoho, Nimbalo, changed yore tune agin? Now yore weepin'!"

The harvest mouse glared at the big Dillypin hog. "No I wasn't, I was sneezin'. Jus' some cider went down the wrong way. So wipe that stoopid grin off'n yore face or I'll do it for yer, big as ye are!"

Jurkin held up his paws, feigning terror. "No offense, matey, don't start slayin' anybeast, we're 'avin' a good time. Cummon, Tagg, are ye goin' t'get up an' give us a song or a dance, matey?"

The otter shook his head ruefully. "Where I was brought up, singing and dancing were the last things anybeast was

305

called on to do. I'm only good at the use of weapons, or at using my body as a weapon. 'Tis what I was trained for."

Jurkin waved a paw airily. "Then show us a bit o' that. Stand clear, Dillypins, give my mate Tagg a bit o' room!"

The otter expelled a great sigh and shrugged. "All right, then, if you really must. Keep your eyes on my blade."

Tagg whipped out the beautiful knife and began twirling it with one paw. It spun until it was nought but a shining blur.

"Heyya hupp!"

As he shouted, Tagg struck the spinning blade with his other paw. It flashed off and stuck deep in the cabin wall. With an enormous somersault he was alongside the wall, pulling the knife out almost on the instant it struck. The blade began twirling again. This time he was facing Nimbalo as his paw shot out. The harvest mouse yelled, throwing himself flat on the deck. A concerted "Aaahhhh!" arose from the hedgehogs, who thought Nimbalo had been slain. With a powerful leap, Tagg was at Nimbalo's side, helping him up. The harvest mouse patted his chest, throat and both ears, thoroughly shaken.

"Wh-where's the blade?"

Tagg threw back his head and laughed. "I don't know. Ask Jurkin."

Looking mystified, Jurkin scratched his headspikes. "I dunno, mate. Where'd it go?"

Tagg pointed downward. "Look between your footpaws!"

The blade was there, still quivering. Jurkin jumped back a pace. "Seasons o' spikes'n'stickles, 'ow did ye do that?"

Tagg whipped the blade free and resumed spinning it. His paw flicked out and everybeast ducked. He chuckled. "Where is it now, eh?"

They looked between their footpaws, at the deck and the cabin wall. Jurkin narrowed his eyes. "Stuck in somewheres."

Tagg turned slowly so they could all see. "Aye, stuck in

the back of my belt where I always keep it. Never mess with a blade, unless you've spent fifteen seasons learning how to use one. Now I'll bid you all good night!"

He strolled out onto the deck and found a quiet place to sleep. Nimbalo swaggered out in his friend's wake, but not before saying, "Good, isn't 'e? That's me matey Tagg. I taught 'im all 'e knows!"

Like twin specters, the rocks loomed up out of dawn mist. Tagg woke to the sound of Jurkin calling orders.

"Bring 'er in portside there an' make fast for'ard an' aft!" He presented Tagg and Nimbalo with a bag each. "'Tain't much, some leftover allfruit duff an' a flagon o' cider apiece. Stir yore stumps, mates. Let's go an' find yore vermin tracks, see which ways they're bound."

They leaped ashore onto the base of the two great limestone rocks protruding out of the woodlands. Making their way around the huge monoliths, they entered the deep, silent tree cover. Sunlight pierced the leafy canopy, turning the ground mist into golden tendrils amid the dark green shadows. Jurkin took the center, with Tagg and Nimbalo ranging out either side of him. All three were accomplished hunters and trackers, their paws making no sound as they trod carefully, avoiding dead twigs or anything that could crack or rustle underpaw. No words were exchanged; keeping each other in view, they communicated silently by head and paw gestures. Ranging between the trunks of mighty oaks and lofty elm, spreading beech and stately poplar, Tagg kept his eyes riveted on the ground and his ears alert. Through fern beds, loam and moss-carpeted sward they went, until both river and tall rocks were well behind them. The distant trilling of a tree pipit caused the trackers to halt and listen carefully. The little bird sounded either angry or upset. As three heads turned in the direction of the birdsound, Jurkin pointed and Nimbalo wordlessly mouthed, "Over there!"

Tagg pointed to himself, indicating that he would go ahead and his friends follow a short distance behind. Drawing his blade, the otter clamped it between his teeth and vanished into a low clump of brush. He wriggled swiftly through a broad swath of rosebay willowherb and into the base of a small spreading buckthorn, where he crouched, still as a rock. Peering through the leaves, he found himself looking at the back of a small hedgehog, trimly outfitted in a bright yellow smock and green apron. Tagg reached out and tugged the apron strings lightly. Turning around, the little hogmaid took one look at the tattooed otter holding a blade in his clenched teeth, and screamed.

"Mammeeeeeeee! Daddeeeeeeee!"

Tagg struggled through the buckthorn as everybeast arrived on the scene at a run, Nimbalo and Jurkin from behind and the hogmaid's parents from the front. Jurkin recognized them and shook his quills impatiently.

"Tell liddle miss fussyfrills to put a cork in that wailin', willyer? We're trackin' vermin!"

Smothering her daughter's tearful face in her billowing dress, the mother stared haughtily down her snout at Jurkin. "Tut tut, I might have known it. A Dillypin!"

Her husband, a little fat fellow, peeped out from behind her and repeated, "Dillypin!"

Jurkin spread his paws wide, gesturing at their surroundings. "What'n the name o' spikes'n'stickles are Forthrights doin' in this neck o' the woodlands?"

The mother patted her child's back soothingly. "This is our summer woodland domicile, away from hot sun and open country, if that's any business of yours, Jurkin Dillypin. And as for hunting vermin, how can you possibly be doing that by bringing one along with you? Great tattoo-faced savage with that sword in his mouth, frightening the life out of our little Pecunia. You should be ashamed of yourself!"

The husband popped out and echoed, "Ashamed of yourself!"

She tugged his snout sharply. "Silence, Merradink. I'll deal with this rabble."

He retreated behind her voluminous dress. "Yes, Campathia dear."

Nimbalo pointed at Campathia. "Are you ole Robald's sister or summat like that, marm?"

She gave him a look that would have frozen custard. "I most certainly am not! We are the southern Forthrights. Robald is one of the eastern Forthrights, an indifferent bunch. They are sadly lacking in personal tidiness, not like us!"

Merradink's head poked out again. "Not like us!"

Tagg felt the discussion was getting them nowhere. He became forcefully polite with the prissy Campathia. "Begging your pardon, marm, I am no vermin, despite my appearance. I apologize for upsetting your little one, I didn't mean to. Now, just answer my questions and we'll be on our way and leave you in peace. Have any vermin, with tattoos like mine, passed this way? If so, when and where?"

Campathia pointed to Tagg's blade, which he held in his paw. "Put that . . . thing away, sir. I refuse to converse with armed ruffians. Put it away this instant!"

As Tagg returned the blade to his belt, he heard Merradink. "This instant!"

Placated by the otter's obedience, Campathia answered the question. "Late last night. I was cooking supper, and I heard them before I saw them. Three vermin, two stoat creatures and a disgusting female rat, all tattooed in a similar fashion to yourself. Acting promptly, we left our camp and hid nearby. They commandeered our camp and ate our supper. The rat said that she had smelled the fire from a distance. Their behavior was dreadful, their manners atrocious, and their language! Suffice it to say I had to cover my babe's ears. They were totally uncouth—"

Tagg interrupted her flow. "When did they leave? Where's your camp?"

Campathia gestured over her shoulder. "Over there. After eating everything in sight and taking what they could carry, the miscreants left within the hour."

"Within the hour."

Jurkin peeped around her dress at Merradink. "Come on, echo, take us to yore camp."

Campathia waggled a stern paw at Jurkin. "His name is not echo, as you well know. Follow me!"

The camp was little more than an elaborately embroidered linen square of considerable size, pegged across a low hornbeam branch and a fallen larch tree. It had been ripped to tatters by the vermin, and a small homemade rock oven nearby was smashed down into the ashes of a fire beneath it. Nimbalo sniffed at the ashes as Tagg inspected the ground, pointing out the unmistakable pawprints of Dagrab, Rawback and Gruven.

"They're headed west and a bit south. It's them all right!" He stepped around Tagg to retrieve a scrap of barkcloth fiber that was snagged on a holly bush. "Aye, lookit this, mate!"

The otter took the barkcloth fragment and sniffed it carefully before turning his attention to Campathia. "How long have you been at this camp, marm?"

She sniffed and replied indifferently, "All summer long, if that's any business of yours."

Tagg shook his head at Jurkin, to indicate that she was lying. Jurkin tipped him a broad wink, then launched into a tirade at her, just as Merradink was repeating "Business of yours."

"Yer mealy-mouthed, snake-tongued, bandy-spiked fibber!"

Horrified, Campathia covered Pecunia's ears. "You common riverhog, how dare you use such language!"

"Such language!" her husband echoed.

Jurkin was enjoying himself. He raised his voice and

310

roared, "Then tell the truth, ye fat, icy-snouted, beady-eyed nettlebush!"

Campathia withered under Jurkin's furious salvo. Dropping her head, she brushed imaginary dust specks from her dress. "Day before yesterday. We arrived in the early evening."

"Early eee!"

She stamped on Merradink's footpaw, silencing him.

Tagg nodded courteously. "Thankee, marm. We'll be on our way!"

The three friends cut off through the undergrowth, leaving the snobbish southern Forthrights behind. Nimbalo was curious.

"Tagg, mate, 'ow did ye know they 'adn't been there all summer?"

The otter tucked the barkcloth scrap into his belt. "Because they'd be dead if they had. Just before they arrived and made camp there, Vallug and Eefera passed through. It was Eefera gave the game away by tearing his tunic on that holly bush. I can smell weasel anytime, and his scent was still on the cloth. That means we're tracking Gruven, Dagrab and Rawback, who are tracking Vallug and Eefera. Isn't that nice, mate? We're all going the same way. But what about you, Jurkin? Hadn't you better get back to your Dillypins and the raft?"

The sturdy hedgehog nodded ruefully. "Aye, mate, even though I'd like to stand alongside ye when y'catch up wid those vermints. But I'll take another route back t'the ole scow. Don't want to bump inter Campathia Forthright an' 'er family again!"

"An' 'er family again!"

Jurkin roared with laughter at Nimbalo's impersonation of Merradink. "Hohohoho! I'll miss you, ye liddle rascal. Take good care of each other, now. 'Twas a pleasure meetin' ye both. Tagg, mate, may the stream be smooth an' yore rudder never bust on ye!" The three joined paws for

311

a moment, then Jurkin turned and cut off at a tangent, back to his family and the raft.

The trail was clear now. Tagg knew he was following five vermin. He recalled his dreams, the mouse warrior Martin beckoning him urgently, Vallug firing the arrows at him, trying to slay him, to stop him. The otter knew then, with a ruthless certainty, nothing was going to stop him going to Redwall. Nothing and nobeast!

26

Gruven strode along confidently. He had gradually come into his own since the journey from the mountain. Granted, there had been setbacks. He had lost some face, having to flee the Taggerung, but there was no sign of the otter now. Doubtless he had perished along the way, or got lost. Then there had been the incident with those hedgehogs. He dismissed it from his mind. There had been too many of them and they were experts at stone slinging. It could have happened to any Juska warrior, caught waist deep in a stream, pelted by a mob. He probed with his tongue at a loose back tooth. There was no shame in retreating from that lot. He would go back there one night, when he was clan Chieftain, and burn them alive in their cottage. Other than that, things had worked out well. They had feasted on the best of food from the hog who lived on the flatlands, aye, and left him to die, trapped inside a mudball. Then, just as provisions were running low, they had found the belligerent old harvest mouse and his farmhouse. Gruven had enjoyed that, he liked inflicting pain on others, though he had granted Dagrab the privilege of slaying their victim when the time came to move on. A pity they had not captured the hogs at the latest camp. He harbored a deep-rooted hatred for the spike creatures after his last encounter with them. But again, things had turned out well enough. Having wrecked the place, they had left carrying valuable supplies of food. Not only that, but it was he who rediscovered the trail of Eefera and Vallug, which Dagrab had lost some time before out on the flatlands. Gruven was the one who was showing the way; it was he who was in undisputed charge of the other two. Dagrab and Rawback obeyed his every command, without question.

He exerted his authority now, pointing to a small pool set in a clearing, a welcome oasis in the thick woodlands. "We'll camp 'ere awhile. You two get some vittles ready!"

Dagrab put down her battle-axe and took the sack of supplies from Rawback. Between them they gathered firewood and found a flat stone, and then Dagrab made a fire whilst Rawback ground a paste from nuts, wild oats and barley, taken from the Forthrights.

"This'll make some good flatcakes for us, Chief. I'll bake 'em over the fire on this flat stone. You'll like my flatcakes."

Gruven ignored Rawback's comments and concentrated on what lay ahead. He told himself that he had no fear of Vallug or Eefera. They were the only creatures who could prevent his gaining leadership of the Juskazann, therefore they would both have to die, preferably by ambush. Dagrab and Rawback he could dispose of easily, leaving the field clear for him to return to the clan, with a harrowing tale of the hunt. How his brave companions had all met their deaths, leaving only him, Gruven Zann, to slay the traitor Taggerung and return to claim his rightful place as Chieftain. Gruven Zann Juskazann!

His train of thought was interrupted by Dagrab, tapping him hesitantly on the shoulder. "Can't yer see I'm tryin' to think?" he muttered through clenched teeth. "Go away, leave me alone."

But she persisted. "Lissen, Chief . . . lissen!"

Gruven rose moodily, sneering. "Lissen to wot, yore slobberin' mouth?"

The rat cupped her ear to one side. "Bells! Can't you 'ear 'em? 'Tis bells, I tell ye!"

Gruven paid attention then. His ears caught the warm brazen tones of two bells from afar. Rawback had finished his baking. He jiggled two hot flatcakes in his paws, announcing triumphantly, "Lookit these beauties, Chief. I done a whole batch of 'em!"

Gruven drew his sword, pointing in the direction of the tolling bells. "No time fer that now. Pack 'em up in the sack, we'll eat as we go. C'mon, you two, follow me. Keep yer mouths shut an' do as I say, an' hold yer weapons ready!"

Friar Bobb came scurrying from the kitchens into the Great Hall, panting and scratching his stomach distractedly, peering into corners. Mhera, Broggle and Fwirl were making for the main door when the Friar spotted them.

"Hi there, have you seen a Dibbun about? We've lost one!" He came trundling over to them, mopping at his brow. "Mhera, your mother an' I were watching the little 'uns. We took them to the kitchens and were showing them how to make strawberry flan. Great seasons, those Dibbuns take some watchin'. We'd not got the pastry rolled when your mama realized that little Trey had vanished. Anyhow, she's searchin' the kitchens with Brother Hoben, whilst I'm taking a look up here. Ooh, that Trey, the scamp! There's no tellin' where he'll get to next."

Mhera reassured the anxious Friar. "Trey won't have gone far. Mama will probably find him hiding in the larders and stuffing himself. You keep searching 'round here, and we'll take a look outside. I'll have a word or two to say to Trey if he's out there. All Dibbuns have been told to stay indoors while there's vermin in the woods firing arrows over."

Fwirl swung the main door open. "Mhera, you and

315

Broggle search out in the grounds. I'm going into the treetops to scout out the woodlands and see if those two painted blaggards are still roaming about by the walls."

Broggle patted his friend's paw. "Watch yourself out there, Fwirl. We've already had one injured. Be very careful and don't stay out there too long!"

Fwirl gave him one of her prettiest smiles and saluted. "Yes sir, got it sir, watch m'self sir and don't stay out too long sir. I hear and obey your orders, sir!"

Cregga was sitting in the old wheelbarrow at the orchard entrance, dozing in the late-noontide sun. Mhera could not help shaking the ancient Badgermum a bit sharply. "Marm, what are you doing out here?"

The badger twitched a fly from her muzzle. "Just catching a little nap in the fresh air. It's nice out here."

Mhera wagged a stern paw at her friend. "Maybe, but it's not showing much of an example to other Redwallers. Nobeast is supposed to be outside, except the guards!"

Cregga's sightless eyes turned in the ottermaid's direction. "Then what are you and Broggle doing out here, may I ask?"

Broggle looked disappointed. He had hoped the badger had not noticed his presence. "Trey the mousebabe has gone missing, and we're searching for him. I don't suppose you've noticed him, marm?"

Cregga chuckled. "He's over yonder in the strawberry patch. I was going to catch him on the way back and take him inside. Oh, talking of which, would you help me back inside, please, Broggle?"

Mhera began helping Cregga from the barrow. "Here, I will."

The Badgermum placed her hefty paw on Broggle's shoulder. "No, you go and get Trey. Broggle can help me. Come on, my favorite assistant cook, help an old beast to the dining room. It's almost time for tea."

Mhera found Trey sitting happily in the strawberry

patch, covered in juice and berry pippins. She hoisted him up as he continued stuffing his mouth.

"What were you told about coming outside on your own, you rascal!"

Trey grinned and popped a strawberry in the ottermaid's mouth. "Saved a big 'un for you, Mura. I no on me own, Badgeymum sayed Trey could pick strawbeez."

Mhera hid a smile, glad that the little fellow was safe. "Oh did she, now! Well, I'll have a word or two with Lady Cregga. Just look at the mess of you! Don't wipe your face on that dirty smock. Use your kerchief, you mucky mouse!"

Trey pulled out a strip of green home-woven fabric and began scrubbing at his juice-stained mouth. Mhera took it from him. It smelled of lilacs, and the word KITTAGALL was written on it in the same unmistakable capitals.

"Where did you get this? Tell me, Trey."

The mousebabe wrinkled his brow and whispered furtively, "Dat cloff was hid inna strawbee leafs. I finded it!"

Matching his secretive manner, Mhera whispered back, "Very clever of you, Trey. Did you see who put it there?"

Pulling a large fat strawberry out of his smock sleeve, Trey put his nose up against Mhera's and explained, as if she was the Dibbun and not him, "Frybobb an' F'lorn not let Trey eatta strawbeez inna kitchen, say no, no, they for makin' a flans wiv. So Trey comes out inna strawbee patch t'look for strawbeez. Not look for cloffs, ho no, cloffs jus' there inna leafs, all hided. I no see who purra there." He shoved the big strawberry into his mouth and refused to talk further.

Mhera carried Trey inside, her mind in a turmoil. Who could have placed the green cloth in the orchard, and why had they chosen that spot? Passing through the dining room on her way to the kitchen, she saw Cregga sitting alone in a corner.

"Cregga, can I ask you something?"

The Badgermum yawned. "Won't let me take my nap, outside or inside. Yes, Mhera, yes, you may ask me something. What is it, O curious one?"

"Besides Trey, did you notice any other creature go into the orchard while you were sitting in the barrow? Think hard, it's important."

Cregga gave the impression she was thinking hard, then answered, "Yes, there was one other Redwaller who entered the orchard."

Mhera clasped the badger's paw urgently. "Who?"

"You!"

Vallug Bowbeast centered his shaft on the figure striding the north battlements and let fly. Eefera watched as the Redwaller fell back onto the parapet.

"Good shootin'! You got it. Wasn't that the squirrel who slung stones at us yesterday?"

Vallug fixed another shaft to his bowstring. "She won't be throwin' no more stones. I think I dropped 'er good, but I'm not certain. Right, let's get their attention!" He sighted on the bell tower's top arched window, where the two bells could be seen, and gritted his teeth as he pulled the big bow to its full stretch. "Sittin' target, can't miss. This'll wake 'em up!"

The arrow hissed off upward. It struck one bell, bouncing off the metal and causing a sharp clang. Another arrow followed swiftly, striking the other bell. Ding! The pair dashed off to the northeast wallpoint, shifting their position to avoid slingstones.

As the bells rang, Boorab, who was having an afternoon doze in the gatehouse, came hurtling out. He took the north wallsteps three at a time, bounding up to the ramparts and yelling at the top of his lungs, "Redwaller down! Bearers over here! Quickly now, everybeast lie flat! Redwaller down!"

Mhera heard the bells and came hurrying out, with

Cregga, Filorn, Broggle and Friar Bobb in her wake. Dibbuns poured out after them, shrieking and milling about, frightened by the noise. Gundil, Foremole Brull and four of her moles came scuttling down the wallsteps. Between them, on a stretcher made from window poles and drapes, they carried Fwirl. Broggle bellowed hoarsely, as if the arrow had found him instead. The sight of Fwirl laid out with the shaft still in her side was more than the poor assistant cook could bear. He ran alongside the stretcher, holding his friend's paw and stroking her brow. "Fwirl! They've killed Fwiiiiiiirl!"

"You in there . . . lissen! D'ye hear me . . . lissen!"

Cregga held up both paws for silence, whispering to Brull, "Get her up to the infirmary, right away. Silence, everyone!"

Rough and gratingly loud, the voice from over the wall rang out. "Are ye lissenin'? Answer me!"

Mhera sped up the wallsteps and threw herself down beside Boorab, who was lying flat beneath the battlements. "Answer him, go on!"

Boorab called out, loud and curt. "We're listenin'. Who are you and what d'you want?"

Vallug's voice came back a moment later. "Never mind who we are. Send out the Taggerung!"

Boorab looked at Mhera, who gave a mystified shrug. "What in the blazes d'you mean?" he shouted back.

This time it was Eefera's voice that replied. "We've come fer the Taggerung!"

The hare had been binding his kerchief to the end of the ladle he carried about as a swagger stick. He sprang up waving it. "Truce, chaps, truce!" He sidestepped smartly, but was not quick enough to stop Vallug's arrow slicing a wound in his cheek as it zipped by.

"No truce, rabbit. Send the Taggerung out to us, or yore all deadbeasts, that's all!"

Vallug fired two more arrows over the wall. "That should give 'em summat t'think about fer today."

319

Eefera led the way as they retreated into the woodlands. "Aye, we'll kill another tomorrer. They'll soon send 'im out!"

Sister Alkanet cut the barbed head from the arrow and pulled the wooden shaft out of the wound in Fwirl's side. She gave the arrowhead to Brother Hoben and set about mixing herbs and powders from her infirmary shelves. "It went right through. Never hit anything vital, or this pretty one would be dead. I can clean and dress this while she's still unconscious. Good thing the shock and pain knocked her out. Would you see if that arrowhead is poisonous? Vermin often do that to shafts. This squirrel won't be up and about for a while, but she'll live. You can go and give Broggle the good news."

In the passage outside the sickbay, Foremole Brull, Drogg Cellarhog and Gundil had tight hold of Broggle, who was struggling and pleading with them.

"Let me go and see Fwirl. I must be with her, I must! Please!"

Brull had a strong but kindly paw about the squirrel's neck. "Naow, zurr, doan't ee fret yurrself. You'm h'only be inna way an' ee Sister wuddent never 'ave that, burr nay, she'm surpintly wuddent. You'm be a guddbeast an' be ee still noaw, maister!"

The door opened and Brother Hoben came out. He smiled at Broggle. "Fwirl's not dead, my friend, merely senseless. She'll be fine provided that this arrowhead isn't poisoned."

Drogg Cellarhog took the arrowhead. He licked it and smacked his lips thoughtfully. "'Tain't poisoned. Any good cellar'og can taste badness after a lifetime o' brewin' all manner o' drinks. Nah, that's clean. Cummon, Broggle, me ole bushtail, smile. Yore Fwirl will be right as rain afore the season's out."

Blinking away his tears, Broggle smiled hopefully. "Does that mean I can go in and see her?"

320

Drogg threw a sympathetic paw about the squirrel's shoulder. "Put one paw in there an' ole Alkanet'll physick the tail off ye, young feller. Best come with me t'the cellar, an' I'll give ye a flask of me special tearose an' violet cordial. When miz Fwirl feels brighter, y'can pick 'er a nice bunch o' flowers an' take 'em up with the cordial." They went off together down the stairs, Broggle talking animatedly.

"Is it good stuff, this cordial? Will Fwirl like it? Now, what kind of flowers should I pick? Er, pansy, marigold and celandine if there's any still about. She likes golden-colored flowers."

Foremole Brull nudged Gundil. "Hurr, so does oi, but et be's a long toime since oi 'ad any."

Gundil smiled from ear to ear. "Hurr hurr, oi'll goo an' pick ee summ, marm. Keep Broggle cumpany."

On his way downstairs, Gundil passed Mhera, assisting a reluctant Boorab up to the infirmary.

"Oh, pish tush, m'gel, nothin' a plum pudden won't cure, wot. I'd sooner have a plum pudden than a blinkin' physick off that stern-faced poisoner. I'll bet there's chaps gone in there an' never come out again after one of Sister Alkanet's potions was poured down their flippin' faces. I'll just nip down t'the kitchens. Nothin' a beaker of October Ale an' the odd bucket o' salad won't take care of, wot wot?"

Mhera kept a firm grip on the hare's ear. "Come on, you great fusspot, that wound needs dressing. I'll see that you get extra supper after she's finished with you."

The suggestion of extra food heartened Boorab considerably. "Oh, well, have it your own way, miz. By the way, d'you know what a Taggerung is? 'Cos I'm jolly well blowed if I do."

Mhera's face was grim as she knocked on the sickbay door. "No, I don't know what a Taggerung is, but just let one show its face around here. Mayhap we'll find out more at the elders' meeting tonight. Surely somebeast has heard of a Taggerung."

27

Even though the night was warm and a full moon hung in the sky like a new gold coin, Vallug felt sulky. He had always lit a campfire at night. Eefera crouched in the shelter of a broad beech tree, trying to ignore the ferret. Vallug looked at the small heap of twigs he had gathered.

"Nighttime's miserable when y'don't 'ave a fire!"

Eefera was enjoying the Bowbeast's discomfort. "Well, go on then, you light a fire. But don't expect me t'sit by it. I told yer, those beasts in there ain't stupid. If they've got any good slayers or seasoned warriors, they'll be out searchin' for us right now. It makes sense, don't it? We prob'ly killed two of theirs an' wounded the big rabbit. If they're supposed t'be the fighters Sawney Rath reckoned 'em t'be, they ain't goin' to let that go without strikin' back. You don't need no fire, not on a summer night like this. Yore gettin' soft in yer old age."

Vallug stood slowly. Stiff-necked, he clenched his paws. "Lissen, weasel, d'you want ter try me, see 'ow soft I am, eh?"

"Sssshh, stow it!" Eefera cocked an ear, listening carefully to the sounds of the nighttime woodlands. "See, I told yer," he whispered. "I can 'ear 'em. Lissen!"

Vallug tuned in his senses to the sounds amid the trees.

"Aye, yore right. What'll we do?" He watched a slow, wicked smile spread across the weasel's face.

"Sounds as if there's no more'n three of 'em. Let's light the fire an' 'ide nearby. We'll kill one an' take the other two alive!"

Dagrab sniffed the warm dry air suspiciously. "I kin smell fire. Pine an' dead beech twigs, over yonder."

Gruven drew his sword, signaling the other two to arm themselves. They crept forward, Gruven whispering urgently, "Take no prisoners. Kill anybeast who's by that fire!" Then he dropped back slightly, allowing Dagrab and Rawback to go unwittingly ahead of him.

Stalking carefully between the trees, the two vermin reached the fire and waited until Gruven caught up. Dagrab turned as he appeared between them. "Chief, there's nobeast there."

Gruven crouched down. "Take a look around."

Rawback blinked as he scanned the area beyond the flames. "Dagrab's right, Chief, there ain't nobeast about."

Gruven laid his sword upon the grass. Placing a paw on each of their backs, he shoved them stumbling into the firelight. "Well, if there's nobeast there wot're ye scared of?"

Both vermin gave a panicked squeak, and turned to jump back out of the firelight. Eefera leaped from the shadows and whacked them flat with a long chunk of dead oak branch. Gruven reached for his sword, but it was not there. Vallug's bow dropped over his head from behind and was pulled backward, choking Gruven as the swordpoint prodded at his spine. Vallug marched him into the firelight.

"Well, if it ain't the Gruven Zann Juskazann called to visit 'is ole mates. Isn't that nice? 'E brought Dagrab an' Rawback along too. We're all one big 'appy family agin, eh?"

Any ideas Gruven had harbored of killing Vallug and

323

Eefera by ambush collapsed. Pangs of fright caused him to flop down on the ground. His cowardly nature took over, and he emitted a choking sob.

"Th-there's f-food in the sacks."

Eefera grabbed the supply sacks from the stunned vermin. He shook their contents out in front of the fire. It was the remains of the provisions they had plundered from the southern Forthrights.

"Hoho! Flatcakes an' nuts; fruit, too. Wot's in the flasks? Cordial? Looks good, eh? Aha, a fruitcake, a nice big 'un! Bet you was keepin' this fer yerself, Gruven, bein' Chief an' all that."

Vallug dug the swordpoint into Gruven's back a little. "Oh, this 'un's a real Juskazann all right. Did ye 'ear 'im back there? Take no prisoners, kill anybeast who's by the fire? Then 'e 'angs back an' lets those two dead'eads go forward!"

Still keeping the sword at Gruven's back and the bow around his neck, Vallug leaned forward until he was breathing down his prisoner's ear. His voice dripped contempt. "Yore a gutless worm, Gruven. Go on, tell us wot you are. Say it!"

Gruven's nose was dribbling. He made no attempt to hide his tears, and his voice sobbed brokenly as the bowstring pulled tighter. "A gutless worm. Please don't kill me!"

Munching cheerfully on a flatcake and drinking cordial, Eefera sat next to Gruven and winked at him.

" 'S all right, mate, we ain't goin' t'kill ye. Yore goin' to be useful to me'n Vallug. Wipe y'nose an' stop blubbin' now."

Vallug had every intention of killing Gruven there and then. But he wanted Eefera to think he was clever also. He loosed the bowstring and withdrew the sword, kicking Gruven flat. "Aye, stop slobberin'. You'll fit in nicely with our plans!"

Eefera made the three sit together by the fire, with

Gruven in the middle. He bound Gruven's paws, one to Dagrab, the other to Rawback. Taking the free paws of Dagrab and Rawback, he bound one to the other behind them.

"There now, all nice'n'comfy. Ye can't run anywhere among trees tied like that. Y'see, we killed a few creatures from that Abbey over yonder. They might 'ave warriors out lookin' to kill us, an' that's enough t'stop anybeast gettin' a good night's rest, ain't it? So 'ere's the plan, mates. You sit by the fire, an' I'll pile a bit more wood on so it won't go out. Now, if'n there ain't warriors out lookin' fer tattoo-faced Juskas, you'll be safe enough. But if'n there is, well, luck o' the game, ain't it? Either way, me'n'Vallug can sleep easy 'til dawn. Good, eh?"

Vallug was impressed by Eefera's plan, although he never said so. But just to emphasize that he too was smart, he checked the captives' bonds for tightness, warning them, "Don't try to escape. We'll be somewheres close by all night, an' you won't know if'n one of us is awake, watchin' yer!" Then the pair retired into the shadows, leaving their three decoys bound together in full view of the fire.

"Vallug was right, Gruven," Dagrab muttered savagely. "You are a gutless worm!"

Though still frightened, Gruven had recovered some of his bad temper. "Shut yer snivelin' face," he snarled. "I'm tryin' to think!"

Rawback laughed ironically. "Huh, snivelin' face, you should've saw yerself a moment ago. *I'm a gutless worm, please don't kill me.* Think about that! We musta been mad t'follow you, Gruven. Y'never change, do yer? Once a coward always a coward, that's you!"

Gruven's eyes blazed hatred as he glared at Rawback. "You'll die fer that, I promise!"

Rawback bared his teeth at Gruven. "We might all be dead by mornin', bigmouth!"

*

Torches and lanterns burned late in Cavern Hole. All who were able attended the meeting. Cregga addressed the anxious-faced assembly.

"First things first. Does any Redwaller know what the word Taggerung means? Apparently those vermin will leave us in peace if we send them out a Taggerung."

Mhera gazed around at the silent puzzled faces. "I never heard the word until today. It's probably a vermin term for something. Could it mean loot, or booty, do you think?"

Tentative suggestions started to come.

"Aye, they might think we keep treasure here?"

"Mayhap it means somebeast in authority, an Abbot or Abbess?"

"But we don't have an Abbot or Abbess, and even if we did, the last thing we'd do is turn them over to a mob of vermin!"

"Hurr, who'm said they'm wurr ee mob? Miz Furl said she h'only see'd two of ee vermints."

"How is Fwirl? Have you seen her yet, Broggle?"

Sister Alkanet fixed the speaker with a stern eye. "No he has not. I'll say when that squirrelmaid is fit to receive visitors. Old Hoarg is well now, he'll be up and about by tomorrow morning, but I wish to complain about that hare—"

Boorab, who had a bandage under his chin reaching up to a bow tied off between his ears, rapped the table and interrupted. "You're gettin' away from the point, marm, though if you'd nipped out an' physicked those two vermin bounders, they'd be well on their way, wot! A Taggerung, eh? Well, with our knowledge of vermin type slang, they may's well have asked for a bucketbung or a jolly old bellwotrang, eh, eh?"

Cregga's booming voice silenced the hare. "This is no time for joking. Kindly keep any silly remarks to yourself, sah. If we don't know what a Taggerung is, then we cannot deliver it to the vermin. But they are murderous beasts; it was only by pure luck that Hoarg and Fwirl weren't slain. Have you any thoughts on the matter, Mhera?"

The ottermaid had, and she made them known. "I think we'd be best concentrating our attention on the vermin. Fwirl said there were only two, with heavily tattooed faces. However, although that may have been all she saw, who knows how many of them are out there? I don't wish to scare anybeast, but we could be in real trouble if vermin have come in numbers. We don't have any real warriors at the Abbey now that Skipper and his crew are away. So, can I suggest three things. One, we must all stay indoors, except the wallguards, and they must not show themselves above the parapet. Two, we must send a good runner, somebeast who is fleet of paw, to find Skipper and bring him back here with his crew. Finally, three. If we cannot fight the vermin, then we have to get them to parley, so that we can understand what it is they want from us."

Sister Alkanet had immediate objections to Mhera's last point. "Give vermin what they want? Why not just fling our gates open wide and let them march into the Abbey? I've never heard anything like it. Parley with vermin? Never. I'd fight them to my last breath!"

Drogg Cellarhog grabbed the Sister's paw and sat her down. "An' wot good would that do, marm? Mhera never said anythin' about lettin' vermin march in here. Why don't you listen? She's tryin' to do the best for all of us, tryin' to buy us time until help arrives. Hopin' to find out the full strength of the foebeast."

There were cries of "Well said, Drogg!" and Cregga had to pound the table to restore order.

"When I had eyes I slew more vermin than you've ever seen. Make no mistake, vermin are cruel, heartless murderers. Mhera is right in what she says: we must do what is best for all. Tomorrow we'll try to ascertain just how many vermin are at our gates, then we can decide

327

calmly what must be done. Meanwhile, everybeast will stay inside and the guard patrol will continue, but they must not expose themselves to danger. Now go to your beds, please, and get a good night's sleep. We'll need clear heads to see this crisis through. Friar Bobb, Filorn, Broggle, will you see that the guards have sufficient food and drink for the night? Boorab, do you still feel fit enough to command the sentries?"

The hare threw an extremely smart salute and winced slightly. "Fit as a physicked frog, marm, as long as they sling portions of this an' that to keep the old energy up through the darkened hours. Chap can get hungry in the dreary night watches, wot! Can't have us guardian coves perishin' at our posts, y'know."

Filorn reassured the gluttonous hare. "I'll see you're well supplied, Mr. Boorab. Sister, is there anything special our Guard Commander must eat for his injury?"

Alkanet cast a frozen glare at the hare. "Just food!"

Boorab bowed and smiled broadly at her. "Just food, eh? Wonderful thought, marm, wot!"

That night Mhera had the strangest dreams she had ever experienced. In the meandering pathways of sleep she saw a beloved face from the past: Rillflag, her father. The ottermaid ran toward him through a misty early morning field. He smiled, holding his paws wide to embrace her, and she called out, "Papa, Papa!"

She recalled his face so well, yet it was not exactly as she remembered it. There was something different. He looked younger. He vanished bit by bit as Mhera tried to run faster, calling his name. Down, down he sank into the swirling, milky-hued vapor. She ran to the spot and knelt down. It was the bank of a river. Sunlight dispersed the foggy tendrils, and the ottermaid stared into the cool dark waters. But it was not her own reflection gazing back at her, it was Martin the Warrior. He held up one paw pad foremost, pointed at the front of it with the other, and spoke just one word. "Taggerung!"

328

Then she was sitting on her mother's lap, on the old wheelbarrow in the orchard. Deyna, the little brother she had lost many long seasons ago, was beside her. Filorn looked radiant, young and beautiful, happy as any ottermum with her young ones. Mhera stopped tossing and turning in her sleep. She lay still and contented, listening to her mama sing.

"Bells o'er the woodland
Sound sweet and so clear,
They peal across meadows and streams.
Small birds sing along,
Hear their echoing song,
Whilst bees hum about their small dreams.
So slumber on, little one,
Safe here with me,
All in the warm afternoon.
When the long day is done
And deep night's shade is come
I will bring you the stars and the moon!"

28

Tagg woke up scratching. He was itching all over. Still with his eyes half closed, he wiggled a paw in his ear and spat out something that was wandering over his lip. Nimbalo was sitting by the fire, cooking breakfast, his fur plastered wetly against him. He watched the otter scratching madly and shrugged apologetically.

"Sorry, mate. It was dark, 'ow could I tell I'd picked a campsite right inna middle of a bloomin' ant trail? Pond's over there."

Tagg tore past him and did a bounding dive into the still waters of a small lake, ignoring Nimbalo's shout of "Wouldn't mind a perch or a fat ole trout fer brekkist, mate!"

Swimming powerfully, Tagg crossed and recrossed the waters, and then he sped back to the lake's center and dived. It felt so good that he frisked about like an otterbabe, performing underwater somersaults and chasing his rudder playfully. Nimbalo left off cooking to gaze on the unbroken sheet of lake surface, muttering to himself as he waited for his friend to surface.

"C'mon, you ole riverdog, this scoff'll be cold if'n ye stay down there all day!"

Breaking the surface on the far side of the lake, Tagg

330

leaped out shaking himself, then bent down and was lost to sight. Nimbalo snorted impatiently, shouting as he went back to cooking, "Wot's goin' on over there, matey? Found more ants t'play with?"

Tagg came bounding back with his tunic slung over one shoulder. He spilled the contents out in front of Nimbalo. "Look, button mushrooms and cress. I found them growing over there. Anything nice to eat? I'm starving!"

Nimbalo served the food, chuckling. "Pancakes an' honey an' pear cordial, but don't tell the ants!"

Tagg smiled ruefully at the thought of the insects. "You little puddenhead, fancy picking a camp in an ant run!"

Nimbalo shuddered and wriggled. "Ugh! I really earned me title durin' the night, mate. I must've slayed about two 'undred ants every time I rolled over!"

The cress was sweet and fresh, and the mushrooms had a wonderful nutty flavor. They finished breakfast by eating as many as they could.

After breaking camp, the two friends headed into the woodlands, still following the vermin tracks. It was a golden morning, with vagrant breezes chasing small fluffy clouds across a soft blue sky. A vague excitement was stirring in Tagg's mind. He did not recognize the country, yet it felt friendly. He stopped for a moment and leaned against an ancient hornbeam.

"Nimbalo, have you ever had the feeling that you know a place, yet you haven't been there before? I mean . . ."

The harvest mouse nodded confidently. "I know wot y'mean, Tagg, though 'tis 'ard to explain. I used t'make a rhyme about it when I was rovin' the flatlands. Lissen.

"There's many's the patch that I ain't trod,
Nor ever been before there,
An' yet it seems as close to me,
As some ole coat I've wore, sir.
Some streams'n'rivers, rocks'n'fields,

331

That I have come upon, sir,
I'm seein' them for my first time,
Yet I knows every one there.
Now was I here ten seasons back,
Did I sit 'neath that tree there,
An' if I pass this way agin,
Then will I meet meself, sir?"

The harvest mouse had saved a few mushrooms. He tossed one up and caught it deftly in his mouth. "Y'see wot I mean?"

He tossed another mushroom up. Tagg nudged him out of the way and caught it in his mouth. "Aye, it's as clear as porridge on a winter's morn. Nimbalo!" The harvest mouse had suddenly rushed ahead. "Come back here. What is it?"

Dodging between the trees, Nimbalo was pointing upward. "Look, mate! Look!"

There in the distance was Redwall Abbey, the morning sun reflecting off its old red sandstone bulk, rearing into the sky.

Within a short distance of the outer walls Tagg and Nimbalo halted, breathless at the sight of the colossal Abbey up close. Nimbalo strained his head back, staring up at it.

"Great seasons o' swamps'n'streams, ants never built that lot, mate!"

Tagg could hardly believe his eyes. It was a dream coming true. "I'm getting that funny feeling again, mate!"

Nimbalo reminded him of their mission. "Let's git outta the way for a bit an' figger out wot we're goin' t'do. Get be'ind these bushes, Tagg."

The otter came back to reality. He took his friend's wise counsel and ducked down behind a coppiced hazel bush. "You're right, we can't go marching up and banging on their door. Nobeast in there would know us. Then there's

332

the vermin, five of them if the tracks are to be believed. We could be ambushed by them as we stood gawking at that place. So, what's the plan, Nimbalo?"

His friend made a calming gesture with both paws. "We takes it slow'n'easy at first. This is the way I sees it. We'll split up an' take different ways, keep t'the trees, not let ourselves be seen. I'll meet ye back 'ere in the late noon. If one of us makes contact with anybeast inside an' gets hisself welcomed in then we're both all right. But keep yore eyes peeled for those vermin. If y'see them, don't go mad an' start slayin' the villains, an' I won't either. When we meets back 'ere, then we'll make another plan an' set up an ambush on them. Right?"

Tagg took Nimbalo's paw and shook it. "Right. Good plan, mate. Oh, here, you take my blade."

The harvest mouse was puzzled. "Why's that?"

Tagg did not want Nimbalo to be unarmed if he met the vermin, but to save his friend's pride he gave another reason, one that was just as valid. "It won't matter so much if the Abbeybeasts see a harvest mouse with a knife, but a big otter like me, with a tattooed face, if they see me carrying a weapon, what then, eh?"

Nimbalo thrust the blade through his belt. It looked like a sword on his tiny frame. "Yore right, mate. Hmm, this is a nice blade. I could get used to it. Jus' the sort o' thing Nimbalo the Slayer needs."

They split up, Tagg taking the east wall going south, Nimbalo going in the opposite direction.

Egburt came dashing into the Great Hall, colliding with Mhera and Cregga, who were going to the infirmary to visit Fwirl. The Badgermum leaned on Mhera as she halted the hedgehog in his tracks.

"Whoa there, speedy, where are you off to in such a hurry?"

Egburt thrust a wooden serving tray into Mhera's paws. "It's Mr. Boorab, he's gone. See for y'self, miz!"

333

Cregga tapped the tray impatiently. "Gone? Where's he gone and what's that thing? Tell me, Mhera!"

The ottermaid studied the tray briefly before replying. "It's a serving tray. Boorab has written a message on it with a charcoal stick. Listen. 'Dear chums'n'chaps, gone to get help from Skipper and co. Dashed silly but brave I know. Don't go weeping and wailing for me, only if I don't make it back, then I hope you'll bawl your bonces off for a blinkin' season, wot. Tell Filorn to start cookin' now, yours truly will be rather peckish on his return. Also, if one knows there's stacks of grub waitin', then one will try one's hardest to return. Rather! Regards to all, keep a light burnin' in the jolly old window. Yr faithful probationary music master and Guard Commander, Bellscut Oglecrop Obrathon Ragglewaithe Audube Baggscut. PS. Tell Drogg to keep my haredee gurdee well greased. PPS. Tell miss Fwirl to refuse any physicks if she wants to live. PPPS. I hope old Hoarg's bucket recovers from that arrow (haha). Only joking, got to go, chin up, chest out, wot!'"

Cregga shook her head and leaned down more heavily on Mhera. "The flop-eared idiot. I knew many such hares long ago. Brave, foolish and reckless, or perilous, as the Long Patrol would say. Let's hope fervently that he makes it! Egburt, I'm promoting you to Commander of the Wallguard in Boorab's absence. Are you able for the job, young hog?"

Egburt performed an excellent parody of the hare. "Able, marm, able's my second name, wot wot. Your wish is my command, I won't say another word, attention, smart salute, eyes right, and I'll bid ye a good day. Quick march, one two one two, pick that step up there, laddie buck!"

Eefera released his prisoners and issued them with their weapons. They stood looking bewildered. Vallug sounded almost friendly as he addressed them.

"Surprised t'find yoreselves alive an' kickin' today, eh?

Well, so am I. Those beasts be'ind the walls must be softer'n we thought they was, which is all the better fer us. Now, we're goin' to take a nice liddle walk, up north a bit, across the path an' into the ditch, then back down t'the main gates o' Redwall. Keep yore 'eads down low; they can use slings from those walltops. We've given ye back yer weapons, so try an' look just a bit like Juska warriors. I'll be be'ind youse all the way. First one makes a wrong move an' I'll spit 'em with an arrer. Wot are yew lookin' at me like that for, Gruven? Cummon, speak up."

No matter how hard he tried, Gruven could not shake of his fear of Vallug. It was as if the Bowbeast was looking for an excuse to kill him. Gruven's paws trembled uncontrollably as he tried to speak around the lump of panic welling in his throat.

"I, er, wasn't lookin' at ye."

Vallug brought his face close to Gruven's. "Say sir."

"I wasn't lookin' at ye . . . sir."

Vallug grinned wolfishly at Eefera. "If only 'is mammy could see 'im now. Come on, let's get goin'."

Eefera went ahead to show the way; Vallug followed in the rear, keeping the three sandwiched between them. They had not gone far when Eefera raised a paw and halted them. He signaled Vallug to hold the three in silence, then ducked off amid the shrubbery.

Nimbalo scarce had time to do a half-turn before Eefera's spearbutt crashed down upon his skull. Slinging the little fellow over his shoulders, Eefera made his way back to the others. He dumped the unconscious harvest mouse on the ground in front of them.

"See wot I found, mates. Lookit wot's in the mousey's belt, Vallug. Now tell me the Taggerung ain't inside Redwall Abbey!"

Vallug took the knife almost reverently from Nimbalo's belt. "Sawney Rath's blade! Well, slit me gizzard an' stew me tripes! Yore right, this is where Taggerung's got to be!"

None of them had ever seen Nimbalo before, so they

took him to be a Redwaller. Vallug prodded the field mouse's limp form with his bow. "Makes yer wonder wot this 'un's doin', totin' the knife around, don't it? I 'ope you ain't killed 'im."

Eefera took a prod at Nimbalo with his spearshaft. "Looks dead. No, wait, I think I seen 'is nose twitch. Dagrab, you'n'Gruven can carry 'im. If'n the mousey comes 'round 'e'll be valuable to us. Must be somebeast special if'n that otter give 'im the blade. Come on, we ain't got all day."

They trekked off north, to where they could cross the path and gain the safety of the ditch without being seen from the Abbey.

Between them, Drogg Cellarhog and Broggle helped old Hoarg up the east wallsteps, though there was no real need to. The ancient dormouse was fully recovered and felt very spry after his welcome discharge from Sister Alkanet's sickbay.

"By hokey, there must've been somethin' in that physick, I feel like a Dibbun this mornin'. Heeheehee!"

Drogg allowed Hoarg to scamper away up the steps. He shook his spiky head admiringly and clapped Broggle's back. "Wish I felt like that. Miz Fwirl will soon be up an' about, I 'ear. 'Ow did she look when ye visited 'er?"

The assistant cook smiled thankfully at Drogg. "She's fine, thank you, and ten times better since I gave her the flowers and your wonderful flask of cordial. Sister Alkanet shooed me out after a while, because Cregga and Mhera had come to visit. You know the Sister, said she didn't want a crowd 'round Fwirl's bed. I'll go up and see her again later." He turned and looked up to the ramparts. "I don't think Hoarg likes it up there. He's coming back down."

Waving his paws and making exaggerated shushing noises, Hoarg descended the steps nimbly. "Keep yore voices down. I just saw a vermin roamin' about in the woodlands. Come an' take a peep, he might still be there!"

Three heads popped over the battlements, watching Tagg moving toward the southeast wallcorner. The otter looked back over his shoulder, causing the spies to crouch down swiftly upon the parapet. Hoarg shuddered.

"Real vermin, that 'un. Did y'see his face, covered in tattoos! He looks as nasty savage a piece o' work as ever I set eyes on. Bet he's killed more'n a few pore innocent creatures!"

Drogg interrupted the old Gatekeeper's tirade. "Wot was the vermin up to when ye first saw 'im, Hoarg?"

"Couldn't see clear, but it looked t'm like he was tryin' the east wickergate below us. Good job 'tis well locked."

Broggle was shaking, though not with fear; the rage was plain on his face. He clenched his paws resolutely. "That vermin could be the scum who put an arrow in my Fwirl. Great tattooed scumfaced coward, let's capture him!"

Drogg stared at the squirrel incredulously. "Capture him? An' how are we goin' t'do that, pray? Did you get a proper look at the beast? He could eat the three of us!"

But Broggle was not to be denied. He bared his teeth viciously. "We won't give him the chance, friends. He's already tried to open the east wickergate. I'll wager an acorn to an oak that he'll try the south wickergate when he reaches there. Well, the blaggard's going to find it unlocked. We'll be waiting just inside the doorway with clubs, to welcome him to Redwall!"

Drogg's face was serious. He took hold of Broggle's paw. "It's dangerous. Are you sure ye want to do this?"

Fired by Broggle's plan, old Hoarg suddenly became belligerent. "I say let's do it. Those cowards are goin' t'pay for stickin' an' arrow in my ear. We'll show 'em that Redwallers aren't fools they can shoot at as they please. I'm with ye, Broggle!"

Drogg became infected by the warlike pair. "Then count me in too, mates! We've got a bit o' time, the rascal didn't look to be in any great 'urry. You two nip down an' open the wickergate bolts, quietly as y'can. I'll go an' get us some weapons. We'll make the vermin sorry they ever messed about with Redwall warriors!"

Tagg strolled slowly and silently along the outside of the southern wall, keeping alert for any sign of the Juska vermin. He stopped often, running his paws across the massive sandstone blocks, awed by the colossal scale of Redwall. Tree cover thinned out, and he found himself on open ground. Crouching close to the wall, he made his way carefully, ever watchful for the foe. About halfway along he encountered a recess in the stonework. It was a small door, stoutly made from seasoned oak. This was a wickergate, similar to the one he had encountered in the east wall. Bending low to avoid hitting his head on the peak-arched lintel, Tagg gave the door an experimental push. It opened slightly. He pushed harder, crouching down and poking his head inside to see what lay beyond the wall 'twixt ramparts and Abbey building. A wooden barrel-coopering mallet and two hard ash axe handles hit the back of his head simultaneously. He dropped like a log.

Hoarg did a little victory dance. "Heehee, poleaxed by an axe pole, heeheehee!"

Broggle silenced the old Gatekeeper sternly. "Stop that, Hoarg, or we'll all be in trouble!"

Drogg placed a footpaw on the back of their fallen foe. "Trouble? How so?"

Broggle, who had come down from his peak of anger, explained, "If Cregga or Mhera finds out, we'll be in for the lecture of our lives. Endangering the Abbey by unbolting a wallgate and almost letting in the vermin. Then it'll be why didn't we let them know, so that the thing could be planned properly, instead of running off in haste on spur of the moment madcap schemes? You know the sort of thing they'd say."

"Aye, I know exactly, young feller." Hoarg stared down at the stricken Tagg. "Ugly-looking great beast, ain't he? With all them tattoos it's impossible to tell what kind of creature he be. So, what do we do with him now, slay him?"

His companions shook their heads vehemently.

"How could any Redwaller murder a fallen beast, vermin or not?"

"None of us have ever taken a life, and I don't think we're about to now. Huh, we've got ourselves into a right mess here."

Drogg decided to take charge. "We can't just leave him lyin' here. Does that ole wheelbarrow by the orchard still work, Broggle?"

The squirrel nodded. "I think so. What's your plan?"

For no apparent reason, Drogg dropped his voice to a whisper. "Go an' get it. There's a little cellar door, where I brings in wood for barrels an' tools. It leads through to my cellars. We'll take him through there an' lock him up in my supply room. Then we can make up a story about how we caught the rogue. I think Cregga an' Mhera will be glad to have a hostage to bargain off against the rest o' the vermin."

Tagg regained consciousness in complete darkness. At first he thought he had gone blind. Lying on a hard stone floor, he brought his paw up in front of his eyes, but he could not see it. Panic set in and despite the abominable aching inside his skull, he sat up. Relief flooded through him when the sight of a pale thin strip of light from beneath a door assured him his eyesight was not gone. With extreme caution he stood upright and began to investigate his prison cell. Holding both paws high, he leaped in the air and barely touched the beam of a ceiling. He landed, sending an agonizing jolt through his head. Stone floors and stone walls, with a single door that felt as solid as the rest of the place and would not budge a fraction. Then he bumped into something and went sprawling. He felt it gingerly, and made out a huge barrel-shaped structure. Putting his weight against it, he shoved. It moved fractionally, and a swishing sound came from within. It was a barrel, and almost full to its brim. He felt around it for some kind of stopper, and found a wooden bung. However, it had been firmly hammered home and was immovable. Dizzy with the effort, he felt the back of his head, where there was a sizable lump and a minute dampness of blood. Pain enveloped him, and he slumped down on the floor and allowed his body to drift into a half stunned sleep in the silent gloom.

Eefera and Vallug crouched in the ditch across the path from the main outer gate. Gruven, Dagrab and Rawback had made slings and collected heaps of pebbles. Vallug had an arrow laid across his bowstring, and several more were stuck point down in the ditchbed, close to paw. Eefera gave the orders.

"You three just keep slingin' stones over the wall, I'll tell ye when t'stop. Vallug, keep yore bow at the ready. Righto, me buckos, get slingin'!"

Nimbalo lay to one side, still out to the world, but breathing.

Egburt came marching into the infirmary, where Cregga and Mhera were drinking medicine beakers of cordial with Fwirl and chuckling over some private joke. The young hedgehog saluted smartly and proceeded to make his report in hare style.

"Ahem, sorry to intrude like this, marms, but the jolly old door was open, so I tootled in, wot!"

Cregga turned her face to him. "Young Egburt, eh? Well you can just tootle out again and get on with commanding the wallguard."

Egburt put on his sternest face, which was wasted on

Cregga. "It's about the wallguard I've come, marm. Confounded vermin are slingin' stones over like spring rain. So I've ordered the guards to stand down an' get themselves inside under cover, wot!"

Mhera threw up her paws in dismay. "You've left the walls unguarded, Egburt? That's an excee—"

Her speech was cut short by the sound of breaking glass from downstairs. An extra long shot had obviously hit one of Great Hall's large stained glass windows.

Mhera bounded for the door, calling back, "Stay there. I'll see what's going on down below!"

Cregga shuffled after her. "You two stay here, I'm going down too."

Fwirl tried to hoist herself out of bed, but Egburt shoved her firmly back and gave her his commander's glare. "You're not even walkin' wounded, miz. Best stay put. I'll send Broggle up to sit with you."

Sister Alkanet appeared in the doorway. "You certainly will not. I'll say who comes and goes here!"

Egburt bowed his head and threw six swift salutes. "Er, quite, er, mister sarm, I mean Sister marm, I'll just, er, tootle off, wot!"

Alkanet stood, paws akimbo, blocking his way. "Why are you talking in that silly manner? You're not a hare."

Egburt kept saluting and trying to squirm by the Sister. "Only temporarily, marm, sort of harehog, or a hedgehare y'may say . . ."

The severe Sister placed a paw against Egburt's snout. "Hmm, dry and quite hot, probably with dashing up and down those wallstairs all the time. A good physick should cure that!"

Nimbalo came awake suddenly. He lay in the ditch, unmoving, his eyes riveted on the battle-axe that stood leaning against the ditchside next to Dagrab. She turned and saw him.

341

"The mouse 'as come 'round! Look, 'e's awake!"

Vallug drew back the shaft upon his bowstring and leaned forward. The arrowpoint was less than a pawslength from Nimbalo's face.

"Move jus' a whisker an' yore dead, mouse. I couldn't miss from 'ere if'n I wanted to. Eefera, tie 'im up."

As Eefera bound Nimbalo's paws behind him, the harvest mouse's eyes shifted from the battle-axe to Dagrab. His voice was calm but deadly cold as he addressed the rat.

"Is that yore axe?"

Dagrab fitted another stone to her sling. "Aye, 'tis. D'yer like it, mousey, eh?"

Vallug stamped on Dagrab's tail. "Less o' the jawin' an' more o' the slingin'!"

Dagrab began whirling her sling as Nimbalo spoke again. "I'm goin' to slay you with that axe, rat!"

The stone clacked sharply against Dagrab's paw. She had forgotten to throw it in astonishment at the harvest mouse's flat statement. Vallug stamped harder on her tail. "Keep slingin', I said! I want these Redwallers to think we got a pile o' clanbeasts out 'ere, not just you dozy loafers!"

Eefera checked Nimbalo's bonds to make sure they were tight. "So then, bucko, wot do they call you?"

Nimbalo looked at him as if he were dirt. "My name's Nimbalo the Slayer, as that there rat's soon goin' to find out. Wot do they call you, maggot breath?"

Vallug threw back his head and laughed. "Hoho, we got a feisty one 'ere. Tell me, mousey, wot d'ye know about an otter they call the Taggerung?"

Nimbalo directed his scorn at the Bowbeast. "A lot more'n you do, slobberchops, but I ain't tellin' ye!"

Eefera dealt Nimbalo a stinging blow to the face. "Yore insolent. We don't like that. You'd better tell 'im wot we want ter know, or it'll be the worse for yer, me liddle 'un!"

Nimbalo licked blood from where the blow had knocked his teeth against his lip. He winked at Eefera.

"If'n I was yore liddle 'un I'd have killed meself from shame long ago. An' wot could be worse than sittin' lookin' at yore face, yer great shamble-toothed snotnosed excuse for an idiot!"

Vallug had to throw his paws around Eefera to stop him from leaping upon the harvest mouse. "Leave 'im be fer now. 'E ain't much use to us dead!"

When Eefera was released he took his spleen out on Gruven, slapping him repeatedly about the face and ears. "Who do ye think yore smilin' at? I'll wipe the grin off'n yore face. Ye don't laugh at me an' get away with it!"

Vallug took a few kicks at Gruven also. When he was allowed to carry on slinging stones, Gruven found himself wishing that he had half the backbone of the little harvest mouse.

Vallug fired an arrow over the wall and roared out his ultimatum: "Give us the Taggerung or yer all goin' to die!"

Tagg awoke in his dungeon with thoughts crowding his mind. Was it night or day? How long had he been here in the pitch dark? Who had clubbed him senseless? When were they going to let him out, or were they just going to keep the door locked and leave him imprisoned here? Where was Nimbalo? The otter could not remember ever being anywhere where he could not feel the wind on his face, see the sky or walk freely. Stumbling about in the blackness, he found the door and began battering on it with clenched paws, roaring for all he was worth, "Let me out! Why have you got me locked up in here! You've got no right to imprison me, d'you hear? Let me ooooooooouuuuuttt!"

29

Mhera stood in the Abbey doorway with Cregga. Redwallers crowded behind them, ordered to stay inside. Brother Hoben uttered what Mhera was thinking.

"Look at those stones. Two vermin couldn't do that alone. I'm afraid Fwirl made a mistake when she said there were only two."

Cregga leaned on the doorpost, stroking her striped muzzle. "So it seems. How many would you guess there were out there?"

The good Brother shrugged. "Who knows, marm? Certainly more than we first thought."

Mhera made her way to the broken window and climbed onto the redstone sill, gazing out to where the slingstones battered down constantly onto the Abbey lawn. She noticed that they followed a certain pattern, all falling around one central area, apart from the odd long throw, or occasional short casts that landed on the gatehouse path. Gundil peeped over her shoulder, his homely face anxious as he guessed her intent.

"You'm bain't a goen owt thurr, mizzy? They'm slingenrocks wudd crack ee skullbones. Stop ee in yurr wi' us'n's, noice'n'safe."

The ottermaid shook her head. Her mind was made up.

"I've got to go out and speak to them, Gundil. We must find out what a Taggerung is. This state of affairs cannot continue; it's only a matter of time before some Redwaller is slain. Even vermin must realize that they've got to communicate with us at some point, if only to clear the whole matter up."

Gundil raised his digging claws in despair. "Ho, lackeeday, bain't no use a talken to ee, miz, oi'm bounden to go owt thurr with ee!"

"And so am I. That makes three of us!"

"Beggin' y'pardon, marm, but as jolly old rankin' officer I'm comin' too, so that makes four, wot!"

Mhera had not noticed Cregga and Egburt below on the floor. She climbed down from the windowsill. "There's no need for you to put yourself in danger."

Cregga reared to her full height, which was considerable. "You seem to forget, Mhera, I am acting Abbess in charge. I would be neglecting my duty if I let you go out there alone."

Gundil reared to *his* full height, which was not much at all. "Hurr, an' oi'd be agglectin' moi dooty to ee. You'm moi friend!"

Mhera patted his velvety head, forestalling Egburt. "Don't tell me. You'd be neglecting your duty as Wallguard Commander if you didn't accompany me. So we'll all go together, my good friends. Thank you for your support."

By now more Redwallers were gathering in Great Hall, and Mhera and Cregga had to fend off their curious inquiries.

"Egburt said you're going out to talk with the vermin?"

The badger nodded. "Yes, Friar, though I wish he'd kept quiet about it."

"D'you need any help out there, Cregga marm?"

"None, thank you. We're going to parley, not to fight."

Broggle, Hoarg and Drogg were holding a whispered meeting.

"You tell her about our prisoner, Drogg, go on."

"Who, me? I'm not much good at explainin'. You tell 'er, Hoarg."

"Tell who, Mhera or Cregga?"

"Either one'll do. Tell Mhera, she ain't as fierce as Cregga, go on!"

"Er, I wouldn't know what t'say. I think young Broggle should do all the talkin'. 'Twas his idea in the first place."

Sister Alkanet was wearing Cregga's patience thin. "That Fwirl, already she wants to get up. Will you come and tell her she must remain in bed until I say!"

Cregga distractedly released a Dibbun who was clinging to her. "Sister, leave Fwirl alone if she feels well enough to get up!"

Friar Bobb sounded a touch officious as he cornered Mhera. "Will you be back for lunch, miz? Shall I serve it in Cregga's room for you both, or will you eat in the dining room?"

Mhera already had her paw on the latch of the Abbey door. She looked pleadingly at the Friar. "Yes. I mean no. We'll be back shortly, I hope. We'll take lunch in the dining room like everybeast; don't go to any trouble on our behalf, Friar. Now we really must go out there!"

Hoarg and Drogg pushed Broggle forward. In the stress of the moment, his old stammer returned. "Er, er, M-Miz M-Mhera . . ."

She whirled on him rather sharply. "Now what is it?"

Broggle stared guiltily at the floor.

"I . . . I w-wanted t-to . . ."

Mhera's patience was close to the breaking point when she caught Filorn watching her. The ottermum smiled and shook her head. Mhera bit her lip, and patted Broggle's back gently.

"Forgive me, Broggle. I know you've got a lot on your mind too. Yes, you can go up and visit Fwirl whenever you like, tell Sister Alkanet I said so. You two have a nice time. G'bye now." She kissed Broggle's cheek and threw the door open. "Gundil, Egburt, help our Badgermum, come on. We'll go along the walltops; there's no stones falling there. Keep low, though!"

The door slammed and they were gone.

Gruven, Dagrab and Rawback were paw weary, but Eefera and Vallug would not allow them to stop slinging. Eefera flicked at them smartingly with a whippy twig. "Cummon, put yer backs into it! Sling those stones 'arder!"

Vallug cupped both paws around his mouth and bellowed, "Yer under siege! Give us the Taggerung!"

Nimbalo pulled a face of comic despair. "Under siege? Haha, that's a good 'un. They couldn't 'it a pond if they was standin' in it, the picklepawed oafs!"

Eefera slashed at him with the whippy twig. "Shut yer mouth, you, or I'll cut yer tongue out!"

Nimbalo grinned crookedly at Vallug, a long welt on his face causing him to squint. "Ain't yore pal the tough 'un? 'E's very good at beatin' bound up prisoners. Wonder if'n 'e'd like to try it with me paws free, eh?"

Vallug grabbed the harvest mouse and heaved him bodily out of the ditch onto the path in front of the Abbey's main wallgate. "Think yore safe in there, don't ye?" he shouted out to anybeast who was listening inside. "Well, lissen t'this. We've got one of yore mice 'ere, a prisoner. Name o' Nimbalo the Slayer. If'n ye don't give us the Taggerung then Nimbalo's goin' to die, nice an' slow. So make yore minds up!"

Sister Alkanet fixed Broggle with an icy stare. "Well, Broggle, I'm surprised at you. Oh, I heard it all. Sneaking and speaking to Mhera behind my back like that. If you wanted to visit Fwirl, you only had to ask me. I'm just trying to do my best by her so she'll get well soon. It wasn't very nice of you to go over my head like that!"

Broggle was amazed at the Sister's accusation. "I never went behind your back, Sister. I wasn't even talking about Fwirl, it was Mhera's idea for me to visit anytime. I wanted to tell her something entirely different. Honestly I did!"

Alkanet narrowed her eyes. "Are you telling me the truth?"

Drogg spoke up in his friend's defense. "Of course he is. Broggle was tryin' to tell Mhera about the prisoner we took, him'n'me an' ole Hoarg."

Alkanet folded her paws, turning the frozen stare on Drogg. "Prisoner, what prisoner? You'd better tell me everything!"

Tagg's paws were throbbing from banging on the door, and he had shouted himself hoarse. He leaned against the big barrel, contemplating turning it on its side and rolling it hard at the door, but he soon realized it was a foolish idea. The room area was too small for rolling a barrel of its size with sufficient speed to damage the stout wood. Then he heard pawsteps. A short silence, followed by voices.

"A big vermin, you say?"

"Aye, Sister, big strong-lookin' rascal with a faceful of tattoos that'd frighten the life out of ye!"

"Hmm. And you knocked him out with a mallet and axe handles, then locked him up down here. Why didn't you tell anybeast?"

"We were waiting for the right moment, Sister. I was trying to tell Mhera and Cregga about it when they dashed off."

"I see. What type of vermin is this creature? Is it armed?"

"Er, I dunno. I've never seen many vermin. 'Spect they all look the same, savage an' murderous. He wasn't carryin' any kind o' weapon, but he had a big heavy tail, like an otter's rudder. But I've heard o' weasels an' stoats that had hefty tails. Remember what we learned at Abbey

348

School about that rat, Cluny the Scourge? Didn't he have a big heavy tail?"

Tagg listened intently to the speculation going back and forth. If he had been branded as a vermin, it might make matters worse if he began shouting. They could be frightened off. He decided to hold his silence until somebeast addressed him directly.

Nimbalo lay on his back, shutting his eyes against the sun. He felt furtively around the path until his tightly tied paws encountered what he had hoped to find. A sharp-edged piece of stone, not very big, but sufficient to his needs. Keeping his body as still as possible, he curled both paws inward. Then, gripping the stone securely, he began rubbing the broken edge against his bonds, hoping the vermin would not notice.

Eefera took Gruven's sword and leaned over the ditch's edge to lay it against Nimbalo's ear. "Wot's the matter with ye all in there?" he called out. "Don't ye care about yore liddle friend Nimbalo? Come an' see if yer don't believe us. Come on, ye lily-livered craven, we won't sling or fire arrows, ye've got my word on it!"

Cregga and Mhera lay flat beneath the threshold battlements, flanked by Gundil and Egburt. "What d'you think?" Mhera whispered to the Badgermum. "You know more about vermin than us."

Cregga placed a cautionary paw upon Mhera's shoulder. "Don't trust them, that's the first rule I learned about vermin. I don't know who this Nimbalo creature is, but it may be a trap, so here's what we'll do. Gundil and Egburt, you go back into the Abbey. Tell Drogg and any other able-bodied beasts to arm themselves and come up to the gate. They should be safe enough now the slinging has stopped. If the vermin have got a mouse prisoner, we might get the chance to open the doors quickly, dash out there and rescue him. But tell Drogg to stay by the gate, quietly, until I give the word. Go now."

Eefera's voice sang out from the ditch. "Pore liddle Nimbalo. I wouldn't like to be 'im, if'n one of youse in there doesn't make some kinda move soon. Hahahaha!"

Cregga gave her instructions to Mhera. "I'm going to stand up in plain view. I know how to parley with those scum. You stay low, just so you can see over the wall; that way you can let me know what's going on. Now don't argue, pretty one, do as I say."

Mhera pressed the badger's big paw to her cheek. "All right, but please be careful. You're our only Badgermum!"

Sister Alkanet tapped lightly upon the storeroom door and spoke in her no-nonsense voice.

"Listen to me, vermin, I want straight and truthful answers, or you can stay locked up in there until you perish. Understood?"

She was surprised that the answering voice was not a gruff snarl but a level and reasonable-sounding baritone. "I understand. What do you want to know?"

"What do you and your friends want at Redwall Abbey?"

"There are five vermin outside. They are not my friends, they are my enemies. I am not a vermin, I'm an otter."

Old Hoarg stamped his footpaw and chuckled. "Heehee, I knowed he was an otter, moment I set eyes on him!" He wilted into silence under Alkanet's skeptical stare. She continued.

"They say you have a tattooed face, like the two vermin one of our creatures saw in Mossflower Wood. Why is that?"

Tagg stood with his forehead against the door. He shrugged. "It's a very very long story, if you have the time to listen. Let me ask you a question, marm. Have you seen a harvest mouse lately? His name is Nimbalo the Slayer."

The Sister's severe voice left him in no doubt. "No, we have not! I'm asking the questions, otter, if that's what you are. Do you have a name? What is it?"

"You can call me Tagg. It's what I've been known as for as long as I can remember." The silence that followed was so long that Tagg asked, "What's the matter, marm? Don't you believe me? My name's Tagg!"

This time the Sister's voice sounded a little shrill. "Tagg? Is that short for something? What's your full name? The truth now, I want no lies!"

"Zann Juskarath Taggerung!"

Four voices echoed the last word. "Taggerung!"

Egburt came hurtling into the cellar at that precise moment. Forgetting all his hare impressions, he cried, "Brull said she saw you go down here. Quick, Drogg, an' you too, Broggle an' Hoarg! We're all needed up at the front gate. The vermin have captured a mouse an' they're goin' to kill him!"

Tagg banged upon the cellar door and shouted, "This mouse, d'you know his name?"

Egburt gaped at the door, wide-eyed. "Nimbalo the Slayer they said his name is. Why?"

Suddenly the door shook as the otter smashed his body against it. "Let me out of here, d'you hear me? I must get out! I won't harm anyone, I swear it! I've got to save my friend! It's me the vermin want, me, the Taggerung of the Juska!"

Sister Alkanet shook her head stubbornly. "We'll have to report this to the elders for a counselors' meeting. I'm afraid you'll have to stay locked up until they decide."

It was then that Broggle did something totally unexpected. He pushed the Sister to one side and heaved the bolts back. "Then go and save your friend. Hurry, Taggerung!"

Cregga stood up in full view of the vermin. "We have no mouse here named Nimbalo, but if you are holding him prisoner I beg you not to harm him!"

Vallug rose, an arrow notched full stretch on his bow.

"Yore not in any position to make demands of us, stripedog. We'll chop this 'ere mouse inter fishbait if'n yer don't give up the Taggerung!"

Mhera peeped over the battlements and saw the five tattooed vermin and Nimbalo lying bound on the path. Cregga spread her paws. "I don't understand what you mean. There is no such thing as a Taggerung in our Abbey. How can we give what we don't have?"

Eefera whispered to Vallug as he watched the badger's face. "That ole stripedog's blind. See, she's lookin' right past us at the flatlands be'ind. I tell yer, she's blinder'n a stone!"

Vallug laughed scornfully at the old blind badger. "Hohoho, 'ow d'you know you ain't got a Taggerung in there? You couldn't see yer paw in front of ye, y'ole fool!"

Cregga could feel anger coursing through her veins. "Listen, you thickbrained scum, it's you who's the fool. You can stand out there shouting for a Taggerung until you're blue in the face. We haven't got a Taggerung and we don't even know what a Taggerung is. So use what little brain you have and tell us, what in the name of all seasons is a Taggerung, eh?"

Nimbalo sawed through the last of his bonds and burst loose. Bloodlust shone from his eyes as he leaped for the battle-axe sticking up over the ditch's edge. "Death t'the vermin!" he roared.

He grabbed the axehead. The shaft went sideways and struck Vallug on the elbow, and he released the arrow instinctively. Cregga stood stock still, the shaft buried in her chest. Mhera leapt up, screaming.

Tagg came up the stairs like a thunderbolt. Dashing through Cavern Hole, he collided with an ottermum. Stopping momentarily, he held her steady by the paw. "Sorry, marm!" Then he was off up the stairs into Great Hall, leaving Filorn looking as if she had seen a ghost. As he bounded through the Great Hall toward the Abbey door, the otter's eyes flicked left and right, looking for a weapon. He saw the warrior mouse on a huge wall tapestry. Perched above it on two silver spikes, Martin's sword shone like fire on ice. There was no time to stop. Bounding forward, Tagg gave a mighty leap. He snatched the sword and sped out of the door.

Brother Hoben was already at the gate. He saw the big painted otter charging toward him, shouldering Redwallers aside as he came. Broggle was dashing to keep up with Tagg, waving his paws at Hoben, yelling, "Open the gates, Brother! Let him through, open the gates!"

Hoben kicked the wooden bar up and threw open Redwall's gates. Like lightning the otter charged past him, whirling the sword, his voice roaring like thunder upon the wind.

"Vallug Bowbeast, 'tis death to you! I am Taggerung Juskaaaaaa!"

Vallug already had another arrow on his taut bowstring. He let fly at Tagg. The shaft buried itself in the otter's chest, but he kept coming, his mighty wrath unstoppable. Vallug was reaching for another arrow when the great sword flashed downward. Tagg's shout was the last thing the ferret heard in his life.

"For my father!"

Vallug's body remained standing; his head thudded into the ditch, alongside the severed bow. Eefera was up out of the ditch, running across the flatlands. Tagg spanned the ditch in a bound and went after him. Dagrab fled south along the ditchbed, with Nimbalo hard on her heels wielding the battle-axe. Gruven snatched up his fallen sword and ran, terror coursing through him. He ran as he had never run before, north up the ditchbed, away from the melee. Rawback paused, but only for an instant, before he chased after Gruven. As soon as the woodlands came into view on his right, Gruven left the ditch and scrambled into the tree cover, with Rawback in his wake. Together they hurried north, following the woodland fringe until more tree cover appeared on the west side. Recrossing the path hastily, the two stoats stumbled through the ditch and entered Mossflower's west thicknesses, Rawback some way behind as they struck inward. When he ran out of breath Gruven halted. The ground beneath his paws was soft, and immediately he began sinking. With his final effort he pulled himself clear and found dry ground. When Rawback came staggering and panting along, Gruven leaned against a tree, puffing, and waved him on.

"That way, mate. I'll catch me breath an' wait 'ere awhile to stop anybeast followin' us. You go on, I'll catch ye up."

Rawback plowed wearily on. Gruven waited until he heard the terror-stricken screams from the swampland, and then he sat down until he regained enough breath to carry on. When the screaming had stopped, Gruven felt quite recovered. He cut off around the swamp edges, chuckling to himself.

"Dead, all dead an' gone, only me left. Gruven Zann Juskazann!"

30

Rose-blushed skies and scattered creamy cloudbanks softened the western horizon with early evening. Twoscore seasoned otters, armed with slings and light javelins, dogtrotted tirelessly on, their footpaws thrumming over the flatlands. Grim-faced and silent, Skipper and Boorab led the column. The otter Chieftain took a bearing from the low-slung sun.

"Chin up, bucko. We'll make it t'the Abbey by nightfall!"

The hare's breathing was ragged. He had not slept since he left Redwall, but stubbornly he fought the weariness that threatened to overwhelm him.

Skipper could not help but notice his plight. "You drop out an' take a blow, mate, carry on when yore rested."

Boorab picked up his pace, snorting defiantly, "Never, sah! Officer never lies down an' naps on a mission, wot. We'll enter the blinkin' Abbey together, side by jolly side!"

Skipper's eyes were never still when he and his crew were on the move. He was constantly reading the land ahead and to both sides. The otter's roving gaze fixed on a bright glinting object, ahead and slightly south. At first he took it for a flame, but as he drew closer he recognized it as a metal object reflecting the reddening sunrays. He veered a point, taking his contingent in its direction.

"Over there, mates. Keep yore javelins ready. At the double!"

Boorab dropped behind slightly, then found himself in the center of the crew, supported by two burly females who rushed him along.

"Let yore footpaws go loose, matey. We'll do the runnin'!"

Skipper was first at the scene, and his keen eyes took it all in at a glance. Death had visited the flatlands.

The weasel Eefera lay slain, mouth lolling open, sightless eyes staring at the sky. Tagg sat slumped nearby, a broken arrow protruding from his chest. His head was bowed, but he still held on to the sword of Martin the Warrior, the blade pointing over his shoulder, resting against his cheek.

Boorab joined Skipper, and surveyed the tableau gravely. "By thunder, sah, now that's what I call a Warrior, wot!"

Skipper reconstructed what had taken place from the tracks and bloodstains round about. "The weasel ain't carryin' bow'n'arrows. This big feller, the tattooed otter, that broken shaft's been in him awhile. See, the weasel's wounds are much fresher." He called to one of his crew who was tracking further forward. "Which way did they come?"

The otter jerked a paw over his shoulder. "Back thataway, Skip, prob'ly from the Redwall direction!"

Skipper picked up the broken halves of Eefera's spear. "Hmm. The way I sees it is that the otter chased this weasel clear from the Abbey. That's a big strong weasel, but he couldn't outrun the otter, even though our friend 'ere 'ad taken an arrow right in his chest. This otter chased the weasel almost a league, aye, an' caught the vermin too. I don't know 'ow he did it, but a terrible fight took place 'ere. That otter slew the weasel, then sat 'imself

356

down an' held the sword up. 'Tis an ole trick: the sun shines off'n the blade, like a signal to let yore mates know where y'are. But nobeast came, so the otter died there, sittin' up holdin' Martin's sword, alongside his dead enemy. But 'ow did he come to be carryin' the great sword o' Redwall?" Skipper knelt and tried to prize the weapon loose from Tagg's grasp. "Like y'say, Boorab, 'ere's wot y'call a Warrior. I can't budge the blade from his paws, an' I ain't no weaklin' . . . by the roarin' river, this bucko's still alive!"

Tagg lifted his head a fraction, one eye flickering half open. "Juska . . . leave me 'lone . . . now." Then he slumped over, still gripping the sword.

Boorab called out, "You chaps, take off y'belts. Use 'em with those javelins to make a stretcher. He's comin' back to the Abbey with us. Look sharp there, jump to it now, no time t'waste, wot!"

Skipper stroked his whiskers thoughtfully. "Juska, eh? I've seen Juskas afore. They go in clans, tattooed murderin' thieves. But Juskabeasts are all vermin: rats, stoats an' the like. 'Ow did an otter come t'be mixed up with 'em? See, 'is face is all tattooed up, even more'n an ordinary Juska."

The hare had got his second wind and was feeling impatient. "Won't matter if the chap's tattooed from rock to rudder, looks like he's goin' to peg out soon if we don't get him help. Besides, who knows what's goin' on back at the Abbey, wot? They could be besieged, battered an' waitin' on us to arrive!"

With a renewed sense of urgency they set off again. Borne between eight stout ottercrew, Tagg lay on the stretcher clasping the sword, mercifully unconscious as they traveled at the double.

Nimbalo made his way back along the ditchbed in the failing light, using his battle-axe as a walking staff. He went into a fighting crouch at the sound of a gruff voice.

"Halt, who goes there?"

Brandishing the axe, he answered in equally gruff tones, "Nimbalo the Slayer, so stan' aside, whoever ye be!"

Drogg Cellarhog held out a paw to help him from the ditch. "Yore the 'arvest mouse who went after that rat. C'mon up, friend. Did ye have any luck?"

Nimbalo scrambled up onto the flatlands, where a party of Redwallers were waiting. He winked knowingly at them. "Oh, I 'ad all the luck in the land, 'twas the rat who ran outta luck. She won't be slayin' anymore, y'can bet on that, mates!"

Egburt held up a lantern he had just lit. "Nimbalo, have you seen anything of your otter friend? He ran out here somewhere, chasing a weasel. We've got to find him because he took the sword of Martin the Warrior with him."

Nimbalo leaned nonchalantly on his battle-axe. "Don't worry, matey, if'n Tagg's out 'ere, then he'll find us."

A cry rang out of the darkness. "Ahoy the lantern there! Egburt, is that you, laddie buck?" Skipper and Boorab loomed up out of the darkness, with the otter crew at their back. The hare shook Drogg's paw.

"Well met, old chap, as y'can see I made it. What's the situation back at Redwall? Any problems back home, wot?"

The Cellarhog's spikes rattled as he shook his head, bright tears glistening in his eyes. "This mouse 'ere, Nimbalo, 'twas him an' the otter called Taggerung, they drove the vermin off, but not afore one o' the scum shot Cregga Badgermum with an arrow. She's hit real bad! I don't suppose ye came across the otter? He was carryin' the sword of Martin. We're out searchin' for him."

The ottercrew parted ranks, allowing the stretcher bearers to carry Tagg into the lantern light. Skipper patted his paw. "We found yore otter, lyin' by a slain weasel; there's an arrow in his chest too. But he's still breathin' an' the sword's safe. Though he's got some sort o' death grip on it."

Nimbalo ran to Tagg's side, suddenly feeling frightened and lonely. "Tagg, mate, it's me, Nimbalo. Say somethin', Tagg. 'Tis me, Nimbalo the Slayer, yore ole matey!"

Tagg did nothing. Nimbalo collapsed, grief-stricken, against him.

Boorab detailed two more otters. "Put your shoulders to that stretcher. We can't let this brave beast die. Get Nimbalo up there with him. He can keep his pal company on the way back to the Abbey."

Redwall's main gates were still open. Filorn stood out on the path with old Hoarg, holding a lantern each. Noting the ottermum's drawn, anxious face, Hoarg murmured, "Go an' sit in my gate'ouse, marm. Put your paws up an' have a nice 'ot beaker o' motherwort tea. You'll do no good standin' out 'ere. I'll give ye news, soon as I see them returnin'."

Filorn shook her head, smiling at the kindly dormouse. "No, I must wait here, but you go in, Hoarg. It's been a long weary day for you. Please, go in. I'll be fine right here."

Hoarg tugged his grizzled whiskers courteously. "If yore sure, marm. I ain't as young as I used t'be."

He shuffled slowly inside to the gatehouse, where his supper was awaiting him. Filorn drew her shawl tighter around her shoulders. It was the otter. Something about his tattoo-covered face, the deep sound of his voice, the way he moved. She had to wait and see if the search party had found him. Worry piled upon worry in her mind. Brother Hoben had said he saw the otter hit by an arrow. Was he badly hurt?

"Ho the gate! Is that the pretty young Filorn waitin' to greet me?"

Filorn knew Skipper's gruff voice. She ran south down the path toward a small lantern gleaming over the ottercrew and the Redwallers who had gone searching.

They entered the Abbey, with Filorn holding Tagg's

359

paws, still clasped upon the sword. Nimbalo was aching from supporting his friend's head against the bumping and jogging of the journey. He looked up into Filorn's face. "Don't fret, marm. Tagg's my matey, I won't let 'im die."

Foremole Brull's moles were laying mattresses and cushions upon the floor of Great Hall. Filorn fussed about the ottercrew as they lifted Tagg from the stretcher. "Easy now, lower him gently, try not to bump him, please."

Mhera appeared at her mother's side. "Mama, what is it? Who is that creature with his face all tattooed like a vermin?"

Filorn drew her daughter close, leaning forward with her until Mhera could feel the unconscious otter's shallow breath on her brow. "Look, my child, look. Does his face mean nothing to you?"

Even in repose, Tagg's features looked barbaric because of the red, black and blue markings ingrained into them. The dream came back to Mhera as she stared harder and harder.

"Father . . . is it Papa? He looks something like him."

Filorn did not reply, but much to Mhera's astonishment began singing and caressing Tagg's paws, which were still locked onto the sword hilt.

"Mountains rivers valleys seas,
Whose little paws are these, are these?
Meadows, woodlands fields and shores,
These little paws are yours, are yours!
If you don't give me a kiss,
I will tickle paws like this!"

It was many a long season since Mhera had heard her mother sing a baby song. Now Filorn was tickling the big rough paws. Mhera was totally startled by what happened next.

Tagg was still senseless, but he smiled and opened his paws, pads upward. Just like any babe who wanted its mother to do it again. Nimbalo quickly removed the sword. There on Tagg's open right paw was the four-petal mark, pink and distinctive as the day he was born with it.

Filorn hugged Mhera. "I knew it deep inside me, ever since I saw him yesterday. This is my son! He's returned home. He's your brother, Mhera!"

The ottermaid clasped the flower-marked paw between her own, and spoke his name loud and clear. "Deyna!"

Nimbalo scratched the end of his nose. "Deyna! Y'mean Tagg's name ain't Taggerung no more?"

Filorn shook her head, smiling at the harvest mouse. "His real name is Deyna; he has no other."

Nimbalo mused over the new name. "Hmm. Deyna. I don't know whether I like that or not, it ain't like Nimbalo the Slayer. Huh, just Deyna? Couldn't we call 'im Deyna the Deadly or Deyna the Dagger or Deyna the Dangerous? Hoho, I likes that 'un. Deyna the Dangerous, great name!"

Filorn tweaked the little fellow's ear. "If I hear you calling him Deyna the Dangerous I'll tell everybeast that your name is Nimbalo the Nuisance. Understood?"

The harvest mouse shrugged unhappily. "Jus' Deyna it is, then, marm."

Sister Alkanet arrived with Broggle and Friar Bobb, who were carrying bowls of warm water, dressing cloths, ointments and herbal remedies. They waited to one side as she cleaned and inspected the wound. Her pronouncement was not a happy one, though she tried to sound optimistic.

"The arrow has gone too deep, I haven't the skill or experience to remove it. Though I must say, Deyna is the strongest and fittest beast I've ever seen. I've heard in the past of creatures living quite a normal life with arrowheads or spearpoints still in them. Deyna will live, but he'll have to take things easy. I can cut away the arrow shaft, but the point will have to stay in him."

Skipper had been listening, and voiced his opinion. "Beggin' yore pardon, marm, but Rukky Garge could fix Deyna up. Ole Rukky is the best otterfixer on earth."

Sister Alkanet waved her paws dismissively. "Rukky Garge is just some legend. There's no such otter!"

Filorn was inclined to agree. "I believe there was such an otter, but I heard she passed on many long seasons ago."

Skipper merely smiled and pointed to his rudder. "I was scarred deep there when I was a liddlebeast, but Rukky made the scar go away. I still goes to see ole Rukky, takes 'er freshwater shrimp an' 'otroot soup now an' agin. She's like a gran'ma to me, marm. Hoho, she's still kickin' right enough."

Filorn clasped Skipper's paw anxiously. "If she could heal my son I'd take her a hundred pans of shrimp and hotroot soup! I'd give her anything!"

The otter Chieftain understood Filorn's anxiety. "No need t'do that, but I know Rukky likes bright trinkets. She's like a magpie, loves anythin' bright'n'shiny, Rukky does."

Filorn opened her broad apron pocket. "I found this lying in the ditch this afternoon. Perhaps she'd like it, what do you think?"

Skipper inspected the knife of Sawney Rath, with its brilliant sapphire, amber handle and bright silver blade. "I think she'd make a skeleton dance fer this beauty, marm!"

Mhera shifted anxiously from paw to paw. "Let's take him to her straightaway!"

Skipper appeared rather uncomfortable with this suggestion. "Be more'n my life's worth, miz. Rukky's a loner, very awkward pernickety ole body she is, won't 'ave anybeast within a league of 'er. She don't treat nobeast save otters these days, an' then only as a favor to me'n'a few other otters. Look, you leave this to me. I'll take Deyna an' persuade Rukky to cure him. My crew can carry him most o' the way, an' we'll drop in from time to time t'let you know 'ow he's doin'. Mhera, you an' yore mama trust me, I'll take care o' Deyna. I think you'll be needed 'ere, ain't that right, Sister?"

Alkanet pursed her lips, bound, as usual, to have her say. "Correct, Skipper. Cregga is not young and full of energy. I took the arrowhead from her, but she's slowly fading. She needs you by her side, Mhera. Filorn, you know how much Friar Bobb relies on your help, and the others too. I beg you to stay at the Abbey."

Filorn was impressed. She had never heard Alkanet beg anything from a living creature, so she gave in to her request.

"Well, we've come through all these seasons not knowing whether Deyna lived. Now we do know, I suppose we'll have to be patient a little longer, Mhera."

The ottermaid bowed obediently. "We'll be patient, Mama, but it won't be for long, I hope."

This time a bigger, more comfortable litter was made to transport Tagg. Sister Alkanet waited until they were ready to set off and then pulled Skipper to one side.

"I'm surprised that a creature like you still believes in that old relic and her mumbo jumbo of spells and charms. Shame on you! Though I'll be even more surprised if Deyna returns alive. How could you raise the hopes of Filorn and Mhera on stories and tales like that?"

Skipper winked at the Sister. "Maybe I'll surprise you again before too long, marm. Take care!"

Nimbalo joined the otter crew. Skipper looked inquiringly at the battle-axe-wielding harvest mouse. "Belay, mate, where d'you think yore off to?"

The little fellow nodded at the litter. "Wherever me matey goes, that's where I'm off to. Any objections?"

Skipper was very tactful in dealing with the truculent mouse. "I can't stop ye, 'specially since yore the one they calls the Slayer. But this ole otterfixer, Rukky Garge, if she sees anybeast that ain't an otter hangin' about her den, she'll turn us away. No matter wot condition yore matey's in."

Nimbalo's face was the picture of dejection. His lip quivered. "But me'n'Tagg's always been together. Wot'll I

363

do without 'im? We stuck by each other through thick'n'thin, an' now yore goin' to take me matey away. Wot'll I do 'ere, all on me own?"

Mhera's heart went out to Nimbalo. She took his paw. "Wait here at the Abbey with us. You'll like it, I'm sure. It's like being part of a big happy family."

Unknowingly, Mhera had mentioned the wrong word. Nimbalo growled. "Don't talk t'me about families. I ain't part of no family!"

Skipper and his crew slipped quietly off with Tagg, leaving Mhera to practice her diplomacy on the irate harvest mouse. Tactfully, Filorn stepped into the breach.

"I never met a warrior yet who wasn't hungry. Come to the kitchens with me, Nimbalo the Slayer. Let's see what I can find for you. Redwall food is the best anywhere, come on."

Boorab, who had been gently nodding off, came awake at the mention of food. "Ahem, charmin' an' kindly marm, permission to accompany you, wot."

Filorn was never less than gracious to her friend the hare. "Why, of course, sir, you are cordially invited."

Mhera went to sit on Cregga's bed. It had been impossible to carry the wounded badger upstairs, so mattresses had been laid for her beneath the tapestry of Martin, and she lay propped up on them. Sensing Mhera's approach, the Badgermum smiled weakly. "Your mama could charm the birds from the trees. That little harvest mouse doesn't know it, but he's got all the qualities of a Redwaller. You must help to make him happy here, Mhera."

The ottermaid plumped up her friend's pillows. "You mean *we* must help to make him happy here, Cregga."

The badger stroked Mhera's cheek. "Maybe, if I'm still around, but nobeast lives forever."

Mhera sniffed and straightened the coverlet busily. "Now you can just stop that sort of talk, silly old badger.

Deyna's going to get well and so are you. I won't listen to any morbid rambling ab—"

Cregga put out a searching paw. "Mhera, what is it? What's the matter?"

The ottermaid held a green strip of cloth close to Cregga's muzzle. "It's one of those pieces of material. Faded green, homespun and scented with lilac. I found it just now, in the folds of your bedspread. I wonder who put it there. Do you know?"

Cregga shook her great striped head slowly. "A blind creature who can hardly move, with a deep painful wound. How am I supposed to know anything? What does it say?"

Mhera read the crude vertical capitals written on the fabric. "FITTAGALL. Oh, dear. What's it all supposed to mean, Cregga?"

A lot of Redwallers joined Nimbalo and Boorab in the kitchens, as there had been no proper meals served, owing to the day's unusual events. Friar Bobb and Filorn aided by Broggle and Fwirl (now much recovered) managed a good makeshift buffet. Nimbalo sampled everything, from soup to desserts. Filorn sat down with him, encouraging the harvest mouse as he ate.

"I'm sure you've got lots of wonderful tales of the adventures you and Deyna had together. Perhaps you could tell us some? Here, let me fill your tankard with October Ale."

Nimbalo was suddenly in his element: lots of good food and drink, and an attentive audience. He shovelled turnip'n'tater'n'beetroot pie into his mouth and washed it down with a huge draft of the best October Ale.

"Aaaahhhh! That's the stuff t'give yer muscles like boulders, marm. Thankee. Now, where was I? Oh aye. Tagg, that's Deyna, an' me was surrounded by snakes one time."

Foremole Brull shuddered. "Burr, surrpints. Oi carn't aboide ee gurt snakey beasters!"

The harvest mouse gave her his reckless nonchalant grin. "Snakes, marm? Me'n'Deyna was never afeared of 'em!" He rose and swaggered about outrageously.

"There was one time me'n'my mate,
We nearly met our fate,
One dark night, midst a storm,
Just to keep us dry an' warm,
We found a cave an' a cheer we gave,
We rushed in straightaway,
'Twas full of snakes, for goodness' sakes,
All silvery black an' grey.
There was big snakes, small snakes,
Every one was wide awake,
Wrigglin' an' a-hissin' there,
Tongues a-flickerin', tails a-snickerin',
Enough t'curl yore blinkin' hair.
One bit me so I bit it back,
An' my mate gave one such a whack!
We fought the serpents tooth'n'claw,
For every one we slayed there was a dozen more.
Then my ole mate, he took two sticks,
An' in the space of two short ticks,
We grabbed those snakes, me'n'my chum,
An' knitted them up into an apron for his mum,
Chuck one, hurl one, knit one, purl one,
We never went there again,
Don't try to sleep, where the snakes are tummy deep,
Take a snooze out in the rain!"

Nimbalo took a bow amidst the applause and roars of laughter. Boorab presented him with a damson cream pie.

"Top hole, sah. You're a born weaver of yarns, wot. Try some of Friar Bobb's damson cream pie. Bet y've never tasted anythin' as scrumptious as that, wot. Wot wot, hawhawhaw!"

366

Nimbalo bit into it and smacked his lips. "Thankee. It's good, very nice, but tell me, did ye ever taste a snakeyfish pie?"

The hare looked at him aghast. "Snakeyfish pie, sir? What in the name o' puddens is that? You haven't eaten one yourself, have you, old chap?"

Nimbalo winked at the horrified listeners. "Ye wouldn't believe me if'n I told yer!"

31

Tendrils of blue smoke curled through the trees of south Mossflower Wood, wreathing upward from a fire of dead pinecones and fir branches on the rocky ledge of a riverbank. Skipper stirred the contents of a big pot, set on a tripod over the flames. He tasted it and waved his rudder.

"Swash, bring more watershrimp. Blekker, chop more 'otroot an' peppers, an' sliver some o' them scallions in with it!"

The two sturdy otter sisters, Swash and Blekker, brought the ingredients to him and watched as he stirred them into the pot of freshwater shrimp and hotroot soup. Skipper held out the ladle to the pair, proud of his cooking prowess.

"Sup that an' tell me wot ye think?"

They took turns, blowing on the ladle's contents and sipping.

"That's the stuff, Skip. It'd melt moss off'n a boulder!"

"Aye, only you can make shrimp'n'otroot soup like that, Skip!"

Skipper chuckled. "Don't tell yore ma that!"

Deyna was still unconscious. He lay strapped to the litter, scarcely breathing and woefully thin and pale looking. Swash mopped his fevered forehead with some moss she had dipped in the river. His muzzle was hot and dry to the touch.

"Skip, this pore feller ain't eaten in three days now. D'you think we should try an' feed him somethin'?"

But Skipper remained adamant, as he had since they left Redwall. "No vittles for Deyna, just a drop o' clear water now an' agin. We got to leave him like that until Rukky sees wot's best. I don't want to do the wrong thing by feedin' a bad-wounded otter. Right then, clear the decks, me buckos, fill yore bowls an' wait back by the bend for me. Mind an' leave plenty o' the soup for the otterfixer. Don't want 'er in a bad mood."

The crew filled their bowls and took off to await Skipper's return by the riverbend. When they had gone the otter Chieftain went to a massive old larch tree. It was long dead but still standing, its core rotted and eaten away by insects. Standing half a pace off, Skipper swung his rudder and whacked it against the hollow trunk.

"Whock! Whock!"

Behind him on the riverbank an incredibly ancient otter materialized from amid the rock ledges. Her fur was totally silver white, mostly hidden by a heavily ornamented black cloak and hood sewn with crystal shards, seashells, globules of amber and small bright polished stones. Her body was bent with age, and she leaned upon a knobbly stick. From beneath the hood of her cloak she peered out at Skipper. There was not a single tooth in her mouth, but the two eyes that watched him were brighter than her hooped gold earrings.

Skipper bowed. "Rukky Garge, me ole friend, 'tis a pleasure to see ye."

She sucked hard on her gums before replying. "Ahhr weel, 'tis der young riverpup. Did yeer famine-gobbed crew ayt up all Rukky's soup?"

The otter Chieftain helped her courteously up the bank to the pot. "Only the hard tasteless bits, me ole queen. I saved the best for you. Try a taste."

Rukky Garge spooned a ladleful, boiling, straight into her mouth and gulped it down. She licked her lips. " 'Tis a fact, ye kin make d'soup better'n myself can. So, well, ye never came to see Rukky fer nought. What izzit dat ails ye?"

Skipper pointed to the still form of Deyna. "I fetched this pore beast from the Abbey. He took an arrow; see the broken shaft still stuck in his chest? Yore the best otterfixer, my ole charmer. Can you make Deyna better agin?"

Rukky Garge sniffed the wound in Deyna's chest, pushed one of his eyelids up and looked at the upturned eye, rubbed his muzzle, felt all four paws, picked up his rudder, weighed it in her paw and let it drop, all the time muttering away. "Ahhr weel now, Redwall Abbey an' all de clever cratures. Couldn't be curin' a waspy sting atween dem, ahhhr no!"

Skipper broke his respectful silence. "So ye say, me ole darlin', but could you?"

Rukky went back to the pot and supped two more ladles of hot soup. "Dis a Juskabeast. Pictures'n'patterns on de face. Baaaad! Why you ask Rukky to do de otterfixin' for dis varmint, eh?"

Skipper gave his explanation as she made inroads on the soup. "Deyna's the son of an ole mate o' mine. He was taken by Juska when he was a cub. Rillflag was his father an' Filorn's his mother; she still lives at the Abbey, with his older sister Mhera."

The ancient otter repeated Mhera's name, drawing it out. "Meera, Meeeerraaaa! I like well dat name. I fix him!"

Skipper stood where he was, knowing that Rukky did not like shaking paws, or being touched in any way. "My thanks to ye, Rukky Garge. I'll keep the soup goin', good an' hot, night'n'day, whenever ye needs it."

She leaned forward on the knobbly stick. "Ahhr weel now, ye'll need lots o' d'soup. Dis Deyna won't be fixed in wan day. 'Twill be when de russet h'apples fall."

Skipper tried not to look surprised. "That's a long time, marm?"

She attempted to chew on a watershrimp. "So y'say, so y'say. Need longen time to be fixin' arrowhole. Gotta take varmint pictures off da face too, ho yerssss!"

Skipper raised his eyebrows. "You can do that, take off the tattoos?"

She gave up chewing and swallowed the watershrimp. "So I can, so I can. I make dat picture on yore paw, 'member!"

Skipper looked at the pike tattooed on the back of his paw. "Aye, you did, a long time ago I recall."

Rukky shrugged. "So, I put pictures on wid dye an' needle. I take dem off too. An' dat flower on Deyna's paw, I fix it up good, you see. Den he looken like yew, proper riverdog again, not varmint!"

Skipper had to carry Deyna into Rukky's cave and lay him on a long moss-covered shelf. The otterfixer's cave was like her cloak, studded from floor to ceiling with crystal, metal and semiprecious stones, amber, carnelian, peridot and black jet. Two firefly lanterns reflected off the decorations, making the interior dazzle and shine.

Skipper took out the blade of Sawney Rath. "This is for you, Rukky my ole sweet. A liddle gift."

She recoiled, drawing her paws into the voluminous cloak. "Pretty an' bad, baaaaad! I'll not touch d'thing. Stick in inna wall. Dat blade's shedded blood. Baaaaaad!"

Skipper buried the knifepoint in the cave wall. "Fair enough. Now wot d'ye want me to do?"

The ancient one made a dismissive gesture. "Geddout, go you! Make d'soup for Rukky, an' tell yore crew keep 'way, far 'way. Mebbe call if'n I need ye, young pup."

Skipper left the cave as Rukky began building a fire of special herbs and dried roots. Deyna lay motionless on the ledge, oblivious of all around him. Pale whitish smoke wafted around the cave, fragrant and exotic. The otterfixer opened a dark lacquered box and began choosing her instruments.

*

Blekker and Swash were making a rush net to catch freshwater shrimps at the riverbend when Skipper loped up. The others of the ottercrew gathered around to hear his report.

"Rukky sez she can fix Deyna up, but he won't be fit to travel until early autumn, when the russet apples start t'fall. I'm goin' to stay an' keep the soup pot goin' for 'er. Blekker an' Swash, you carry the news back to Redwall. Deyna's mama an' sister'll want to know he's goin' to live. Oh, an' take a score o' the crew with ye. They can stop at the Abbey just in case any more vermin turn up at the gates!"

There was fierce competition among the ottercrew. A stay at Redwall with the best of food and comfort was preferable to several weeks' wait at the riverbend. Skipper got things finally organized, sending Blekker and Swash off with twenty that he had picked himself. The otter Chieftain ordered the rest to keep the soup ingredients coming daily, then he went back upriver to his lonely vigil outside Rukky Garge's den.

Six days had passed since Cregga took Vallug's arrow. She still lay on her large pad of mattresses beneath Martin the Warrior's tapestry in Great Hall. Brother Hoben and Sister Alkanet stepped outside for a breath of the late summer air. Alkanet tucked both paws into her wide habit sleeves.

"Six full days and she's still alive. Can you believe it, Brother?"

Hoben smiled and nodded his head in admiration. "Good old Cregga Badgermum. She's indestructible!" He knew he had said the wrong thing by the look on Alkanet's face.

"Hmph. Typical Redwaller, just like the rest of them, all winks and nods and smiles, telling themselves that Cregga will live forever. Now listen to me. Nobeast knows how old she really is, but that badger has lived more seasons than any four of us put together. 'Tis about time you all realized that. She took the full force of a vermin arrow close to her heart. I removed the shaft and dressed it, so only I have seen how deep and serious the wound is. Cregga hasn't long to live; her seasons have finally run out. You must realize this!"

Hoben kept his voice calm, staring levelly at the Sister. "I assure you, most of us do realize all of what you've said. But hope springs eternal, and where there's life there's hope. So we don't go about telling each other that our Badgermum is about to die. It's very hard for the Dibbuns, and those close to her, like Mhera, Broggle and Fwirl, to accept that soon they'll lose a beloved friend. So I beg you, Sister, please don't start preaching the fatal message to them."

The severe mouse fixed him with her frozen stare. "As you wish, Brother, as you wish!" She stalked off with her head erect.

Mhera and Fwirl were sitting on the mattresses with Cregga. The badger only spoke when it was necessary, and she slept a lot. But Mhera had stayed by her side the whole six days, constantly looking after her friend and chatting to her of what was going on in the Abbey.

"Guess what, Cregga? I hear that there's going to be a little celebration in your honor this evening, isn't that right, Fwirl?"

The pretty squirrelmaid looped her tail over her eyes. "Oh, Mhera, it was going to be a surprise, and now you've gone and given the secret away. What will Friar Bobb and Broggle say?"

Cregga chuckled hoarsely. "I already knew. My hearing is still good as ever. I heard them discussing the menu this morning. I hear quite a lot lying here—like now, for instance. Trouble's headed our way, the rascals." The old badger smiled as Boorab and Nimbalo marched up and seated themselves beside Mhera and Fwirl.

Despite his initial reluctance, the harvest mouse had taken to Abbey life like a duck to water. He was

373

everywhere at once, down in the cellars picking up hints from Drogg, working in the kitchen, learning from the cooks, or out in the orchard, helping with the growing of berries, nuts and fruit. He spent quite a bit of time with Boorab. They got along famously together, usually trying to outfib one another. Today they were both in garrulous form.

"What ho, ladies. Couldn't resist the chance of a visit to three jolly pretty charmers, eh, wot wot!"

"If that oaf thinks I'm a pretty charmer he's blinder than me!" Cregga whispered to Fwirl and Mhera. She turned her attention to the new visitors. "So then, what's your real reason for bothering us? You tell me, Nimbalo. I can't believe a word that hare says."

The harvest mouse stuck his chest out proudly. "Ho, I'm an even better fibber than Boorab, marm, but I'll tell the truth this time. It's that pair in the kitchen, ole Friar Bobb an' Broggle. They won't let us 'elp with the vittles. Run the pair of us off, didn't they, mate?"

Boorab's earbells jingled as he nodded agreement. "Rather. Sent us packin' on our way, an' what for, may I ask? Huh, a couple o' pawfuls of candied chestnuts, a measly taste of summer trifle, a few sips of elderberry wine, an' . . . an' . . . what else was it, Nimbalo old scout?"

"Er, a mushroom'n'gravy flan, bowl o' salad an' some o' that soft white cheese with celery an' hazelnuts in it. An' a—"

Mhera interrupted the harvest mouse. "Stop! That's quite enough. It sounds as if you tried to clean the pantries out between you. No wonder you were chased out. If I'd been there I would have showed you the way out with a broom, and you'd still be smarting from it, you pair of gluttons!"

Nimbalo wiped crumbs from his whiskers, saying sorrowfully, "Ah, 'tis an 'ard cruel life, matey, to 'ear those words from the luvly lips of my mate Deyna's own pretty sister. Well, that's wot we get for tryin' to 'elp out a little with the chores!"

Boorab's ears drooped pathetically. "Harsh words an' harsher treatment, laddie buck, that's all you can expect in this bloomin' Abbey. An' I speak as one who's a fifteen-season probationer, always the caterpillar an' never the frog. Or is it always the tadpole an' never the butterfly? I can never jolly well remember. I don't think miz Mhera deserves to see what we found, after that harsh outburst, d'you?"

Fwirl darted forward and tweaked the hare's ear. "Give it to her this instant. Come on, out with it!"

"Owowow! Me flippin' delicate shell-like lug! Give it to her, Nimbalo, quick, before I'm a one-eared relic! Owowow!"

The harvest mouse passed a strip of green fabric to Mhera. "We found it stuck t'the bottom of Friar Bobb's sandal. When he kicked us out of the kitchens it stuck to me tail."

The ottermaid felt the green homespun material. "Hmm, some honey got smeared on it. Apart from that 'tis like the others, green homespun and a scent of lilacs. Let's see what this one has scrawled on it. SITTAGALL! All in capitals."

Fwirl released the hare's ear. "SITTAGALL? That's a strange word. Sounds like the name of some odd creature. SITTAGALL. Are you sure that's not one of the long list of funny names you have, Mr. Boorab?"

The hare massaged his ear ruefully.

"It certainly is not, miz. Jolly strange, though, isn't it? You've collected quite a few others like that, Miz Mhera. HITTAGALLs, PITTAGALLs, SITTAGALLs an' whatnot. I wonder what it's all supposed to mean? A real puzzler, wot?"

Mhera folded the fabric and put it in her beltpouch, with the others that had been found over that summer. "Indeed

375

it is. I've tried to solve it, but I can't. I've dreamed and thought of it until I'm weary."

Cregga's heavy paw reached out and covered the ottermaid's smaller one, dwarfing it completely. "I've a feeling you'll find out very soon, my friend. Go away now, all of you, out and enjoy the sunshine while it lasts. I'm tired. I need to take a nap."

Mhera stopped in the open doorway and looked back at the Badgermum, lying propped up on pillows beneath the Abbey tapestry. Cregga's observations always turned out to be true. But how soon would it be before she found out the solution to everything?

32

They placed the long banqueting tables, one at the bottom of Cregga's bed and one on either side, leaving a space between the latter two and the tapestried wall. It was to be a memorable feast in honor of Cregga. Every little thing Friar Bobb and Filorn knew the Badgermum liked to eat was placed by her, close to paw. Hot scones, soft cheeses, candied fruits and summer salad. Drogg Cellarhog commandeered the willing paws of Boorab, Nimbalo and Foremole Brull. Between them they brought all Cregga's (and quite a few of their own) favorite drinks to the tables. This involved a good amount of choosing and tasting, in which they all took part cheerfully.

"Yurr, this'n strawbee fizzer be's a good 'un!"

"Hmm, y'don't say, marm? Let me taste a smidgen. Nimbalo, old scout, tell me what y'think of this October Ale, wot?"

"Prime stuff, matey. 'Ow d'ye brew this stuff, Mister Drogg?"

"With tender lovin' care, friend. 'Tis a secret known only to Redwall Cellarkeepers, passed down over countless seasons. Now, take a drop o' this pale cider, sweetened with heather'n'clover honey. Ole Cregga Badgermum's very partial to it."

Sister Alkanet appeared in their midst, paws akimbo. "Then perhaps you'd better leave a drop in case she's thirsty!"

The tasters shuffled about like naughty Dibbuns caught in the act.

"We were just doin' a spot of checkin', marm, wot. Right, chaps, let's get this lot up to Great Hall. 'Scuse us, Sister, wot wot!"

Mhera and Fwirl were getting the Dibbuns ready, helped by Egburt and Floburt. Soapwort, blended with rose petals and almond oil, created a sweet aroma around the dormitory. Fwirl and Mhera washed and dried the little ones, passing them on to Floburt and Egburt, who dressed them in spotlessly clean smocks, amid loud protests.

Brother Hoben popped his head around the doorway. "Great seasons, who are all these nice shining creatures? Surely not the mucky little Dibbuns who were playing in the orchard this afternoon!"

Trey the mousebabe waved a tiny paw at Hoben. "You nex' t'get washed, Bruvver. Looka you, ole muckybeast!"

Hoben allowed the Abbeybabes to drag him in, and good-naturedly pretended to protest as Fwirl readied a soapy flannel. "No, please, I haven't got time. I'm very busy. What'll I do if soap gets in my eyes?"

The little mousemaid Feegle scoffed at him scornfully. "Keep you eyes closed then, an' don't cry."

Hoben allowed Fwirl to wash his paws and face, wincing as she dried him roughly and combed the tats out of his whiskers. The Dibbuns roared with laughter at his mock sulks. "Ouch, ow! There's soap in my eye an' you're hurting me!"

Mhera and Fwirl played along with the Brother.

"Be still, you silly great mouse, let me dry down those ears!"

"You should be ashamed of yourself, Brother. Look at these Dibbuns, they never made half the fuss you're making!"

Early evening bells tolled out over Redwall Abbey, calling all its inhabitants to the feast. Filorn took her daughter's paw as they crossed Great Hall together. There was a tinge of regret in Mhera's voice.

"I wish Deyna was here tonight. I've never really met him and I only saw him for a short time."

The ottermum patted her paw gently. "Don't fret, Mhera, there are many seasons ahead for you both to get to know one another. Skipper is a good beast. I trust him. He'll bring Deyna back to us safe and sound, you'll see. Now smile, my pretty one. Don't let our Badgermum feel that you're unhappy in any way."

Sister Alkanet shuddered visibly as a discordant jangle grated on her nerves. Boorab and a half-dozen otters lugged the haredee gurdee across the stone floor toward the tables. She sniffed. "I hope you don't intend making a din with that infernal contraption and ruining the evening?"

The irrepressible hare saluted and jingled his earbells. "Din, marm? Beggin' y'pardon, I'm an expert musician, I don't make dins. Never know when one needs a trusty old haredee gurdee at a party, wot. Gangway, you chaps, make way for a priceless instrument an' a valued an' talented creature. Master of Ceremonies, y'know. Miss Mhera said I could perform the honors. Charmin' young gel, that 'un, bit like her dear mama, wot!"

When everybeast was seated and the bells had ceased tolling, Boorab arose and pounded the tabletop with a ladle. "Good evenin', chaps, chapesses an' goodbeasts all. Ahem! Pray silence whilst Brother Hoben says the grace!"

Hoben nodded to the hare and proceeded.

"Seasons of plenty at Redwall,
Yield their bounty to us all,
From the good earth's fertile soil,
We who bent our backs in toil,

Reaped Mother Nature's rich reward,
To bring unto this festive board,
This food which we have labored for,
What honest beast could ask for more,
Save that kind seasons never cease,
And hope to live long lives in peace!"

Midst a loud and fervent amen, Boorab's ladle hit the table again. "Well done, sah! Redwallers, kindly be upstandin'. I propose a toast, to the creature we are here to jolly well honor. Cregga, Badgermum of this Abbey!"

Everybeast, even the smallest Dibbuns, arose and raised a profusion of beakers, cups, goblets and tankards. The roar almost shook the rafters as they took up the toast.

"To Cregga, Badgermum of this Abbey!"

Gundil, quite overcome by the moment, scrambled beneath the table, hurried across to Cregga and shook her paw heartily. "Hurr, mum, ee be's gurtly luvved yurr. Doo ee say a speech!"

Several more came forward to prop the badger up on her pillows. Cregga's sightless eyes turned this way and that, as if she could see every creature sitting around her.

"Thank you, Gundil. I hope you'll bear with me, friends. I have quite a few words to say, some of great importance."

Boorab quaffed off a beaker of redcurrant cordial. "Then say on, old gel. We're all ears, wot!"

"Yore the only one 'ere who's all ears, mate!"

Cregga waved a paw, silencing the laughter Nimbalo's remark had caused. "Thank you. Please, sit down and eat. You must all be hungry, and I know a lot of hard work went into the making of my feast. Eat and listen, for I have a lot to say."

The food was served and the feasting began as Cregga continued, "The seasons of Abbess Song were finished before any of you were born, I think. I was her greatest friend and she left me in charge of our Abbey. I didn't take the position she offered me as Abbess, but chose instead to be a caretaker, until a likely candidate appeared as Abbot or Abbess. I was guided by the teachings and wisdom of my friend Song in my search. Though you did not know it, I waited many many seasons, always listening and paying attention to all about me. One day I discovered a likely prospect. At first I was not sure, so I had to wait longer, observing the young Redwaller who attracted my interest. Then I set about educating my candidate, leaving clues, giving hints and always paying attention to the creature of my choice. Nobeast, not even I, can live forever; since I took that vermin arrow this fact has become quite plain to me. So tonight I propose to elect, with your approval, a new Abbey leader."

Immediately, all Redwallers, including Boorab and Nimbalo, ceased eating to hear Cregga's announcement.

"Mhera, daughter of Filorn, would you come over here to me, please."

The ottermaid stood up amid wild applause, cheers, whistles and ladles pounding upon tables. Willing paws pushed her forward.

"Congratulations, my dear! Oh goodness, to think a daughter of mine is going to rule Redwall!"

"Hurr, miz, ee Badgermum knowed whut she wurr a doin' when she'm chosen ee, ho aye, boi okey she'm did, hurr hurr hurr!"

"Jus' like yore brother, missy, yore a nat'ral leader, but far prettier than 'im, even though 'e is me matey!"

"Oh I say, top hole, m'gel, spiffin', wot! Does this mean I'm not on probation any longer? Well played, you young . . . er, I mean O respected leader an' all that, eh wot!"

"Mhera, best wishes from Fwirl and me, and Friar Bobb!"

Sister Alkanet thrust a clean kerchief into Mhera's paw. "Stand up straight now, miss, and no tears. I'd have chosen you too if I was Cregga. Go to her now."

Mhera made it as far as Cregga's bed, then sat beside the Badgermum and broke down sobbing. "Oh, Cregga, you're not dying, are you?"

The great badger chuckled. "Dry your eyes, pretty one. I'm not going to pass on in the midst of my own feast and leave that hare with all the food. Look here." She brought from beneath her robe an object bound with strips of green cloth. She unwrapped the scraps of fabric and gave them to Mhera, together with the small bark-bound volume that had been hidden inside them.

"There's the rest of your mysteries. All the ITTAGALLs old Hoarg and I didn't have time to hide around the Abbey. You can read all about them in the book, but leave that until the morrow. We're right in the middle of a celebration; I can't have ottermaids weeping and riddles unraveling." Cregga raised her voice so everybeast could hear. "Your new Abbess Mhera is going to make an announcement."

In the silence that followed, Trey the mousebabe piped up. "I 'ope it not that alla Dibbun get anuvver wash!"

Mhera burst out laughing at the cheeky infant. "Hahahaha! No it's not. As Abbess of Redwall Abbey I request that you all carry on feasting and have a wonderful time!"

Cregga waited until the roars of approval had died down. "Attention please, friends. I have only a little more to say before I retire and leave Mother Abbess Mhera to watch over Redwall. I would like to confirm that Boorab's probation is now over, and he is a fully fledged Master of Abbey Music."

With his mouth still full of plum pudding and cider, the hare leaped up and went sprawling. He bolted upright and saluted. "Thank you, marm. I wish to say . . ."

Drogg Cellarhog blinked and wiped a paw across his face. "Don't you mean you wish to spray? Finish eatin' first!"

Boorab swallowed hastily and looked regally down his nose at Drogg. "Mind y'manners, old chap, wot! Er, where was I? Oh yes. Blinkin' long probation, but thank you, marm, and you too, Mother Abbess. I say, flippin' ottermaid young enough t'be one's daughter an' one's got to call her Mother. Bit thick, wot! Ahem, in honor of the jolly old occasion, marm, I shall play my haredee gurdee and sing for you. Now what is your pleasure? A ballad, a dirge, a song of unrequited love, wot?"

Cregga lay back and smiled fondly. "Nothing mournful or sad, if you please. Play me . . . a rousing old marching song, so I can . . . remember the good old days when I ruled the hares of the Long Patrol at Salamandastron. A special . . . favorite of mine was 'The Battle of the Boiling Water.' Do you . . . know it, Boorab?"

The hare was already making complicated adjustments to his cumbersome instrument. He chuckled confidently. "Know it, marm? I learned it sittin' on my old grandpa's lap. You remember him, of course, old Pieface Baggscut, the most perilous an' greedy hare in the regiment. 'Twas his favorite song, too. Ah, those were the long sunny days, marm—"

Foremole Brull twitched the hare's bobbed tail. "Stop ee jawin' an' sing yurr song, zurr!"

Boorab twiddled the strings, struck a small drum and wound a handle. Three ladybirds flew out of the instrument in a cloud of dust. He launched lustily into the song.

"Well I have to sing of a day in spring,
When I kissed me wife an' daughter,
Then marched away to join the fray,
At the Battle of the Boiling Water.
With a tear in me eye and an apple pie,
I roared the jolly chorus,
As the drums did roll for the Long Patrol,
We conquered all before us!

There was Colonel Stiff an' Sergeant Biff,
Who had a wooden leg sah,
And in the lead, oh yes indeed,
Stood Lady Rose Eyes Cregga,

There was Corporal Black the big lancejack,
An' meself a half ear shorter,
An' a small fat cook with a dirty look,
At the Battle of the Boiling Water!"

As the drums on the haredee gurdee boomed out and
Redwallers pounded the tabletops to the jolly marching
air, Cregga went back in her mind. She was young and
strong, her sight was perfect, and she was striding the
dusty flatlands at the head of a thousand young marching
hares, carrying her enormous axepike. No day was too
long then, no march too tiresome. Like smoke, a dust
column rose in a plume in their wake on that high far-off
day, long long ago. She hummed the jaunty tune, reveling
in the summer heat, glad to be alive and so full of strength.
Smiling and nodding to her trusty officers, every one
dashing and perilous, the sight of their faces delighting
her. Sight. What a glorious gift it was. Blue skies, the sun,
like a golden eye, watching over white mountaintops,
green valleys, clear meandering streams. The misty figure
of Boorab's grandsire appeared before her on the march
and threw her a gallant salute with his saber blade.

"All present an' correct, marm. Where to now?"

Cregga heard herself saying, "Into the setting sun, over
the hills and far away."

Boorab's voice, and the music of the haredee gurdee,
faded slowly as she marched off into the sunny afternoon
long gone.

"So we ate our scoff an' the war kicked off,
'Twas a day of fearsome slaughter,
An' a skinny rat shot off me hat,
At the Battle of the Boiling Water.
Then the good old sarge just yelled out 'Charge!'
Ten thousand vermin scattered,
While the puddens flew 'til the air turned blue,
All steamed an' fried an' battered!

Well, I knocked the socks off a fluffy fox,
An' walloped a weasel wildly,
I snaffled the coat off a snifflin' stoat,
An' flattened a ferret finely.
We whacked an' thumped an' kicked an' jumped,
We showed the foe no quarter.
'Til they ran away an' we won the day,
At the Battle of the Boiling Water!"

Mhera was holding the Badgermum's paw, and felt her slip away at the end of the second verse. The ottermaid sat at her friend's side, still holding her limp paw and staring at her smiling face. Cregga looked so peaceful and happy. Boorab finished his song, bowing and posing outrageously as the haredee gurdee groaned and wheezed to a halt amid the cheering and stamping of applauding Redwallers. Sister Alkanet saw Mhera sitting dry-eyed at the badger's side, looking into her still face. Sensing something was wrong, the Sister hastened over, followed by Filorn, who nodded to Boorab, indicating he should sing the song again as an encore. Nobeast noticed, amid the gaiety, what was going on at the bed beneath Martin the Warrior's tapestry.

Alkanet leaned close to Mhera and whispered, "What is it? Has Cregga Badgermum fallen asleep?"

Mhera touched the sightless eyes, closing them for the last time. "Aye, Sister. Our Badgermum has finally gone to rest forever."

A tear brimmed from Alkanet's eye. Mhera wiped it away. "Not now, Sister, we'll weep later. Don't let them know Cregga is gone. Carry on with the feast in her honor; that's what she would have wanted. Chin up now, be brave!"

Sister Alkanet turned to Filorn, and there was awe in her voice. "Truly your daughter is the Mother Abbess of Redwall!"

33

Soft autumn mists swathed the dunes, awaiting their banishment under a blossoming sun. Gruven sat atop one of the sparsely grassed dunetops, listening to waves breaking upon the shores below him. He had spent more than a score of days tracking betwixt dawn and nightfall. The trail was becoming distinctly easier to follow as he traveled south. For some reason, unknown to him, the Juskazann had moved location. He had arrived at the original camp only to find the site abandoned. The clan had traveled south, skirting the tideline and dunelands.

Gruven picked the last crumbs of a pasty from his chair, gulped the final dregs of cordial from a flask and hurled it away into the mist. His supplies were exhausted for the moment, but he could always find more. Several mornings ago he had sighted wisps of woodsmoke. A family of mice had dug their cave into the side of a wind-sculpted sandhill, and were sitting in the entrance cooking breakfast. Gruven sneaked up to the hilltop overhanging their home. His callous method of murder was simple: he collapsed the sandhill on them by jumping up and down on the overhang. After taking a few hours' nap, he had dug out all the food supply that was not spoilt, leaving the occupants smothered beneath the stifling avalanche of sand that had snuffed out their lives.

Watching the sun spread welcoming warmth and light, Gruven sat mentally rehearsing his story, cutting parts and embellishing bits until it sounded good to him. Next he practiced indignation and righteous wrath at the moving of camp during his absence. Perhaps he would root out the culprits and slay them, just to establish his authority as clan Chieftain, Gruven Zann Juskazann.

Leaving the dunes, he took to the firm damp sand of the tideline for better walking. There was no real need of further tracking. He knew the clan would establish another camp among the dunes; all he had to do was look out for the smoke of cooking fires. Around early noon, Gruven became bored. It was a warm day with virtually no wind. He sidetracked listlessly into the dunes and lay down in a sandy crater. It was pleasantly warm, and he allowed his eyes to shut and drifted into a comfortable nap.

He had only lain there a short while when he was rudely awakened. He was rolled roughly over, and the sword was snatched from his belt. A noosed rope was thrust over him, pinioning both paws to his sides. There were four of them, two weasels, a stoat and a rat, and they looked lean and tough. Gruven felt fear rise sourly in his throat, but he did his best to put on a hard face and a gruff voice.

"Wot's the meanin' of all this? Who are ye?"

The bigger of the weasels, a female named Gruzzle, prodded him with the point of his own sword. "Shut yer mouth an' get up off yer behind!"

Struggling upright, Gruven recognized one of his old clan, the rat Wherrul. However, he looked different. His facial tattoos had been overlaid with green wavy lines on the brow and a yellow circle on either cheek. Gruven felt a surge of relief.

"Wherrul, mate, wot are you doin' with these beasts? Yore a Juskazann, just like me. Wot's 'appened?"

Wherrul began yanking Gruven along on the rope. He did not sound at all friendly. "I ain't Juskazann no more. We got taken over. I'm part of a big clan now, the Juskabor!"

Further conversation was cut short as Gruzzle prodded Gruven with the sword. "I've already tole you t'shut yer mouth, I won't tell yer agin. Now get movin'. You can do yer talkin' in front o' the Chief!"

It was late noon by the time Gruven was hauled stumbling into the new camp. Right away he noticed that the number of tents had increased fourfold, enough to accommodate at least three hundred Juska. Familiar faces from his old tribe stared at him as he was dragged along. They all had their former Juska marks tattooed over like Wherrul. All in all they looked a warlike mob. There were a lot more foxes in evidence, too. Gruzzle halted in front of a large well-made tent, painted with lots of colored symbols, and kicked Gruven flat in the sand.

"Stay there, you three, an' watch 'im!"

She threw back the tent flap and entered. A moment later she marched out again, three others with her. One was Grissoul the old vixen Seer, accompanied by another equally wizened vixen, who carried all the paraphernalia of a seer or soothsayer. But it was the male fox that Gruven instinctively knew was the Chieftain.

Ruggan Bor was an impressive figure, a big male fox, golden rather than reddish furred, with no black tip to his tail. His face was inscrutable, but one glance informed Gruven that the hard golden eyes were those of a born slayer. He was dressed simply, in a short black shoulder cloak and a black kilt. A saber was thrust through his broad chain-linked belt. Ruggan Bor gave Gruven the briefest of glances, then turned to Grissoul.

"Is this the one who took over from Sawney Rath?"

Grissoul bowed fawningly. "That he be, lord: Gruven Zann, the stoat who vowed to slay the Taggerung."

Ruggan nodded to Gruzzle, who leaped forward

388

promptly. "Loose yonder rope an' return his weapon."
The weasel obeyed immediately and without question.

Gruven realized he was not going to be executed on the
spot. The knowledge gave him fresh confidence, and he
decided to bluff his way along. Ruggan Bor obviously had
him tagged as a warrior. Swaggering forward, he faced the
Juska Chieftain, leaning on the sword and narrowing his
eyes like a veteran killer. However, he did not attempt to
speak. Something told him that Ruggan was not a beast to
be taken lightly. The big golden fox had not moved a
muscle, yet his eyes looked Gruven up and down.

"You are the son of stoat they called Antigra?"

Gruven had to swallow visibly before he answered.
"Aye."

Ruggan Bor's paw strayed close to his saber. "I am
Ruggan Bor of the Juskabor, Lord of the South Coasts. I
took your clan, the Juskazann, and added it to my own.
Antigra, your mother, plotted against me. I slew her."

Gruven found it difficult to keep up his attitude of
bravado as Ruggan continued, his face still expressionless, "So, Gruven Zann, do you wish to take revenge for
your mother? Are you going to challenge me as Chieftain
of these Juska? You stand armed and free before me. If
you are going to do anything, now would be the time to
do it."

Gruven's nerve had already failed him. He knew he was
a deadbeast if he lifted the sword. Yet if he was ever to
become leader of the clan he could not lose face, so he
played his ace card, hoping bluster and bragging would
impress the fox warrior. Swelling his chest, he snarled
aloud, "My name now is Gruven Zann Taggerung. Eight
warriors left camp to track him with me. Only I have
returned; the others lie dead. I slew the Taggerung!"

Ruggan turned to his own vixen Seer. "Ermath, what do
your omens say?"

The vixen shrugged. "Nought, lord. I saw no signs of a
Taggerung's death."

The burning golden eyes faced Grissoul. "And you?"

She averted her gaze humbly. "I cannot say, lord. Who knows if the Taggerung still lives?"

Gruven interrupted her harshly. "I do! The Taggerung still lives because I am Taggerung now. Did you not say that the beast who slew him would take on his name? You said it to me before I left!"

Grissoul was caught between two fires. Maybe Gruven had done the deed, but then maybe he had not. She preferred to go with the one she knew was a Warrior Chieftain, tried and tested. Ruggan Bor.

"Gruven Zann, thou vowed to bring back the Taggerung's head. Where is it?"

Gruven sneered. He had already thought of this answer. "The days have been hot, more than a score and a half of them. What warrior in his right mind would carry such a thing that long? I gave it back to the flies when I reached the old camp!" Thoroughly roused now, and carried upon the surge of his manufactured anger, Gruven turned upon Ruggan Bor. "My word is my honor as a Juska warrior. I tell you 'twas I who slew the otter they called Taggerung. With this sword!"

The golden eyes stared levelly at him out of the expressionless face, though the fox's paw was now on his saber hilt. "So you say, Gruven Zann. But you have not answered my first question. Are you going to avenge your mother or challenge me for the chieftainship?"

Gruven had been doing some quick thinking. "We are both mighty warriors," he shot back. "The clan would gain nothing by our loss. You know of the Taggerung, of his reputation. When you cannot find him you will realize I am the real Taggerung. Then we will let the whole of the Juska decide who is leader!"

Ruggan Bor signaled to Gruzzle. "Take six Juska, find Gruven Zann a tent of his own, give him food and guard him well." He turned his back on Gruven, dismissing him. "I will give you my answer tomorrow. Attend me here to break fast." He strode back into his tent, followed by the two Seers.

Gruven was taken care of. His food was of the best, roasted seabird and barley wine. He sat eating, his mind racing. Was he an honored guest or a prisoner? Did Ruggan Bor regard him as a warrior and a slayer, or had he seen through the bluff? Were the vermin outside an honor guard or jailers? Gruven decided he had some serious thinking to do.

Ruggan sat with his Seers, watching them toss bones and shells, sometimes tracing patterns in the sand, occasionally burning feathers and herbs as they chanted by the fire. He waited patiently until they were finished and listened to the verdicts.

"Lord, 'tis still the same. The omens are cloudy."

"Aye, lord, mayhap time will reveal the answers."

The golden fox looked from one apprehensive face to the other. "Time reveals all, but this one looks like a born plotter with a ready tongue, too ready methinks. I have not got time to wait while he schemes behind my back. There is something I do not like about that stoat. If I was the slayer of a Taggerung, nobeast would dare stand against me. Why did he not choose to fight if he is such a mighty one? I slew his mother, took over his clan. Anybeast who did that to Ruggan Bor would be feeding the sea fishes by now. Leave me. I will reach my own conclusions on this!"

Dawn crept in like a misted ghost. Ruggan Bor sat impassive by the fire embers in his tent. He narrowed one eye and stared at the back of the guard's neck until the ferret outside his tent turned and saluted with his spear. "Lord!"

It was a trick Ruggan had learned through long seasons of commanding Juska vermin. They always felt his eyes upon them.

"Tell my cook to bring vittles for two, then go and bring Gruven Zann to me here."

Gruven had got into the habit of sleeping late, and he was still blinking and stifling yawns when he was marched into Ruggan's tent. Hiding the contempt he felt for lazybeasts, Ruggan nodded.

"Sit, eat, and answer my questions truthfully, Gruven Zann!"

Gruven sat down and began eating, a cornmeal porridge with shellfish in it. He felt rather resentful that his host should ask him to answer truthfully, even though he was prepared to lie at every turn.

Ruggan did not eat as he interrogated his guest. "Where was it, this place where you slew the Taggerung?"

Gruven slopped down blackberry wine mixed with water. "At the old campsite, I think."

"But you said you carried the head until you reached the old camp and threw it away there."

Gruven drank long and slow as he prepared an answer. "Oh, yes. That was where I first saw him. I tracked him north for three days before I killed him. Then I returned to the old camp, to see if anybeast had come back there. There were still no signs of Juska back at the camp, so I threw the head away." He waited with bated breath while Ruggan considered this.

"I see. Then you found our tracks and followed them. Tell me, why did you not notice the traces of us breaking camp when you first arrived there?"

"Oh, that," Gruven explained hastily, the food and drink forgotten as he cursed himself inwardly for his silly mistake. "Well, er, I was tracking a Taggerung, a dangerous and savage beast. I wasn't looking for other trails. Would you?"

Ruggan Bor slowly poured himself wine, mingling it with water. "Hmm, I see, that makes sense. Finish eating, we have to go."

Gruven wiped a paw across his lips, taken by surprise. "Go? Where to?"

The fox's eyes stared at him over the goblet rim. "To the

392

old camp, of course. We must find the Taggerung's head. If you have spoken the truth, you have done what no other warrior alive has ever done. Slain a Taggerung. Have you eaten enough?"

The food turned to ashes in Gruven's mouth. He could only nod.

Leaving a few Juska vermin to guard the tents, Ruggan Bor set off north into the fading mists. Gruven walked slightly behind him, surrounded by six hefty Juskabeasts. Close to three hundred armed vermin accompanied them.

34

It was the most glorious of autumn mornings at Redwall Abbey. Old Hoarg and Brother Hoben were hard at work in Great Hall. Mother Abbess Mhera could not bear untidiness, and she had cajoled them into doing the job they had been promising to do for the last ten days, repairing two windowpanes that had been smashed by vermin slingstones. Hoarg held the ladder, whilst Brother Hoben fitted the second small sheet of carefully knapped crystal into place and began closing the lead flashing around it by pressing with a smooth block of beechwood. The task completed, he climbed down from the ladder and helped Hoarg to sweep up the broken shards. "There, old friend. Good as new, eh!"

The inseparable pair Fwirl and Broggle came skipping through from the kitchens. They waved to Hoarg and Hoben.

"Good morning! It's another lovely day outside!"

Old Hoarg raised a wrinkled paw as they opened the Abbey door. "If you're goin' out, please don't slam that door. Give these new panes time to settle in; don't want 'em jumpin' out."

The squirrels made a great show of shutting the door carefully and skipped off toward the orchard, chuckling.

Fwirl pulled Broggle up at the orchard edge, her eyes shining as she took in the beautiful season. "Oh, isn't it pretty! Look at those leaves, golden and brown and scarlet, and the colors of the fruit: yellow pears, red apples, purple berries. There's our Abbess. Mhera, good morning to you!"

Mhera was standing with several Dibbuns, grouped around a russet apple tree, heavy with fine rust-colored fruit. She waved a paw absently at her two friends, her eyes never leaving the tree. Trey put a paw to his lips and reprimanded the two squirrels.

"Shush, Muvver h'Abbess says not to shout or stamp y'paws. H'apples fall when they be's ready, not afore!"

Fwirl and Broggle joined the group, curious to know what was going on. "Is it a game?" the squirrelmaid whispered to little Feegle. "Can we join in, please?"

Still staring at the tree, Feegle nodded. "First one t'see a h'apple fall down gets a prize off Muvver h'Abbess, so be shushed an' watcha tree!" As she spoke, an apple fell and hit Broggle on the head.

Wegg the hogbabe whooped with excitement. "Me me, I see'd it, Muvver h'Abbess!"

Broggle rubbed his head. "Aye, but I felt it!"

Fwirl was almost knocked over by Mhera as she dashed toward the Abbey, in a most undignified manner for an Abbess, shouting, "Mama, Mama, the russet apples are falling!"

Squeaking and laughing, the Dibbuns raced after her. Broggle touched a spot between his ears ruefully. "What was all that about, Fwirl?"

The squirrelmaid shrugged. "I've no idea. Oh, look, there are harebells growing by the old wheelbarrow. Let's take some to Cregga."

Between them they gathered a small bunch of the delicate drooping blue flowers and carried them to the sunny spot by the northeast wall corner. Cregga's grave was always bedecked with the most beautiful flowers.

395

Fwirl took a beaker with some water in it and arranged the harebells. Broggle placed it gently on top of the headstone, a smooth slab of typical Redwall sandstone with words engraved upon it.

Sleep softly on, Beloved One,
Take with you all our dreams,
To rest in noontide valleys,
Beside old silent streams.
Cregga Rose Eyes, Warrior Badger of
Salamandastron mountain
and Badgermum of Redwall Abbey for
countless seasons.

Filorn and Friar Bobb were busy in the kitchens, decorating a magnificent redcurrant trifle. The Friar's tongue stuck out at one side of his mouth as he inserted flaked almonds into the golden mound of meadowcream surmounting it. Then he stood back, watching Filorn anxiously.

"Easy now. It takes a good eye and a steady paw, marm!"

Filorn leaned over the trifle, holding her breath. Her paw descended fraction by fraction, until the candied strawberry in it came to rest precisely on the peak of the cream.

"That's perfect! But I've seen you do as well, Friar."

Holding out his paw, the old squirrel watched it tremble slightly. "Mayhap when I was younger, but I rely on you now, my friend. Whoa, look out! What's all this stampede?"

Mhera skidded in, her gown swirling as she tried to check herself. Filorn caught her daughter and was rocked back on her paws by the Dibbuns colliding into them both.

"Mercy me, Abbess, there's no need to rush in like that. We've finished the trifle you ordered!"

Mousebabe Trey clambered up Mhera's back and flung

himself into Filorn's paws, roaring, "F'lorn mum, rusty h'apples be's fallin' down inna h'orchard!"

Filorn stumbled backward. Mhera stopped her, but was unable to rescue Trey. The tiny fellow went headlong into the trifle while Filorn stared as if hypnotized at her daughter. "The russet apples are falling!"

Friar Bobb hooked Trey out of the trifle, the other Dibbuns giggling at the sight of the mousebabe with the candied strawberry stuck on his head. Friar Bobb burst out laughing.

"Hohoho, look at liddle Trey! I'll straighten this mess up, marm, you an' the Abbess go an' do what y've got to do. Hohoho!"

They found the otter sisters, Blekker and Swash, with a few of the ottercrew down at the pond, taking a morning dip. At the sight of Mhera and Filorn, the energetic otters bounded out of the water and waggled their rudders politely in respectful greeting.

"G'day, Abbess, marm, wot can we do fer ye?"

Mhera felt dwarfed by the two big sisters. "The russet apples have started to fall. I saw it myself, in the orchard a short while ago. The message you brought from Skipper said that Rukky Garge would have my brother Deyna healed and well by the time russet apples were falling. What do we do?"

Swash placed a broad calming paw on Mhera's shoulder. "You waits, Abbess marm, that's wot ye do. We'll stand lookout on the walltops. Meanwhiles, you an' yore mama go about yore business. Me'n'Blekker'll let ye know the moment anythin' stirs."

Filorn folded her paws resolutely. "My thanks to you, Swash, but we'll be up on the walltop with you, watching for my son's arrival back home."

Blekker shook water from her coat. "I wouldn't advise it, marm. It could take a day an' a night or two. Skipper

397

wouldn't be too 'appy if'n he knew you was up there that long. Best stay inside. Leave it to us."

But Mhera would not hear of it. "You leave Skipper to me, Blekker, we're going up there with you. Mama, tell Fwirl we'll be taking our meals on the ramparts and ask Foremole Brull to bring up blankets for us and the crew."

It was Gundil who led the party bringing blankets to the walltop. He presented Mhera with a soft pink one. "This 'un's furr ee, h'Abbess. Oi'm stayen oop yuur with ee, hurr!"

Mhera felt a wave of affection for her old friend. "Gundil, I'm sorry I haven't had much time with you lately."

The mole rubbed his downy head against her sleeve. "You'm been gurtly busied, bein' ee Muther h'Abbess an' suchloike. But us'n's gotten lots o' toimes agether in ee seasons t'cumm."

Mhera spread the blanket so they could both sit on it. "So we have, my friend. What's that you've got there?"

Gundil produced Abbess Song's book, with the strips of green cloth wrapped around it, and held it out to the ottermaid. "Oi bain't no gudd at ee readen, Muther h'Abbess. Do ee read owt o' ee likkle book furr oi. Uz molers dearly do luvvs to 'ear ee readen."

Mhera laid the fabric strips next to each other on the parapet before she opened the book. "Right, where do you want me to start from? Oh, and stop calling me mother. Call me Mhera or miz, like you always did."

The mole's face crinkled into a deep grin. "As ee wishen, miz. Start ee frumm th' burginnin'!"

Mhera began to read. "I, Song, daughter of Janglur Swifteye and Mother Abbess of Redwall, do leave these thoughts of mine to be read by the creature who is chosen to rule the Abbey in my stead.

"Humility Is The Thing A Good Abbey Leader Learns.
Patience Is The Thing A Good Abbey Leader Learns.

398

Wisdom Is The Thing A Good Abbey Leader Learns.
Understanding Is The Thing A Good Abbey
Leader Learns.
Friendliness Is The Thing A Good Abbey Leader Learns.
Strength Is The Thing A Good Abbey Leader Learns."

Mhera tweaked Gundil's digging claws playfully.
"They're all in here, the ITTAGALLs, Courage, Compassion, Fairness, Decision . . . you don't want me to carry
on reading them all, do you?"

Gundil tweaked Mhera's paw back, but very gently,
because his digging claws were so blunt and powerful.
"Burr nay, miz, jus' ee larst wun. Oi loikes that 'un!"

Mhera turned to the back of the book and read the
rough untidy scrawl, which contrasted sharply with the
other neat script. "I Choose Mhera As The Ottermaid To
Rule Our Abbey."

From where they were sitting the gravestone below was
visible. Mhera smiled at it fondly. "Imagine the time it
must have taken for a blind badger to write that, Gundil.
Granted the writing isn't as tidy as Abbess Song's, but
Cregga Badgermum did it all right. Look here." She
unfolded one last length of fabric from her robe sleeve.
ICMATOTROA was scrawled upon it in identical writing
to that in the book. "It was the last piece I was supposed to
find. This was wrapped around the book the night she
gave it to me at the feast. There there now, my friend,
don't weep. Cregga wouldn't like to think that she made
you unhappy."

Gundil tried bravely to blink away the large teardrops
falling from his eyes. "Oi know, miz, but Creggamum
wurr such a guddbeast. Oi misses hurr!"

Rukky Garge and Skipper sat by the stream's edge. The
old otterfixer tapped her knobbly stick on a boulder.

"Ahhhrrr weel now, Deyna bigbeast, sit ye here by mah
side." Deyna did as she ordered, holding still as she

399

pushed and scratched at his face. She consulted Skipper. "Prithee, frien', what say ye now, eh?"

Skipper took Deyna's face in both paws, peering at it closely. "Rukky me ole queen, I wouldn't believe it if'n I didn't see it with me own two eyes. Not a tattoo mark on 'is face. 'Tis a miracle ye've worked!"

The ancient otter blushed like a maiden. "Heeheehee! Show unto yon riverdog yeer paw, Deyna."

Holding forth his right paw, Deyna allowed Skipper to look at it. There was no sign of a flowered birthmark. The pad was totally dark. Skipper scratched his rudder in disbelief. "Well, blow me down to port an' sink me whiskers. 'Ow did she do it, Deyna matey?"

The former Taggerung stared at the paw. "I don't know, Skip. I was asleep most of the time, but in the moments I was awake it burned like fire, my face too."

Rukky smacked her stick down across Deyna's paw. "Ahrra weel, good now though, mah beauty, no feels of hurt?"

Deyna clapped his paws together hard. "None!"

She struck him in the chest with her stick, right where the arrowhead had been. He did not flinch. Rukky gave a toothless grin. "Ayaah, when Rukky Garge fixes otters, they fixed good!" She pointed out a big boulder. "Dat wun!"

Deyna strode across to it. Wrapping his paws around the large smooth granite rock, he picked it up and flung it into the center of the stream. The spray splattered wide. Rukky Garge wiped her face on her cloak and nodded at the stream. "You strong, riverdog, stroooong! Now bring d'stone back out!"

Deyna dived headfirst into the stream, cutting the water like a pike on the hunt. He appeared in midstream, grasping the boulder, and swam back to the bank with it. Rukky made him perform the feat three more times before she was satisfied. Then she allowed him to make his way back and sit by her, breathing lightly. Skipper slapped him heartily on the back.

"If'n I told anybeast about that they'd never believe me, bucko!"

Rukky tapped the otter Chieftain with her staff. "You make de good soup, mah frien'. Now let dis Deyna make some for us, see wot it be tastin' like, eh?"

Deyna made a cauldron of fresh watershrimp and hotroot soup for them, and then Rukky indicated that he too could share it. They sat eating in silence until it was all gone. Skipper smacked his lips and patted his stomach. "Well, mates?"

Rukky Garge and Deyna answered together. "Not as good as yours!"

Skipper's craggy face lit up with pleasure. "Y'took the words right outta me mouth. Though it was passin' fair, for a beginner. Well, Rukky me ole charmer, I got to get our mate back 'ome to his sister an' mama."

Deyna put a paw around the otterfixer's shoulder affectionately. "Thank you, Rukky. I owe you my life!"

She stiffened and shook his paw off. "Don'ta touch me, riverdog! Ah not like bein' touch by anybeast. Go ye to de cave, take back yeer blade an' get from me sight!" Deyna stood up, a hurt expression on his face. The ancient otter rapped his rudder with her stick and cackled. "Heeheehee! But come ye back when ye learns to make der soup better'n Skip. Rukky be pleased ter see ye den!"

Two days and three nights had passed for the watchers on the walltop. By now they had been joined by everybeast except the Friar and his duty cooks. They took turns at night, some watching whilst others slept. Drogg Cellarhog brought a fireholder up to the ramparts and mulled ale with spices in it to keep up their spirits and to ward off the chill of autumn nights and dawns. They sang many songs and recalled lots of old poems and monologues to while away the time. The Dibbuns thought it was a wonderful holiday, even though they were guarded by Sister Alkanet, who had roped them together. "I don't trust these little rogues on high walltops!" She said it until everybeast grew tired of the phrase and the Dibbuns paraded around, linked together, singing impudently.

"Don't trus' us likkle rogues on walltops,
It be sad when a pore ole Dibbun falls,
Fall on yore 'ead an' die, then you start t'cry,
That's wot 'appen to likkle ones on walls!"

They finally gave up when Abbess Mhera threatened them with bath and bed, and Friar Bobb brought them warm mushroom soup to drink.

Fwirl and Broggle sat with Filorn and Boorab. They had drawn the last watch of the third night. Drogg's fireholder was close by, and they sat wrapped in blankets, talking softly. Several times Boorab had volunteered to go down and work in the kitchens. His requests being refused made him rather sulky.

"Pish tush t'the blinkin' kitchens I say, wot. Measly fat little Friar chasin' the tail off a chap: keep your paws out o' this and don't dare touch that, leave those measly flippin' pasties alone, get y'nose out of that pudden. Yah boo to them says I, wot? I say, any of you bounders know when they'll be bringin' a spot of brekkers around? The old tum's gurglin' away like a drain!"

Somewhere a bird twittered, and the first pale milky light showed, reflecting eerily back off the mist. Fwirl wrapped her blanket tightly and scooted nearer the fire. "Isn't it strange being up here in autumn mist?"

Broggle yawned. "Aye, it gives me a floaty feeling when it's thick all around me."

Boorab snorted. "Fiddlededee, laddie buck, y've never been in a real pea souper of a fog. I remember one time I got caught in a fog so bally thick I had t'cut my way out with a knife, wot!"

Nimbalo loomed up like a small blanketed ghost and sat with them. "Huh, that's nothin'. I was in a mountain fog once, they're the worst kind, couldn't see me paw behind me back, or me tail if'n I looked forward. 'Twas so thick I saw a frog walkin' on it!"

A voice spoke from behind Nimbalo. "Mountain fogs are mere wisps compared to a good marsh fog. When I was younger we used to go out looking for marsh fogs, they were so thick and soft. I'd take my needles with me and knit them into blankets for the infirmary!"

The speaker came forward. Wide-eyed with astonishment, the friends sat staring at Sister Alkanet. The stern Infirmary Keeper was smiling. Filorn opened her blanket for Alkanet to share.

"Hahaha. Well done, Sister, you've certainly stopped those two fibbers in their tracks. Blankets for the infirmary, eh? Hahaha!"

Foremole Brull shuffled up, tiny dewdrops forming on her velvety fur. They twinkled in the firelight. "Yurr cumm ee sun. Fog's be a-liften naow."

Within a short space of time it was a soft autumn morning. Warm breezes took faded leaves from the trees, drifting them down to earth. Swallows swirled and soared in patterned flights beneath a clear sky of powdered blue. Gundil took a fallen sycamore seedpod and spun it into the air on its two perfectly shaped wings. Mhera stood between the battlements, watching the woodland fringe and flatlands skirting the path to the south. Blekker stood by her side, leaning on her javelin. Mhera sighed impatiently. "When do you think Deyna will come?"

The big otter squinted her left eye against the sun. "Sorry, Abbess marm, can't say for certain. When ole Rukky Garge said it'd be the time that russet apples fall, she was only sayin' it as a rough guide. Could be another two or three days. Friar's servin' brekkist, marm. Why don't ye go an' eat? I'll keep watch 'ere. Go on, liddle Abbess, y'look tired."

Mhera clenched her paws in frustration. "Oh, if there were only some way to make him come back!"

"Ye could try singin' them 'ome!"

Mhera was puzzled by old Hoarg's remark. "What d'you mean, singing them home?"

The old dormouse took a sip of his morning dandelion tea. "It always seemed t'work when I was a liddle 'un. We often stood on the walls and sang to bring travelers safe 'ome."

Blekker and Swash agreed with Hoarg.

"Aye, marm, otters believe in 'ome singin'."

"Skipper said it always works. Try it, Abbess marm. We'll sing the verses if'n you an' yore Redwallers 'elp out on the choruses!"

A smile spread gradually on the young Abbess's face. "What a lovely idea. Listen, you Redwallers, we're all going to join in and help sing my brother home."

Everybeast agreed, with only one exception. Boorab. "I say, bit thick isn't it? I've waited all flippin' night for a bite o' breakfast. Now I've just been served, what've I got to do, eh, wot? Abandon my scoff an' start tra-la-laain' away to some chap who won't even jolly well hear it. Blinkin' liberty if y'ask me, wot, wot wot?"

Mhera tried imitating Sister Alkanet's famous frosty glare. "Sir, you may do as you please. Fill your face by all means, but if you do not join in the singing I will have you barred from the kitchens henceforth. Take note of my decree, Friar Bobb!"

The good Friar nodded vigorously. "Noted, Mother Abbess!"

Boorab cast aside his plate and beaker. "Steady on, chaps, confounded blackmailers . . . er, I mean, lovely day for a bit of an old warble, wot. Count me in. You otters there, what're you waitin' for, eh? Sing away, me buckos. Sing!"

Blekker and Swash, together with the other otters

Skipper had sent back to the Abbey, lined up. After a bit of throat clearing they went at it lustily.

"When will you return me darlin', are you homeward bound?
See the golden sun a-smilin', warmin' up the ground,
Here I stand an' wait me beauty, though 'tis gettin' late,
Listenin' for the weary paws, a-marchin' to my gate.

What if the sky goes dark! Well, I'll light for you a lamp!
So I'll see you comin' dear. Tramp! Tramp! Tramp!

Are the drums a-beatin' bravely, o'er the lonely moor?
Are ye thinkin' of your mother, standin' at the door?
Do the banners stream out boldly, have the days been long?
Are you marchin' down the road, listenin' for my song?

What if the sky goes dark! Well, I'll light for you a lamp!
So I'll see you comin' dear. Tramp! Tramp! Tramp!

Is that a dusty cloud arisin', out across the plain?
Is that me bonny rover now, come back to me again?
O Grandma turn the blankets down, an' put the kettle on,
I've sung him home, no more to roam, my only one.

What if the sky goes dark! Well, I'll light for you a lamp!
So I'll see you comin' dear. Tramp! Tramp! Tramp!"

Everybeast enjoyed the song so much, they called for more. Mhera and Broggle picked up the verses as well as the chorus. They stood with the otters, singing out for all they were worth. Behind them, the Dibbuns led a march, backward and forward along the south ramparts, making a great show of shouting tramps aloud at the end of each chorus. Halfway through the third rendition, Nimbalo pulled Boorab out of line. The harvest mouse whispered to the hare, pointing south, to where the woodland jutted out in the distance to connect with the winding path. Mhera watched Nimbalo scramble up onto Boorab's shoulders. He held on to Boorab's ear with one paw, gesturing out with the other, then he started shouting. Filorn saw it too, and had a quick word with Blekker. The otter halted the singing, howling out in her stentorian baritone, "They're on the path! Comin' thisaway! I told ye it'd work!"

Boorab lifted Nimbalo down and took charge. "Well, what'n the name o' sizzlin' seasons have y'stopped singin' for, eh? Don't want to break the jolly old magic spell, do you? Hoarg, get down an' open the gates. Throw wide your portals, old lad. The rest o' you ditherin' duffers form up behind me. Jump to it, now! We'll march down the road singin' to meet 'em, by the left, right'n'center we will, wot wot!"

Boorab sidestepped into the gatehouse, but he soon caught up with the singing marchers. He carried a banner made from an old tablecloth tied around a long window pole. Swaggering along jauntily, the hare was in his element, bellowing aloud, "Anybeast with a frog in their throat, let the frog do the singin'. Hawhawhaw! C'mon now, let's rip the roof off . . .

"What if the sky goes dark! Well, I'll light for you a
   lamp!
So I'll see you comin' dear. Tramp! Tramp! Tramp!"

The ottercrew coming the other way saw the Redwall singing parade and doubled their march speed. Then they were trotting, and the pace hotted up even more, until they were running to meet the welcoming committee. Not to be outdone, Boorab waved his banner and yelled out orders.

"Look at 'em go! Hah, we'll see who meets who first, chaps. If it's a bally charge they want, we're the ones who'll show 'em. Lay back the kitchen sink! Forward the buffs! Blood'n'vinegar an' flyin' fur! Eulaliaaa! Redwallers chaaaaaaaarge!"

They thundered down the path in a headlong stampede, and Boorab was knocked flying into the ditch. But even the fastest of runners were not as fleet of paw as Mhera and Filorn upon that day. The pair were well out in front, hurtling toward the ottercrew charging up from the south. Way out in front of them was one, a big strong figure who could outrun the wind. Filorn could see the dust pluming in his wake, Mhera could even hear his footpaws slamming the hard earth as he streaked toward them like summer lightning. They screamed together. "Deynaaaaaaaa!"

He swept them up as though they weighed nothing and ground to a halt, hugging them both close. Then Nimbalo pounded up like a small juggernaut. Unable to stop himself, he bulled straight into Deyna, Mhera and Filorn, sending himself and them sprawling in a heap together. Instantly they found themselves surrounded by other Redwallers. Then they began to laugh, as happiness flowed from them, infecting everybeast. They laughed until the tears ran down their dusty faces, hugging one another as if they would never let go. The laughter rose into the air, startling birds in the soft autumn morning.

From that long-ago day when his father carried a babe out of the Abbey gates, Deyna, son of Rillflag, had returned home.

35

Gruven was in trouble. However, like all liars and cowards he kept on convincing himself that he could wriggle out of it and end up on top. The fact that Ruggan Bor had slain his mother meant little to him. Antigra had always been too pushy, constantly berating and nagging at him. Gruven was glad she was out of the way. What really rankled was the golden fox's taking over his clan, but he could think of no way to reverse their positions. He was wholly frightened of Ruggan, an inscrutable creature, unlike anybeast Gruven had ever met. Ruggan Bor never showed any extremes of wrath or joy, never smiled or snarled. His fascinating golden eyes seemed to detect untruths without a single blink. Gruven could not face him for more than a moment. Every Juskabeast under his command knew Ruggan Bor to be highly intelligent, a redoubtable warrior Chieftain, and a ruthless killer. Gruven was gradually coming to realize this, and it made his blood run cold.

Double time was the order of the long trek back to the old camp. All the vermin kept up the pace without question or complaint. They slept little, ate frugally and went heavily armed. Ruggan Bor strode out at the head of his clan, talking to nobeast save to give orders or consult his Seers. At first, Gruven tried to establish some authority over the six Juska who were detailed to guard him. His efforts went unrewarded. When he complained of the marching speed, a tough lean vixen looped a rope about his waist and growled, "Keep up or we'll drag ye the rest o' the way!"

Gruven was forced to suffer the indignity. His blustering fell upon unsympathetic ears. "You dare to do this to a Taggerung? Hah, I could snap this rope with a single bite! My teeth are like knives!"

A big scar-faced rat prodded his bottom with a lance. "Yew start chewing that rope an' ye'll be wearin' this lance fer a spine. Shut yer mouth an' keep movin', stoat!"

Gruven turned and spat at the rat's footpaws, trying to act tough. "I won't ferget yore face, rat. Remember this: my name's Gruven Zann Taggerung. I use lances like that as toothpicks!"

A muscular ferret marching alongside Gruven jabbed an elbow hard into his ribs, grinning at Gruven's wince of pain. "Ye won't 'ave no teeth t'pick if'n I land a kick in yer mouth. Now stow the gab an quit slackin'!"

Gruven dragged on the rope, halting the vixen who was pulling him. "I'm not takin' any more o' this. I demand to speak with Ruggan Bor!"

He did not see the blow coming. The vixen belted him across the jaw with her carved spearbutt, snarling nastily, "Do ye, now? Well, 'e don't want ter speak with you. Get marchin'!"

When they stopped for the night, Gruven was set apart from the rest, tied to a tree, with all six guards circling, watching his every move. The scar-faced rat thrust a bowl at him. It contained only water, with a stale crust of barley bread floating in it. The rat eyed him contemptuously. "Get that down ye an' then sleep. We'll be on the move agin soon as 'tis dawn!"

Gruven ate and drank swiftly, then huddled down to rest. His mind was still racing, rehearsing explanations.

Where was the imaginary head of the slain Taggerung? Oh, it probably landed in the stream when he threw it away, it would be washed to the sea by now. Then what happened to the body? Ruggan Bor was no fool, he was certain to pose the question. The body? He would have to think about that one, and think fast too. They were covering ground at a rate three times quicker than his laggardly pace. It would not be long before they arrived at the old campsite. Gruven closed his eyes tightly. Think . . . think. Of course! He threw the body into the swamp. Yes, that was the place, the swamp where he sent Rawback to his death. Hahaha! Let them try to search a swamp. Ruggan Bor, huh, the pan-faced fox, aye, him and all his thick-headed lackeys. None of them were a match for Gruven Zann Taggerung. They couldn't find their tails if they grew out of their noses! He would outthink them, he would outsmart them, the same way he had defeated Eefera and Vallug Bowbeast and the rest.

Gruven did not realize he had fallen asleep and was murmuring aloud, "What d'yer mean, never slew 'em? They're all dead, ain't they, an' I'm the only one who's left alive. Oh, I slew 'em right enough!"

The vixen leaned on her spear, watching Gruven. "Wot d'yer suppose that 'un's babblin' about?"

The muscular ferret scoffed. "Sez 'e's slaying all kinds o' beasts."

Looking up from the lancepoint he was sharpening against a stone, the scar-faced rat commented dryly, "Aye, in 'is sleep. That's the only time that 'un's slayed beasts. Got a coward's streak, wider'n an oak trunk, from tip ter tail!"

Only one fire burned in the vermin's makeshift camp, that of Ruggan Bor. He needed it for his Seers to predict. The golden fox sat watching the two old vixens casting shells and stones, burning feathers until the air smelled rank, and mumbling, always mumbling as they tried to read the omens. Which invariably had to be in the Juska

Chieftain's favor. He listened awhile, then stretched out, his saber close to paw. "Tell me that last bit again."

Ermath's toothless face looked ghastly in the firelight. "Is the fox not related to the wolf, lord? There is none among vermin who can equal the fox for stealth, guile and ferocity. He alone carries the blood of the Great Vulpuz, Ruler of Hellgates!"

Ruggan ignored his old soothsayer. He had heard all that before. "No, you, Grissoul, what did you say?"

Sawney Rath's former Seer stared at the bones she had cast down.

"He who has the Taggerung slain,
Shall take on the champion's name,
Zann Taggerung, lord of Juskas all,
Beware the bells within Redwall!"

Ruggan's golden eyes reflected the dancing flames. "What does all that mean? Tell me!"

Grissoul remained hunched over the scattered bones, unmoving. Ruggan Bor had witnessed Seers in a trance before, and he repeated the command. "Say the lines again and explain to me what they mean."

Ermath was not overfond of Grissoul. The other vixen had been slowly usurping her position since Ruggan took over her clan. Ermath scuffled across to Grissoul and shook her roughly. "Answer the question. Speak when my lord commands ye!"

Grissoul did not respond. She slumped forward until her muzzle touched the ground. There was shock in Ermath's voice. "Lord, she is dead!"

Ruggan Bor used the flat of his saber blade to lift Grissoul's head. He inspected the dead vixen and let her head drop down again. "She was old. Creatures die when they grow too old. Did you understand what she said? Can you remember the lines?"

Ermath cringed back into the shadows. "Nay, lord, 'tis not for me to read the omens of another Seer. Who knows what anybeast sees at the sight of Hellgates, where rules the—"

Ruggan cut her short as he lay down to rest. "Get my guards to bury her. 'Tis of no matter, the ramblings of a dying vixen. Leave me now, I will rest."

Any dreams of bells, Taggerungs or Seers that crossed Ruggan Bor's trails of sleep were forgotten when the impressive fox woke at dawn's misty light.

Four days later, on a morning dampened by fine warm drizzle, the Juskabor clan reached the old campsite. Fires were lighted in the lee of sheltering dunes, and cooks began preparing the first hot meal they had eaten in a while. Ruggan Bor stared around. Pacing the ground, he unsheathed his saber. "Bring the stoat Gruven here to me."

Gruven was hauled forward on his rope by the six guards. He knew it was no good blustering to the golden fox, so he put on a casual air, as if he was in command of the situation.

"Ah, Ruggan, the very beast I've been wanting to see. Well, here we are at last, eh. You know, I left this camp a simple warrior and returned as the Taggerung . . ." His voice trailed off under Ruggan Bor's unblinking stare.

"The head, Gruven. Where did you leave the head?"

Again Gruven changed his attitude, drawing himself up regally. "My name is Gruven Zann Taggerung. I protest at your treatment of me. I will not speak until this rope is taken from me!"

The saber whipped through the air, slicing the whiskers from the left side of Gruven's muzzle. Ruggan Bor's expression had not changed. "My next stroke will take off your ears, then I'll start working down your body, bit by bit. Where is the Taggerung's head?"

Gruven sat down on the sand and wept like a babe. "I threw it in the stream."

"What stream? There's no stream around here."

"The stream! The stream! It's back there in the woodlands!"

"Which woodlands? Those northeast of here?"

"Yes, yes! Over that way, that's them!"

"So, what did you do with the body?"

Unexpectedly, Gruven began to laugh. He looked straight up into the fox's golden eyes, giggling and sobbing. "In the swamp! I threw it in the swamp! Heehee, the head too, all in the swamp, gone forever, heeheehee!"

Ruggan nodded to the guards. "Get him up on his paws. Let's go and find this swamp."

Birds were singing, drizzle slackened off and the sun broke through as they entered the woodlands. Ruggan gave orders for his Juskabeasts to fan out and search for the boglands, whilst he and the six guards rested close to the tree fringe, with Gruven in their midst. Halfway through the afternoon a youngish fox came loping back to report.

"Sire, we found the swamp, it's a big 'un. First we thought there was nothin' about 'cept a few frogs'n'lizards. But then we caught this crazy stoat. The rest are bringin' 'im. Be 'ere soon, sire."

"That's two crazy stoats we'll 'ave now, hawhaw!" the scarred rat whispered to the muscular ferret. He went silent as the golden eyes swept by him and came to rest on Gruven.

"Do you know of a crazy stoat hereabouts?"

Gruven's mood had changed. He looked completely mournful. "They're dead, all dead, I killed 'em. All dead an' gone!"

Ruggan heard the party bringing the prisoner in. He did not turn, keeping his eyes fixed on Gruven. Behind him a weasel called out, "Lord, this is the stoat, but 'e's right off'n 'is skull, mad as a toad with a tail!"

The stoat was thrust forward, tightly bound. Ruggan saw Gruven's eyes go wide in horror, his voice screeching hoarsely, "Rawback? Go 'way! Yore dead! Dead, I tell ye!"

413

Rawback looked plump and well, owing to a plentiful diet of frogs, lizards and other swamp inhabitants, but his eyes burned feverishly, and it was obvious his sanity had snapped at some point of his swampland sojourn. He put his head on one side and poked his tongue out at Gruven, then he turned to Ruggan Bor, as if sharing a confidential secret.

"That'n there thought 'e'd done fer me, y'know. Aye, thought 'e'd sunk ole Rawback in the swamp. Hohoho! Right up ter me nose 'twas, but I ain't no fool, I got out. Big branch, luvly branch, growin' right over me 'ead. I grabbed it. Two days! Two days I was, pullin' meself out, liddle diddy bit by liddle diddy bit. Hohoho! Fooled yer, didn't I, Gruven? You ain't no mate o' mine no more. You wouldn't push nobeast in a swamp, would ye, sir?"

Ruggan signaled the guards to untie Rawback. "Of course I wouldn't, my friend. Sit down here by me. Bring him food and some blackberry wine, we're going to talk together."

Rawback clutched Ruggan's paw and kissed it. "Blackberry wine an' real vittles! Seasons smile on ye, sir. Ye don't know wot this means t'me. Talk? I'll talk to ye, me good sir. Wot d'you want ter know? Ole Rawback'll tell ye!"

Gruven thought of making a dash for freedom, but the scar-faced rat's lance tickled the nape of his neck and the muscular ferret's spearpoint was a hairsbreadth from his stomach.

Rawback ate like a ravening wolf, ripping into warm ryebread and a roasted woodpigeon, guzzling blackberry wine until it dripped down his chin. Ruggan patted his back. "You're one of the old clan, I can tell by your tattoos. Eat up, there's plenty more where that came from. I want you to tell me about Gruven. Did he slay the Taggerung?"

Half-chewed food and wine sprayed from Rawback's mouth. "Wot, you mean Gruven? Hohohoho, d'ye think 'e killed the Taggerung?"

Gruven tried to drown Rawback out by shouting,

414

"Don't lissen to that crazybeast! He's mad! You wouldn't believe anythin' that fool says, would ye?"

The tough lean vixen grabbed Gruven in a headlock. She stuffed his mouth with a sod of earth and grass, holding it shut whilst the scar-faced rat bound the stoat's muzzle shut with his own belt. Ruggan pushed more wine at Rawback. "He won't disturb us, friend. Now tell me everything, right from the start when you left camp."

The blackberry wine swiftly loosened the stoat's tongue, and it seemed to restore his powers of recall also. Rawback related the full tale of the hunt for the Taggerung. Ruggan Bor listened carefully to it all, particularly the episode of what took place at Redwall. For a madbeast, Rawback had an excellent memory.

"Well, there we was, see, all in the ditch outside o' Redwall Abbey's front gate. Eefera an' Vallug's shoutin' fer them to bring out the Taggerung. Then this mouse we was 'oldin' prisoner breaks loose, an' it all goes wrong. Vallug slays an ole blind stripedog with an arrer, an' the mouse grabs a battle-axe an' goes after Dagrab. Nobeast's watchin' me'n'Gruven, so 'e snatches 'is sword an' runs off north up the ditch. That's when I escaped too. I follered Gruven. I chanced to look back to see if we was bein' chased. I saw Vallug Bowbeast lyin' dead, an' I saw the Taggerung too. But 'e was chasin' Eefera westward o'er the plain. It was the Taggerung, though; I'd know 'im anywheres. There was an arrer stickin' out of 'im, but a bowshaft wound wouldn't stop a warrior like 'im. Redwall beasts was floodin' out the gates, yellin' an' shoutin'. I knew it was all over then. So I kept me 'ead down an' ran north along the bottom o' that ditch after Gruven, fast as I could. Next thing, we leaves the ditch—"

Ruggan Bor had heard enough. "Finish your vittles now and rest, Rawback. You can join my clan as a Juskabor."

Unused to so much food and wine, Rawback was soon snoring. Gruven was ungagged and brought before

415

Ruggan Bor. The golden fox stared implacably at him. "You heard him. What have you got to say now?"

Gruven spat out soil and grit. He had recovered from his hysteria, and had his story ready. "Rawback's mad. Even you must be able to see that. His mind is fuddled. That was the Taggerung he saw lyin' slain in the ditch, not Vallug. His head was severed from his body. I know, I chopped it off with my own sword!"

Sipping from a flask of blackberry wine, the Juskabor Chieftain thought for a moment, then shrugged. "Why didn't you tell me this at first, instead of making up a lot of foolish lies?"

Gruven went into another of his acts. This time he was the honest warrior, rough and ready, but a little embarrassed. "Sire, I did not want you to know that I fled in the midst of a battle. But I had to, we were greatly outnumbered. I give you my word of honor, though, I slew the Taggerung outside Redwall's gates. There you have it, the truth!" He stood trembling, averting his gaze from Ruggan Bor.

A long silence followed before the Juskabor leader spoke. "I am always prepared to listen to the truth. Since you were first brought to my camp you have wriggled and lied your way all around it, Gruven. I believe Rawback. He had nothing to lose by telling the truth. My Juska warriors are wondering why I haven't slain you before now; they've seen me deal with liars and cowards before. But if you are really the Taggerung, I must allow you every chance to prove it. A Taggerung is a mighty legend among Juska clans, one to be respected and honored. I must tell you that when I first heard an otter was the chosen one I was very disappointed. My clan and I always wanted to see a fox as Taggerung. If you slew him as you say, then a lot of creatures must have witnessed the deed. We will find out the real truth, Gruven . . . when we reach the gates of Redwall!"

416

36

Darkness fell earlier each day as the season drew into mid-autumn. The trees were bare and the harvest was in. Deyna strolled round the Abbey lawns, paw in paw with his sister and mother, savoring the moonlit night. He caught Filorn's glance. "What is it, Mama? Have I sprouted an extra ear?"

Filorn looked away quickly, embarrassed at being caught staring. "No, son, it's just that you're so like your father, a big handsome riverdog." She shuddered slightly in the night air. Deyna swept off his cloak and placed it around her shoulders. He smiled fondly.

"And you're so like my mother and Mhera's so like my sister. Except that I'm supposed to call her Mother Abbess now. I like having two mothers, I get treated twice as well."

Deyna was very tall; Mhera looked up at him, chuckling. "Start calling me Mama and I'll kick your rudder into the pond. Isn't it time we were going inside? I can feel rain."

Deyna placed his sister under the cloak with Filorn. "Sorry. I've spent so long out in the open I hardly notice the weather. Come on, we'll take a slow walk back to the Abbey."

Filorn measured each pace deliberately. Deyna laughed. "I didn't mean that slow, Mama. Come on, I've seen you running. Don't come the old ottermum with me, my beauty."

The Abbey bells tolled out softly, one ring apiece. Filorn suddenly speeded up. "That's what I was waiting for. Come on, you two, I'll race you!"

Shoulder to shoulder with Mhera, she sped off across the Abbey lawn as the first drops of rain fell. Deyna caught up with them, sweeping both off the ground and running for the Abbey door. Mhera and Filorn were laughing, kicking and shouting.

"Hahaha, put me down, you great lump, put me down!"

"I'm the Abbess, you can't do that to me, put me down, baby brother! Hahaha, oh dear, hope nobeast sees us. Hahaha!"

Deyna joined in the fun. "I can't, Mama, you'll get your paws wet, and you too Mother Abbess. Got to keep my little old sister dry. Hohoho!"

Boorab and Nimbalo were waiting in the warm shaft of light from the open door. The harvest mouse shook his head sadly. "Lookit me pore ole mate, forced t'carry 'is wicked family 'round fer the rest of 'is life. Shame, ain't it?"

The hare fixed them with a disdainful glance as they arrived on the doorstep. "Dreadful goin's on, wot? Here's me in me dwindlin' seasons, but I notice the bounder hasn't offered t'carry me around!"

Deyna set his mother and sister down lightly. Then he lifted Boorab up and set him on his shoulder. "Right, where d'you want me to carry you to, sir?"

"I say, jolly decent of you, wot. Straight inside, laddie buck. I can't wait to get at the jolly old harvest feast they've set up in your honor. Absoflippinlutely famished I am!"

The others followed Deyna and Boorab inside, Mhera

calling, "You puddenheaded hare, you've given the surprise away!"

Great Hall was decorated with multicolored lanterns and sheaves of flowers, and the tables had been laid beautifully. Everybeast from Dibbun to elder raised a hearty cheer at Deyna's appearance, and he was forced to feign surprise.

"Great seasons of thunder! What a marvelous spread! Thank you, friends one and all. Thank you!"

Boorab tugged Deyna's ear. "I say, old scout, any chance of lettin' me down, wot?"

"Hurr hurr, you'm stayen oop thurr, zurr, give us'n's a chance at ee vikkles. 'Old on to ee gurt glutting, zurr Deyna!"

Boorab bared his teeth at Gundil. "If he does I'll scoff his blinkin' ears one at a time!"

Deyna sat at the head of the big table, with Filorn, Mhera, Nimbalo and Hoarg, Redwall's oldest inhabitant. It was a feast to remember, happiness and friendship enhanced by the best of Redwall fare. Puddings, pies, pasties and cakes were arranged between fruit, berries and nuts, both fresh and preserved in honey from last autumn's harvest. Salads, breads and soups of every variety jostled for position with trifles and flans. Drogg Cellarhog had outdone himself with his selection of ales, cordials, teas and fizzes. But the highlight was a great cheese, produced by Filorn, Boorab, Nimbalo and Gundil. The hare watched anxiously as it was served from the table's far end.

"Steady on there, you molechaps, leave a smidgen for the Master of Abbey Music. Have a bit of respect for my cheese, you rotters!"

However, there was still almost three-quarters of the huge cheese left when it reached the much-relieved hare. He cut a large wedge, arranging it on a platter with some salad, pickled onions and a farl of warm ovenbread, and passed it proudly along to Deyna.

419

"Try that, sah. Go on, taste it and tell me if you've ever scoffed anything so good, wot?"

Deyna cut the cheese and tossed half to Skipper, so they could both sample it. Filorn smiled at their delighted expressions. "We made a new yellow cheese and spiked it with nuts, celery and herbs, then we soaked it for three days in boiling carrot and dandelion juice mixed with pale cider. Mr. Boorab gave it a name, but it's too complicated to say."

The hare bowed gallantly. "Quite simple, marm. We made it together, so I took a bit of our names, all four. It's a filboonimgun. Nice title, wot?"

Mhera nudged her brother. "I'd never get any if I had to remember that name. I think I'll just call it the nice big tasty cheese."

Nimbalo winked knowingly. "That's 'cos you ain't got a memory like me, Abbess. Ahoy, Friar Bobb, pass me the floggingrumble cheese, will ye?"

Fwirl corrected him. "It's called the grungleflingboo cheese, isn't it?"

Others joined in, complicating the name Boorab had so painstakingly invented.

"No no, miz Fwirl, 'tis the floogenbumble, I think."

"Nay, zurr, et be's ee groggenfumble, oi'm surrpint!"

"Don't be silly, the cheese is called the fumblegroogen!"

"The groggenflingbull, that's what Boorab said!"

Sister Alkanet rapped the table for silence. "Stop this, please! Mr. Boorab, tell them the correct name."

Everybeast sat watching the hare. They had to wait until he had eaten the big lump of cheese in his mouth. There was an expectant silence, then Boorab smiled foolishly. "Er, sorry, but I've completely forgotten, wot. Hawhawhawhaw!"

The entertainment was opened by Skipper and his crew performing a hornpipe, the finale of which saw them all in a circle facing outward, their rudders entwined in a pattern behind them. Fwirl and Mhera were called upon to sing a duet. It was a comic one, but they sang it seriously, with demure looks, fluttering eyelashes and paws joined sedately.

"There's a hedgehog who lives down the lane, down
  the lane,
And I'm longing to see him again, once again,
I wait by the old log, for that handsome young hog,
Through the cold stormy wind, and the drizzle and fog,
But his mama won't let him come out, him come out,
I can hear every shout from her snout, what a snout,
'Don't you raise a paw, to go out of that door,
Go and tidy your room,' I can hear his ma roar.
Through the window I see his dear face, oh dear face,
By that window a ladder I'll place, I will place,
Then just wait and see, he'll climb down here to me,
We'll go strolling together, how happy we'll be.
So I crept to the window that night, cruel dark night,
I was standing the ladder upright, what a fright!
When his mama rushed out, crying, 'O lackaday,
That naughty young Spike has gone running away!'
So I sit here and weep for my hog, faithless hog,
'Cos they say he's run off with a frog, with a frog?
Take a maiden's advice, if you want to look nice,
Just turn yellow and hop once or twice!"

Fwirl and Mhera hopped primly back to their places amid laughter and applause. Deyna did not wish to do any warrior's tricks that he had learned with weapons, as they might frighten the Dibbuns. Instead he sat twenty of the Abbeybabes on a long form, took it on his shoulders and walked the full length of Great Hall. Amid the cries of admiration and wild cheers, Nimbalo announced, "I taught me mate to do that, y'know, but I used to carry twoscore o' liddle ones!"

Boorab was not to be outdone. "Oh did you indeed? Well, I used to do it with that same number, old lad, plus me fat auntie an' two kegs of ale. Oh yes!"

It was a fibbing contest. Everybeast sat back and enjoyed the pair, each trying to cap the other's achievements by lying outrageously.

"Hah, that's nothin'. When I was only a liddle sprig I could stand in a bucket an' carry meself 'round all day!"

Boorab waggled his ears airily. "Pish tush, laddie. You've seen how high this Abbey is, wot? Well, one time I stood on the lawn outside and landed on the roof with a single flippin' jump. Did it very slowly, of course, had to wait an' rise with the mornin' mist, y'know. If y'don't believe me, ask old Foremole. She saw me do it, didn't you, marm?"

Foremole Brull smiled from ear to ear. "Aye, zurr, oi see'd ee do et wi' moi own three eyes, so oi did!"

Mousebabe Trey decided to take part. He clambered up onto Filorn's lap and wagged a tiny paw at the two fibbers. "Chah! Dat nuffink, I climbed right up on F'lorn an' felled inna big big trifle, so I eated meself out of it. You ask Frybobb!"

Friar Bobb nodded sagely. "He certainly did. I was there, it was no fib."

"You fell into a giant trifle an' ate your way out?" Boorab stared at the mousebabe with something akin to hero worship in his eyes. Trey patted his small fat stomach.

"Yip, h'I did, sir!"

The hare's gaze misted over as he imagined what it would be like to fall into a monster trifle and eat his way out. "You lucky little blighter. Wish I could've had a try, wot!"

Nimbalo pushed a fair-sized trifle across the table. "Let's see 'ow ye did it, Trey me ole tatercake!"

Sister Alkanet stepped in, catching the little fellow almost mid-dive. Boorab and Nimbalo wilted under the famous icy glare.

"I once physicked a hare and a harvest mouse so

422

severely that they swelled up and couldn't go out through the infirmary door. Then I had to double physick them back to normal. I can still do it. Ask Abbess Mhera, she'll tell you."

"Oh believe me, Sister Alkanet certainly can," the Mother Abbess of Redwall assured them solemnly. " 'Tis a fact!"

Boorab's ears fell flat, either side of his face. "Stone me! A joke's a joke an' all that, but, er, wot wot!"

Nimbalo lifted one of his friend's ears and whispered into it, "Fizzick? Wot's a fizzick, matey?"

"Take the word of an officer, sah, you do not want to inquire further. The good Sister could stop a horde o' stampedin' frogs with just a spoonful of the jolly old jollop she brews up!"

Rain pattered against the warm-lit Abbey windows as the night wore on. Elders loosened their belts and talked of the old days, drowsy young ones were carried off to the dormitories by Skipper's ottercrew. Bearing the famous cheese between them, a cluster of moles, Boorab, Nimbalo and Gundil followed Drogg downstairs. It was an experiment, to see how the cheese complemented the Cellarhog's remaining stock. Old Hoarg and Brother Hoben drifted off to the gatehouse for a game of nutshells and pebbles. Friar Bobb had fallen asleep in his chair, while Floburt and Egburt crept away to the kitchens with Sister Alkanet to bake scones for next morning's breakfast. Others shuffled off yawning to their beds. Deyna was happy just to sit with Mhera and Filorn. He gazed up at the ancient high-raftered ceiling while Abbess Mhera watched him.

"So, do you like our Abbey?"

The former Taggerung ran a paw over his unmarked face. There was no evidence of any tattoo on it. "Like it? I never imagined any place could be so wonderful. I've got you here, and Mama too. It's like living in the midst of a beautiful dream!" He hugged his mother and sister close. Filorn sighed happily.

"The dream will continue. We are a family again, together, here at Redwall."

Several mornings later, Nimbalo was out early, taking a morning stroll along the walltop. He liked rising before dawn and helping in the kitchens amid the good-natured bustle and delicious aromas wafting from the ovens. Friar Bobb would slice some hot bread and pack it with button mushrooms cooked in a savory herb sauce for him. The harvest mouse climbed the east wallsteps with his sandwich and ambled along the ramparts. He was fascinated by everything about the imposing architecture of Redwall, and munched away, his bright eyes taking in every detail. An early frost rimed the red sandstone battlements. Dawn was breaking slowly, calm and windless, tingeing the horizon orange and peach. Below the north wall, rowan trees were clustered thick with red and cream berries; further away he could see the fir cones, now turned brown. In leisurely fashion Nimbalo reached the northwest wall corner. His gaze swept over the flatlands and back to the path that ran alongside the west wall.

There standing in front of the main gate was Ruggan Bor at the head of three hundred armed Juska vermin. They stood immobile and silent, barbaric tattooed faces tight-lipped, awaiting their Chieftain's command. Not a spear or a blade clanked against a shield. Ruggan Bor, the golden fox, leaned on his saber hilt, his inscrutable gaze assessing the walls.

Nimbalo dropped flat below the battlements, his breakfast forgotten as he scrambled away to the north steps.

37

Icy ditchwater squelched beneath Gruven's footpaws as he stood in the ditchbed, surrounded by his six guards. His mind worked furiously as he tried to figure out what would happen when Ruggan Bor made his presence known to the Redwallers. Gruven shivered, more from fear than cold, and the ditchwater gurgled and made a sucking noise as he changed position. The tough vixen cuffed his ear and whispered viciously. "Quit hoppin' 'round an' be still or I'll knock ye senseless!"

Slowly the sun rose over the vast thickness of east Mossflower. Ruggan kept his Juska clan close in to the west wall, not wanting to be out on the flatlands with the sun in his eyes. He would wait until the sun got higher and lessened the handicap. Behind him, Rawback gave a slight cackle. Ruggan gave a nod to two of his foxes. They did not bind Rawback, merely gagging the crazed stoat and muttering a few warning words to keep him silent. Ruggan Bor was an experienced leader. Always calm and patient, he could wait until he felt the moment was right.

No sound came from within the Abbey walls, nor from the outside, where massed Juskabeasts lined the path. An hour dragged slowly by. Ruggan checked the wall shadow. It had extended over path and ditch onto the flatland. A single gesture from him sent his troops noiselessly back to the edge of the ditch. Ruggan Bor drew his saber. The time had arrived. He signaled four spear carriers. They ran forward and thudded their spearbutts against the great oaken doors of Redwall.

Boom! Boom! Boom! Boom!

Ruggan had expected to wait until some old gatekeeper appeared on top of the wall to see who was knocking. Instead the doors swung open and he was faced by a wall of over twoscore otters, tough capable beasts, armed with slings and javelins. An array of squirrels, moles, mice and hedgehogs peered over the battlements, armed with all manner of throwing implements. They were led by a hare carrying a long hooked window pole.

An otter stepped forward, half a head taller than the rest. Ruggan's attention was caught by the sword he carried. It was slightly short for such a big creature, but a magnificent weapon nonetheless. The big otter looked as though he could use the blade. His gaze swept over the Juskabor, then back to their leader.

"What do you want here, vermin?"

Ruggan walked forward until he was but a pace away from the otter. "I am Ruggan Bor, Lord of the Southern Coasts and Chieftain of the Juskabor clan!"

The big otter too stepped forward until his face was a whisker away from the golden fox. His voice held no fear. "And I am Deyna, Warrior of Redwall. I asked you what you want here?"

Ruggan took a pace back, to stay out of sword range. "I want information. Do you have an otter here with his face tattooed in this manner?"

The six guards heaved Gruven out of the ditch. The stoat stared at Deyna, bewildered. The voice was the same, but the face was different from that of the Taggerung. It had not been tattooed.

The strange otter gave Gruven a dismissive glance. He recognized his old adversary immediately, but kept deliberately silent. Fixing his attention on Ruggan Bor, Deyna answered the fox's question levelly. "There is no creature within these walls with vermin tattoos on his face. Why do you ask?"

Ruggan did not like the way his interrogation was going. The otter Deyna was staring him down with cold ruthless eyes. He had an air of confident authority about him. Ruggan decided to turn the tables. His saber was longer than the otter's sword, and he pointed it threateningly in Deyna's face. "Do not lie to me. I have three hundred at my back. We could overwhelm you and search your Abbey!"

Deyna moved like lightning, backward, sideways and forward. Ruggan stood with his saber pointed at nothing, the otter's blade across his throat. Deyna was alongside him, a paw hard on the nape of his neck, so he could move neither forward nor back.

"Nobeast sets paw into Redwall Abbey without my permission. Now take your vermin and begone, or stay here and die!"

Ruggan's expression did not change. "I can only go if I have the information I came for. This otter was called the Taggerung. Was he here? Tell me, Deyna of Redwall."

Deyna nodded. "He was here once, but he is gone now. The Taggerung no longer exists. As far as I'm concerned, he is dead."

Gruven seized the opportunity. Pushing the guards aside, he cried, "I told you he was dead. I slew him right there in that ditch! I am Taggerung now. Gruven Zann Taggerung!"

Nimbalo climbed up onto a battlement, pointing at Gruven and yelling aloud, "Aye, that's the one. I saw 'im slay the big painted vermin!"

Gruven could hardly believe his ears. Here was somebeast, a little mouse, agreeing with his lies. He waved to Nimbalo. "Thank you, my friend, thank you! Hahahaha! Ruggan Bor, did you hear that? Now who d'you believe, crazy Rawback or me? I have a witness, you heard him. I slew the Taggerung!"

Ruggan placed his paw to the blade at his throat. "Put up your sword, otter. We are leaving!"

Ruggan ordered his Juskabeasts across the ditch onto the flatlands. Deyna stood warily, his sword still at the ready. Gruven was jubilant. He grabbed back his sword from the vixen who had taken it and sawed through the rope around his waist, laughing all the time.

"Hahahaha! Gruven Zann Taggerung. Bow before me! Nobeast is mightier than the Taggerung!"

Ruggan stood to one side, holding a hasty whispered conference with his Seer Ermath. Waving his sword and laughing hysterically, Gruven confronted the six Juska who had been his guard.

"Now, you scum, I'll show you what happens to anybeast who treats a Taggerung the way you treated me. Hahahaha! Kneel, all of you, kneel and bow your heads before me. Hahahahaha!"

"Zann Juska Taggerung! He who slays the Taggerung becomes Taggerung himself!"

Gruven half turned as Ruggan Bor swung his saber. And Ruggan Bor kicked Gruven's headless carcass into the ditch.

Ermath the old vixen Seer spread her paws wide to the waiting vermin and called in a reedy trembling voice, "Lord of the Southern Coasts! Chieftain of the Juskabor! Ruggan Zann Taggerung!"

A mighty roar erupted from the three hundred clanbeasts. "Ruggan Zann Taggerung! Taggerung! Taggerung! Juskaaaaaaa!"

Then something happened that nobeast had ever seen before: Ruggan Bor smiled. He grinned from ear to ear and threw back his head, laughing over the spears clattering on shields, over the waving swords and blades of all kinds, over the lances thrust upward at the sky as his laughter mingled with the roar of the Juskabor clan.

Abbess Mhera came to the open gate and wriggled between the ottercrew to her brother's side. "What is it, Deyna? What's going on out here?"

Deyna ushered his sister gently into Skipper's waiting paws. "Go back inside quickly, Mhera. Those vermin are working themselves into a frenzy!"

Deyna was right. Ruggan Bor turned to face him, standing at the ditch edge and whirling his saber. The Juskabor vermin leaned eagerly forward, pointing their spears and blades. Deyna knew that three hundred Juska could not resist the temptation of an Abbey defended by less than a third of their number. He signaled Skipper. "Get everybeast inside and bar the gates, Skip. I think there's going to be trouble!"

Mhera had made her way up to where Boorab was standing on the walltop, balancing between two battlements. "Are the vermin going to attack the Abbey?" she called. "Is Deyna inside?"

Boorab did not answer. Shading his eyes, he peered down to the southern bend of the path at the dustcloud arising betwixt woodland and flatland. He turned back to Mhera with an odd smile on his face.

"Beg pardon, Abbess marm, but best cover your ears. I'm goin' to shout." The hare's narrow chest puffed out to its fullest extent as he sucked in air. Placing both paws around his mouth, he bellowed mightily, "Eulaliiiiiaaaaaaaaaaaaa!"

Nimbalo wiggled a paw in his ear. "Wot's all the yellin' for, matey?"

Boorab pointed to the dustcloud, grinning like a madbeast. "C'mon, laddie buck, and you, Abbess. Filorn, marm, would you be so kind as to oblige me? You too, Hoarg, Drogg, Hoben. In fact everybeast, all shout together, loud as y'can. Eulalia's the word, pronounced yoo lay lee ahh, long on the ah. One, two, shout!"

"Eulaliiiiaaaaaa!"

Boorab had them shout another five times. Then he held up his paw.

429

Down at the main gate the Juska were about to charge at the still half-open doors, the gap packed with otters prepared to take down as many vermin as they could before the gates closed. The whole scene suddenly became a frozen tableau. A colossal roar, like a tidal wave breaking against a cliff, came up from the south.

"Eulaliiiiaaaaaaa!!!"

The roaring continued and the very ground beneath the Juska began to thrum. Through the massive dustcloud emerged a giant Badger Lord at the head of a thousand fighting hares.

Boorab chortled with delight. "I say, you rotters are in for a jolly good pastin', wot," he called down to the vermin. "Here comes the Long Patrol an' a blinkin' Badger Lord t'the rescue."

Redwallers hung over the parapets, cheering. Mhera had never seen a real live Badger Lord before; he was an awesome and frightening sight. Deyna threw open the gates, marching out with Skipper and the ottercrew. Ruggan Bor and his three hundred Juska were completely taken by surprise. They had no option but to put up their weapons and stand still. The hares had split and swirled out in a massive pincer movement, leaving the vermin surrounded, their backs to the open gate, which was blocked by warlike otters. It was all done with startling speed, a smart military example of outflanking the enemy.

Filorn buried her face in her apron. "Mhera, don't look. There's going to be a dreadful slaughter!"

Boorab chuckled reassuringly. "Not at all, marm, those fightin' hares aren't led by some berserkin' Bloodwrath creature. Oh dear me no, that giant beast is none other than the Lord of Salamandastron, Russano the Wise!"

Lord Russano was twice as broad and half as high again as any creature present. He towered over all, like an oak among aspens. He was dressed humbly, in a plain brown cloak and tabard, and his wide woven belt showed no evidence of sword or other blade. In his huge right paw he carried a short length of dark polished hardwood like a scepter. Quiet confidence and immense calm radiated from him. An older hare, with stiff whiskers and a fierce glint in his monocled eye, marched smartly up to the badger and saluted with his lance.

"Position secured, everythin' present an' correct. Sah!"

Russano nodded. "Thank you, Colonel. Who is the Chieftain of these Juska vermin?"

Ruggan Bor was marched into the Badger Lord's presence. Russano looked across to Deyna, who was obviously in charge of the defenders. "Have these Juska harmed or slain any of my Redwall friends?"

The otter gave a small courteous bow. "None, sire, thanks to your timely arrival. We were just about ready to do battle; you spared us a lot of bloodshed."

Russano turned his attention to the Juska Chieftain. "Had you attacked Redwall Abbey it would have been your most fatal mistake. What do they call you?"

The golden fox's voice trembled as he stared up at the Badger Lord. "I am Ruggan Bor."

Russano tapped Ruggan's chest with his hardwood stick. "I have heard your name spoken as Lord of the South Coasts. I am Russano of Salamandastron. Will you challenge me?"

Ruggan Bor laid his saber carefully at Russano's footpaws. "I too have heard of you. Only a fool would attempt such a thing."

Abbess Mhera could not take her eyes from the Badger Lord. She watched, fascinated, as the Juska laid down their arms, wondering what Russano would do next. He pointed to the flatlands beyond the ditch, his voice rumbling out, stern and majestic. "Take your creatures out there and line them up in ranks a score long facing this Abbey. Stand out in front of them, Ruggan Bor!"

Whilst the vermin slunk wordlessly across the ditch,

Russano issued orders to his colonel in a low tone. Boorab winked at Abbess Mhera. "By the left, marm, takes a real Badger Lord to make those villains sit up a bit, wot!"

Trey the mousebabe had sneaked up onto the walltop. He tugged Boorab's paw urgently. "Do the vermints all getta tails chopped off now an' buried inna big 'ole?"

The hare picked Trey up and set him on a battlement to watch. "Indeed they do not, you bloodthirsty little bounder. You pay attention now, laddie buck. This'll be somethin' y'can tell your grandmice about, wot!"

Guarded by the colonel and five hundred armed hares of the Long Patrol, the Juskabor clan were ordered down on all four paws as Lord Russano addressed them.

"I have spared your miserable lives. If ever any of you are seen within a season's march of Redwall Abbey again, I will not be so merciful. Go back to your South Coasts and stay there!"

The fierce colonel saw Ruggan Bor starting to rise. He placed his lance on the back of the fox's neck. "Stay on all fours, vermin. This is the way you and your heroes will travel until sunset. Make no mistake, fox, myself an' five hundred o' the best'll go with you to make sure you do. I ain't as easygoin' as Lord Russano. Make one false move an' ye'll soon find that out to your cost, wot! Right now, listen up at the back there, you cads, wait for my sergeant's command!"

Two gimlet-eyed sergeants with ramrod backs and gruff voices began barking at the thoroughly cowed vermin. "Now then, you scruffy misbegotten lot, about turn! On the double, you dozy drooping daffodils! On all fours, heads down, tails cringin' . . . wait for it, wait for it . . . south'ard crawl!"

Away went the Juskabor in shameful banishment, with Ruggan Bor their Chieftain not at their head but at the rear.

Russano stood with Deyna and Abbess Mhera, watching the vanquished enemy raising a dustcloud over the plain. As she curtsied lightly, Mhera noticed that she did not even come level with the badger's waist.

"Lord Russano, I am Mhera, Mother Abbess of Redwall. Surely fate must have sent you to our Abbey today."

Russano knelt and kissed the ottermaid's paw respectfully. "Fate it was, Mother Abbess, that and a dream of Cregga Rose Eyes. She told me that her seasons had run. Cregga had a great and loving heart. I have made a long march from my mountain to visit her resting place, here at the Abbey of Redwall."

Boorab, who had been listening nearby, stepped forward and threw an elaborate salute to the Badger Lord. "Stap me vitals, sah, you arrived in the bally nick o' time!"

With a smile, Russano returned the salute. "We might not have. Our pace was very slow until we heard a fine military-sounding voice giving the war cry. If that was you, then you deserve the compliments of everybeast."

Boorab clicked his footpaws together so hard that he winced. "Thank you, sah. Most kind of you to say so, sah. Only doin' one's duty, wot wot!"

Mhera ushered the Badger Lord inside the gates. "You knew our Cregga?"

The Badger Lord's warm dark eyes smiled. "She nursed me when I was a babe. I recall that for a blind badger Cregga had enormous wisdom and patience, despite the fact that she had once been the wildest of Warrior Badgers ever to march from the mountain. She taught me many things. I lived at this Abbey with her for a while and acted as her eyes when she was blinded in battle. Then I journeyed to Salamandastron and ruled in her stead. This place has many wonderful memories for me."

Deyna held out his paw to Russano. "Abbess Mhera is my sister. I am Deyna, Warrior of Redwall."

The badger shook Deyna's paw cordially. "I knew that as soon as I saw you wearing the sword of Martin. I observe by your eyes that you are used to weapons,

Deyna. I think you have led an adventurous life, my friend."

Deyna put a paw about his sister's shoulders and winked at Russano. "I'll tell you about it sometime, though you'd have trouble believing the half of it, matey."

The Badger Lord shrugged his wide shoulders. "Oh, I've seen and heard a few things that would make even your rudder curl, laddie buck!"

When they reached Cregga's grave, Russano took a medallion and chain from around his neck and hung it over the headstone's edge. It had been made at the forge in the mountain of Salamandastron, and was of burnished steel, quite large and heavy. On it was graven a likeness of Cregga, with two rubies for eyes. Russano touched his big striped muzzle to the stone and murmured gently, "My lady, your memory will live forever, both here and at the mountain you once ruled. Sleep in peace!" Standing straight, he breathed deeply and wiped his eyes. "Deyna, I'm sorry I won't have time to hear your story. I've visited Cregga now, and tomorrow morning I must leave. I'm sure you'll forgive me, Mother Abbess."

Mhera arranged the medallion a little more tidily upon the stone. "Why must you hurry away, sir? Don't you like our Abbey?"

Russano waved a paw across the lawns. Hares were flooding through the gate, greeting the Redwallers and playing with the Dibbuns. "Like Redwall Abbey? I love the place! But I have a thousand Long Patrol hares with me, and that would strain even the most generous hospitality of anybeast!"

Placing both paws within the wide sleeves of her habit, Abbess Mhera shook her head reprovingly at Russano. "We owe our lives to you and your hares, lord. This Abbey has more than enough to feed and accommodate your hares for many seasons. I will not hear of your leaving tomorrow for such an absurd reason. You are our honored guests. Surely one of the first things Cregga must have taught you was that the gates of Redwall are ever open to all our good friends!"

The great Badger Lord, Russano the Wise of Salamandastron, sat down beside the grave. He patted the earth, gazed up at the soft autumn afternoon and picked the delicate pink flowers from a vervain growing between the back of the headstone and the wall. Mhera watched him as he smelled its elusive fragrance. Russano looked for all the world like a happy Dibbun, as he must have been when he lived at the Abbey.

He offered her the flower. "Oh, yes, Cregga said that to me often. You sounded just like her then. Say it again for me, please, Mother Abbess."

Deyna felt proud of his sister as she accepted the vervain flower and smiled at Russano. "The gates of Redwall are ever open to all our good friends!"

EPILOGUE

Extract from the diary of the squirrelmaid Rosabel.

I did not know that my story would be so long. It took me four evenings to read it. Cavern Hole was packed to the door with Redwallers each time. It was a huge success; the congratulations and cheers are still ringing in my ears. Of course, there were questions to be answered. Many Dibbuns wanted to know why the Taggerung allowed Rukky Garge to remove his tattoos and cover the speedwell flower birthmark on his paw. I told them that this was so he could live out his life in peace, unknown to any Juska vermin, under his original name of Deyna. However, being what they are, the Dibbuns found this most unsatisfactory. The idea of having a wild name like Taggerung and running around with a fierce tattooed face appealed to them immensely. Our Abbey Warrior, Deyna, stayed silent throughout my reading. When I was finished he came over and kissed my cheek, and presented me with an old polished bone tailring that he had worn in his wild seasons. He told me to keep it as a souvenir. I think he was profoundly moved; I saw tears in his eyes.

Now, wait until you hear my good news! Abbess

Mhera and Brother Hoben asked to see me in Cregga's old bedchamber. I went up there wondering what it was all about. Brother Hoben began by saying that my manuscript was to be placed in the Abbey archives. He said it was a remarkable piece of work. Then he told me he was retiring as Recorder, to help old Hoarg in the gatehouse, as the poor old fellow hardly ever leaves his bed these days. Our Mother Abbess then promoted me to the position of full and official Recorder of Redwall Abbey. She told me that Cregga's chamber was to be made into my office! Will somebeast please pinch me? I keep imagining I'll wake and find it's all a dream. Foremole Gundil and his crew are fixing up a desk, shelves and cupboards, all just for me. I am going to keep Cregga Badgermum's big comfortable bed. Fwirl my mother is making me a beautiful coverlet for it, and my father Broggle is helping her with the embroidery. He's very good with needle and thread, though where he finds the time since taking over as Head Cook from Friar Bobb, goodness knows. Everybeast except Filorn said that my father should not have appointed Boorab as Assistant Cook. Boorab respects Abbess Mhera's mum greatly. That hare behaves himself perfectly when she is about. So, who has become Redwall's new Master of Music? Nimbalo, who else? Do you know, he has actually learned to play that great creaking antique known as the haredee gurdee.

Right, I must wash the ink from my paws. Our two new Infirmary Keepers need me to copy out some more remedies for their sickbay records. Sister Floburt and Brother Egburt make the nicest-tasting physicks; Dibbuns invent ailments just so as they can drink a dose or two. Who said that medicine always has to taste nasty? You'll never guess what Sister Alkanet is doing now: she has become old Drogg's assistant in the cellars. I must tell you that some of our cordials have been tasting decidedly odd of late. Boorab put aside a beaker of pennycloud and violet tea at supper last night. He remarked that he would sooner be physicked than have to drink it (wot wot!). Some of us started to laugh, but we soon stopped. Sister Alkanet may be only an Assistant Cellarkeeper, but she still retains her legendary icy glare. Great seasons, is that the dinner bell already? Good job I washed my paws. Sister Floburt and Brother Egburt will have to wait until after dinner. Even Recorders have to eat, you know. I must go, but here is my gift to you, my first signature in my new position.

Rosabel, daughter of Broggle and Fwirl,
Recorder of Redwall Abbey in Mossflower Country.